STRANGE
LOYALTIES

STRANGE LOYALTIES

WILLIAM McILVANNEY

CANONGATE

Edinburgh · London

This edition published in 2013 by Canongate Books Ltd, 14 High Street,
Edinburgh, EH1 1TE

www.canongate.tv

6

Copyright © William McIlvanney, 1991

Extract from *The Crime Interviews Volume Two: Bestselling Authors Talk About
Writing Crime Fiction* (Blasted Heath) © Len Wanner 2012

The moral right of the author has been asserted

First published in Great Britain in 1991 by Hodder and Stoughton Ltd

British Library Cataloguing-in-Publication Data
A catalogue record for this book is available on
request from the British Library

ISBN 978 0 85786 993 7

Typeset in Perpetua by Palimpsest Book Production Limited,
Falkirk, Stirlingshire

Printed and bound in Great Britain
by Clays Ltd, St Ives plc

For Liam

Here's a nice jungle: glades of trust
Disturbed by parakeets of lust,
Pools of deceptive calm where need
Bathes among crocodiles of greed.

ONE

1

I woke up with a head like a rodeo. Isn't it painful having fun? Mind you, last night hadn't been about enjoyment, just whisky as anaesthetic. Now it was wearing off, the pain was worse. It always is.

I didn't want this day. Who sent for it? Try the next house. I burrowed into the pillow. It was no use. A sleepless pillow. What was it they called that? Transferred epithet? My teachers. They taught me everything I don't need to know.

I got up and went on safari for the pain-killers. There weren't many places they could be. The bedroom was unlikely. That left the sitting-room, the small kitchen, the hall and the bathroom. The hall was out. There was nowhere there to keep them, unless I had cunningly hidden them under the carpet. The places were the kitchen or the bathroom. Deductive reasoning. Lucky I was a good detective.

After checking cupboards that held old razor blades and more dishes than I would ever use, I found the magic bottle. It was in the sitting-room behind the tiers of the change I hated keeping in my pockets. I got a glass of water and took two pills, feeling they wouldn't be enough – like sending in two rookie policemen to quell a riot.

I came through and sat in the sitting-room. As memory returned, I wished it wouldn't, because I did it again. I started to cry. For about a month now I had been doing that. The day would begin with tears. Maybe other people did exercises. I cried. Nothing dramatic, no wracking sobs. Just quiet and remorseless tears. They wouldn't let up on me. The good thing was they didn't last long.

After a few minutes they stopped. I wiped my face with my hand and stood up. At least today was the day I had decided I would start to do something about my tears. One of the two people I'd told of my intention had said I was crazy. But I've never said I was sane – just no more mad than anybody else I see around me. When we breakfast on reported mayhem and go to sleep having ingested images of national catastrophe like Mogadon, don't anybody call me crazy.

I ran a bath and lay in it as if it were a ritual of cleansing more than physical. Heal me, holy water, and prepare me for the things I have to do. I don't think it worked but the hot water helped my head. As the whisky sweated out of me, the miasma round my mind drifted up and mingled with the rising steam like mist clearing.

Maybe Brian was half-right. I wasn't crazy. But maybe I was daft. We had a corpse. But did we have a crime? If we did, it wasn't one you would find in the statutes. But then I didn't believe in the statutes too much anyway. Mr Bumble got it wrong. The law isn't an ass. It's a lot more sinister than that. The law is a devious, conniving bastard. It knows what it's doing, don't worry. It was made especially to work that way.

I've seen it go about its business too often – all those trials

4

in which you can watch the bemusement of the accused grow while the legal charade goes on around him. You can watch his eyes cloud, panic and finally silt up with surrender. He doesn't know what the hell they're talking about. He can no longer recognise what he's supposed to have done. Only they know what they're talking about. It's their game. He's just the ball.

I've been at trials where I had put the man in the dock and, fifteen minutes into the thing, I wanted to stand up and speak for the defence. 'Listen,' I've wanted to shout, 'I caught this man on the streets. That's where he lives. You lot ever been there?' But they went on with their private party, listening to precedents like a favourite song, playing word games, applauding one another. Occasionally, the voice of the accused will surface among the gobbledygook, small and often wistful and usually sounding strange, like a Scottish accent heard in the midst of Latin. It's a glimpse of pathetic human flesh, freckled and frail, seen through a rent in ermine robes, but quickly covered. Who's this interrupting our little morality play? He doesn't even know the script.

Those judges, I thought, as the water cooled around me. I do a lot of my thinking in the bath. Maybe that was one advantage of having rented an apartment with no shower. They lived as close to the world as the Dalai Lama. Never mind having little understanding of the human heart, they often didn't have much grasp of the daily machinery of the lives they were presuming to judge. Time and again the voice had quavered querulously down from Mount Olympus, asking the question that stunned: 'A transistor? What exactly do you mean by that?' 'UB40? Is that some kind of scientific formula?' ('Not a

5

formula, Your Honour. A form. An unemployment form.') 'An unemployment form? And what is that?'

Did you have to check in your head at the door when you joined a club? Under those wigs, what strange heads mulled in port and pickled in prejudice?

'Lawyers,' I said to the ceiling above my bath. Who could trust them? They stuff their wallets with crimes and declare themselves the pillars of society. Their fees are often fiscal robbery but who can nail them but themselves? 'A brilliant lawyer' was a phrase I had often heard. That was all right if all you meant was an ability to play legal games. But what did that mean? Intelligence as a closed circuit. Intelligence should never be a closed circuit. Take them off the stage that is a law court, where the forms are all pre-set, and a lot of them wouldn't know tears from rain.

I suppose you could say I was getting disillusioned with my job. I got out of the bath and pulled the plug, wiping away any suggestion of a tide-mark as the water drained. That was a technique I had learned since being on my own. It made the bath easier to clean. (Laidlaw's Handy Home Hints For Single Men: first edition in preparation.)

I towelled myself. Naked, I didn't like the softening belly. It wasn't so bad with the clothes on. And besides, among others you usually pulled it in a little, put on the corsets of vanity. In the bathroom I just contemplated my navel and found it a bigger subject than I wanted it to be. Ah, those now gone days when I could eat a house and drink a brewery and still have a stomach like a plank nothing could warp.

Intimations of mortality bulged under the towel. Time was I seemed forever. Time was time hardly was. My life was an unknown continent and I was its only explorer. And what had I discovered? Eh, well, eh, life is . . . Thingmy. Give me another few years and I'll have it sussed. But how many years were left? These days they passed so quickly. It was as if you stopped to mend a fuse and when you looked up another year had gone.

I remembered reading somewhere a theory about why time passed more quickly the older you got. The gist of it was this: when you're ten, a year is a tenth of your life; when you're forty, a year is a fortieth of your life. A fortieth is a lot less than a tenth. I was over forty. I didn't try to calculate the decimal points. I just agreed with the principle.

But it was strange. Awareness of my own mortality gave me a boost. A shot of psychic adrenalin pumped through me and blew the last remaining tendrils of mist out of my head. If you stayed true to your experience, you needn't fear age. It was only bringing you closer to understanding. I had always wanted understanding. Let's see if we could find it.

I put on a clean pair of underpants. From small beginnings . . . I put a new blade in the razor. I squeezed shaving soap onto my palm from the dispenser. I soaped my cheeks, my chin, my upper lip. I had done away with the recent moustache. It made me look too much like a policeman – standard issue, along with the identity-card. I looked into the small round mirror like a porthole and a floating face stared back at me, bearded white. By the time I was as old as I looked in the mirror, I hoped I would have the wisdom to match the appearance.

As I shaved the fuzziness of my face into definition there came into focus with my jaw the time ahead, hardening round the purpose I had given it. I had one week. It was a month since the bad thing had happened and it had taken me that time to win a week away from police work, at least from official police work. I had earned my busman's holiday.

It would be a kind of investigation, but my kind. Since I had been a policeman in Glasgow, the expression just about every superior had used to describe me, as if they were reading from my file, was 'maverick'. It had become equivalent to some kind of rank: Jack Laidlaw, Maverick. Well, they were right. I *was* a maverick. They didn't know how much. If I wasn't fond of lawyers, I was less fond of policemen. For years I had been working against the grain of my own nature.

How often had I felt I was working for the wrong people? How often had I felt that the source of the worst injustices wasn't personal at all but institutional and fiscal and political? It was the crime beyond the crime that had always fascinated me, the sanctified network of legally entrenched social injustice towards which the crime I was investigating feebly gestured. 'When a finger points at the moon,' a Paris graffito had once said, 'the fool looks at the finger.' Maybe I had been watching fingers for long enough.

All my prevarications had come home to roost, my personal harpies to foul my sense of my own worth and mock the work I had been doing. If I was a detective, let me detect now. It was time to put such skills as I had into overdrive.

For I was faced with a death I *had* to understand. It was a death I had to investigate, not for police reasons, though perhaps with police methods. Investigator, investigate thyself. A man was dead, a man I had loved perhaps more than any other.

Nobody had said 'crime'. But that dying seemed to me as unjust, as indicative of meaninglessness as any I had known. And I had known many. For he had been so rich in potential, so much alive, so undeserving – aren't we all? – of a meaningless death. I knew.

I should know. He was my brother.

The doorbell rang. The sound changed the meaning of my thoughts. It's one thing to psych yourself up inside your own head, to threaten to bring experience to book in your own mind. It's another to translate the mental vaunting into event, to bring the intensity of your feelings against the facts and see what results. It's the difference between the gymnasium and the championship fight. The bell said, 'Seconds out'. You're on your own. The proximity of someone else only made it clearer.

I padded barefoot to the door with shaving-soap round my ears and on my upper lip. In the doing of it, I had a small revelation: a dangerous world. This was how we lived now. The flat I had rented was in an old, refurbished tenement. When it was built, it had a door on the street that anyone could enter. Now it was different. The outside door was locked. You pressed a bell. Someone lifted a phone. If they knew who you were, they pressed a buzzer. You were allowed inside and came to their door. They checked you through a peep-hole. If you passed the test, they opened the door.

This was a tenement on the edge of Glasgow, not the Castle of Otranto. Anyone who lived here couldn't have much worth stealing. Maybe a video. We had become afraid of ourselves. There was a time a man or woman would have taken pride in being able to open the door to anyone. What was happening to us?

Was even this relevant to my brother's death? The way I felt, anything might be. I put my hand on the phone. Come in, strange world. And I'll be watching you more closely than I ever have before. I lifted the phone.

2

'Hullo?'

'Hullo. Jack?'

It was Brian Harkness. It would be, as early as this. My recent condition had brought out the social worker in Brian.

'Okay, Brian.'

I pressed the release buzzer and left my door open. I was finishing shaving when Brian came in and closed the door. He came through and sat on the edge of the bath.

'Aye, Brian.'

'Jack.'

He was giving me a look that should have had a stethoscope attached.

'How you doing?' he asked. 'You been on the stuff?'

'Define your terms.'

'You been on the stuff?'

'Brian. I get it on prescription.'

Jolly wit: the balancing pole with which we walk the tightrope. I was rinsing the last of the soap off my face.

'Jesus, I worry about you. What you doin' to yerself? Nobody knows where you are any more. You're as popular with the squad as a ferret in a rabbit warren. The only time we see you's on the job. Then you disappear. To this?'

He was looking round. I was drying my face.

'Brian,' I said. 'Why are you not wearing an ample floral frock?'

'What?'

'You're going to play at being my mother, dress for the part.'

'Piss off and listen once in your life, will ye?'

'Ma mammy never spoke like that. Times have changed.'

'Jack. You'll have to pull yourself together.'

'She spoke like that, though. If you really want to be mother, make us something to eat. I have to get ready.'

He stared at me the way relatives sometimes look at patients in a hospital, when they think they're not being observed. But I'm not a detective for nothing. I saw that expression that wonders if the patient knows how bad he really is. He shook his head and went through to the kitchen.

I was glad to see him go for the moment. It took the pressure off. The truth was I wasn't feeling too sure of myself. As I started to comb my wet and rumpled hair, I absorbed, in a kind of delayed action, the things he'd been saying, the reality of his concern, the valid reasons for it. The snarled hair tugged at the comb and some came out on it but I didn't miss it. At least my hair was staying. It seemed as thick as ever and had no grey. But if my hair was there to remind me of who I had been, what else was?

Brian was right. My life was one terrible mess. Miguel de Unamuno had written something that applied to me, if I could think what it was. I read quite a lot of philosophy in a slightly frenetic way, like a man looking for the hacksaw that must be hidden somewhere, before the executioner comes. It was something about continuity. Unamuno says something like: if a man loses his sense of his own continuity, he's had it. His bum's out the window. Sorry, Miguel, if I'm not quoting accurately.

That was me all right. I had lost the sense of my own continuity. I was improvising myself by the day. I didn't know who I was any more. The life I had thought I was constructing had fallen apart. Family, for example. I had always thought that was the lodestone of my life. Now I was irrevocably separated from Ena and I saw my children by appointment. My relationship with Jan lived in a kind of sensual limbo – a free-floating bed that wasn't anchored to any social structure. Beyond the act of love, I wasn't sure what I had to offer her. I survived by a job I doubted every day. And just when I thought I might be going under, when I needed every scrap of confirmation of life's meaningfulness I could get, my brother, who in my worst times had seemed more substantial to me than myself, my brother had walked into a random car. Or was it so random?

Something in me had to believe it wasn't. I wasn't saying it was suicide. What was I saying? I didn't know. Maybe part of what I was saying was 'guilt'. Every time someone I love has died, I have felt guilty. I didn't spend enough time with them, I didn't appreciate them fully when they were here, I hadn't given enough to them.

But the guilt, I believed wildly enough, wasn't just mine. I've always been generous in that way. In just about every case I've investigated, I've wanted to implicate as many people as I could, including myself. My ideal dock would accommodate the population of the world. We would all give our evidence, tell our sad stories and then there would be a mass acquittal and we would all go away and try again. (But don't tell the Commander of the Crime Squad that I said that.)

Scott, my dead brother, had become the focus for that manic feeling, so long suppressed in me. I needed his death to mean more than it seemed to mean. If the richness of the life in him could be snuffed on the random number-plate of a car, and that was all, I was ready to shut up shop on my beliefs and hand in my sense of morality at the desk. The world was a bingo stall.

But I didn't want it to be. I needed Scott in death as I had needed him in life. I needed a reunion in meaning between us.

I was completing my pretence of tidying up the bathroom when I realised that Brian was standing in the doorway, watching me. He covered his surveillance with talk.

'Make something to eat?' he said. 'With what, like? Your fridge might as well be in a shop-window. There's bugger-all in it. What you want me to do? Make soup out the curtains? I put the kettle on. At least you've laid in a stock of water, I see.'

'The frugal life, Brian.'

'Frugal? You're a one-man famine.'

'Eggs,' I said.

'That's right. Four eggs in a wee plastic container. That's your whack.'

'So boil them. And make some toast. Two eggs each. With toast and coffee.'

'The bread's like bathroom tiles.'

'You don't notice when it's toasted.'

'Okay, Egon.'

While he rustled up a gourmet breakfast in the kitchen, I went through to the bedroom. I dressed and laid my black leather jerkin on the bed — multi-purpose gear, suitable for cocktail party or dog-track. I didn't know where I might be going. I found the travelling-bag in the cupboard. What to put in it was the question. I'm hopeless at packing. I usually leave it to the last minute so that I've got an excuse for making a hash of it.

I might be away for a week. There were five clean shirts on hangers in the wardrobe. I kept them like that because I didn't have an iron. God bless the tumble-drier. But it meant I had to work out how to fold them. Button each one first, lay it face down on the bed, fold each side in very slightly from the shoulder, fold the sleeves the other way, fold up the tail slightly, double up what's left and an object of beautiful neatness was before you. (Personal column: home-help for hire, all domestic skills.)

Five shirts should be enough, plus the one that I was wearing, if I packed a couple of pullovers to hide any second-day grime on the collars, should that prove necessary. I put in whatever else I thought I would need and then applied Laidlaw's Infallible Packer's Law: check everything from the feet up and the inside out. I had forgotten an extra pair of shoes. I put them in. All right. Shoes. Seven pairs of socks. Seven pairs of underpants, unironed. Five shirts. Two tee-shirts to wear under the polo-neck if the shirts proved unwearable a second day. Two ties, in case I was feeling formal. Two extra pairs of trousers, rolled cunningly to prevent creasing. A blazer jacket.

The toilet bag. I went through to the bathroom, put what I needed in the toilet bag, brought it back and packed it. The travelling-bag didn't look well. It was tumoured in a lot of places. But the zipper closed. I found my migraine pills and squeezed them into a side pocket. St George was ready.

So was Brian. We sat at the table by the window and had breakfast. It looked a nice day. I hadn't packed a raincoat.

'This toast's exhausting,' Brian said. 'The kind of stuff you should eat in groups. Too much for one person. Team chewing.'

'I like it. Makes you appreciate food. You don't just pop this in your mouth and swallow it. It demands your attention.'

But I knew the vaudeville couldn't last. The serious act was waiting in the wings.

'Jack. What do you hope to prove doing what you're doing?'

'Whatever I prove.'

'That's very good. Come on, Jack. Scott's dead. He just got knocked down. He was drunk. You blame the driver?'

'I don't blame the driver, Brian, be your age. Why would I blame the driver?'

'So what's the score? Are you going to indict the traffic system?'

'It's just something I want to work out. I'm doing it in my own time. Who am I harming?'

'Yourself. I would think.'

'Anyway, what'll you be up to?' I said, changing tack.

'Working with Bob Lilley. His neighbour's off work as well just now. But not for reasons of insanity.'

'Uh-huh. Anything on?'

'There's a body been found near the river. Across from the Rotunda. Not identified yet. Wearing a rope cravat.'

The Rotunda was an old building that had been turned into a trendy eating-place, symbol of the regenerating Glasgow.

Across the Clyde were some of the derelict sites where industry died. I thought of people eating and drinking in the high brightness while, in the darkness across the water where the light didn't reach, a dead man lay abandoned. Maybe it was just my mood but the conjunction of those two images came to me like a coat-of-arms for the times, motto: live high on the hog and don't give a shit about other people.

'Advance word is he was an addict. Bob's got the report. His arm had been broken recently. And they seem to have given him a sore time before they killed him. Like breaking his fingers one by one.'

'I think my egg just addled,' I said. 'My compliments to the chef. If you would just ask him not to talk during the meal next time.'

We cleared up the debris of the meal and, at Brian's insistence, washed the dishes.

'This place is depressing enough to come back to,' he said. 'Come back to dirty dishes into the bargain, and the first stop could be your head in the oven.'

'It's electric.'

'So you could cook yourself to death.'

'I didn't realise the time,' I said as I hung up the dish-towel. I would have to wash it some time soon. It was beginning to make the dishes dirtier. 'I got up later than I thought. Jan should be here soon.'

'Jan coming?'

'We thought we would go to the Lock. Have some lunch there. Then she would run me to the station.'

'Which station?'

'Central.'

Brian held up his hand.

'Tell me no more,' he said. He held his hand to his chin like Sherlock in an old print, pointed his finger at me. 'Graithnock.'

'Jeez, you're good,' I said. 'It's only where Scott lived.'

'Revisiting the scene of the crime. Except that there is no crime.' He was kind to my silence, covered it with words. 'So Jan's coming.'

'That's the idea. A farewell lunch before I venture into the outback.'

'What's going to happen with you two?'

'Ah she's great,' I said. 'What a marvellous woman.'

'That's not what I asked.'

'Brian. I'm in enough shit to fertilise Russia. How do I know what I'm going to do? I know I love her. Whatever that means. But what I do with that, I'll have to find out. Put your question on hold.'

'Anyway,' he said. 'That gives me a problem. Jan coming. I was going to give you my car.'

'You'll need it.'

'I'll use Morag's. She can't drive anyway, the way she is. She'd need to steer from the back seat.'

Morag was eight months gone. It was their second. Stephanie was fifteen months. They weren't loitering.

'You sure?'

'Be like driving a dodgem car. But I'll be all right.'

'Hey, thanks. That would help. You're not so hard-bitten after all, are you?'

'I've got a soft spot for lunatics. You should never have given Ena the car, anyway.'

'She needed it more than I did. For the kids.'

'But how do I get home now? I was hoping you'd drive me there.'

'I will.'

'But you're seeing Jan.'

'Then you come too.'

'Oh no. That's private business.'

'Brian. We're going for lunch. Not to the back row of the pictures. We're all sophisticated adults now, wee man. I think we'll manage.'

While we waited for Jan, Brian asked me about Ena and the children. I had seen them the day before, Sunday: the day of the child, the new agnostic sabbath when all over the western world diffident fathers turned up to catch a glimpse of the only things they still believed in from their marriage. They brought gifts of ill-fitting clothes and books that would never be read and membership-cards for leisure centres.

I was enlisted in their ranks. The idea depressed me. How about years of that stuff? If I died on a Saturday, they would be losing a stranger. I turned away from the contemplation, bruised. I had bumped into another bad thought. Too much of the furniture of my mind seemed to be constructed these days from despair.

I was glad when Jan tooted the horn. I picked up my travelling-bag, a week in prospect, and Brian and I came out into bright sunshine. Brian waved to Jan and held out his hands and nodded at me. The translation was 'Blame him'. She smiled. Her smile was a beautiful absolution.

In the car Jan and I kissed, nothing too hot, just checking that the pilot light was still on. After she had pulled away, she referred to the rear-view mirror.

'Yes,' I said. 'He's following us. He's coming too.'

'You feel you need support?'

'Brian's lending me his car. I've got to drive him back home. What else could I—'

'Jack.' She could stroke you with your name. 'I'm kidding. All right? Just as long as we get some time together to talk.'

With that voice and the smell of her, a few of the hormones started to bristle: okay, we might be needed here.

Just when you think you're dead, life tickles your feet.

3

Where do they come from, those times? They are no respecters of persons. You've decided a day's just bad business. You've coloured it grey, when suddenly it's blinding you with hues you didn't know were there. You're ambushed by pleasure. It was like that at Lock 27.

We ate outside at the wooden tables. It was a place that had meant something to Jan and me a few times before, slow drinks and long talk that was winding to bed by a devious route, pausing to pick the odd flower from our different pasts, while her mouth turned into an astonishing organism, exotic as a sea-anemone, and I became briefly infatuated with the lobe of her left ear. Those times.

Today was like an orchestration of them all. The particulars that created the effect didn't seem too great. But then the notation to Solveig's Song doesn't look like a lot, at least not to me. (A music teacher once showed me when I was at school.) Heard, it can melt you.

Jan and Brian shared a bottle of white wine. I, as prospective driver of some distance, was on Perrier. We ate some kind of food. And we talked. That was about it.

But then May was out, laying tracks of scent in the air like mysteries you would want to follow till they buried you and the sunlight was showing off with the canal – see what I can do with water? – and a young couple were walking up and down the bank with a child and people were talking and laughing and you felt this wasn't such a bad species to be part of and I thought, what a game this is to play. Freeze the frame. This'll do.

After Jan and Brian had delicately kidded me throughout the meal about my incompetence in living alone (no mention of Scott), Brian insisted on paying and went off for a walk along the canal.

'Do you know what you're doing?' Jan said.

'I think so.'

'That should make a change.'

'Come on, Jan. Not you as well.'

'Me especially.'

Her eyes were in the sunlight and she had a stare it wasn't easy to confront. She looked as if she could see, as the man says, 'quite through the deeds of men'. With me, that must have been easy for her, I thought. She had a lot of confessional moments to draw on. But she contradicted me.

'Who are you, anyway? I still don't know. I thought I did. But watching you lately's been like trying to find someone in a crowd. By the time I get hold of what I think is your arm, it's someone else. It's not just Scott's death. It was there before. But it's worse now. Look at what you're up to now. What made you decide to do this?'

'I think it was the funeral.'

'The funeral?'

'I think it was. You don't get any good ones, Jan. But this

was the worst. Scott wasn't there. Don't smile. I didn't expect him to walk in with the mourners. I mean, among the mourners I didn't feel him there. Except maybe with David and Alan. And the kids didn't know what was going on. But at least their shock was real. Anna was hurt, of course. But, Jesus, she was cold with it. You know there was nothing afterwards? Nothing. Not a sausage roll, not a cup of tea. We stood outside the crematorium a couple of minutes. A bunch of strangers, looking as if the host hadn't turned up. The man who was his headmaster spoke to me. "You must be the brother. He was a fine teacher." A fine teacher? Shove it up your arse. He was a lot more than a fine teacher. Anyway, we all know he wasn't such a fine teacher towards the end. What we don't know is why. None of us there had a clue. "Fine." That word pisses me off. It's not a personal response. It's a box in a report card. Poor, fine, excellent. Tick the appropriate place. Some of the rest of them spoke to me. There was a John Strachan. I need to speak to him for starters. I was too numb at the time. We all just got in our cars and came away. We might as well have been at a football match.'

'Jack. That's what those things are like.'

'You don't bury a dog that way, Jan. You don't bury my brother that way. That's for sure. I may have been numb at the time but I knew even then. This won't do. Did they know what they were dealing with? This was some man, you know. I knew him when he was him. A head busier than an anthill. He painted. He tried to write. He wanted to be into everything. He was thirty-eight when he died. How the hell did that happen?'

'It was an accident.'

'I know it was an accident, Jan. But where did the accident begin? That's what I want to know. In the middle of the road? At the kerb? In the pub before he went out? In the fact that he drank too much? In the reasons why he drank too much? When did the accident begin? And why? When did my brother's life give up its purpose? So that it could wander aimlessly for years till it walked into a car? Why? Why did it lose itself until we found it lying in front of that car? I want to know, Jan. Why do the best of us go to waste while the worst of us flourish? I want to know.'

That was on Perrier water. It was lucky I wasn't on the whisky. A few minutes before, I had been wanting to stay here. Now the idyll was broken. I had rained on it with my words. The sun was still there and the people, but they didn't look the same to me any more. I think I resented them a little. I think Jan resented me.

'I don't know how much longer, Jack,' she said.

The remark should have been surprising. But love has its own grammar. Unspoken clauses pass between you, understood. I wasn't surprised. A familiar dread appeared in the sunshine like a fin in a bright bay.

'I never intended to fall in love with a band of guerrillas. You take up a new cause every day. Group sex was never my thing. We make love the best. But outside of bed, who are you? I never know who's getting out of bed, never mind who's getting in. I need a Jack Laidlaw of my own. I'm thirty now.'

She had been talking lately of having a child. I knew I was first choice as the father, but only first choice. She seemed to think there was potential in my genes, given the right training, which obviously I hadn't had. The clairvoyance of women amazes me. They can project a smile into a relationship and some embraces into a future. They can nest in a promise you didn't know you had made. Jan saw a future in us but, if I didn't, she still saw a future. I could understand her impulse. I wasn't the only one who stared into the darkness above the bed and heard age whispering around me. Jan had her own dark voices. Somewhere inside her, she knew the faces of her young glowing hopefully, featureless as candle flames. If the features didn't take after me, they would take after someone else. Time was running out for her, too. Wasn't it always for all of us?

'You go and have your week,' she said. 'I'll see you when you get back.'

I had a temptation to plead my case but I resisted it. I didn't know which way to plead. I sensed which direction she was going and it might well be away from me. She had given up working in the hotel and was in partnership with two friends in a small restaurant. Her life was orderly and successful. Me, I seemed to be moving backwards. I sometimes get the feeling that I'm on foot while everybody else is driving. It's as if my life still hasn't invented the wheel. Maybe this week it would. At least Jan would be waiting. Court was in recess for a week.

Brian was loitering close at hand and I called him over. At Jan's car she and I took an assessing farewell and she mouthed through the windscreen that she loved me. I drove Brian home.

We didn't talk much in the car. Outside his house, he stood with the car-door open.

'Remember, Jack,' he said. 'Polismen have even less unofficial freedom than civilian punters. Don't do anything daft, or not too daft. And keep in touch, if only to tell me how the car's doing. I want to hear from you. And I might need your advice on the case.'

It was a prepared speech. I found that moving.

'I'll phone every mile, on the mile,' I said.

'Oh, yes. And take a tip from a good detective. Always check the glove compartment of a new car.'

We waved and I drove off. It wasn't until I had gone some way that I thought of what he had said. I pressed the switch and the flap of the glove compartment came down and a bottle of the Antiquary fell into my hand. I put it back in and closed the flap.

I thought of people setting out on journeys in fables: warnings from beautiful, dark women and magic potions given to help them through.

4

Graithnock isn't far from Glasgow, just over twenty miles. But it took me about fifty minutes. I wasn't breaking any speed records. The nearer I came to the place, the less confidence I had in what I was doing.

I had to think that Anna wouldn't be delighted to see me. I had phoned her a couple of times soon after the funeral and had been talking to a freezer. Each answer had come back small and cold as an ice-cube. She had had no questions of her own. The third time I phoned there was no answer and no answer any time since. I hadn't much idea what was going on with her. I felt as if I was driving into a fog bank. That slows you down.

I tried to establish landmarks. It wasn't easy. If I hadn't known Scott so well by the time he died, what chance did I have to know Anna? The closest I had come to Scott lately had been a couple of months ago. He had phoned and then appeared at the flat. He was at that stage of drunkenness where you are being amazingly sober. His mouth was carving its words like a stone-mason. I was rather condescendingly solicitous for an hour until I began to get drunk as well. We finished what I had in the house.

We had some night. We went out and started hitting pubs as if they were beachheads. It became a competition to see who could talk the most crap in the shortest possible time. We were pretty evenly matched. Like a lot of benders, it was mainly about hilarious pain, using the alchemy of alcohol to convert grief into farce.

We succeeded rather well in different styles. Scott became ludicrously charming. I didn't. He kept addressing strangers with great formality, calling them 'dear sir' and 'my good, good man'. Ordering a drink was ceremonious enough to have been accompanied by heraldic trumpets. He placed coins on the counter in the manner of an antiquarian displaying rare objects. He proposed elopement to four different women in four different bars. But if he was Sir Galahad of the Bevvy, I was Mordred. My mood became dressed in black. Anyone addressing a remark to me would find me staring into its innocence and seeing bad meanings there. I was so obnoxious I could hardly bear to sit beside myself.

There is a blessedly hazy memory of one of the last pubs we went into. It was Reid's of Pertyck, I think – at any rate, a bar with a kind of raised balcony section with tables and chairs. I was at the bar. I must have been ordering. Scott was sitting at a table on the balcony part. Perhaps the setting confused him, transported him to another time and place. For he started to order drinks from where he was sitting in a manner that cocked a few quizzical heads. Some Glasgow pubs don't go in for the grandiose.

'My round, I believe,' Scott was shouting. 'Another bowl of mead, mine host. Minion.' Fortunately, he was referring to me. 'The reckoning.'

He threw a crumpled fiver towards the bar. A small man picked it up and held it in his closed hand. I wasn't noticing much by then. But I noticed that. Mordred had a kind of malicious tunnel vision by this time. Only the bad things got through. I held out my hand, palm up. The small man looked at me questioningly. I tapped my right palm with my left forefinger, no mean achievement given my condition.

'That,' I said and closed my hand into a fist. 'Or that.'

The small man handed over the fiver but he didn't like doing it.

'It was a joke,' he said.

'That was a joke,' I said. 'Well, you're about as funny as Arthur Askey.'

I paid and brought the drinks back to our table, not mead but gin and tonic for Scott and for me a Bloody Mary, which was a logical expression of my mood, since I never drink it. I gave Scott his fiver back.

'No, no,' he was saying. 'Give it to the people. Let the people drink.'

'Behave yourself,' I said.

The small man was back.

'Hey, you. That was a joke,' he said.

'What are you?' I said. 'A bloody budgie? That all they taught you to say? Come back in a month when you've learned another sentence.'

'Listen, you,' the small man said and grabbed my arm.

I shook him off and he sat down on the floor. Things could have turned, as they say, ugly, except that I helped him up.

'It was a joke,' he said again.

'So was that,' I said. 'Let's forget it.'

'All right,' he said. 'Just so long as ye know it was a joke.'

The repetition of that statement reanimated the demon.

'Sorry Ah knocked you off your perch,' I said.

Thankfully, the small man didn't turn back. But there followed many mutterings while Scott beamed upon the sotto voce threats as if they were a concert in his honour. Miraculously, we got out of there without any more trouble and out of the next bar as well and eventually bought a carry-out and took a taxi back to the flat.

The evening resolved itself into what it had really been about. We were matching disasters. I think Scott had come to see me for some kind of joint exorcism, a mutual laying to rest of some of the wilder dreams we had spawned together lying in our shared bedroom in our parents' house. He had started to admit to himself how badly his marriage was failing and he needed to share the admission with me, the keeper of his old dreams, as he was the keeper of mine. Also, he knew my situation and I think he suspected it might soon be his and he was perhaps checking out the terrain with someone who already lived there.

I wished now that I had been more help. We were both too sore at that time. As we drank and talked into the night, we discovered a new kind of sibling rivalry. You think you've got wounds? Look at mine. Your compass is broken? My ambition's got gangrene. Women came in for much meandering analysis. Weighty pronouncements on the nature of relationships were made and forgotten. Past girls who had long since vanished into unknown marriages and for all we knew divorces were conjured from their names and seen in the maudlin glow of nostalgia and knelt before, like shrines we never should have lost faith in. We battered ourselves against the incomprehensible and the unsayable and lay back exhausted.

At about half past three in the morning, Scott sat up suddenly on the floor where he'd been lying. He stared ahead like a visionary.

'I came here to tell you something,' he said. 'I should have told you this before.'

He looked at me and looked away. Whatever he had to say was not something he found easy to say.

'I am leaving Anna,' he intoned and lay back down and went to sleep.

Next morning he sheepishly washed himself and shaved with my razor and went back to her. I had seen him a few times since then but only over the shoulder of other people's events.

That was my last real memory of him alive and it wasn't such a bad one. Let those who think life is measurable by its propriety wish for nicer last remembrances of the ones they love. That crazy night stayed with me. It made me smile. For in spite of all the hurt, he had somehow stayed above it. The size of the pain was the size of the dream he felt denied in him. To hold the pain yet was yet to hold the dream. That was one reason why I couldn't forgive his dying. That was one reason why I was driving towards Anna.

Who was Anna? I had never quite worked that out. I knew what she looked like all right. She was small and fine-boned and sweet-faced. Since her marriage to Scott, she and I had always exchanged pleasantries like sealed envelopes. Who knew what implications were inside them? Perhaps I would find out now.

On my left I saw Fenwick, where Brian Harkness had lived with his father before marrying Morag. I had met the old man several times. I liked him. I was tempted to go in and see him, postpone my descent into whatever Graithnock had in store for me. Brian's father and I had things in common. He wasn't sure of policemen either. But Graithnock was only minutes away — too late to hide.

I went round the one-way system until I saw a phone-box. Then I had to find a parking place. I had decided that, before I spoke to Anna, I would get in touch with John Strachan. He had told me at the funeral that he had been with Scott before he died. I think I was taking out insurance against the possibility of Anna's monosyllabic responses. If she didn't want to tell me anything, I could defy her silence and still make my journey worthwhile. I phoned Scott's school.

'Good afternoon. Glebe Academy.'

There was a typewriter in the background and a voice saying something I couldn't hear — those delicious sounds of normalcy that are sweets in the shop-window to an obsessive and he's a boy again, only able to stare in, without the currency to purchase.

'Glebe Academy. Yes?'

'Good afternoon. Could I speak to Mr Strachan, please?'

'Who's calling, please?'

'My name's Laidlaw. Jack Laidlaw. I'm Scott's brother.'

I had nearly said, 'I was Scott's brother.' Grief is often so mannerly that it ties itself in knots. I heard a silence I didn't understand at the other end.

'Oh, Mr Laidlaw.' Then she said something that stuck to my chest like a badge. 'You had one terrific brother, Mr Laidlaw. A lot of us miss him. Pupils and staff alike.'

I loved not just the statement. I loved the breathlessness of her voice, the spontaneity with which she said it, the breaking through the barrier of her own embarrassment. It wasn't something she had said by rote.

'Thanks,' I said.

'I'll get Mr Strachan for you.'

When he came, I didn't recognise the voice and I realised I might not know him if I saw him.

'Hullo. Mr Laidlaw?'

'Mr Strachan. I'm sorry to disturb your day. I know you must be busy. But I'm in Graithnock today. And I just wondered. Would it be possible to talk to you? About Scott. I just would like to understand it better. I'm sorry to impose on you. But could I see you sometime? Even just for half-an-hour?'

He hardly paused.

'You could come to the house tonight,' he said.

'You sure?'

'I'm sure. You'll still be around later on?'

'Definitely.'

'Okay. I'm sorry I haven't time to warn Mhairi. Or you could eat with us. But you could come after that. If that's all right.'

'That's great.'

He gave me the address. I was relieved. That meant I was bound to recognise him.

'Say about seven o'clock. Let's hope we've got the kids down by about then.'

'That's great. I'll see you then. I appreciate this.'

'It's no problem. Scott's worth talking about.'

His words and those of the secretary were ointment on my mind. Two people agreed with the feeling in me. I felt as if I was a member of a cadre against the indifference to Scott's death. I was ready to talk to Anna now, invested with more authority than my own mania. I went back to the car.

5

Scott and Anna's house was the end one in a street of terraced houses. There were trees in the street, emerging from the buckling asphalt defiantly. As I parked between two of the trees, I noticed the sign. It was stuck in the sandstone chips of the front garden. It said 'For Sale'.

I got out and went up the path and rang the bell. It was one of those rings you know will never be answered, tirling into hollow silence. It was, appropriately enough, like calling at a mausoleum. I looked in the curtainless front window. The room was completely denuded. There were lighter patches on the walls where Scott's paintings had been hanging.

My memory rehung one of them. It was a big canvas dominated by a kitchen window. In the foreground on the draining board there were dishes, pans, cooking utensils. Through the window was a fantastic cityscape of bleak places and deprived people and cranes and furnaces. The people were part of the objects, seemed somehow enslaved by them. I remember a face looking out of a closed tenement window as if through bars. It was meant, Scott had told me, to be an echo of the face that was looking at his painting. I remember a man's face seeming liquid in the glow of his own blowtorch,

34

as if he were melting down himself. The whole thing was rendered in great naturalistic detail, down to recognisably working-class faces below the bonnets, but the total effect was a nightmare vision. On the left of the kitchen window, like an inaccurate inset scale on some mad map, was a small, square picture. It was painted in sugary colours in vivid contrast to the scene outside. It showed an idealised Highland glen with heather and a cottage pluming smoke from the chimney and a shepherd and his dog heading towards it. Scott had called his painting 'Scotland'.

The painting became the empty patch on the wall again. So easy was it to erase that fiercely felt vision. The room was anybody's, nobody's. Even the carpet had been lifted. Anna had always been thrifty.

I crunched across the chips and went round the side of the house. There was a wooden door set in the wall around the garden. It was locked. I put my foot on the door-handle, pulled myself up and dropped over. The back area was just an outhouse, a garage and a patch of grass. Gardening hadn't been one of Scott's passions.

I wandered around a while, peered in the kitchen window. The place was empty and clean. Anna had always been a good house-keeper. I looked at the patch of grass. I could remember sitting there a few times on travelling rugs during sunny Sundays, with Scott and Anna and Ena. The children were playing around us and we sipped beer. Our desultory talk from those times seemed to hang in the air about me. Our plans had been motes, just sun motes.

The outhouse door wasn't locked. I looked in. There was an old rusted lawn-mower, a rake, some lengths of wood, a small bag of tubes of oil-paint, nearly all of them squeezed empty. This was it so soon?

I felt I might as well have stumbled upon an archaeological site. You would be hard pushed already to tell who had lived here, unless you adopted the experts' technique of constructing an elaborate edifice of theory on a minute base of fact that couldn't support it. Scott's memorial was how much his house fetched and this handful of rubbish.

Then I saw it. I wasn't sure what it was at first. It was behind some pieces of board, face to the wall. I had thought it was just another board itself till I noticed the varnish shining and knew it was a frame. I extricated it. It was Scott's painting, 'Scotland'.

Holding the painting up, I couldn't believe it. What had happened between them that Anna should do this? She knew how much it had meant to Scott. I was angry.

I found an old, black bin-bag and put the painting in it. I came out and closed the outhouse door. I balanced the painting on the garage-roof that abutted on to the garden door. I climbed the door and brought the painting with me on the way down. I was putting the painting in the boot of the car when a neighbour crossed the street towards me. I didn't know him.

'Excuse me,' he said. 'What are you doing?'

'Just visiting,' I said.

'You can only view by appointment.'

'I've seen all I need to see.'

'What's that you've got there?'

'Who the hell are you?' I said. 'The Keeper of the Suburbs?'

As soon as I said it, I felt bad. The man was right enough. He had seen a stranger poking around an empty house.

'Look,' I said.

I took out my identity-card and showed it to him.

'I'm Scott Laidlaw's brother. I'm just collecting something that was left for me. It's a painting Scott did.'

He was waiting for me to let him see it. He had a big chance.

'Well,' he said. He was giving the issue his lofty consideration. He seemed to imagine I cared. Why does a little piece of property make some people act as if they were on stilts? 'Well. I suppose everything's above board.'

'Do you?' I said and locked the boot and got in the car.

Driving, I was annoyed at myself for becoming angry. Muzzle the dog. My anger wasn't for him. But it was for somebody. I could feel it in me, sealed and ready, just waiting for an address.

6

I remembered John Strachan as soon as I saw him, just after ten past seven. I had been hoping to come later but this was as long as I could hold off. I had looked at the new town centre Scott hated. I had taken a meal in a café. I had left the car in a parking lot and walked. But impatience still outmanoeuvred me.

'Jack, isn't it?' he said.

We shook hands.

'I'm John. Come in.'

'This is good of you.'

'No.' He shook his head. 'I feel like talking about it myself.'

He was a tall man with glasses. He couldn't have been more than early thirties but he had a troubled, abstracted air that suggested the sum he was trying to do in his head wasn't working out. He was wearing jeans and a baggy sweater.

He led me through to the living-room and introduced me to Mhairi. Mhairi was small and overweight and she had a shiny, round face, like a dumpling in which you know there won't be any bad bits. She was wearing jeans and a loose, floral top. John introduced me to the children as well, Catriona and Elspeth, or rather he identified them for me as they dervished round us.

The children were doing what children so often do, transforming the banality of the moment into a game. As is usual with such games, nobody knew the rules but them. This one appeared to consist of Catriona, who would be about eight, making the ugliest face she could contrive up against Elspeth's nose, accompanied by a klaxon-like noise. Then she would run in and out of the furniture and stop in the most inaccessible place she could find. Elspeth, maybe five, would pursue her, make her face, her noise, and run away as well. Like so many children's games nobody seemed to have devised a rule yet for deciding when it was over.

The three adults were momentarily transfixed, perhaps by such effortless dissipation of enough energy to light up a small town.

'I hope I haven't come too early,' I said.

'Oh no,' Mhairi said.

She said it with surprise, looking into the strangeness of my remark. The rigid sense of time I had implied seemed alien to her. I had an insight, part observation, part memory, into where they were. Mhairi was standing by the door to the kitchen with a slightly dazed resignation, like someone waiting for a bus she had begun to think might not travel on this route after all. I could imagine the promised places it was supposed to have on its destination board: 'When The Children Are Older', 'More Time To Myself' and 'Some Of The Things I've Always Wanted To Do'.

'I think we should take Jack through to the lounge for a minute,' Mhairi said.

The three of us went through there. Catriona and Elspeth threatened concentration distantly, like gunfire in the hills around a fort.

Moving into the lounge was moving nearer to John and Mhairi themselves, I thought, closer to the control room of what they were up to. It was furnished with a kind of vulnerable eclecticism. The floor was varnished, with an Indian rug on it. The chairs didn't match but were old and handsome, chosen presumably for comfort. Someone had taken macramé. On the walls were an African mask and one of Scott's paintings I hadn't seen before. While I studied it, they didn't speak. Books were much of the furniture. There were two main bookcases and a couple of smaller bookstands. One of them was devoted to black writers – George Jackson, Baldwin, Cleaver, Biko, Mandela, Achebe. I could imagine their friends sitting around here. They would drink wine and talk seriously about important matters. They would be easy to satirise. But I felt I was in one of decency's bunkers, where two people were trying to find values that made their lives honestly habitable.

'What do you think the painting's about?' I said as I sat down.

It was a pastiche of Da Vinci's last supper. Five men were at table, facing out. The man in the centre had no features. His hands were by his side. The other four were bearded. One of them could have been Scott. The meal and the clothes were contemporary. The perspective allowed you to see the five plates, still empty, before them. The plate of the man in the middle was blank. The other four plates had the image of the same face on them, a calm but mournful face of a balding man in his fifties, looking out at you. There were other elements in the picture but I hadn't time to examine them. I didn't like the painting. It seemed too derivative, not of Da Vinci, but of an idea extraneous to itself, an idea it hadn't quite incarnated successfully.

'I'm not sure,' John said. 'Maybe that the four are feeding off the man in the middle? His loss of identity.'

'Something like that,' Mhairi said. 'Anyway, I like it. And Scott never explained.'

We all looked at it briefly.

'It's good to meet you,' Mhairi said. 'Scott talked about you a lot. Black Jack, he sometimes called you. Nicely, though. We miss him so much.'

'So do I,' I said. 'Not that I had seen too much of him lately. But he was always there for me. Like money in the bank. Suddenly it's the Wall Street crash. I feel a bit impoverished without him.'

'He was special,' John said. 'The pupils talk a lot about him at the school. I think a couple of the sixth-year girls had vaguely thought they might marry him.'

'We used to see a lot of him and Anna,' Mhairi said. 'Not so much lately. But he still came round himself.'

'Anna,' I said. 'I tried to go and see her today. The house is up for sale. That was quick.'

They looked at each other.

'You know how bad it was between them before Scott died?' John said.

'I thought I had some idea. But maybe I underestimated drastically. I don't know how you felt about the funeral, John. But I found that hard to take. I know Anna has to cope with it the way she can. But come on.'

'I think I can understand what Anna did,' Mhairi said. 'I don't know if it's what I would've done. But then maybe I wouldn't have had the guts.'

I waited.

'They were really separated before Scott died. They lived in the same house, right enough. But it was all over bar admitting it. What Anna felt must have been close to hate, I think. I think the funeral was a way to avoid hypocrisy as much as possible. She's very strong-willed, Anna.'

'So was Scott, Mhairi,' John said. 'He had a lot of charm with it. But if you ruffled the etiquette, you touched iron quick enough.'

'What do you think went wrong between them?' I asked.

They both smiled and shook their heads.

'I know,' I said. 'Cancel the question.'

'No,' John said. 'I suppose, knowing them as well as we did, we got a few pointers. But how do you referee that stuff? You just see them sometimes coming out of their privacy and you know the game's changed.'

'That's right,' Mhairi said. 'You know what I've noticed? One of the signs is when a couple start to overreact to something in public. A subject comes up and they're both going over the top. And you realise it's not that they're talking about at all. It's something else. That's just the excuse for a much deeper enmity. I think that's when it's bad. Because they've stopped trying to sort out the real problem. They're just using it as fuel to fight about other things.'

'I know what you mean,' John said. 'Know when I noticed that with Scott and Anna? Know one of the first times? The private school discussion? Remember that?'

Mhairi breathed out and shook her head.

'Do I remember the Vietnam War? That was terrible. I thought Scott was going to get violent.'

'He would never have done that. But he took words as far as they would go.'

'Private school?' I said.

'It was Anna's idea,' Mhairi said. 'She said she wanted David and Alan to go to a private school. It was one night they were in here. Just the four of us. I think Anna mentioned it in company deliberately, to see if she could get some support.'

'Fat chance,' John said. 'I teach where I teach because I believe in it. It's not just the money. That helps, though. The little there is of it.'

'Oh, the three of us were agreed. But Anna still had the right to her opinion. But Scott was outraged. By the time he was finished, I was beginning to think maybe I agreed with Anna. Excuse me. But he was out of order that night.'

'Don't worry,' I said. 'I believe you. I think it's a family characteristic.'

'It was as if she was trying to undermine the meaning of his life,' John said.

Catriona and Elspeth entered the room like a Molotov cocktail, exploding in the middle of us.

'Come on, girls,' Mhairi said wanly.

All right, Canute said: turn back, tide. They had devised a different game. This game was less complicated than the previous one, marked a distinct regression in subtlety. What this game was about was simply decibels.

'Nyah, nyah, nyah, nyah,' Catriona sang. 'Nyah, nyah, nyah, nyah, nyah.'

'Nyoo, nyoo, nyoo,' sang Elspeth. 'Nyoo, nyoo, nyoo. Nyoo, nyoo, nyoo.'

The lyrics were a lot better than the tunes. Mhairi nodded to John.

'Sh!' John said, a man trying to blow out a forest fire. 'What Mhairi and I were thinking. You and I could nip round to the pub. Have a blether there.'

Mhairi smiled at me and nodded. I was grateful to them, not just because the shift would make communication possible but because I liked them and I didn't want to repeat the brief vision I'd just had of shooting their children.

'You sure you'll be all right, love?' John said.

I could understand the question.

'I've survived so far. I'll get these two to bed. You won't be too long?'

'No. We'll go to the Akimbo. Okay?'

John kissed her and kissed the children. I thanked Mhairi and waved to Catriona and Elspeth.

'Maybe we'll see you sometime when the circumstances are less sad.'

'I hope so,' I said. 'I think I would like that.'

7

Walking with John Strachan, I found myself surfacing too quickly from the depth of my preoccupation with Scott's death into an ordinary evening. I felt a psychological equivalent of the bends. I couldn't relate to what was going on around me.

I seemed alien here. Yet I knew this town well enough. Our family had lived here for five or six years when my father – inveterate dreamer of unfulfilled dreams – had brought us to make another of those fresh starts of his that always curdled into failure by being exposed to too much harsh reality. But tonight the town didn't feel familiar. Maybe I was seeing it not so much as the place where I was as the place where Scott wasn't, an expanse of buildings that had lost my brother as effortlessly and effectively as an ocean closing over a wreck.

Suddenly I didn't want to sit in the Akimbo Arms, a pub I had known slightly, and be invaded by the anonymity of the town. I needed a place that would give me a stronger sense of Scott.

'John,' I said. 'What you say we don't go to the Akimbo? We could walk to where I've parked the car. And I'll drive us to the Bushfield Hotel. I need a room for the night anyway.'

'Sure,' he said. 'I have the odd pint in there. It's all right.'

The Bushfield was a converted private house. It was mainly a pub but it had perhaps ten bedrooms as well. Katie and Mike Samson, who owned it, had known Scott well. I had spent a few sessions in there after hours, enjoying the singsong. The sweetly ample Katie had been very fond of Scott. Maybe Mike had liked him, too. But with Mike you couldn't be sure. Tall and lean, he sometimes gave the impression that you might need a power-drill to find out what was going on inside his head. Together, they were tune and descant, Mike providing a slightly lugubrious undertow to Katie's joy in things.

I parked the car in front of the hotel and took out my travelling-bag. As John Strachan and I went into the hotel, Katie was crossing the hallway from bar to kitchen.

'Have you got a room here for a wayfaring stranger?' I said.

'Oh, Jack,' she said.

She stood staring at me. I thought I understood what the stare meant. She was reaffirming the death of Scott in seeing his big brother. Scott would never again be standing where I was. Katie being Katie, as spontaneous as breathing, the thought brought tears to her eyes. She approached with her arms open and pulled me down into an embrace where breathing was difficult. The travelling-bag hit the floor. Just when I was going down for the third time, she released me.

'You're thin as a rake,' she said.

'That's just muscular leanness, Katie.'

'Don't dodge. What have you been eatin'? Or what have ye not been eatin', more like?'

'I'm the worst cook in Britain.'

'Ach, Jack. I heard about yer other bothers, too.' She

meant my marriage. 'Trouble always travels in company, doesn't it?'

I tried to introduce John Strachan to her but she knew him already. She would. She treated even casual customers as if they were part of an extended family. She shooed John through to the bar to get a pint and took me upstairs to show me my room. It was freshly decorated and beautifully clean.

'This is the best one,' she said. 'Some of the others are getting done up. Then there's two fellas from Denmark staying the night. And a man from Ireland's been here for nearly a week.'

I didn't unpack the bag. I told her I wanted to phone Glasgow. She wouldn't let me use the payphone. She took me back downstairs to the kitchen. Fortunately, Buster the dog recognised me, although that didn't always guarantee you immunity from threatening noises. She left me dialling Brian Harkness's number.

'Hello?'

'Hullo, Morag?' I said. 'It's –'

'I know who it is all right. I'd recognise your growl anywhere. It's Black Jack Laidlaw, the mad detective.'

It's nice to be recognised.

'Where are you?' she said.

'I'm in Graithnock. I'm still in Graithnock.'

'Whereabouts in Graithnock?'

'I'm just booking into a wee hotel. I just got in there.'

'Don't be daft,' she said. Morag had the kind of directness that often goes with authentic generosity. Kindness was such a natural thing with her she never bothered to dress it in formal clothes. 'You're forty minutes down the road from us. Get your bum in the car and get up here.'

I didn't take time to explain that that was a long forty

47

minutes. The car would make it but not my head. I could hear over the phone the background noises of domesticity, like an old tune I could still remember but had forgotten the words. I didn't want to take any contagion of gloomy obsessiveness into that nice place.

'Well, I've still got a couple of people to see, Morag.'

'Jack. Who do you think you're kidding? You'll sit in a room the size of a coffin and get pissed. Your habits are known. Come up here and get a decent meal and some company. Brian told me about your fridge. He said you could sell it as new. If you can't look after yourself, let other people do it now and again.'

'What it is, Morag,' I said. 'I just tasted whisky for the first time there. And, you know the way you can sometimes just tell right away? I really think I'm going to like it. So what I thought I would do, I'll just stay with it for a while and see if I can acquire the taste. And it's awkward to do that when you're driving.'

'You're hopeless. You not coming up?'

'Not the night, lovely wumman. But it's in my crowded diary. How's Stephanie and the mystery guest?'

'Steph's fine. The other one's kickin' like a football team. Listen. We're going to feed you properly soon. Even if we have to put you on a drip. No escape. You want to speak to Brian?'

'Please, Morag. He's in, is he?'

'Yes. I don't swallow all that Crime Squad stuff about having to work late all the time. The fate of the nation hanging on a break-in in Garthamlock. I'll get him. You watch yourself, you.'

'Like an egg in a cake, Morag. Cheers.'

'So Morag's seductive tones didn't persuade you?' Brian said. 'Actually, the way she's goin' on at me. D'you mind if I come down there? Can you get me a room?'

'I'd change places any day,' I said. 'So how did it go today?'

'You first,' Brian said.

I started trying to give him a brief outline and began to feel as if I was drawing pictures in the air with my finger. I found myself interpreting Brian's silence as the sound of scepticism. Maybe obsessions are essentially incommunicable. What did I have to tell him? I visited an empty house. I found an abandoned painting. I met a schoolteacher and his wife and family. It was all as interesting in the telling as one of those childhood compositions: What I Did At The Weekend. Even to myself it seemed that I was not conveying my experiences so much as my symptoms. Brian's response wasn't a hopeful diagnosis.

'Christ, Jack,' he said. 'What's the point of what you're doing?'

'I'm not telling you,' I said. ''Cause you're not a nice man. Anyway, what about you?'

I think Brian was relieved to get back to talking about the real world. Buster was looking at me from the floor as if he shared Brian's opinion of me.

'Meece Rooney,' Brian said. 'You know him?'

'Meece? I know him.'

'Well, you did,' Brian said. 'He's dead.'

'You mean he's the one? On the waste ground?'

'Meece Rooney. Listen. Somebody said he was supposed to have studied medicine. Would you know about that?'

'Meece did about a month at university,' I said. 'Before he decided there must be quicker ways to fulfil yourself. If Meece was saying he studied medicine, he must've meant he had been reading the label on a cough-bottle.'

I found myself shrugging. Grief can be selfish. I didn't dislike

49

Meece. I hadn't disliked Meece. By the rule of thumb you sometimes applied to the troublesome people you dealt with, he wasn't the worst. The thumb was almost up. He had been in my experience more victim than perpetrator. He was a fantasist who had decided to sublimate his fantasies in heroin. But if my brother's dying was a sore thing, why not his? His death was someone's mourning.

'He was dealing, you know,' Brian said.

The thumb went down. It's one thing to find your own way to hell. But when you start directing the traffic there, it's different.

'I'd lost touch with him,' I said. 'I didn't know he was a dealer. It's a natural progression, right enough. So what else have you got?'

'Not a lot so far. We traced him to a bedsit in Hyndland. He was supposed to be living there with a woman. By the way, the pathologist's report shows he had a broken arm recently. The neighbours aren't saying a lot. We don't even have a name for her yet. But she seems to have been on the stuff as well. Only thing is, she's not there any more. And her clothes aren't either. But one of the unwashed cups has lipstick on it. And the remains of a coffee that hadn't even hardened.'

'So you think she knows who did it?'

'It looks that way.'

'And evaporated for the good of her health.'

'You're a genius.'

'I'm just thinking aloud. Don't get smart-arsed.'

'You taught me,' he said.

'No. That's maybe what you learned but it's not what I was teaching. But that's interesting. At least it narrows the focus.'

'What do you mean?'

'Well, with a junkie you've got problems, haven't you? They're good at keeping bad company. There's a lot of that stuff out there. And their motivations are like mayflies. They can be born and die the same day. That can make a motive hard to trace.'

'Uh-huh.'

'But the way Meece died looks planned. Breaking fingers one by one doesn't smack of spontaneity. It might mean questions were being asked. Or just some special rites of passage into death. Either way, Meece's murder was arranged. And the vanishing woman confirms that. She maybe knew it was going to happen or that it had happened. And whoever did it frightened her out of her life. And into another one.'

'So?'

'So it's a guess. But you're looking to move towards official sources in their world. The big fear. What's the biggest fear an addict has?'

'No more of the stuff.'

'Correct. Who's god for those people?'

'The man who gives the goods.'

'I don't think you're looking for some lost soul who took a bad mood. I think you're looking for more important people.'

I didn't know whether Brian's silence meant awe at my forensic brilliance or just that he had fallen asleep.

'Well,' he said. 'Thanks for taking so long to tell us what we knew already.'

We both laughed.

'You might just about get a pass-mark at detective school for that lot.'

51

We talked some more but that was enough of that. Brian's reaction had punctured my self-absorption. Other people's problems seem so much simpler than our own. Maybe I had enjoyed playing at detectives with Meece Rooney's death because I couldn't begin to understand Scott's. I had been like a man in a real war who finds relief in playing chess. I had become involved in a case that for me was purely abstract. I didn't want to be. I had my own worries. What did Meece have to do with me just now? He was Brian and Bob's problem. It could stay that way.

'Okay,' Brian said. 'Oh, by the way, Bob Lilley says when you've stopped taking the fits, we'd love to have you on this case with us.'

'Aye,' I said. 'Tell him if he could take the odd fit, it would be a hopeful sign. It might prove he was alive. Tell him he could live in Madame Tussaud's and nobody would notice the difference.'

'I feel like a Valentine card,' Brian said. 'Passing on all these loving messages.'

'Cheers,' I said.

I put down the phone rather noisily and Buster growled at me, his Dobermann ears erect.

'Shut your face, Buster,' I said. 'The world's queuing up to have a go at me and you're at the end of the queue. I'll see you after.'

We stared at each other. One of the advantages of having big worries is that smaller problems seem irrelevant. It's all a question of perspective. I felt as if I could give Buster a sorer bite than he could give me.

8

I imagined a party. That is not a difficult thing for me to do. It has always been a word liable to send my mind off in pursuit of its fabulous nature, like El Dorado.

This was a big party. It took place in a house in Marrenden Drive, which is a street in Troon, a town not far from Graithnock. Troon is an interestingly Scottish town. It has for a long time had a shipyard. It has also for a long time been a fairly popular coastal resort, where quite a few well-off people have chosen to live. Therefore, it has, like most things Scottish, a dual nature. It is both rough and genteel. Visitors may have to find the roughness for themselves. The gentility will be more obvious. A passer-by might be forgiven for wondering if they toilet-train the seagulls.

But then that modest gentility sub-divides itself into its own duality, for it conceals not only the fact that some people have much harder lives than the town suggests but the fact that some people have much softer ones. There is considerable wealth here. Marrenden Drive is where some of that wealth resides. In the slightly Calvinist forthrightness of the place, Marrenden Drive is a well-hidden softness, like a secret and surprisingly lush garden where discreet riches bloom into stone.

The house where the party was held was large and sat in its own grounds. That night it must have been lit up like a small city. Its owner was known for a certain lavishness. His name was Dave Lyons and he had many business interests, though perhaps only he knew what they all were. Besides the house in Marrenden Drive, he appeared to have a place in Edinburgh, where his business was conducted.

There were maybe sixty or seventy people present at the party. The guest-list was varied. Dave Lyons was a self-made man who had, like a lot of us, played at rebelliousness in his youth and had continued to maintain loose friendships with people from different areas of society. The party would be an expression of his socially eclectic life, with all its disparate elements seemingly reconciled in an atmosphere of warmth and celebration.

As the evening progressed, the whole house came into use. The party broke up into side-shows, as parties often will. People stood in the kitchen, trapped in one of those drink-assisted debates that seem at the time like the most important issue in the world. In the dining-room, some were pecking at the remains of the very impressive buffet. Music was playing in the spacious lounge, where disorderly dancing was taking place. Who knows what else was happening in other rooms? But upstairs, in what Dave Lyons called the television room, some four or five people sat around, watching a programme. They seem not to have noticed that someone had come in and stood behind their chairs, looking over their heads at the images on the screen. But they couldn't help noticing what he was soon to do.

The room was in darkness apart from the light of the

television set. In that peaceful dimness, where people lolled with glasses in their hands, what happened must have been like an air-raid on a pleasure beach. A very large crystal vase passed above their heads in a deadly trajectory and converged with the television screen. The set, balanced on one ornately decorative, spindly leg, keeled backwards on to the floor, where it is reported to have expired in a not un-musical jangle of guts. Someone dropped a glass. A woman screamed. Panicked movements took place in the dark, suggestive of the aftermath of a terrorist attack. Someone put on the light. There, nodding benevolently at everyone, was a man who appeared to think he was on the rostrum at a march-past in his honour. He was identified as Scott Laidlaw.

The fuel for my imagination had come from Anna, through John Strachan by way of Mhairi Strachan. But I suspect my sense of the event isn't too wildly divergent from the facts. Anna, it seems, outlined the entire evening for Mhairi in vivid detail. The whole thing was, Anna had said, carved on her memory. It must have made a fair impact. Those were dramatic words for Anna, whose normal social discourse seemed to me to have all the authenticity of an air-hostess's smile. She had also said that the night had been the last straw for her and in that less resonant phrase I thought I recognised her more habitual tone.

Anna had assiduously collected the contextualising details of Scott's social philistinism and relayed them at length to more than Mhairi. I thought the reason was perhaps the need for self-justification that tends to come to people prior to the foreseen break-up of a relationship, like an outrider warning them to cover their flanks. I could imagine her going the rounds in that way that I've known friends of mine to do, holding a public roup of their former commitment, so that it may become clear that there is no longer any reason for them to stay.

I had to admit she seemed to have a case. The impossibility of living with Scott appeared to have been caught in flagrante. After John Strachan had told me, we both sat silent for a while, in the lounge of the Bushfield. He sipped his pint, I sipped my whisky. The grandiose folly of Scott's gesture was both arresting and incomprehensible. It replayed itself endlessly in my mind like some demented fiddle-tune – Laidlaw's Farewell to the Social Life. But were there any words to it? What did it mean?

'This Dave Lyons,' I said. 'I've heard of him. But not from Scott himself. Just sometimes from Scott and Anna together. Had Scott fallen out with him?'

'I don't know. I think they knew each other better when they were younger. Maybe it was one of those relationships that just survive on habit. Past any reason that either of them understood any more.'

'I was wondering why Scott attacked his telly. Was it a resentment of his money? But that seems a pretty pathetic target to go for. Who hasn't got a TV? It's not exactly the first thing you'd associate with Rockefeller.'

'No,' John Strachan said. 'You're not going to get them to man the barricades with that one. Death to the telly-owning oppressors.'

'Do you know him yourself?

'Dave Lyons? I've seen him. But I don't know him personally.'

'So you obviously wouldn't know his phone number.'

John Strachan looked at me and started to laugh. He shook his head.

'You're a very indirect man, aren't you? What are you going to do? Phone up and say, "Hullo, it's about your broken telly"?'

'No,' I said. 'I wouldn't be as abrupt as that. I could phone up and say, "Hullo. It's nice to meet you. *Now* it's about your broken telly."'

'Oh, that's fine,' he said. 'Given that reassurance, I can help. I know somebody who should have the number. I'll try him.'

He went out to the pay-phone in the hall and I crossed to get us in another drink. Things were picking up at the bar. Gestures were becoming more expansive. Three separate groups had connected up loosely. I was introduced to one of the Danish residents. His name was Søren, which endeared him to me immediately. But unlike Kierkegaard, he seemed never to have experienced angst. He had a face like a baby which has just discovered tickling. His mood was infectious. A late night in the Bushfield looked to be in the offing.

John Strachan came back with the number and the address. The sight of a fresh pint seemed to make him nervous. He would have to be getting back to Mhairi. I thanked him for his help and we talked a little longer and I told him how much the painting of the five men at the table had interested me.

When he was gone, I went to the pay-phone and dialled the number he had given me. The voice that answered was strong and self-assured.

'Yes?'

'Hullo. Is that Mr Lyons?'

'It is. Who's this?'

'I'm sorry to bother you. My name's Jack Laidlaw. I'm Scott Laidlaw's brother.'

'Ah, hullo. I was really sorry to hear about Scott. It was a terrible loss.'

'Yes. I was wondering, Mr Lyons. I'm in Ayrshire just now. I suppose you could call it a kind of sentimental journey. I'm just trying to sort out my feelings about Scott's death. And I wondered if I could talk to you some time this week.'

He hadn't sounded like the sort of man who would hesitate as long as this.

'Excuse me. Where did you get my number?'

It was my turn to hesitate, since I didn't know where his number had come from. I could hear what I thought was Mozart faintly in the background.

'I was going through some of Scott's papers. And your number came up.' I was embarrassed by the way it came out. I had made it sound rather ominous: this is death on the line. 'I mean, I found your telephone number. And I thought, as a friend of Scott's, you were somebody I would like to talk to. I had lost touch a bit with him at the end. I'd just like to see him more clearly.'

'Papers?' he said. 'What kind of papers were these?'

It was a strange question, not to say impertinent. That interested me. It seemed to imply that there might be papers Dave Lyons would be worried about. My casually evasive movement might have bumped against something solid. I decided to move carefully.

'Just some of Scott's things.'

'Well, I'm very busy this week. Normally, I'd be in Edinburgh and it wouldn't be possible anyway. But I'm working from home this week. I'm sorry but the schedule's pretty tight.'

'It wouldn't take long, Mr Lyons. There's something in particular I'd like to talk to you about.'

'What would that be?'

Papers, significant papers, I hoped my pause was suggesting.

'It's a bit complicated to go into on the phone.'

I suspected his silence was debating whether it was better to close me off now or to check out what I thought it was I had. There was something here. I sensed it.

'Tell you what. I really am busy this week. There's not much time I can give you. But tomorrow. I have a business lunch. At Cranston Castle House. If you're there round about twoish. We can maybe have a few minutes. But only a few. It's the best I can do.'

'It's great,' I said. 'I appreciate it.'

'You know where it is?'

'Not exactly. But I'll find it.'

'All right, then. I'll see you then.'

I was looking forward to meeting him. When I came back into the lounge, my evening went into a higher gear. The talk covered a lot of ground fast. The Happy Dane and I found we both liked Kris Kristofferson. A stranger offered me his condolences and told me that an old man called Sanny Wilson had met Scott in a bar the night he was killed. Sanny had told the man something he remembered. Scott had said at one point, 'The man in the green coat has died again.' I was intrigued. The man said that, if I was still here tomorrow night, he would try and bring Sanny Wilson in to tell me about it himself. I said I thought I would still be here.

After closing time, the residents stayed on in the lounge. A guitar-player who had come in after doing a gig in another pub decided to become a resident as well for the night. We had a sing-song. In the pauses during it, I had a long, rambling, self-revelatory conversation with Katie. I sang 'Cycles' when it was first my turn. Later, when the mood had been established by the right amount of alcohol, I gave them 'The Learig', perhaps Scott's favourite song. As a reward, I received a lot of advice on how to locate Cranston Castle House.

I might have been in the lounge yet, so good was it, except that I wanted to keep some brain-cells for tomorrow. I took my farewell of everybody as if I had known them all my life. Before going upstairs, I went out to the car and collected Scott's painting and the bottle of whisky. It seemed a matter of tremendous urgency there and then. When I came back in, I had a brilliant idea. It did not occur to me at the time that it was the same kind of brilliant idea that Caesar had when he decided to go to the Capitol. I rang Jan's number. Fortunately, no one answered.

In my room, I unveiled Scott's painting and set it up against the wall. I stripped and sat on the bed and looked at those images of Scotland. I opened the bottle of whisky. I communed with art and had a long conversation with the Antiquary, recalling old times. I put out the light and went to bed.

I woke up suddenly in the darkness with two thoughts, distinct as nightlights, in my mind.

The man in the painting of the five at supper was wearing a green coat.

How do you die twice?

TWO

9

A kitchen in the morning: it can be a garden of the
senses. The sunlight is shafting in through the window,
as if William Blake has been given the commission
today and is announcing the sacredness of the everyday. The
coffee-percolator is putt-putting like the pulse of normalcy.
The aroma it gives off is wandering aimlessly somewhere,
inviting anyone to follow. A woman stands in the sunshine,
chopping vegetables. The rich smells they release make a
meadow in a room. A man sits at a table, drinking coffee. The
warmed clay of the cup in his hand warms him fraternally,
telling him we're all part of the same process. I'll be your cup
today, you can be someone else's later. The man has eaten a
good breakfast. A dog drowses on the sunlit floor, occasionally
opening one lazy eye on the world. The room around the
woman and the man is sustaining. The feeling it engenders is
of hope, old failures buried, new possibilities to be born.
Perhaps God has taken the twice bitten apple from Adam and
Eve, gently healed it with his hand, hung it back up on the
tree, said, 'Try again.' That kind of feeling.

If place were only place and the present only the present,
but we invade them with the past, complicate them with our

futures. For I was the man at the table and Katie the woman at the worktop. To individualise the moment is not perhaps, as we think, to save it but to lose it. The room was still the room but we were an unhappy woman and an angry man within it. That melted it into flux. If the world was a new red apple, I was the worm inside.

I was just Jack Laidlaw finishing his coffee and wondering what to do next to assuage a need for understanding. Katie was an over-worked woman making soup. Even the dog was no canine ideal. It had its own fleas of banality. This was Buster, who had a serious aggression problem. We were accidentally sharing some space. Mike was somewhere mysterious, as he usually was even when he was with you.

I had wakened with a thought that was still around. While I had a bath and shaved and changed and heard Katie giving the other residents their breakfast, the idea had continued to play about the edges of my mind. During my breakfast in the kitchen, I called it home for a serious confrontation. It seemed to me, in my obsessiveness, that it was a new, important angle from which to confront the mystery of Scott's last month. I thought I should invite Katie to consider it. So I did.

'Women, Katie,' I said.

It must have sounded more like a wistful expression of longing than the question I was asking myself aloud.

'Sorry?'

'Women. Scott. The way he was at the end, there had to be a woman in there somewhere.'

'There was Anna.'

'Did you know her?'

'I knew who she was. I'd had her pointed out to me in the

street. But I never spoke to her. I don't think she mixed a lot with the servants.'

The adder's tongue of malice flicked and withdrew. I knew how much Katie had cared about Scott. Maybe the caring hadn't been entirely platonic. Maybe she had seen in him the wastage of a man she might have saved, as women sometimes will.

'Nah,' I said. 'That's not what I mean. It was gone between him and Anna. Somebody else. He was living raw. There's only one ointment I can think of for that kind of pain. And he wasn't that different from me.'

Katie was finding the chopping of the vegetables an act of total concentration.

'What do you think?' I said.

'What would I know about that?'

'Katie. What you don't know about the people around you, it wouldn't even cover a penny. And watch you don't include a couple of fingers in the soup. You're going at it hard there.'

The knife nearly came down strong enough to split the bread board in two. She turned towards me, the knife still in her hand. She was a formidable woman. I thought I could hear The Ride of the Valkyries starting up faintly in the background. I pretended to duck behind the table.

'Don't throw it,' I said.

Buster, with his finely honed sensitivity always aware of everything except what was going on, began to growl. Jokes seemed to be lost on him. A nuance to Buster was whether to bite your right leg or your left.

'Your dog's daft, by the way,' I said. 'You should get him a brain transplant. I'll pay for it.'

'Leave Buster alone. You don't understand him. He's got a lot of affection.'

'He's a dumb bastard. You should shave his head and tattoo National Front on it.'

She put down the knife. She stared at the wall immediately in front of her.

'Jack,' she said. 'Why are you so angry? It's only a dog. And that stuff you're asking. That's personal. Any talks Scott and me had are between us.'

'What's this, Katie? The sanctity of the pub confessional? Who do you think I am? An income-tax inspector? I'm his brother, for Christ's sake. I loved him.'

'Do you want another cup of coffee?' she said.

'I want some answers,' I said.

She sighed and wiped her hands on her apron. She took a fresh cup and saucer and put them on the table across from me. She collected the percolator, filled my cup and filled her own. She replaced the percolator. She came and sat at the table. She took a cigarette from my packet, lit it and gave it across to me. I love the way a woman can make a ceremony out of a passing moment. Maybe society is a masculine distortion of reality but civilisation is feminine. I felt disarmed by small kindnesses.

'What is it. Jack?' she said.

'Katie,' I said. 'My life's collapsed about my ears. And I'm trying to rebuild it. Simple.'

'When do men grow up? I can still see you in short trousers.'

As if on cue, I went in the huff.

'We're in different plays,' she said.

'What?'

'Men and women. We're in different plays. Women are realistic. You lot are trying to act out some grand drama that isn't there.'

She sipped her coffee black. She looked at me steadily. Her mood had taken off the morning and its preoccupations like so much make-up. I saw her clearly, maybe for the first time. She seemed thoughtful and understanding and slightly tired of it all. Where she had been and what she had gone through came out to settle on her face and the tension in her between her past and her refusal to give in to it gave her a dignity.

'It's like Mike,' she said. 'So we can't have any children. What's that? It's a sad thing you learn to live with. Like a dark place in your head. But you can make brightness round about it. Not him. It's like a holy curse to him. The world picked him out specially, it seems. To blight his life. We could've adopted years ago. But he had to fight things on his own terms. To prove himself. It's too late for us now.'

A door swung gently open on her words. Beyond it was the mustiness of dead dreams, an attic of ghostly aspirations, children's clothes no one would ever wear. I saw her pain and the courage with which she bore it. I thought of Jan and understood her a little more clearly. She would be trying to avoid going where Katie was. She was right to try.

'Mike,' Katie said. 'Drama, drama. Different plays.'

Mike came into focus for me, all that bleak tenseness in him. He was a silent and furious quarrel with the world, a raging stillness. I sensed him as one of life's obsessive litigants who, isolating one slander on his sense of himself, expends everything fruitlessly on trying to have it retracted. But I sympathised.

'It's funny, Katie,' I said. 'But I see it the other way round. I think it's often women who live among melodrama. Melodrama to me's effects exaggerated beyond their causes. I've known women sing opera because the arse had burned out a pan. I'm going crazy because my brother's dead. Not because there's a button off my shirt.'

We looked at each other across the table, as if it was no-man's-land, acknowledging truce.

'But I love them just the same,' I said.

Katie smiled and leaned over and touched my hand. 'I can tolerate you as well,' she said. 'Ask.'

'So were there any women? With Scott.'

'He didn't tell you?'

I thought of what he had been trying to say that night in my flat.

'I think maybe once he came close. But I don't know. We had lost touch a bit. For whiles we might as well have been on different continents.'

'There was somebody,' she said.

The significance of the words materialised before me, solid as a door into a mysterious chamber of Scott's life where I hadn't been. It was a door I hesitated at, even as his brother. I would be rifling his privacy in his absence. But something in me needed it to open. Only Katie could do that and she wasn't making any moves. I waited. She waited, sipping her coffee. There were rules here, I understood. You didn't just blunder in. There was a ceremony of respect to be performed and Katie would conduct it.

'I think I was the only one he told,' she said.

She was staring at the table, cuddling the secret to her one last time before she would release it. I thought I saw what it must have meant to her. Trying to tell people who you really are is always a kind of love letter. It invests them with importance in your life. Enlarged by Scott's trust in her, Katie didn't want to betray it. She had to talk herself towards sharing it with me.

'I loved him in some way, you know,' she said. 'I think a lot of people did a bit. He could be a pain in the bum could your Scott. But even while he was doing it, you could see how vulnerable he was. I fell out with him very badly a few months back. It wasn't like him. He didn't come in for two weeks. You've no idea how much that upset me. I thought a part of my life was gone. When he walked in that door, it felt like Christmas for me. And you getting the best present you'd ever had. Oh, he could brighten the day.'

She finished her coffee.

'Her name was Ellie,' she said suddenly. 'She was a teacher. She didn't have any children. That's all I know.'

'She worked beside him?'

'Jack.'

She made my name a long, slow accusation. Having admitted me to the sanctum, she didn't want me trampling all over it.

'What do you think Scott did. Jack? Show me pictures? Maybe three or four times in here, in the early hours, he mentioned her. Always just "Ellie". No second name. And I didn't ask for it. I know she mattered to him a lot. I know the guilt was damaging him. I know it seemed to have broken up between them. I was sharing his pain. The details weren't what

69

mattered. He was bleeding for somebody. Was I supposed to ask for her phone number? He needed a bandage. I was a bandage.'

'But who is she? Where did she live?'

As soon as I said it, I knew I had closed the door on myself. She stared at me as if focussing the lens on the microscope. What strange creature have we here? She spoke with carefully muted anger.

'Why don't you go to the crematorium and sift the ashes?'

'If I thought it would help, I would,' I said.

I stared back through the lens at her. What strange creature thinks I'm a strange creature?

She stood up and lifted her cup and lifted mine, though it wasn't empty, and crossed to the sink and rinsed them out. She went on with making the soup. I wondered, perhaps unworthily, about Katie. Maybe her motives for not wanting to talk about the unknown Ellie were less noble than she made out. Maybe jealousy was one of them. I always suspect self-righteousness. I think it's usually a way of cosmeticising the truth of self, like a powdered periwig on a headful of lice.

Katie had brought her pot of soup to the boil and turned it down to simmer.

'Buster,' she said.

Buster recognised his name. He wasn't as dumb as I had thought. Katie took the leash that was draped round a hook on the kitchen door.

'If that starts to boil over,' she said, 'turn it down some more, will you? I'm taking Buster out to clean himself.'

I thought about the euphemism when they were gone. It was an expression my father had used. 'Take Bacchus out to clean himself,' I could remember him saying. Or Judie. Or Rusty. Or Tara. We had a lot of dogs, which is why I have always liked them as long as they don't develop delusions of grandeur and begin to think they're the householder. The phrase reminded me of my family, the four of us living together. I thought of the possibilities there had seemed then and how strangely they had led to me sitting alone in the kitchen of the Bushfield Hotel. The other three were dead. I was glad my parents hadn't known Scott's death. I felt somehow responsible towards the other three. We had tried to make some kind of honest contract with the world and it seemed to me the world had cheated on us. The least we were due was some retrospective understanding. I decided I was here to collect.

I lifted the phone and dialled Glebe Academy. It was the same nice woman from yesterday who answered. John Strachan was with a class. They would have to fetch him. While I waited, I reflected that I had to know more about that closed room of Scott's life Katie had allowed me to glimpse. If I couldn't go through the door, maybe I could get in a window. But I would have to be careful in speaking to John Strachan. I wasn't sure what John knew. I wasn't even sure what I knew yet. Approach by indirections.

'Hullo?'

'Hullo, John. It's Jack Laidlaw.'

'Hullo, Jack.'

A session in a pub can be a great force-feeder of intimacy.

'Look. I'm sorry to bother you again so soon. Especially taking you away from a class.'

'No problem. It's one of my more civilised groups. The room should still be there when I get back.'

'What it is –' is something I'll have to work up to. So let me cover my tracks a little by saying – 'I was just wondering. Scott must have left some things at the school. I mean, he didn't exactly know that he was leaving. I'm thinking of papers and stuff like that. Something that might help me to understand what he was going through at the end.'

'It's possible.'

'I know it's probably a terrible nuisance for you. But do you think you could check it out for me? Take a look at his room? And see if there's anything there at all? That would give us a clue.'

I was trying to read the pause that followed. I wondered if he was going to refuse.

'Actually,' he said, 'his room's been taken over. You know? There's somebody else in it now. It was a coveted room. Terrific windows for an art room.'

I understood his hesitation. He hadn't wanted to convey to me how quickly Scott's dying had converted to administrative practicalities. One man's death is another man's sunlight.

'So I think it's been cleaned out,' he said. 'But I'll go up there today and have a look. I suppose there might be something.'

'Thanks, John. Oh. There's something else,' which I casually mention since it's why I phoned. 'Ellie Somebody? It's a woman I thought I might try to speak to. But I can't get her second name. Does that name mean anything to you?'

This time the pause was impenetrable. Did he know about Scott and her? Was he instinctively deducing what I had just learned about them? Was he simply baffled by the name? The slowness of his answer, when it came, suggested alien matter caught up in his thoughts, grinding the machinery to a halt.

'Well,' he said. 'I don't know. It's not an unusual name. But there was a woman who worked here at one time. Ellie. But I don't know if that's who you mean. She's left now. Ellie Mabon. Do you mean Ellie Mabon?'

I didn't know. But if all you have are shots in the dark, you'd better check out anything you hit to see if it's what you're after.

'I don't know,' I said. 'It could be. Anyway, thanks.'

'All right,' he said at last, perhaps not sure what I was thanking him for. 'I'll see about Scott's room. I'll phone you if there's anything.'

'I'll be out and about today, John.'

'Well. If I can't get you personally, I'll try and look in at the Bushfield. Sometime in the evening. All right? I better go and see if the natives are getting restless. Cheers.'

'Cheers.'

I put the phone down and went to look for Katie's phone-book. I could hear someone walking about upstairs and imagined Mike pacing the psychological prison he seemed to have made for himself. The phone-book was behind the bread-bin. With Katie, it would be. We weren't so different from each other as she thought.

I was on my third Mabon before I found an Ellie. The first one hadn't answered. The second was what sounded like an amazingly old man who insisted on telling me about a mix-up with the plumbing in his house. I promised to look into it. The third was at a good address in Graithnock. The voice was brusque but with interesting undertones, like a sensuous body in a business-suit.

'Hello?'

'Hello. I'm sorry to bother you. I may have a wrong number here. I'm looking for Ellie Mabon.'

'Speaking.'

I knew this was the one. The realisation paralysed my mouth for the moment. She didn't know how closely we were connected, what I knew about her.

'Hello?'

'I'm sorry,' I said. 'My name's Jack Laidlaw. I'm Scott's brother.'

She practised breathing for a little.

'God,' she said. 'Your voices are so alike.'

'You knew Scott,' I said, not one of my more illuminating remarks.

'Well, I didn't just speak to him on the telephone.' Then I sensed her realise she was showing too much of herself too soon. Her voice, when she spoke again, was like a woman who has readjusted her dress. 'I taught beside him, you know.'

'Yes, I know. Could I meet you and speak to you about that?'

'I beg your pardon?'

'I'm sorry. This must sound pretty bizarre to you. But I found Scott's death hard to take. I'm just trying to come to terms with it. Talking to people who knew him. You know? I thought maybe we could talk.'

'You're right,' she said. 'It does sound pretty bizarre.'

'I thought it might.'

'What am I supposed to tell you?'

'I don't know.'

'Well, if you don't, neither do I. All right?'

'Not really,' I said. 'Come on. Please. It's not such a wild request.'

'Wild? Listen. As far as I'm concerned, it might have come straight from the Amazon jungle. Why don't you go back there?'

The conversation wasn't going well. I felt myself within seconds of losing this hand. But a couple of things had registered with me: the remark about not just speaking to Scott on the telephone was an admission in code and she knew it; if she was as angry as she acted, why hadn't she put down the phone? Her whole game-plan was set on keeping me away from her life. I understood that. I even sympathised. But I couldn't afford to agree. I might need something that she could tell me. Her weakness was that she didn't want to put down the phone until she was sure she had frightened me off. I knew there was only one card I could play.

'You live at 28 Sycamore Road,' I said, reading from the phone-book. 'I'm sure I can find it.'

'What? Listen, you. I'm a married woman.' She thought about it, made an emendation. 'A happily married woman. I don't need you messing up my life. What would my husband say?'

'When does he come home?' I said.

'6.30.' She had said it before she realised the impertinence of the question. That made her angrier. 'What the hell does it have to do with you?'

'Mrs Mabon,' I said. 'I don't want to mess up your life. What good would that do me? I just want to talk. I can come in the afternoon. Nobody needs to know.'

'I do have neighbours.'

'We can stand on the doorstep.'

'What about the children?'

'Mrs Mabon, you don't have any.'

There was silence.

'This afternoon. Okay?'

'I don't think I believe you.'

'Maybe you should.'

'No way. You can go to hell,' she said and put down the phone like a punch on the ear.

I sat holding the phone and feeling ashamed of myself. By the time I put down the receiver, I had decided I couldn't go through with what I had threatened. I had no rights here. Katie was right. I was sifting ashes. Let them lie.

Katie came back in with Buster. She looked as if she knew she was right. I was guilty about what I had been doing in her absence, feeling I had proved her case by being so insistent. It didn't help that I had let the soup bubble over slightly. When Katie didn't say anything but just adjusted the gas, I felt even worse. Buster was the most welcoming thing in the room. That made it time to get out.

I went upstairs for my jacket. When I came back down, I looked into the kitchen. Katie was tenderising meat as if it was my head.

'That's me away, Kate,' I said. 'Thanks for the breakfast. I'll see you later.'

She turned her face, looking past me.

'You going to be away all day?' she said.

'Is that a question or a request?'

She started almost to smile and waved me out of the room.

10

'Gus. Right? So you probably think that my real name's Angus. But that just shows yer cultural parochialism. Guess. On yese go. Ah'll give yese a hundred guesses. An' ye'll no' get near it.'

There were some less than serious accepters of the challenge (offering, among others, 'Angustura') but I wasn't one of them. I stood among the jocularity and wondered what I was doing here, what I was doing in Graithnock, what I was doing in my head. The Katie Samson effect was still with me.

Leaving the Bushfield, I had parked the car in the town centre and taken my obsession for a walk. The town wasn't interested. I had wandered for a while among the normal business of the day and felt as marginal to what was going on around me as if I had been a religious fanatic wearing a sandwich-board with a message only he could understand.

Coming in here, I felt worse. Maybe Katie was right about the way we inhabit different plays. I certainly seemed to be appearing in a different drama from anybody else. Obsessively following the script of some gloomy revenge tragedy, I had wandered into a vaudeville show. I had no lines here. All I could be was part of the audience.

'Wrong. Wrong again. Let me enlighten your abysmal igno-rance. The answer is . . . Wait for it . . .'

The answer was, apparently, Gustavus – 'as in Adolphus'. Well, the truth was that his name was actually Gustave, since his ancestors had moved from Sweden to France and natural-ised the name accordingly. But it had been originally Gustavus. The heavily built man who had been outlining his exotic origins looked as Scottish as a haggis. His ability to decorate the truth with lies and the appreciative response his talent evoked confirmed my sense of the hopelessness of my quest.

We're all experts in concealment, hailing one another's disguises as if they were old friends. Among this jostling crowd of masks, many of which were my own, I couldn't expect to look upon the truth of what had happened to my brother. There's nobody here but us liars.

But by the time the cabaret was over a small revelation had given me renewed hope. Although it was as insubstantial as misting on a mirror, it meant my belief in understanding wasn't quite dead. I realised who had been speaking.

Scott had mentioned him to me more than once and I had a conviction of having seen him around the town when I was younger, though the effects of his aging made me uncertain about that. His name was Gus McPhater. Presumably Gus was short for Angus. The fact that he had just spent several minutes elaborately denying that this was the case made it seem likely.

He was the Baron Münchhausen of the Akimbo Arms. The lies he told were local legend. According to Scott's intermit-tent reports to me, Gus McPhater had designed the Queen Mary ('But some bastard altered the plans. Never was the boat it shoulda been!'), had written the James Bond books ('Ian

Fleming paid me a lump sum. Ye can shove yer publicity') and designed the first mini-skirt, foisting it on an unsuspecting public for his own voyeuristic purposes ('At my age, ye take yer pleasure where ye can get it'). He was a former merchant seaman.

I was standing in the public bar. Through the arched doorway that joined this gantry to the one in the lounge, I could see that the lounge was almost empty. Two elderly women with plastic shopping-bags beside them on the cushioned bench-seat were tippling quietly, nodding into each other's remarks. The bar wasn't much busier. Besides the artiste and myself, there were two men studying the horses as well as a young man distant enough to be into transcendental meditation and a vociferously unemployed bricklayer, wearing a boilersuit, as if the call to build something might come at any moment. From things Scott had said, I recognised the tall barman as well. His name was Harry and he looked as happy as a Rechabite at a wine-tasting. I recalled one of Scott's quotes from Gus McPhater: 'Harry does for conversation what lumbago does for dancin'.'

It was that time just after opening when a pub begins to come awake, starts a new day inside the old one, as if the morning had a stutter. The ice was brimming the bucket. The linoleum floor was devoid of cigarette-ends. The moted sunlight coming in the window was clear enough to see through.

But, imagining Scott's nights here, I populated the emptiness. This had been one of his places and some small part of his spirit had been left here. Holding my own brief seance for my brother, I conjured vivid faces and loud nights. I saw that smile of his, sudden as a sunray, when he loved what you were saying. I saw the strained expression when he felt you must agree with him and couldn't get you to see that. I caught the way the laughter would light up his eyes when he was trying to suppress it. I heard the laughing when it broke. He must have had some nights here. He had lived with such intensity. The thought was my funeral for him. Who needed possessions and career and official achievements? Life was only in the living of it. How you act and what you are and what you do and how you be were the only substance. They didn't last either. But while you were here, they made what light there was – the wick that threads the candle-grease of time. His light was out but here I felt I could almost smell the smoke still drifting from its snuffing.

I looked across at the preposterousness of Gus McPhater. He, too, however marginally, had moved within the orbit of that light. He was sitting at a small, round, formica table, a third of a pint in front of him. He was staring at the floor. His short performance was over. He had the emptiness of an actor who has just divested himself of his role. I believed in who he was in silence more than who he had been in noise, despite the laughter of the others.

Watching him, I saw more than a vaudeville turn. He might be able to tell me something about Scott. Yet what was the point of talking to a professional liar? Then I remembered something else Scott had told me about him. He had a daughter who died young and it had made him a recluse for years. When he re-emerged into life, he came complete with armour-plated lies. I remembered Scott, lover of paradox, saying, 'His gift is modesty.' I think he meant that he chose to be a variety of people that he wasn't rather than just be himself. 'His patter's a lapwing,' Scott had said. 'It leads you where he isn't. Because where he is is too vulnerable.'

I went over to where he was.

'Excuse me,' I said. 'You're Gus McPhater?'

He looked up slowly and by the time his eyes met mine he had remembered his lines.

'This is correct, young man,' he said.

He showed no surprise that a stranger should come up and know his name. Perhaps he was used to it. Perhaps he thought I was an autograph-hunter.

'Can I buy you a drink?'

'This is permissible behaviour.'

'A pint of McEwan's?'

'This is correct.'

He drank off what he had left and handed me the glass. I went across to the bar. Harry accepted my order as if it was just another small boil on the bum of Job. I brought the pint of heavy over to Gus McPhater and put my fresh glass of soda and lime on the table beside him. As I sat down, I saw him analysing the contents of my glass.

'Are you an alcoholic, son?' he said.

I couldn't help laughing at the innocent decadence of his assumption.

'Not yet,' I said. 'Give me another fortnight. No, I'm driving.'

'Well, that's good thinking,' he said. 'The bar and the car don't mix. Eh? The bevvy and the Chevvy. No way.'

The words were so obviously rehearsed and delivered so archly that I had a momentary dread that the list wasn't finished. I foresaw, in a second of panic, having to endure McPhater's

Thesaurus of Drinking and Driving – the poteen and the machine, the bender and the fender.

'I'm Jack Laidlaw,' I said. 'Scott's brother.'

I knew in his immediate reaction that Scott's assessment had been accurate and my hope had been justified. This was a man who knew the public from the private. He only gave guided tours of himself to tourists. I wasn't there as one. He grimaced and exhaled for several seconds, as if he was emptying himself of all the things he might have said to the stranger I wasn't. When he looked at me, his eyes were a shyness making my acquaintance.

'Of course,' he said. 'Ah should've known ye from Scott. Actually, Ah saw ye a few times a lotta years ago. Ye were just a boy, really. But a wee bit tasty, Ah recall.'

I had a noisy youth.

'You're the polisman.'

'Not today, I'm not,' I said.

'Ach, Scott,' he said. 'Ah was sorry to hear that. Ye know what Ah thought when Ah heard it? This is no crap. Ah thought, here's me. Ah mean, Jeanie an' me get on well enough. Minus the occasional re-run of Waterloo. But Ah've done what Ah'm gonny do. Ye know what Ah mean? That Scott had a lot to do yet. Ah think maybe Ah would've volunteered tae take his place. Given the chance. Maybe not, mind ye. But maybe Ah would. An' he's the only one outside ma own Ah could even think that about. There's a few Ah wouldn't've minded helpin' to shove under the car. Your Scott was different.'

'Well, you won't get any argument from me.'

'Thanks for the drink, son. It seems to be a Laidlaw habit. Ah got enough of them from Scott.'

He took a sip of his beer.

'That was a bad one. They're all bad. But that was a bad one.'

'Did you see him much before he died?'

He looked round the bar as if establishing in his memory Scott's location there.

'Well,' he said, 'Ah hope you don't mind me sayin' this. Jack, isn't it? But Scott wasn't the same man before he died. Ah mean, Ah know it was an accident an' that. But it was like he was the accident already. He just hadn't found the address. Ye know what they say. Like lookin' for a place to happen.'

He continued with that theme and I listened interestedly enough but it wasn't anything I didn't know. At least I was talking to someone who had known Scott and who made me feel less alien to the town. But it was all so general, as if the complexity that had been my brother was already, within a month, being processed into plastic clichés – 'not happy in his marriage', 'hitting the bottle', 'a waste of a good man'. I was looking for Scott, not an identikit of disillusioned West of Scotland man.

Then Gus McPhater, like someone digging a vegetable garden who turns up a human bone, said something that was specific to Scott and which I wanted to examine.

'Ah saw him that night.'

'Sorry?'

'Scott. Ah saw him that night.'

'Where?'

'Where else would Ah be?' he said. 'In here. Ah saw him in here. The night he was killed.'

'Was that long before he died?'

83

'Be a few hours, Ah suppose.'

'What was he like?'

'He was well on. That's what he was like. He was givin' the gin and tonics a terrible lacin'. No wonder he fell out with people. He had been a few places before he came in here, Ah'd say. High as ye get he was. He came in here as if it was a saloon an' he was Billy The Kid.'

The image of aggression didn't suit Scott. I remembered his archaic chivalry the last time we had been drinking together. That was central to my sense of him. But Katie Samson had mentioned his untypical quarrel of a few months ago. There had been the incident at the party. And now Gus McPhater was describing him as if he were someone else. As a stalwart of the Akimbo Arms, Gus must have seen some angry men in his time. His assessment of the wildness of Scott's behaviour had the authority of a connoisseur behind it. I watched him hold the moment in his mind, weighing it appreciatively.

'My God,' he said. 'Ye see them all in here. If ye just wait long enough. The ones that are just lookin' for a face to waste. The ones that are lookin' for where they used to be at the bottom of the glass. The ones that've only a pint between them an' slittin' their wrists. An' Ah'm tellin' ye. That was some Scott that night. That was a man wi' bad things in his head.'

I wondered what the bad things were. A part of me argued that they were probably only the general unhappiness of his life. But I suspected an acceleration of despair towards the end of his time, as if another, final ingredient had been added to the brew of grief that was poisoning his being. It was that ingredient I wanted to isolate. I was wondering if it could be the man in the green coat's miraculous act of dying again.

'You said he fell out with people,' I said. 'Was there anybody in particular?'

'Oh, yes. There was.'

'Who was it?'

'Well, the way Scott came in, ye would've thought it could be anybody. But when Scott exploded, Ah remember thinkin' that's who he had been lookin' for all the time.'

'So who?' I was hungry for another name on which to focus, some specific that would bring my suspicions into clearer perspective. 'Who was it?'

'Fast Frankie White.'

I had a name all right but it blurred things further. The irony was that I knew the name and it should have clarified things. Fast Frankie White ('the ladies' delight') was a petty criminal. He belonged to my world, not to Scott's. I could think of no reason why Scott should have fallen out with him. Perhaps it was something just born of the moment.

'Was there a fight?' I said.

'Just words. Bad words.'

'What about?'

'That, Ah don't know.'

'You must have some idea.'

'Well.'

He finished off his pint. I bought him another aid to memory.

'See, Scott was in here first. Before Frankie, like. He was drinkin' doubles. He wasn't exactly fightin' at that time. But ye could see the safety-catch was off. The eyes were swivellin' a lot. He seemed to be lookin' for something. When Frankie came in, he was it. Scott made a beeline for 'im. Ah don't hold too much wi' Frankie White. You know him?'

'I know him.'

'Well, ye'll know what Ah mean then. He's not the worst. But ye don't introduce 'im to yer daughter. But it was Scott that started it all right. Frankie hadn't even ordered a drink. An' Scott's right into his ribs. They're arguin' hot an' heavy. Then Frankie breaks away an' Ah hear him sayin', "Tae hell with it. Ah don't need this. Ah'm barrin' maself." An' he's off. An' Scott shouts after him. "Aye," he's shoutin'. "You should bar yerself from everywhere. You should bar yerself from the human race. Ah know what you've done." An' that's about it. Some of the other boys were askin' Scott what all that was about. But he wouldn't say. An' he didn't hang about much longer. Ah wondered maself if he went lookin' for Frankie. Whatever that was about, it wasn't over for Scott.'

It was now, but he had left some weird hieroglyphs of behaviour behind him that I couldn't decipher. A quarrel with Fast Frankie White was one of the weirdest. They shouldn't have had enough in common to nod to each other, let alone argue. That Scott should feel passionate enough about Frankie to anathematise him was incomprehensible. Also, according to my information, Frankie was supposed these days to be living somewhere in London.

I questioned Gus McPhater some more but the mist didn't clear. I ordered a pizza from the bar ('They're classic,' Gus McPhater had said) and, while my mouth engaged it in combat, my mind was trying to work out where this new information took me. It wasn't much. But it was strange enough to re-invoke the demon in me that insisted there was more to Scott's death than a road-accident. My appointment with Dave Lyons might be worth keeping. I was already trying to see beyond it.

'Fast Frankie,' I said to Gus McPhater. 'Do you know where he comes from originally?'

'Does anybody?' he said. 'It's round these parts somewhere, right enough. But he was never too strong on solid information was Frankie. Mainly, he comes from his own imagination, Ah think.'

My respect for Gus McPhater grew some more. He knew Frankie White down to his fingerprints. I left him another drink behind the bar and came out. Mind you, Gus was a better judge of people than he was of food. I hadn't quite finished my meal. It was a classic pizza, all right – say, first century AD.

11

Life is like a journey, saith the preacher. It's corny and he's been saying it too long but you can see what he means. I was thinking that as I came nearer to Cranston Castle House. Only, with the Irish in me from my mother's side, I turned the image on its head. A journey can be like life, I thought. Take this one.

I had left the decaying industrialism of Graithnock on the north side and was driving past green fields right away. Graithnock is like that these days, an aridity surrounded by the green world, a desert in an oasis. I turned right before I came into Kilmaurs at the place I had heard my father call the Old Stewarton Road-end. From there I was moving uncertainly and unhurriedly and vaguely towards Stewarton. Never take directions from a committee. That way, you're looking for a place that exists only in the abstract. The gathered wisdom of the Bushfield left me looking for landmarks that weren't there and gradually becoming aware that I would know where Cranston Castle House was when I found it.

But the weather was good and, though I didn't know where I was, I knew, in the countryside around me, where I had been. For I was driving through my past. These might not be the very places where Scott and I had played but, given the mythic quality of childhood terrain, they might as well have been. It was to places like this that we had come from the town to imagine more than the streets gave us, to replenish our horizons. The infinite innocence of our dreams was growing all around me.

I remembered the promise of those times, how the world had seemed to belong to everybody and the possibilities were anybody's for the taking, and then, uncertainly at first among the camouflage of the trees but slowly gaining substance, I made out the crenellations of what had to be Cranston Castle House. As I found the entrance to the driveway and came nearer to the place, its solidity grew more and more to feel like the hidden meaning of the countryside, the definitive clause in the statement of the place you might easily have overlooked. That was why I had been thinking that a journey can be like life, Scott's and mine. Here was where all the paths we had hoped to follow led, to entrenched property and status and wealth. The very ground we walked on had been owned, and not by us. The mirages of youth evaporated and confronted you with this. I parked the car among the few other cars in front of the building. Brian's Vauxhall was a Shetland pony in the Winners' Enclosure.

The building was big, one of those nineteenth-century attempts to re-invent the past, capitalism imitating feudalism. I opened the large wooden door and came into a small, wood-panelled entrance hall – Lilliputian baronial. A couple of floral armchairs and a brass-topped table were arranged tastefully beside the huge empty fireplace. The Akimbo Arms it wasn't. On my left, through an open, arched doorway, I could see the dining-room. Three men were finishing a meal with a lot of empty, freshly set tables around them. Through an arched doorway on my right was the bar. Everywhere, there was wood. If you could have replanted the interior of this place, you would have had a forest.

Going into the bar, I experienced a moment of confusion. That happens to me quite often. Throughout my boyhood, I was shy to the point of embarrassing other people – given to frozen silences and good at blushing. Perhaps we never quite grow out of the children we have been. Certainly with me adulthood seems to be a veneer that hasn't quite taken. Patches of the raw wood keep showing through in unexpected places. I'll walk into a party, dressed in maturity and nodding suavely, and suddenly realise that I don't know what the hell to say. Panic breaks out in me like pimples. This was one of the times.

I had recourse to my usual solution. I headed for the drink, even though that was a defensive reflex that clicked on an empty cartridge. I was on soda and lime. The girl behind the bar helped. She was dressed in what I assumed must be the uniform of the staff – black skirt, white blouse, a tiny scarf like a floppy bow tie. But the naturalness of her manner gave me some ease and made me feel I had an ally against all this supposed sophistication. As I sipped my drink, I tried to find my bearings.

This was where the diners took coffees and liqueurs. It didn't look as if it had been a very busy day. There were two tables with a couple at each. The only other people were two groups of business men – four at one table, five at another. I didn't know where Dave Lyons was. I had been hoping he would give me some sign when I came in. But nobody had moved, nobody had glanced towards me. I had made all the impact of the pheasant carved in wood above the gantry.

Gradually, impatience led me out of the time-lock of my adolescent awkwardness back into what I take for manhood. After all, I had been waiting long enough to grow a beard. I decided on the group of five and crossed towards their table. As I came nearer, I noticed one of them become very still. He didn't look towards me. He seemed to be listening to one of the other men but his listening, I thought, became a perform-ance of listening. I concluded that he was the man. I also concluded that he wasn't keen to see me.

When I stood beside them, the man who was talking even-tually looked up at me. He took me in vaguely, seeming slightly annoyed at my intrusion. Perhaps he thought I was a waiter.

'Excuse me,' I said. 'I'm looking for Dave Lyons.'

The acting listener was amazed. He snapped his fingers and pointed at me. His face couldn't have expressed more surprise if I'd dropped in through the roof.

'Scott's brother,' he said. 'Right? Of course, you are. Of course, you are.'

It was nice to have his confirmation of the fact. He stood up and shook hands.

'I'm Dave Lyons. It's great to meet you. Even if it's sad about the circumstances. Gentlemen. This is . . .'

'Jack Laidlaw.'

'Jack. That's right. Jack Laidlaw. He's the brother of a friend of mine. A friend unfortunately recently deceased. Jack. This is . . .'

He gave me the names. I was glad he didn't ask me to repeat

them. All I was aware of about them was the proximity of a lot of rubicund flesh, well-fed faces, heavy hands.

'If you'll excuse me, gentlemen. I have to give Jack here a little of my time. Please. Have more brandies if you want.'

He lifted his own brandy glass from a table with other glasses on it and coffee-cups and a sheaf of paper with mysterious figures on the top sheet. I caught the whiff of Aramis aftershave. I'd know it anywhere because Jan had once given me a bottle as a present. I had spent a fortnight trying to get used to it. I finished up leaping away from the smell as soon as the cork came off. I'm sure it's lovely but I had to admit eventually that I was allergic to it. Jan wasn't too pleased. Perhaps that's where our relationship had begun to founder: I couldn't inhabit her ideal sense of me. Maybe I could introduce her to Dave Lyons. Was this the kind of man Jan wanted?

'We'll sit over here,' he said to me. 'You have a drink?'

'It's at the bar.'

I collected my drink and joined him at the table in the corner, well away from everyone else. He looked at my glass.

'Soda and lime?' he said. 'I take that myself occasionally. When I want to stimulate my taste buds for a real drink. Abstinence makes the heart grow fonder.'

Dave Lyons was small, getting heavy. The features were thickening but that didn't diminish their attractiveness. It was a very positive face, the kind you could distinguish from fifty yards. The dark eyes didn't flicker. Neither the lack of height nor the thinning hair caused him any problems. When he had stood up to shake my hand, he had seemed to be on a podium of self-assurance. Perhaps he was standing on his wallet.

'I was sorry to hear about Scott,' he said.

We talked about Scott's dying. He accepted as something easily understood my need to bother the people Scott had known. But there wasn't much he could offer by way of insight. He had lost touch with Scott in any serious terms many years ago. Mainly, they had been friends when they were students. And everybody had changed a lot since then. He had been hearing for a few years how badly things were going for Scott. But the end had come as a shock. Didn't it always, though?

His even voice had a mesmeric quality. It almost put my misgivings to sleep. I felt again that I was being stupid. I had interrupted a man's business lunch in order to have him tell me the platitudes with which we respond to the death of those friends who, due to time and circumstance, had more or less died to us already. What more could I expect?

Only two things niggled at the lassitude of purpose into which his voice had put me. One was something he said. One was something he didn't say. He said, 'I was sorry I couldn't make the funeral.' That was understandable. But the deliberateness with which he said it, right in the middle of no context, made me notice. It made me wonder if the deliberateness of the apology was a response to the deliberateness of the absence. What he didn't say was anything about the party Scott had disrupted.

'You had a party not too long ago,' I said. 'Scott was there.'

He paused, stared at me, shook his head and smiled sadly.

'You know about that?' he said.

'I heard.'

'I wasn't going to mention it. I thought it might be too painful for you.'

'No, that's all right,' I said. 'It's not quite as painful as his death.'

'I can see what you mean. Well, you'll know about it then. It was no big deal, really. Scott just got steadily drunker. Argued with a few people. Finished up in the television room. Some of the guests were watching something. And for some reason Scott threw a heavy crystal vase at the TV. It sent a certain frisson through the party, you might say. Didn't do the telly a lot of good either. Or the vase. Still, they were replaceable. Could've been somebody's head. Anna had to get Scott out of there. I think she was afraid he might set fire to the curtains next. He was wild that night. But then I think he usually was towards the end.'

'The television. You wouldn't know what was on at the time?'

He looked at me and his expression distanced itself from the remark. He seemed measuring me for a strait-jacket. It did sound like a ridiculous question, I had to admit to myself, and his eyes, taking on a sheen of amusement, confirmed my feeling.

'You know,' he said. 'That's something I neglected to find out. That's a bit remiss of me. But maybe that's it. You think that might explain it? Scott was just practising to be a television critic?'

The comforting cosiness of his presence had changed suddenly. In a few sentences he had turned the mood of the conversation from warm to cold. I saw how much he disliked me. In my modesty, I wondered why. Quite often, I don't like me either. But I couldn't see what I had done to earn such quick contempt – unless I was encroaching where I shouldn't. So I encroached further.

'You don't see the point of the question?'

'Well,' he said. He sipped his brandy. 'It does seem about as relevant as asking what colour of tie he was wearing.'

'Not really. The people I know don't usually go to parties to watch television.'

'I have big parties. Very big parties. The house is populated like a village. There are people doing lots of things. Maybe we don't go to the same kind of parties.'

'I just wondered if there was any special reason for them to be watching television. If maybe the programme had special associations for the people at the party. Including Scott.'

'I really wouldn't know. In the mayhem after it, nobody thought to check the *TV Times*.'

He sighed. He took some brandy. He glanced across to where his friends were sitting. He was effortlessly making me look silly. I had given him a lot of help. I gave him some more. If he thought my last question was a weird one, wait till he heard these.

'Do you know Fast Frankie White?'

'I beg your pardon?'

'Fast Frankie White. Do you know him?'

He put his hand to his head.

'What is this? Am I appearing on "Mastermind"? Specialising in the works of Damon Runyon?'

I waited.

'I do not think I've ever had that pleasure,' he said.

'Where's Anna?' I said.

'She's not in Graithnock now?'

'No. She's selling the house.'

'Maybe she's trying to avoid answering your questions.'

'Maybe she is.'

'I honestly don't know. Perhaps she went home. She comes from the Borders, too, doesn't she?'

'Yes.'

'Why don't you try there?'

'Do you know who the man in the green coat is?' I said.

His head was cupped in his left hand by now. He was talking to the table, presumably since it seemed more sane than I was.

'I imagine he could be quite a lot of people,' he said. 'I also imagine that, if you keep on talking the way you're talking, he may enter this room at any moment in search of you. With a very large net.'

'Before he does,' I said. 'Have you ever had a beard?'

His hand came down over his nose and he looked up at me, seeming genuinely alarmed. He laughed briefly and stood up. He didn't offer to shake my hand. Interview over.

'Well, Mr Laidlaw,' he said. 'It's been interesting meeting you. I hope the pills work soon.'

I stood as well.

'Thanks for your time,' I said.

'Don't mention it,' he said. 'Please. Not to anyone. I must admit I could have spent it more fruitfully. Take care of yourself. Or maybe you should get somebody else to do it for you.'

He had chewed me up nicely. This was him spitting me out. As he walked back to his friends, leaving me standing, I noticed that his stomach had the protuberance of a Russian doll. I wondered how many smaller men were hiding inside the polished confidence of his exterior. I intended to find out.

12

I drove to 28 Sycamore Road. My route was hardly direct. I cruised the countryside for a while. I stopped beside a bridge above the Bringan, an area of woods and fields we had known as boys. I leaned on the parapet and watched the river running. It looked like melting glass below the bridge. Downstream it hit the rocks and the glass went frosted the way glass does around where it has broken. I looked among the trees where gangs of us had played at hide-and-seek. You're hiding again, I said to him in my head, and everybody else has gone home. But I'm still seeking.

I got back in the car and drove some more. Dave Lyons' dismissiveness had been counter-productive. It came too pat, it was too complete. Nobody could justify that much self-assurance. He froze me out too fast. That made me suspicious. If he had lost touch so long ago, how did he know where Anna came from? If he had become such a stranger to Scott, why did he invite him to a party?

I thought I would like to talk to him again with more in my mouth than a series of disconnected questions. To do that, I had to know more. Ellie Mabon might be more. I regretted invading her life. But it was still just late afternoon. There should be no husband. I was apologising to her mentally as I stopped the car at her door.

I parked behind a blue Peugeot and stepped out. The house was big, an odd amalgam of wood and stone. It was an original concept. I hadn't seen another one like it, for which I was grateful. The complicated bell had only begun its symphony of chimes when the door opened. We stood looking at each other while the bell continued pointlessly.

I appreciated Scott's taste. If you were going to lose your head, she was a good place to lose it. She was tall and red-haired with a beautiful mouth even her present expression couldn't mar. The eyes were green as an aquarium and drew you to them in the same way. She was dressed to go out, wearing a black fitted suit, the lapels of which met enticingly across her bare chest.

'Hullo,' I was able to say.

'How dare you!' she said.

'I'm sorry. But I —'

She was glancing down the road.

'Turn right now and get back into your car.'

'Wait.'

'Do it!'

She started to smile sweetly. She was nodding as if agreeing with something I was saying.

'Do it now. Get into your car. Drive in the direction in which it's facing.' She pointed helpfully, still smiling. 'What I'm doing just now is showing the neighbours I'm giving you directions. At the end of the street, you take first right. First left. Then you pull in to the side of the road. You wait till my car comes past. And you follow it. It's the blue Peugeot out there. Move.' I started to walk away.

'That's where it is,' she called after me. 'I'm sure you'll find it. You can't miss it.'

She closed the door quite loudly.

I waited for ten minutes before I saw the Peugeot in the rearview mirror. She was a careful woman. I followed her out of the town. She drove for some time. Just when I thought we might be leaving the country, she took a winding road, turned into another and pulled on to the grass beside the gate of a field. There was room for me behind her.

Outside the cars, we stood looking at each other. As far as I was concerned, it wasn't a bad way to spend the time.

'Hullo,' I said. 'I'm Jack Laidlaw.'

She ignored my outstretched hand.

'Oh, I know,' she said. 'Scott told me about you. But I thought he was exaggerating. He exaggerated about a lot of things. You're the one area where he seems to have mastered understatement. You're off your head.'

It was a day for collecting accolades.

'Do you think we should be telling each other such intimate things about ourselves so soon?'

She stared at me and shook her head, the way people might when watching a disaster on television. She sat against the bonnet of the Peugeot. She had legs from which fantasies are made. I tried not to make any. It wasn't easy. The urge to live is a kind of holy idiot. It finally understands nothing but itself. It has no sense of context. Attending the funeral in all good faith, it may finish up wanting to screw the widow.

Ellie Mabon was staring through the trees and I, supposedly obsessive pursuer of the truth, saw not a source of information but a marvellous woman. The mad, whispering optimist who had arrived in me with my awareness of my own sexuality was talking again: perhaps she's the one. Perhaps with her I could have made the place where I want to be.

'Scott and I used to come here,' she said. 'Why didn't you phone first?'

'I thought I did.'

'I mean again. Before you arrived just now. There could have been someone with me.'

'I didn't want to give you the chance to knock me back again.'

She was still abstracted, presumably remembering the past. It was a good place to have chosen. The roadway was hemmed with trees, high but hidden, a position from which to see without being seen. Below us, some distance away in a small valley, there was a house. It was a modern house with just a little land around it. It wasn't a farmhouse. It was perhaps a townie's dream of the country, urban amenities included.

'We used to pretend that house down there was ours,' she said. 'Pretty pathetic, I suppose.'

Her references to Scott and herself demystified the moment for me. This wasn't just a woman dreaming. This was Ellie Mabon, who had had an affair with my brother and had a husband she was worried about. Seeing the icon animate into someone who breathed the same troubled air as I did, I banalised her further. I noticed the shoes she was wearing. Their high heels were digging into the turf. But she had chosen the location. She must have known where she was coming, with someone she didn't want to meet. Yet she had dressed like a fashion show and worn shoes that were spectacularly unsuited to the place. The reason might be vanity, the need to look her

Waterstones

Unit 1
Thistle Marches
Stirling
FK8 2EA
01786 478756

SALE TRANSACTION

STRANGE LOYALTIES (£8.99
9780857869937
Balance to pay   **£8.99**
Cash   £20.00
CHANGE   £11.01

— — — — — — — — — — — — — — —

THE WATERSTONES CARD
YOU HAVE JUST MISSED OUT ON 0.5 STAMPS
ON ITEMS WORTH £8.99
JUST ONE OF THE MANY BENEFITS
OF THE WATERSTONES PLUS CARD
Apply on our app, online or in any shop

VAT Reg No. GB 108 2770 24
STORE TILL OP NO. TRANS. DATE   TIME
0055 1   780702 349262 19/02/2019 14:32

0 999020055001 3492625 0

Waterstones

Refunds & exchanges

We will happily refund or exchange
goods within 30 days or at the manager's
discretion. Please bring them back with
this receipt and in resalable condition.
There are some exclusions such as Book
Tokens and specially ordered items, so
please ask a bookseller for details.

This does not affect your statutory rights.

Waterstones Booksellers,
203/206 Piccadilly, London, W1J 9HD.

Get in touch with us:
customerservice@waterstones.com
or 0808 118 8787.

Buy online at Waterstones.com or Click & Collect.
Reserve online. Collect at your local bookshop.

Did you love the last book you read? Share your
thoughts by reviewing on Waterstones.com

best before a stranger. Or the reason might be a sense of theatre – wearing the costume of the other woman. Either way, it put her among the rest of us. Speech returned to me.

'Anyway,' I said. 'I'm glad you came. I just need to talk to you.'

'What I can't forgive,' she said. 'What I won't forgive is that Scott told you about us.'

'But he didn't.'

'Then how did you know?'

'I just found out today. Today was the first time I heard your name.'

'Then he must have told somebody.'

'That doesn't mean that what he said was bad. And it was only your first name he mentioned.'

'Oh, that's lovely. I suppose that's what you call discretion. I didn't tell anybody.'

'Well, you wouldn't, would you?'

She threw me a look like a spear.

'If you only had the first name, how did you find me?'

'I'm a detective.'

'I've heard,' she said.

She turned towards me and folded her arms. She had made up her mind.

'Let's get this over with. What is it you want to ask me? You seem to know enough already.'

'No, not enough.'

'Before you start. I'll tell you anything I can about Scott. But don't ask me about us. We stopped seeing each other more than a couple of months ago. It was over for us.'

'Why was that?'

She seemed to be deciding whether my question came within her rules. She made a concession.

'I stopped it. Scott was too serious about everything. He couldn't have an affair. It had to be a grand passion. He was so intense about everything. I could see the whole thing blowing up in our faces. I dreaded that some night he would arrive at the door.' Her eyes returned from contemplating the house that could never be theirs and looked at me. 'Maybe it runs in the family. I mean, I wasn't too wrong, was I? In a way, it did happen.'

Her implied accusation didn't affect me. I was too busy accusing the accuser. She appeared to want a relationship that wouldn't interrupt her meals with her husband or embarrass her in front of the neighbours. Scott had made the mistake of loving her too much, I thought.

'You weren't seeing him at school?'

'I left. I do relief teaching now. I had to get away. It was too painful being so close. Charlie had been suggesting I take it easier for years. He makes good money. And every day I was living with the dread that Scott might announce our forthcoming engagement to the staffroom. Or decide to kiss me in the corridor. He was unpredictable towards the end, you know.'

People whose heads are imploding often are.

'So you've had no contact with him for months.'

She eased her heels out of the mud, found a new position for them.

'He phoned,' she said.

'When?'

'A lot of times. But at least it was during the day. Except for the last time.'

'When was that?'

For the first time I saw her forget her lines. The role she must have chosen to play with me faltered, couldn't hold. Like an actress remembering who she really is in the middle of a performance, she froze. I saw real pain. It made me want to hold her. But she reassumed a kind of composure.

'It was that night,' she said. 'The night he died.'

I waited. She was in a place of her own. No one should interrupt her there. She retracted her closed lips and contrived not to cry.

'He phoned in the early evening. Charlie was out. He phoned from a pub. The pain in his voice was awful. I knew then. I knew how bad he was. I spoke to him for a long time. Till his money ran out. But I could've gone to him. I could've helped. Maybe if I had, it wouldn't have happened.'

She glanced at me and away, as if she couldn't bear to face herself in my eyes.

'No, Ellie,' I said. Her first name came naturally out of the moment. 'No. Don't think that. He was probably too far out by then.'

'But why didn't I? Jesus, sometimes I hate how sensible I am. What did it matter if it was awkward to explain to Charlie? Or if people saw us? Scott was going to die.'

'You didn't know that.'

'Maybe not. But I've thought about that phone-call a lot. I think maybe it's typical of my life. It's what I do. Scott was the most authentic thing that's ever happened to me. Easy to accommodate he wasn't. But he was real. I've thought perhaps that's what bothered me. I wanted him but not the disturbance he caused. And the phone-call sometimes seems to sum it all up. I gave him as much space as wouldn't disturb the routine of my evening. It's what I do. What's wrong with me?'

Perhaps we choose our fears, I was thinking. We frighten ourselves with the smaller things so that the bigger things can't get near enough to bother us. Perhaps Ellie Mabon chose the fear of breaking the pattern of her life to avoid confronting one of the biggest fears we have – the fear of feeling. Let go the reins on that one and where might it take us?

'What did he say that night? Can you remember?'

'It's not the kind of call you can forget. He wasn't talking about the weather. But it wasn't too coherent either. Mainly what I remember is the pain. Most of it I could only half-understand. Oh, it was terrible.'

'Can you remember anything?'

She thought, staring at the grass in front of her.

'Where would you start? It was all so confused. Something had happened recently. I know that much. I don't mean just us breaking up. That hurt him enough. But something else. Something had happened recently. That almost destroyed him. He had always told me the only faith he ever had was in people. And I think that was gone.'

'Happened here? In Graithnock?'

'I don't know. It was recent. It happened to somebody he knew. So maybe it happened here. Somebody he admired very much. Because he kept saying, "The best of us. He was one of the best of us." The person he was talking about must have died.'

'Does the man in the green coat mean anything to you?'

'Who *is* that?'

'I'd like to know.'

'He used that expression.'

'In what context?'

'I think he said it was the man in the green coat all over again.'

'But you don't know who he is?'

'No idea. But I'll tell you something. Whatever had happened made him hate Dave Lyons. He had never liked him much. But he was so angry with him that night.'

And so angry with Fast Frankie White. I found it difficult to make a connection between the Dave Lyons I had just met and Frankie White. I asked her if she had heard of Frankie. She hadn't.

'Dave Lyons,' I said. 'You know him?'

'No. I know *of* him. Scott had spoken about him.'

'Did Scott still seem to be in touch with him?'

'As far as I knew he was. He seemed to be lumping him along with two other people that night. As if they were all together. It was something that happened – when he was a student, I think. One of them was a name I'd never heard him mention before. Blake, I think it was. Andy Blake? He said a strange thing about him. "Physician, heal thyself," he said. The other man he didn't name. He just said I had seen him, but I didn't know him. He said I had seen him all right. Don't worry about it. It was all like that. He was telling me and he wasn't telling me. It was weird.'

'But what did he lump them together *for*? Was it something they had done?'

'I wouldn't know. I honestly think that's all I can tell you. Believe me, I've gone over that call in my head a hundred times. Look. I think I'd better be going. We're going out tonight. I've got to get ready.'

I couldn't imagine what else she could do to make herself look better. I took out my cigarettes. She didn't smoke. Hardly anybody did these days. I would soon be in quarantine.

'Do you know where Anna is just now?'

She shook her head, looking up at the trees.

'We weren't that close.'

'Listen. I really appreciate what you've done. It's meant a lot to me. I can imagine how sore this has been for you.'

'I doubt it,' she said. 'I really did care about him, you know. You know what I said to him when we split up? "I'm saving both our lives." That's what I said. That's irony, if you like.'

The wind had risen. I smoked and listened to the leaves and watched some cows in a field. In this place where Scott had been and wouldn't be coming back, I learned his absence again. It was a lesson from a bad teacher who taught by rote, not caring how well you understood it. You didn't have to understand, only to know. Ellie Mabon put her arms round her shoulders and shivered.

'Well,' she said. 'I'd better be going.'

I looked at her and nodded. She smiled and pointed to the ground behind the cars. There were tread-marks on the grass.

'Those,' she said. 'They'll always remind me of Scott. Him and me here. I wonder how long they'll last. What is all this about for you really? I mean. What is it you're doing exactly?'

'I don't know exactly. I suppose I'm trying to make my own peace with Scott's death. I suppose this is how I do it.'

'How do *I* do it?'

She started suddenly to cry.

'Damn,' she said. 'Will you hold me one time for him?'

I crossed and held her. It was a small, chaste ceremony of

mutual loss. Her hair in my face gave off a melancholy sweetness. Clenched to her, I felt the tremors of her body, how the edifice of beauty was undermined from within with deep forebodings. In the embrace I experienced our shared nature – so much questionable confidence containing so much undeniable panic. That was me, too. Some of my colleagues and bosses liked to say I was completely arrogant. They misunderstood the language of my living. Arrogance should be comparative. Humility was total. Faced with simplistic responses to life that tried to fit my living into themselves, I was arrogant. I seemed to meet them every day and I knew I was more than they said I was. But when I sat down inside myself in the darkness of a night, I knew nothing but my smallness. I knew it now and shared it with hers.

She subsided slowly, sighed and moved away. Her mascara was spiked with tears. She sniffed.

'Where is it you're living anyway?' she said in a watery voice that suggested the tears had invaded her larynx.

'I'm in the Bushfield Hotel tonight. I might still be there tomorrow night. I don't know.'

'If there's anything else I can think of, I'll 'phone you there. I'd like to help you if I can.' Her voice was submerging. 'Oh, God.'

She fumblingly opened the passenger-door and leant inside. She came out with her handbag and put it on the roof of the car. She went back inside and brought out a dispenser of quickie cleansers, from which she pulled a handful of connected, wet tissues. She put the dispenser on the roof of the car as well. She stood, breathing deeply and trying to make sure her tears were over. She wiped her face carefully, especially around the eyes. She opened her handbag, took out her compact and checked her face. She finished off wiping it clean and threw the dark-stained tissues away. She very carefully put on her make-up. She took more tissues and wiped the heels of her shoes. She put the stuff back in the car, closed the door and went on tiptoe to the driver's door. She looked at me. She was Mrs Mabon again.

'You want me to move my car?' I said.

'No,' she said. 'I've done this before. I can do it one last time.'

She pulled into the road, reversed back close to the gate and drove off without waving. I lit a new cigarette off the old one and stood on the stub. In the car, I rolled down the window and smoked, looking out at the country. The indifferent permanence of the place, where all the times they had been here had left no mark, told me nothing that I did would make any difference. But I started the engine. My ability to go on fed off that of the car as if it was a life-support machine. One mechanical purpose led to another. I would phone Brian Harkness.

13

'Meece was dealing, right? But he was dealing funny. He was putting quite a lot up his sleeve. Literally. He was using more and more of the stuff and selling less. It looks as if the woman and him were stashing too much away in their own veins. Or maybe saving it up for a rainy day. Keeping a private account. The story is that when he came to pay off his suppliers, the books didn't balance. They warned him.'

'That could've been the broken arm.'

'Right. It looks as if it didn't help his memory tying a knot in his arm. So they closed the account. With a warning to all bad debtors.'

'Where did you get this?'

'Asking around. Ye know Macey? Ernie Milligan's tout.'

'Well enough. I test every penny he gives me with my teeth. But that sounds real enough. Though it's nothing you couldn't have guessed. No names yet?'

'Not yet. Macey's listenin' for us.'

Like a visual aid to my understanding, Buster cocked an ear. Listening? You get it? Thanks, Buster. In contrast to what I was hearing, even he seemed an emblem of domestic cosiness, as if he were a dog stitched on a sampler: Buster, Sweet Buster. The kitchen was warm and pleasant with residual smells of cooking. We had both been well fed by Katie, who had forgiven the tetchiness of my morning.

When I had come in late, she gave me a cuddle and told me to sit down. 'What you need,' she said, 'is a poultice for your stomach.' She made me a good one. Doing the dishes had let me feel temporarily a part of her sweetly dishevelled orderliness, where preoccupations were put up like shutters and kindliness was lit like a fire.

In the brightness of the room I had rested from the darkness of my head. Phoning Brian had changed that. Now a chill wind was blowing in my ear from bad places where they broke your arm to encourage concentration and turned a life into garbage if it wasn't serving their purpose. And I realised a part of me was still out there in the cold looking for something, picking among the waste.

'You've got no information on the woman yet?'

'Not yet.'

'I've been thinking a bit about her,' I said.

'You mean how she managed to get away?' Brian said.

'If she did.'

'I think we would have found her by now if she was dead.'

'I don't mean that. When you think about it. Let's say they didn't do her. That would be sloppy workmanship, wouldn't it?'

'Maybe they saw her as an innocent bystander. Maybe they knew she was too frightened to say anything.'

'Maybe. But it's not how I would bet.'

'All right, master,' Brian said. 'What do guru say?'

I could imagine him smiling. He had me in a role that was

familiar to him. It must have seemed like old times to be able to make professional fun of me. I quite enjoyed pretending I was back in what had passed for normalcy with me.

'What if whoever did it was told to leave her alone? I mean, a good tradesman would've done the job right. He's got his reputation to think of. That's how you stay in business. Not leaving anybody who can lodge a complaint.'

'So?'

'So why don't you think that way? That the head man's got a soft spot for the woman. Something like that. That gives you another possible point of connection. It's always the part that doesn't fit that you should follow. Here's an obvious, unimaginative pattern with one piece missing. Why? It shouldn't be. If you're prepared to kill one for money, what's the difference with two? Just the price. Unless the instructions were specific that you shouldn't.'

'I gaze in wonder,' Brian said. 'Your fee's in the post.'

'Just a small deductive sketch I have dashed off,' I said. 'Like Leonardo doodling. It doesn't help anybody, right enough. It doesn't help you. And it certainly doesn't help me.'

'What about homeopathy?' Brian said. 'I know a homeopathic doctor in Ayrshire who's supposed to be very good. That's maybe the cure you need.'

'Let's try more conventional help first. This could take the place of the fee in the post. Fast Frankie White.'

'What about 'im?'

'I want to find the latest on him.'

'I thought he was in London?'

'So did I. But I'm not so sure now. You think you could check it out? And, Brian. I need to know where he comes from. Originally. That's important. It's Ayrshire. But where-abouts in Ayrshire?'

'If you were up here, you could find the answer to the question for yourself. Instead of wasting your time down there. You would know the answer by now.'

I had wondered when he would get round to that. Knowing what was coming had the same effect as seeing the digits on a payphone register zero. I had to go.

'Brian, use your loaf,' I said. 'If I was up there, I wouldn't have known the question, never mind the answer. I better not cost these people a fortune. Tell Morag that I'm asking for her. And Bob Lilley that I'm not.'

I phoned Ena and we exchanged formalities briefly before she let me speak to the children. Moya was out (she often was out to me these days, even when she was in) but Sandra gave me a detailed account of the cat's latest ailment and Jackie checked as usual on my whereabouts. I had once made a joke to Ena about his having a map in his room with flags to mark my movements but, when Ena suggested it would need to be an awful big map, I didn't repeat the reference.

I tried to phone Jan at the restaurant. It was Betsy, one of her partners, who answered. When she knew it was me, her voice – always distant – more or less emigrated. The only thing Betsy and I had in common was a mutual dislike. She thought Jan was wasting her time with me and I thought everybody was wasting their time with Betsy. She spoke like an elocution class on trivia, elaborately enunciating triteness. She was one of a new breed of Glaswegian who thought the city was a taxi-ride between a theatre and a wine-bar. She enjoyed telling me Jan was out having dinner. I said that wasn't much of an advertisement for their place. She begged my pardon. I asked who was having dinner with Jan. She had no idea. I asked if it was Barry Murdoch. She had no idea. I asked when Jan might be back. She had no idea. I asked, saying I was keen to find a question it wouldn't be too hard for her to answer, what time it was. She hung up the phone. Maybe she had no idea.

I had an idea. The idea was Barry Murdoch – a big, suave phoney who seemed to have been born encased in a Porsche. Betsy had introduced Jan to him, presumably as an alternative diet to the unhealthy regimen of weekly traumas she was having with me – muesli for bacon and eggs. I had met him once in the restaurant and suggested afterwards to Jan, 'Dress by Gucci, head by mail order catalogue.' It was not a remark that had earned me maximum Brownie points.

Someone must have opened the lounge-door, for there were the sounds of talking and laughter suddenly heard and suddenly gone. It was like hearing a party in a strange house you were passing and wanting to go in. I needed a furlough. Thinking of Jan at dinner, I wanted to go to some strange place and maybe see a woman I had never seen before and discuss with someone I had never met the oddness of things. I was hungry for fun.

'Buster,' I said. 'You fancy a night on the skite?'

He didn't seem interested. I decided to go out. I had done what I could for Scott for the moment. John Strachan would be coming into the Bushfield later on. He had phoned twice during the day. Sanny Wilson might appear. But I had some time before that happened.

I stood up and put on my jacket. Before I could escape to

whatever new and exotic experiences were waiting out there in Graithnock, Katie opened the kitchen door.

'Sanny Wilson's here to see you,' she said.

I was back in the tunnel and excited about the possibility of seeing some light. The excitement didn't last long. When I went into the lounge, I realised that Sanny Wilson was so well insulated with liquid from serious contact that he might as well have been a fish in an aquarium. His mouthings had much the same clarity of meaning.

He would be about seventy, a marvellously benign man with sweet, open-handed gestures that seemed to be an attempt to embrace the world. He had obviously loved Scott and generously included me, as Scott's brother, in his affection. That was touching but it was not hugely helpful. We drank and talked for a while and what I gleaned, beyond the frequent repetition of the opaque statement that the man in the green coat had died again, could have been written on my thumbnail.

Still, he wasn't a bad show to be with. He smoked with a great flourish of the hand, holding the cigarette between thumb and forefinger, the palm towards you. With each successive cigarette, his waistcoat looked more and more as if it had been tailored from ash. His soft hat assumed a jauntier angle on his bald head. He had a Dickensian turn of phrase, which tended to include words like 'peregrination' and 'pharmaceutical' and – my favourite – 'clientiele', spoken in what Sanny had apparently decided was a French accent. Only a Philistine would have resented his lack of direct communication. I had lost a source of information but I had found a pleasure to be with. You don't ask Brahms to tell you the news.

I was still enjoying his recital when John Strachan came in.

John was carrying a wrapped painting that turned out to be the five at table. Mhairi and he had decided I should have it, in memory of Scott. I liked that. John had also found a piece of paper in the waste-basket of Scott's old room. Everything else seemed to have been cleared out. The new teacher had just emptied the last of the stuff from a drawer into the basket today. Most of it, John said, had been related to school administration. Only this one sheet had looked like something personal, though what it was John couldn't understand. Glancing over it, I could see why. It was a strange piece of writing. It wasn't just the crumpled nature of the paper that made it difficult to read.

I bought John and Sanny a drink and left them together while I took my treasure trove upstairs. I unwrapped the painting and looked at it and I read the piece of paper again. They yielded nothing much at the moment. I would have to study them more carefully.

When I came back down, John Strachan was already preparing to leave. I thanked him and Mhairi and we threatened to meet again. Sanny Wilson couldn't last much longer. He was beginning to keel over, still mouthing polysyllables as he went, like a pedant dying bravely at his post.

I offered to see him home. Fortunately, he lived close at hand. It was an upstairs flat in an old tenement. Inside, it was a sad and lonely place. The bedroom had no lights.

'Ah'll fix that maybe tomorrow,' Sanny said.

He was nodding off on his feet. But there must have stirred in him some instinct of dignity that was determined I shouldn't take away the wrong impression.

'I am,' he said suddenly, 'festooned with friends.'

I managed to get his shoes and his jacket off. The rest, he insisted, could stay as it was. I left him propped up in bed and made to leave.

'Jack,' he said. 'Jack.'

I turned at the door and saw him in the light from the street lamp outside. He still had his hat on. He had a wonderful, dilapidated dignity, his hand making a vaguely papal gesture in the semi-dark, as if he were granting absolution to the world.

'You are a gentleman,' he said.

'If you say so, Ah must be, Sanny. For you're sure as hell one. Cheers.'

I was at the door when he spoke again. His voice was very tired.

'Jack.'

I turned. Even as I looked, his head relaxed on the pillow and he went gently to sleep, breathing noisily. I was very quiet in closing the outside door.

At the Bushfield I by-passed the lounge. I didn't feel like company.

14

And in his throne room sat the demon king. The braying revelry beneath him touched him not. He had forsaken the courtiers of pretence and the retinue of folly. Dark was his purpose and his broodings deep. He sipped of the magic liquid men cleped Antiquary and felt its fluid alchemy transform the very reaches of his being, flooding him with the freedom that bringeth wisdom in an instant. But not enough.

I could act out in my head the postures of a dedicated searcher for truth but I couldn't find the stuff. I could abandon the jollity of the Bushfield lounge. I could come upstairs to sit alone. I could take my whisky carefully, like a mind-expanding drug. But, no matter what attitudes I struck, I stubbornly remained just a puzzled middle-aged man sitting in a hotel room, looking at a piece of paper and two paintings. The best thing about the sheet of foolscap John Strachan had given me was the familiarity of Scott's handwriting. The message was pretty cryptic.

'I have developed a compulsion to wonder what he was like, what he was really like. I mean, even in simple things. God knows an understanding of the simplest things would do me. The older I get, the fewer certainties I have.

'I mean, did he drink beer, keep pigeons, have a favourite colour, curse a lot, know many women, have some kind of faith?

'My social plumbing stopped working some time ago. I offend a lot of friends. Right in the middle of some hygienic conversation, I open my mouth and there's sewage on their carpet. It has a lot to do with him. He has become like an eccentric hobby. The bank-clerk who's an authority on match-box labels. The teacher who's writing a monograph on wheelbarrows.

'He's no longer just himself, of course. Maybe he never was. Maybe there were always more of him. Maybe he's everybody else.'

This was not for other people's understanding. It was an entry in a diary, written in a code that only the writer would understand. Its purpose was secrecy, a troubled mind whispering to itself. I wondered when Scott had written it. Apart from its crumpled state, the paper looked fresh enough. It bore no discolouration of ageing. I thought about 'no longer just himself'. Did that refer to dying twice? Anyway, I was convinced I was reading a kind of minimalist biography of the man in the green coat. If Scott had known almost nothing about him, I surely knew less.

I looked at the painting again. Even his face didn't belong to him, transubstantiated four times over into the means of food for others. The beards were presumably a metaphor for disguise. The private identities the four had escaped into? If one of them could be Scott, who might the others be? They would presumably know what Scott had known, the thing he had never told me, the thing he had perhaps never told anyone, the thing that had gnawed him to death. Find them, find the means to understanding.

There were clues all right but I didn't know what they meant. The figure I took to be Scott was holding the stem of a flower that blossomed into petals that contained the small, neat head of a snake. The hand of another showed a prominent ring on which there was a carved shape. I thought I could make out a stick with a snake twined round it. Was that the rod of Aesculapius, symbol of medicine? 'Physician, heal thyself.' Was he a doctor? But the snake seemed to have two heads. Why did the snake have two heads? The third man held a bitten apple in his hand. The fourth man had a badge on his lapel. It was the twin masks of tragedy and comedy.

The snake and the apple were Christian, the rod and the masks were pagan. Was that significant? I would have given much for an hour with Scott, and not just to talk about the painting. In his absence, I had another glass of the whisky and toasted his troublesome nature. It looked as if he had earned it.

If he couldn't tell me and I didn't know who the other men were, there was only one road I could take. There was only one person I knew who might possibly have had access to what Scott had kept so secret. I had to find Anna. I didn't know where she was but I knew where her parents lived. Talking to her father would be like interviewing a cardboard cut-out. My only hope was her mother, a woman about whom I had sometimes felt that, if we could have synchronised our youths, we might have meant a lot to each other.

I would leave for Kelso very early in the morning. The decision to do something felt almost like an interim solution to

the problem. I relaxed slightly. I undressed. I finished my drink
and rinsed out the glass. I put out the light and went to bed.
As I lay becoming drowsy in the dark, the sounds of singing
downstairs faded slowly like lights on the shore receding from
someone moving out to sea.

THREE

15

Driving out of Graithnock, I came into sudden rain. It didn't last long. But by the time it had stopped and the neurotic insistence of the wipers became still, an unsought memory was with me and I was travelling in two ways – the car in space and me in time, passing through the changes of my own internal weather.

I remembered another car and other rain. Maddie Harris sat in the car with me. Windscreen and windows were misted blind, as if we were in a world in which there only existed our shared breathing. I was staring ahead. Maddie was talking. The talk was painful for her. Her mouth was naming the hopes she had had for us – each one like an orphan I had fathered. I rubbed a slow peephole in the glass to look at nothing. There was only the rain.

I said, 'No. No, Maddie. I'm sorry.'

In memory my own voice made me grue. It sounded harsh and unrelenting, a sound track run too slow. Something in me, like a child at the films, wanted to shout advice to the preoccupied man in the car. But films can't hear.

I watched her – as I had watched her so often – put her hand on the door. She stood outside and turned, her hand still on the door. Beyond her, spring leaves were on the trees of the park beside which we had stopped. The rest of the world was there after all. I had insisted on bringing it in, like air to the womb of her dreaming. She stood looking at me. The rain fell on her. She didn't open her umbrella. She closed the door and walked slowly away, receding in the space I had cleared in the misted glass to watch her going.

She didn't open her umbrella. That quirky fact, that small malfunction in normalcy had always haunted me. The dignity of it shamed me, its dismissal of what didn't matter. It taught me the contemptibility of my pragmatism. I could love her but not give my life to the loving. If I couldn't put my children at risk, why had I put her at risk? I could care about my children. But where were Maddie's children? Wandering fatherless and disowned in her head. Better indifference than to love and not love fully, Maddie's back was telling me as it went.

Where I had been had an effect on where I was going. I took with me my guilt towards Maddie, towards Ena, towards my children, towards the just man I had always hoped to be. I was travelling through green country in an attempt to find a kind of truth. But perhaps I blighted the promise of the greenery as I passed and would find the purity of the destination fouled by the fact of who arrived there. Perhaps the nugget of understanding we look for is tarnished by the fallible humanity of the hand that finally holds it. How do the false gain access to the true? I was certainly one strange searcher for justice – the polluted avenger, knight of the rusted sword.

But I still drove recklessly fast, as if I could outrun my unworthiness. And still I was driving into my own guilt. I remembered another car with Scott and me in it.

I had been driving him home from an amateur football match we had both played in. Scott's team were a man short and he had phoned me in Glasgow to ask if I wanted a game. I had been good at football in my teens and momentarily forgot the years in between. We had played the game in Ayr and won 3–2, not especially thanks to me. My main contribution had been to manage not to die of exhaustion in the second half.

We had gone into Troon for a pint with some of the other players to replace lost sweat. Then Scott and I bought fish suppers and came along the shore road at Barassie. As we sat in the car with the windows down, eating out of the grease-stained paper, there happened one of those moments that belie their own banality. I saw what he was, not what he seemed to be.

What he seemed to be was a trainee art-teacher who was also a reasonable mid-field player, still ruddy from recent exertion, fingering chips and pieces of fish into his mouth. What he was was a stunningly alive young man, unselfconsciously handsome, the eyes lit up with the search for horizons they hadn't found. I saw the cage the car was for him. All he wanted was everything.

Perhaps it was the sea laid out beside us that moved him, with its mocking immensity. But he talked with such passion about the things he wanted to do, simultaneously inspired by the possibilities and afraid of never grasping them.

He was twenty-two then and about to marry Anna. He wanted to paint. He had plans to live abroad. They had discussed it together and agreed that they would make some money first and then they would go. He would teach wherever they found themselves, earn the space to put his easel. She could teach

125

English anywhere. Their children would be Scottish cosmo-politans. I remembered him explaining to me very precisely how, if Anna became pregnant, they would both come back to Scotland for a time. No matter where they might live, any children would have to be born here. He was like an innocent visionary telling me the telephone number of the house where he would live in a Utopia that hadn't been discovered yet.

Even as he told me, there was a kind of distant panic in his eyes, as if he dreaded his sense of the future was doomed to live alone. It was a dream that needed company. He was right to dread. Anna's idea of their future changed gradually once they were married. She wanted more and more time to make sure of where they were until no room was left for where they might have been. For all I knew, she was right. Maybe the attractiveness of Scott's plan, like that of a lot of plans, lay in the impossible symmetry of its idealism. Maybe so much changed between them that the future they had seen couldn't happen because they were no longer the people who had seen it. I didn't know. I couldn't blame her.

But I could blame me. Remembering him sitting in the car, framed against the grey water that shifted behind him like a mirage of endless potential, I felt I had failed him then. There wasn't much I could have done for him, of course, but I could at least have been less indifferent to his obvious intensity. I had been rather phonily worldly-wise, the older brother offering him a response that was about as specific as 'Things'll sort themselves out, son.' I suppose I was too full of my own problems at the time, as usual.

That time came back to me as an encapsulation of our relationship: an almost utterly vulnerable idealism that was trying to connect with an idealism that had learned some rules of survival. I had started out as wide-eyed as he was. We had both grown up in a house where we were taught to believe the best about people. You gave the world what you had and the world gave back. But I had had to learn quickly that there were plenty of people around who, once you had given them what you could, would pick your pocket to see what you had left. I hated that with a terrible anger. Love of others was a gift, not a steal. You could only give what wasn't forcibly taken.

So I had tried to teach my generosity how to live without becoming embittered. If I can spare it, you can have it. But don't take it behind my back. Don't pre-empt my right to give. It's what makes me me.

Scott hadn't learned that then. I don't think he ever did. That day at Barassie I left his vulnerability naked. I didn't try to teach it to protect itself. Maybe I didn't want him to change because I admired him a lot more than I admired me. He was the way I had been and sometimes wished I still was. I loved the sheer openness of his living. But such admiration can be a luxury the ones we admire have to pay for. It leaves them to endure the storms of experience out in the open while we sit in shelter and applaud. Perhaps I had let him do that.

I came through Moffat for Selkirk. Any time I'm in the Borders I like to pass through Selkirk. I don't often stay but I like to pass through. It's where I was born. You should visit your mother. If you lose where you come from, you lose where you're going.

Approaching that small, hard place, where the wind down Ettrick can shiver your bones with a sense of mortality, I was coming nearer to the source of Scott's idealism and my own. I thought of my father, I thought of my mother.

He was a big, dark man of brooding principles. Not many things pleased him. At the edges of his nature there was great kindness but the centre was sombre. He was a cave with flowers round the entrance. He was a Borderer whom the Borders displeased. He felt the place that had defined Scottishness at its weakest edge, where it meets Englishness, had lost its sense of itself and blurred into anonymity. 'What weapons couldn't,' he once said to me, 'trade and money did.' Kelso came in for his special contempt. 'As Scottish as muffins and tea.'

He moved us from Selkirk to Hawick to Graithnock, working in mills. He was maybe following the work. He was maybe looking for Scotland. He was certainly looking for something he was never to find: a place where people behaved towards one another as he believed they should. Treating people shabbily outraged him till he died. The world seemed to him like a rented room not up to his specifications and he couldn't quite settle.

My mother was a warmer presence than he was. She had had a reputation as a beauty in her youth and I think the assurance that gave her didn't leave till near the end. Attractiveness facilitates acquaintance, like a courier predisposing strangers to goodwill, and my mother had acquired early an innocent vanity that let her enjoy being who she was. But the kindness of other people towards her made her as idealistic as my father in her own way. She tended to think the way people treated her was how they treated everybody. She thought the best of them was all there was.

Together, they didn't prepare Scott and me too well for the

everyday world. I remember my mother saying to me towards the end of her life, when she was worried about Scott, 'Maybe your father and me should have told you two what some people can be like. But the truth was, I didn't know.' I think it was essentially through Scott's problems that she finally began to notice darknesses in people she hadn't known were there.

Driving through Selkirk, which doesn't take long, I was blaming them for the inheritance they had given us. Equipping sensitive children with ideals that are too demanding can make them factories for guilt. Look at what had happened to Scott – the pain of his sense of failure. Hadn't they realised what they were doing? I thought of the time when my father had taken Scott aside at the age of fourteen and lectured him on having to toughen up or life would break him. I knew what he meant. As a teenager, Scott took everybody else's suffering personally. But what did my father expect? He spent years tenderising our consciences and then wondered why life hurt us so much.

Once out on the road to Kelso, I generously relented and forgave my parents. They had stayed true to what they believed in and true to each other – perhaps, I had sometimes thought in my father's case, dangerously true. My mother died of cancer after a double mastectomy that left her feeling unwomaned and weary of living. My father lived on for four years. He had developed diabetes and his pancreas was chronically damaged. When he was found dead, I wondered if the carelessness with which he had lived those last four years amounted to a discreet form of suicide. It was an idea that gained new force when I thought of how Scott had died. Maybe harakiri of the spirit ran in the family.

I decided what they had given us wasn't so bad. The way things are, who shouldn't feel guilt? In our guilt is our humanity. But, as sole surviving legatee of the family conscience, I decided that the acknowledgement of your own guilt shouldn't be a means of absolving others. No scapegoats. Everybody shares.

As I came into Kelso, I was looking for sharers. The handsome trigness of the town didn't promise well for my purpose. It was basking brightly in innocent sunshine. But that didn't bother me too much. Innocence is often just guilt in hiding.

16

Martin and Alice Kerr were not at home. The bungalow sat complacent as a well-fed cat in the sunlight. The lawn looked as if it had just had a shave. A neighbour, who had watched me from her window, directed me to where they were.

The bowling green was full. I sat on one of the wood-slat seats round the perimeter. At this time of day there were no younger people involved. I watched the elderly at play. It was a pleasant sight. If this was what age meant, perhaps I should try harder to get there. I didn't take a cigarette.

On a neat and well kept square of green moved neat and well kept people. The colours were mainly pastel – pinks and blues and greys. The gestures were unhurried. The faces expressed satisfaction or dismay at a shot in an almost abstract way – not emotion so much as the reflection of emotion in a mirror. The voices were all muted. The laughter seemed an echo of another time. The occasional knock of bowl on bowl was soothing. The men and women moved from end to end, turning back upon themselves like sand in an hourglass, measuring a morning.

Seeing Martin and Alice Kerr among them, I was tempted

to leave. They were playing with another elderly couple, a bald, brown, smiling man and a grey-haired woman whose roundness remained attractive, as if her femininity had just matured in the cask. They all seemed so happily preoccupied with one another that I had misgivings about disturbing them. The lives of Martin and Alice had surely earned them this time to play in the innocent light. They didn't need me putting my private cloud between them and the sun.

And yet. The old, like children, can disarm us while they keep their own weapons handy. I don't think I've ever known age to perform a character transplant on anyone. The old are usually who they were with less energy to express it. The rectitude of the aged is often just the fancy clothes in which incapacity likes to dress up.

I watched Martin and Alice. Their togetherness looked as cosy as an advertisement for an endowment policy. But I knew something about the terms of the contract, what their undisturbed present had cost in the past. Martin had been a building contractor and a friend of many local councillors. The word was that the two aspects of his life hadn't always been kept effectively apart. There had been several stories about contracts won through political influence rather than the competitiveness of the tender. I didn't know the truth of the stories but, knowing Martin, I could see that, if they were fiction, they were in the realistic mode. They emerged very convincingly from his nature.

Martin was one of the smiling ruthless. Self-interest and callousness had been so effectively subsumed in his nature that they emerged as a form of politeness. He never raised his voice because he hadn't enough self-doubt to make it necessary. He could listen calmly to opinions violently opposed to his own because he never took them seriously. He offered the conventional forms of sympathy effortlessly because there was no personal content to mean they might not fit. He seemed to me one of what was, in my experience, a depressingly large species, those who use manners not as a means of facilitating serious human contact but as a way of forbidding it. They spend their lives coming in an emotional condom in case they breed with life and create something they can't control. Most of all, I hate the way they can sterilise the lives of those around them.

It was my feeling that he had done that with Alice. I liked her a lot. My sense of their relationship came from the time of Scott and Anna's wedding and a few family get-togethers since and things heard from Scott and Anna. The evidence wasn't extensive but it was firm. How long does it take to analyse a vacuum?

I recognised the frozen solidity of Martin's unexamined attitudes and the way Alice could see wistfully beyond them but couldn't quite get out, a maiden trapped in someone else's castle that was moated with stagnant water. I had always enjoyed her company. She was a warm and open woman. But Martin's presence tended to sit on her spontaneity like a scold's bridle. What had heightened my awareness of her position was my worry for Scott. I thought I saw the potential for a reverse image of her parents' relationship in Anna's marriage to my brother. If Scott had the same openness as Alice, Anna was her father's daughter. Self-interest followed her everywhere like a minder, telling her feelings where it was safe to go. I had feared her calculation would always outmanoeuvre Scott's impetuosity.

Watching from my seat, I remembered something I had said to Jan before leaving Glasgow on Monday. Why do the best of us go to waste while the worst of us flourish? Maybe I had found a clue. I could think of one reason why people as potentially rich in life as Alice and Scott seemed to fare less well and be apparently less successful than Martin and Anna. Those who love life take risks, those who don't take insurance. But that was all right, I decided. Life repays its lovers by letting them spend themselves on it. Those who fail to love it, it cunningly allows very carefully to accrue their own hoarded emptiness. In living, you won by losing big, you lost by winning small.

But the grandeur didn't have to be external. As I had seen in Scott a big spirit, I saw in Alice a person of some stature. Her husband might be the public success but she had the substance. Her vulnerability meant that life could still take her by surprise, make moments to remember, leave room where dreams still unfulfilled could grow. The size of the humanity is the size of the person. I was surprised I could make out Martin from this distance.

I saw him look across and do a double-take. He appeared not to say anything to the others. He went on playing. A couple of minutes later, Alice noticed me. She simply walked off the bowling green and came towards me, saying something to the others over her shoulder. In those two instinctive responses, my sense of two distinct natures had been defined.

'Jack, Jack,' she said as I stood up. We embraced. 'I thought I had seen a ghost there. You reminded me so much of Scott. Poor Scott. Listen. I'm sorry about the funeral.'

She and Martin had attended but had left with Anna without our having a chance seriously to talk.

'We had to accept Anna's way of doing things that day. I don't think she could cope.'

I sat back down and she sat beside me.

'You'd better finish your game,' I said.

'To hell with it,' she said. 'It was the last end anyway. They can finish it without me. I don't think my amazing skills will be missed. Poor Scott. I can't believe it. I think of him so much. How are you coping?'

'All right,' I said. 'It's good to see you, Alice. You're looking well.'

The others had abandoned the game. Martin was coming towards us.

'But what are you doing here?' she said. 'I couldn't believe it when I saw you there.'

'I'm looking for Anna,' I said.

'Anna's not here,' Martin said.

His handshake wasn't a welcome. It was a formal declaration of opposition. What was to follow was a kind of extended psychological tag-wrestling match. If he gave me no information, he won. If I found out where Anna was, I did. The other couple, it seemed, were on his team.

'I'm sorry we can't wait,' Martin said. 'We're having lunch with Bert and Jenny.'

Alice, it seemed, was on my side.

'Jack can come with us,' she said. 'Can't you, Jack?'

Of course, I could. I liked her move. She had used his own weight against himself. Martin's only substance was politeness. They had booked lunch in Ednam House. While they went into the clubhouse to collect jackets and change their shoes, I drove on ahead.

Ednam House: a monument to my father's sense of Kelso. While I waited for them in the lounge, my old man's ghost sat with me, saying, 'See what Ah mean?' I did, I did. While I sipped my soda and lime, I heard English voices crested like old school ties and native voices in which the confusedly rich broth of Scottishness was passed through strained vowels until it became the thinnest of gruels. There was much talk of horses. Something was happening today at Floors Castle, maybe a gymkhana. I remembered something that's often troubled me about where I come from. I tend to think of the Borders as the place of the horse. I like horses, especially if they've got Pat Eddery or Steve Cauthen up on them. But I gave up worshipping them before I was born. They're where it was and I don't like the way it was. It's maybe a tribal memory. I'm sure my ancestors went on foot and had to fight the ones that sat on horses. And maybe in my heart I'm still fighting them.

Four people close at hand were discussing the Royal Family in a very familiar way. How can people do that? Who knows who they are? Do *they* know who they are? It's the King Lear syndrome. As soon as people bow or curtsey to you, how can you work out what they think? The existential mirror that is other people's eyes becomes misted.

The others arrived and fitted in perfectly, except for Alice. Bert was divorced and Jenny was a widow. They had only met six months ago and they were getting married in the summer. They were nice enough but they seemed to have started the honeymoon early. They were at that stage of conspiratorial involvement that finds the rest of the world a slightly droll irrelevance, eliciting suppressed giggles and secret smiles. There could have been something endearing about their born-again adolescence if Martin hadn't been so patently making use of it.

'How about these two?' he kept saying. 'Aren't they something?'

Alice and I agreed with Martin. Bert and Jenny smiled at each other. Martin agreed with Martin. But nobody specified what the something was. My own theories about what they were tended to darken as the meal progressed. Martin was making very sure that I could find no way to introduce the melancholy purpose of my visit and talk about Scott's death. It would have felt like turning up in a hearse to drive the blushing bride to the wedding. Every time Alice and I threatened to make serious contact, Martin invited us to appreciate how Jenny was giving Bert a forkful of her salmon or Bert was offering Jenny a taste of lamb.

Feeling excluded for so long, I had been tuning in occasionally to the talk at some of the tables around us. It didn't help. So much of it sounded like variations on the same theme. Just as Bert and Jenny were telling each other, so that we could listen in, about the wonderful house they had offered for, so a boy nearby was explaining that, if he could maintain his saving pattern for three more years, he could buy a Porsche. The different conversations had an underlying coherence, like an orchestra tuning up to play the same music, probably 'Land of Hope and Glory'.

Come the coffee, I had had it. I wanted a polite way out that took the information with me.

'Well,' I said. I nodded to Bert and Jenny. 'It's been nice meeting you. I've got to go. But listen. Let me get this. It'll do as a kind of engagement present.'

There was some polite demurring. But Martin liked the idea. Perhaps it proved to his friends that I wasn't entirely a boor. I certainly hadn't charmed them too much so far. Now that I had Martin relaxing his guard I said it.

'I want to catch up with Anna today. Is she living near here?'

Martin looked at Alice.

'Jack,' he said. 'Anna's trying to get over things.'

'Martin,' I said. 'So am I.'

'But what's the point?'

'I need to try to understand what's happened.'

'I doubt if Anna knows.'

'She knows more than me for sure.'

'Perhaps we should let bygones be bygones.'

'If I needed a wayside pulpit, Martin,' I said, 'I could've got one without driving this far.'

'Edinburgh,' Alice said. 'It's Jack's brother. It's been a month. He needs to talk about it.'

She told me the address.

'It's an apartment,' she said.

'Thanks,' I said.

I shook hands with the others and kissed Alice. I was sorting things out with the waiter when Alice left the table and came up to me.

'Jack,' she said. 'There's something else. Do you know a man called David Ewart?'

I'm one of those people who vaguely imagine they've heard almost every name before. I fed it into the amazing computer of my mind and it came up blank.

'He lives here. In Kelso. Runs a pottery.'

'The Kelso Pottery.'

'No. That's long established. This is another one. More recent.'

She told me where it was.

'I met him about a week ago in the street. He used to know Anna quite well when they were younger. I was telling him about Scott's death. He said he met Scott when he was a student. I think when they were both students. It seemed to make a big impression on him. I don't know what you're doing. But I suppose you're trying to sort out your image of Scott. So that you can live with it. I think I've been doing that myself. It might help you to talk to David Ewart.'

'Alice,' I said. 'I've always believed in you.'

'So do I. Sometimes.'

She went back to the table and I paid the waiter. I asked him to take over a bottle of champagne. I think I felt guilty about not appreciating other people's happiness enough. But I had to admit to myself that I wasn't sure what I was inviting them to celebrate.

For I hadn't liked being there. Looking for the pottery, I found a phrase that helped me to understand why: urbane deprivation, the condition of being so sophisticated that you plumb the nature of most other people's experience out of your life like waste. Your attitudes are so glib and self-assured and automatic, you lose the necessary naivety that is living. That way, you eat everything and taste nothing.

The pottery shop offered shelter from that feeling. It was dimly lit and full of shelves on which glazed artefacts sat – pots and bowls and ornaments and ashtrays. Whoever worked here was making a simple daily contract with his living. I wandered around. A woman came through from the back. She was wearing a smock and flip-flops. She had careless hair. She smiled at me and went behind the cash-desk, waiting. I selected a green ashtray and went up to her. She smiled again.

'On holiday?' she said.

'No. I was visiting people. And they told me about this place.'

She gave me my change.

'Nice to know we're beginning to get talked about.'

'Actually, David Ewart. He works here?'

'That's my husband.'

'Would it be possible to speak to him?'

'David!'

Sometimes interesting truths emerge from the banal. You make a few casual remarks and they transmute inexplicably into passwords and there is called forth a message that will matter to you till you die. The messenger needn't be elaborately dressed.

David Ewart was wearing sandals, jeans and a sweater. He was tall and his hair and beard had decided on a merger. His eyes stared out of the darkness around them like cave-dwellers. I introduced myself and he introduced his wife, Marion, and took me into his workshop. He made three coffees. He carried one through to his wife in the front shop. He and I sat on stools and talked.

He told me a story and I thanked him and we all said goodbye and I came away with my ashtray. As I drove towards Edinburgh, I reflected that a trip to Kelso to find out where Anna was living had yielded an altogether different and more valuable gift. The tedium of the meal in Ednam House had been worth it. Patience pays.

For I believed I had been in a kind of antechamber to the presence of the man in the green coat.

17

When David Ewart was eighteen, he made a trip to Glasgow. It was perhaps his third time in the city. It was certainly his first time alone there. Everything amazed him. 'I may have been eighteen but I hid my advancing years well. For me, travelling from Kelso to Glasgow was like taking the Golden Road to Samarkand. What would I find there?'

He had with him the address of a house in Park Road. It lay in his pocket like a visa to a new life. Anna Kerr had written it out neatly for him on a large sheet of paper which he had folded very carefully. She had also telephoned ahead to say he would be coming. She had spoken to someone called Scott Laidlaw. David Ewart had been with her during the call. The way she spoke to Scott Laidlaw suggested that she did not know him as well as she had pretended but that she would like to know him better. There was a forced familiarity in her manner.

The address was where Scott Laidlaw and three other student friends were living. They had kept the flat on during the summer and, now that a new academic year was about to begin, they were moving out. David Ewart was starting out on the journey they were completing. He was to attend the Glasgow School of Art and he was checking the flat out for himself and three others. He felt important to be the one making the decision on behalf of the four of them.

He decided to walk from the railway station. He did not know where Park Road was but it was a bright September day and he wasn't sure how expensive a taxi would be or if taxi-drivers could be expected to know Park Road. Besides, to walk in the city was an adventure.

'I learned three things fast. The first was how self-confident architecture can be. I mean, this was before old Glasgow got her face-lift. But I loved those big, dark buildings. "We know the story," they seemed to be saying. The people who built those places knew who they were all right. The second was just the energy of the place. My pulse began to quicken. Like plugging into a generator. The third thing was the people. I thought cities were supposed to be anonymous. Everybody I stopped for directions related to me right away. Nobody spoke over their shoulder. Some of them might've looked at me as if I'd stepped out a spaceship. But they looked at me. "Christ, ye're well oot yer road here, son." "Park Road? That's no' a walk, pal. Ye book a flight for that yin." It was love at first patter. Three different people went out of their way with me. They were like Indian scouts escorting you through their bit of the territory. See when I retire? I think I'll reverse the process. This is where I work. But I've a notion. If I can get Marion to come with me. Check out in Glasgow. Die among humane noise.'

By the time he found the place, he was sweating slightly with exertion and excitement, high on new sights and vivid faces. He felt like an explorer. He had climbed to the top floor of the tenement. What further discoveries lay beyond the door he was staring at? They threatened to be strange. On a placard fixed to the door with drawing pins there was a legend in beautiful script: 'Hard Truths Unlimited. Knock and Go Away.' He hesitated. He knocked and waited. The door was ajar.

He thought he heard a muffled voice saying 'Come in' but he couldn't be sure. He knocked again. This time the voice bellowed.

'Entrez. Avanti. Kommen sie in. Entrada. Get a grip. Come bloody in.'

He did. The first impression he had was a smell. It was the smell of oil paint. Several canvases were stacked in the dim hall. He negotiated them respectfully and looked in the door of the living-room. What he saw was to stay with him – 'like a picture of a place where I wanted to live. I was looking at where I somehow wanted to be.'

Sunshine made a window of light on the floor. The room was shabby and poorly furnished but the effect wasn't depressing. The place for him had a romantic dignity imparted to it by the unknown lives that had passed through. There were more paintings scattered around the room, resting in groups against the walls. There were piles of books on the floor. A young man sat with his back towards the living-room doorway, leaning sideways so that he was profiled against the window. It was a striking profile. He was leafing through a book. An attractive girl sat in the chair opposite, her face towards the ceiling. Her eyes were closed. Neither of them seemed to be aware of David Ewart's presence. That impressed him.

'I mean, I had just knocked at the door. And they seemed

to have forgotten already. I could've been robbing the place for all they knew. They had a kind of animal preoccupation. The way a cat might glance at you if you try to catch its attention. But you won't seriously disturb it. It goes back to what it was concentrating on. I don't know. It was just the natural rightness of where they were, what they were doing. I wanted to live with that kind of assurance.'

The man stopped turning the pages. He read carefully for a moment. He held up his finger, though the girl's eyes remained closed.

'This is the bit,' he said.

He read aloud a brief passage from the book. David Ewart could never remember afterwards what the words had been saying. He had never found the book from which the passage came. He regretted that. It was as if he had been listening to the password to where they were, a password he had never learned. The girl didn't open her eyes.

'Maybe,' she said.

'Maybe? Nobody could say it as well as that if it wasn't true.'

David Ewart walked into the living-room. The man looked up.

'Jeez,' he said. 'The ghost of freshers past.'

The girl opened her eyes. They were blindingly blue.

'David Ewart,' the man said, pointing. 'Sorry. I'm Scott Laidlaw. Some welcome that. I'm sorry.' They were shaking hands. 'We thought you were just some of the through traffic we get here. This is Hester.'

He gave her surname but David Ewart couldn't remember it. He couldn't remember very clearly much that followed.

What remained with him was a sense of excitement. His memory of the circumstances that generated it was fragmentary. Hester showed him round the flat. Scott made coffees for them. He learned that Hester was at Art School as well with one year still to go.

'She paints any surface she can find,' Scott said. 'Stick out your tongue and she paints it.'

'I could do a mural on yours then.'

Someone came in who was called Sandy. He was studying medicine. His course wasn't finished and he was going to move in with Hester. Scott Laidlaw had introduced them. Somebody else came in who was called Dave. ('I remember that because it was the same name as mine.') He couldn't remember their second names. The fourth person who was sharing the flat was studying English. He didn't appear. His first name was mentioned to Dave Ewart several times but it was long gone.

The atmosphere became that of an impromptu party. People were teasing Scott about being the only one who still had some stuff to move out. Derogatory remarks were made about his paintings. He said they would fetch millions in years to come. They held a mock showing of them for David Ewart. He liked them. His valuation was significantly higher than the prices the others put on them. In celebration of having found an appreciative patron at last ('Do you mind if I call you Theo?'), Scott collected an amazing hoard of empty bottles from a cupboard. He and David Ewart got the money back on the empties and brought three bottles of suicidally cheap wine back to the flat. The party moved up a gear.

'That first glass of wine was terrible. But the atmosphere

of the place did something to it. It refermented into vintage in the bottle. See the third glass? Nectar, nectar.'

There was a lot of laughter. They formed a solemn committee to decide upon the fate of Scott's remaining property, since he was apparently notorious for his sentimental attachment to places, his inability to leave when his time was up. It seemed to be a seriously entertained possibility that his books and pictures would become a permanent fixture here.

'I can be nostalgic for half-an-hour ago,' he said.

A bonfire was mooted. A pavement sale. Oxfam. ('What do you have against Oxfam?') Finally, it was agreed that Dave's uncle would collect the stuff in his van the next day. Hester and Sandy would store it till Scott could retrieve it.

'Otherwise,' Hester said, 'he'll never move it. He was supposed to be packing these books today. So what does he do? He starts reading them.'

'I *was* packing them,' Scott said. 'In the mind.'

Happy insults flew back and forward like thrown knives which the recipients always seemed to catch by the handle and return. David Ewart enjoyed being a part of it. He even joined in the singing. By the time he was leaving, he had decided this was where he would be living, even if it was just to share in the ghost of this ambience, which he loved. He was ceremonially given a key.

'I had an uncle and auntie who lived in Rutherglen. I was staying the night there. They all chipped in with the best way to get there. Scott walked me to the corner. I remember him waving. He looked to me like a sailor with a lot of voyages ahead of him. I envied him the things that he might see, the possibilities he had.'

Reaching Rutherglen, David Ewart was light-headed with more than the wine. He liked the people who welcomed him but the evening passed him by like a distant parade. He was still full of where he had been, still hearing the laughter, still seeing the faces. Everything else seemed colourless beside them.

'You ever see *The Taming of the Shrew*? The film? Richard Burton and Elizabeth Taylor. The two young men at the beginning. Burton and Michael York, was it? They come into . . . Padua? Anyway. The beginning of that picture. The first few scenes. I loved them. The place is just bursting with life. And there's people everywhere. And noise. And . . . I don't know. I can't remember. But chickens being sold or something. There's just so much *happening*. And the two of them are all over the place. Laughing. And drinking it in. They're eating everything with their eyes. I could tell what they were feeling. I *knew* what they were feeling. Because it's what I felt that night. It's the feeling of beginnings. Beginnings are beautiful. Aren't they? It's the feeling that everything is possible. That night I felt the terrifying energy of a new generation. And I knew that I was part of it. I knew that everything was possible.'

He had been sitting in his pottery when he said that, turning his empty coffee-cup slowly in his hands like a crystal ball that had gone opaque. He looked too young to be so old. He stared up at me, searching for what I couldn't give him.

'And it was,' he said. 'Wasn't it? What happened? I mean, I remember that time. That's just sixteen years ago. Maybe the Yellow Submarine had sunk. But we still had dreams we shared that were worth dreaming. Dreams that made you worthy of being human. Now if you want to dream them still, you dream alone. The communal dreams? You buy them in a fucking supermarket.'

The swearword was shocking in his gentle mouth.

'I hate these times,' he said. 'The shallowness of them. Some of the noblest dreams the species ever had are being drowned in puddles.'

His gaze returned to the empty cup.

'Anyway,' he said. 'I felt different then. That time in the flat with them had knocked me off my horse on the road to Damascus. It was like a conversion. I believed in almost total hope. You know what I kept thinking at my aunt's house? They were going out together for one last night. The four of them. I kept wondering what they would be up to. What they were saying. I was wishing I was with them.'

On the afternoon of the next day he was in Glasgow and he had the key in his pocket and he decided to go there, just to sit in it for a while, to become familiar with where he would be staying. The placard had been taken off the door but the drawing pins remained. He turned his key proprietorially and went in. He wished he hadn't.

'I can't explain how much it affected me. It was like having found your faith and losing it in one night. I knew something terrible had happened. I didn't know what it was but I knew that it was terrible and that it related to me as well. Somehow it diminished my expectations. I felt as if the previous afternoon had been a lie. They had been playing a cynical game with me. All the idealism, all that marvellous positive energy had been phoney. Otherwise, how could it have changed to this in just one night?'

The flat was a litter of debris. Every book had been torn

148

up, every painting smashed. All across the floor of the hall and the living-room sentences had been severed and scattered into irreparable chaos. David Ewart thought that the passage he had heard the previous day must be lying somewhere untraceable among the dismembered wisdom of the dead. All around him were jagged fragments of image with no context to belong in. An eye looked out of nowhere. A guitar was broken in two. A field had no sky with which to connect. Sunshine still made a window of light on the floor.

'I wandered around there. I couldn't believe it. It was like finding the corpse of youth. It had committed suicide. Why? The obscenity of destructiveness like that appalled me. I think denying the past is maiming the future. I thought I was looking at a terrible desecration. The murder of promise.'

He put down his empty cup. He held his hands cupped towards himself and stared at them.

'So now I do my job. It has a purpose. It's all right. But I had intended to do more. Don't get me wrong. I'm not blaming that disillusionment for what I am. I made my own smallness. I house-trained my own dreams. But that experience back there. You know what I think it did? It gave me an easy way out. All the bad times. When I felt I was selling out, I had my escape clause handy. I remembered that wastage and I thought, "Yes. That's what we're like. That's the way it always goes. Let's not pretend we're more than we are."' He was picking dry clay from his fingers. He held up a piece between forefinger and thumb and his eyes lit with an idea. He smiled at me. It wasn't a pleasant smile. 'You know what I mean? Circumstances are the real potter. We're just the clay. We can take any shape they tell us.'

He flicked the piece of clay on to the floor.

'But I would like to know what happened. Oh, that I would like to know. I left the key on a table and closed the door behind me. We all lived somewhere else that year. But I would have liked to understand, still would. Think about it. I've thought about it. It must have been him that did it. Scott. Who else would have done that to his paintings? What could have happened between one day and the next to make him do that? What did idealism die of? That's what I'd like to know. What happened?'

What happened? Was it then that he met the man in the green coat? At least three people would know. Dave Lyons and two others. One of those other two was still unknown. He had studied English. But Ellie Mabon had said, 'Andy Blake?' and 'Physician, heal thyself'. Sandy had been studying medicine. Dave Lyons and Sandy Blake and another man. And presumably sweet-faced Anna. How could Scott, especially when they were young and trusting each other in the beginning, have kept this from her?

18

Anna's address was in Edinburgh New Town. I've always loved the architecture there but there's enough of my father boarding in me still to have misgivings about the pleasure the place gives me. It may be a feast for the eyes but for a Scot it's a Thyestean feast in which at some point you should realise you're eating the death of your kin. If the old man had found Kelso reprehensibly English, what would he have made of the New Town?

This was in its origins the most English place in Scotland, built to be a Hanoverian clearing-house of the Scottish identity. The very street names declare what's happening, like an announcement of government policy in stone: you have Princes Street and George Street and Queen Street with, in among them, Hanover Street and Rose Street and Thistle Street. Any way you count it, the result is the defeat of Scottishness. This was an English identity superimposed on the capital of Scotland, an attempted psyche-transplant: 'Scottishness may have been a life but Britishness can be a career.' You are not where you come from but where you can go. I couldn't help wondering how far Anna fitted in with the original premise of the place.

Her name was written in ink and covered with perspex in the top slat beside the buzzer. It made me pause. It read: Anna Kerr. That hadn't taken long. It was her choice, sure enough. But I wondered how the two boys felt coming home to here. They were presumably still Laidlaws. A primitive feeling passed through me, too darkly irrational to be identified clearly. It was maybe anger. It was maybe hurt. But I felt she had dissolved a part of my brother's life into instant oblivion, as if it had never been. The ancient Egyptians had believed that if you erased a dead man's name from the funeral tablet, you killed his ka. He couldn't live after death. She was getting there. I pressed the buzzer. The briefness of the pause suggested preparedness.

'Yes?

'Hullo? Is that Anna? This is Jack. Jack Laidlaw.'

'Oh, yes. All right. Top floor.'

The release mechanism was growling like a watch-dog. I pushed the door and it clicked open. After being so desperate to find her, I was almost there. The woman who was closest to the secret of what had been happening to my brother before he died was above me. Rapunzel, Rapunzel, let down your hair. I mean, really let it down. But there were still the stairs. I laboured up them as if they were a small mountain. Truth is sometimes said to live in high places. Let's hope so. After all this, I was thinking, just be there, guru of truth. I don't want to be talking just to wind and empty noise.

She was standing with the door open. She was looking good. She was wearing a tight-fitting, V-necked, light cashmere sweater and ski-pants and long leather boots. Her black hair was attractively short and she was beautifully made up. She looked about twenty-five. But the eyes seemed to have been borrowed from someone older. They stared at me assessingly through a grille of caution. You didn't get into the head behind them just by looking.

'Hullo, Anna,' I said. 'I'm glad I found you in.'

She gave me a smile that showed no teeth. Who said she was in?

'Hello,' she said.

It was not an effusive greeting. She stood aside to let me pass. There would be no familial embraces. Coming into the hall, I was already unsure why she was bothering to see me at all. This meeting was obviously not the highlight of her day. Her reaction on the intercom had indicated that she knew I would be arriving. Why had she not just arranged to be out? When I came into the sitting-room I thought I understood. There was another woman there, sitting on a leather chair. She was casually glancing through a magazine.

'This is Carla,' Anna said. 'Carla, this is Scott's brother.'

I thought at first that Carla might be deaf. She seemed to have found something the reading of which couldn't be postponed in her magazine. Maybe it was the Armageddon Weekly. She reluctantly put her glossy aside and stood up slowly and only then decided to look at me. She offered me a handful of dead fish.

'I've heard of you,' she said.

It was precisely what a schoolmistress had said to me when I entered her fourth-year class for the first time. The schoolmistress had meant that my reputation had gone before me, like an air-raid warning. The schoolmistress had meant that all her anti-aircraft guns were primed and in place and that I would be shot down at the first sign of any action that threatened the established order of things.

'Does that mean you have to believe it?' I said.

'It came from a reliable source,' Carla said.

Then she turned to Anna and became with that simple gesture a disciple of Bishop Berkeley. The fact that she couldn't see me meant that I did not exist. She smiled reassuringly and put her hand on Anna's shoulder.

'Are you all right?' she said.

'I'm fine,' Anna said.

'You sure?'

'Of course. I'm all right.'

I thought I might have to wire my jaw to keep it shut. What was I supposed to have done? Molested her in the hallway? All this solicitousness was because Anna's brother-in-law was visiting her. Perhaps I should check myself in the mirror the first chance I got. I couldn't remember fangs or a Phantom of the Opera mask.

'As long as you're sure,' Carla said. 'I'll make us all some coffee. All right?'

'All right.'

'You don't need to put mine in a cup,' I said. 'You could just throw it about me. Maintain the sense of welcome.'

Carla smiled compassionately at Anna. Anna smiled back. The smiles were a tacit conversation that said 'I can see what you meant' and 'Didn't I tell you?'

'Thanks, Carla,' Anna said. 'You know where the biscuits are.'

Carla went out. Anna sat down.

'You want to sit down?' she said to me.

'Thanks,' I said. 'Anna. I've been wanting to talk to you about Scott.'

'Let's wait till Carla comes back,' she said.

'Anna. What *is* this? My brother's dead. I'd like to talk about him. Who needs third-party insurance? It's a conversation I want. Not a lawyer's meeting. We both loved the same person at one time. That's our connection. What can be the harm in that?'

'Let's just wait, please.'

She was studying the ornate fireplace as if it was an Open University programme. She made no immediate further attempt to talk. Neither did I. If they had special house rules here, let's wait and find out what they were. As I sat, I confirmed what had occurred to me when I saw Carla in the sitting-room. Anna had decided to be in when I came so that she could meet me in a controlled environment. Carla was the thermostat. Whatever Anna thought of me, she knew I was persistent. To avoid me now was to have to confront me later, perhaps when she wasn't prepared for it. It was better that she choose the terrain and get it over with.

The terrain was impressive enough. It was a beautiful airy room with a marvellous view that took in, in the distance, the Forth. All that stunning Edinburgh light poured into the place and made it as bright and sharp and self-delighted as a Hockney painting. The real leather furniture showed off its sheen in the glow. A reproduction mahogany desk against a wall, its green leather surface unmarred by any papers, achieved a cool definition. The three abstract paintings distilled the roofs and the shapes and colours outside and stuck them on the white walls. But there was something out of place. I decided it was Anna.

The room had been here like this before she was. It fitted her the way a jock-strap would.

While we were awaiting the coming of Carla the Protector the phone rang. I started slightly and looked at Anna. Her eyes registered and erased, swift as a well programmed computer. At the fourth ring, I spoke.

'I think the phone's ringing,' I said.

'Let it ring,' she said.

We did. It gave up at twelve. This was an interesting house. People spoke to each other as if you weren't there and let phones ring twelve times, as if that's what they were meant to do. What would happen next? Carla came in.

She was carrying a large silver tray with a stylish coffee pot on it, three coffee-cups and saucers, crystal milk and sugar dishes and a willow-pattern plate with small biscuits. She gave no indication that the phone shouldn't have rung twelve times without anybody answering. She smiled at Anna. Anna smiled at Carla.

A small, complicated ceremony began. I'll give this saucer to you. You give it to him. I'll give this saucer to you. You keep it. I'll leave this saucer here. I'll keep it for me. I'll fill out this cup of coffee, you pass it to him. Here is the milk. You pass it to him. I'll take it back. He takes sugar? *Does* he? You pass it to him. It went on. I've had five-course meals that were served with a lot less fuss. When we were finally settled with our cups which, given the trouble it took to get them, might have been filled with the gold of the Incas, I spoke again. I had already refused a biscuit.

'Do you mind if I smoke?' I said.

'Actually, we do,' Carla said. 'This is a smoke-free zone.

We'd like to keep it that way. There are children who live here.'

'Do you mind if we talk?' I said. 'Is that all right, Anna? I mean, do we have a quorum now?'

'What is it you want?' Anna said.

'Just to talk about Scott. I can't get used to it. I don't understand what happened at the end. I just want to make sense of what happened.'

'I tried that for years. It doesn't work.'

'But you must be able to tell me something, Anna.'

'Why would I want to do that?'

'Remember me, Anna?' I said. 'I was the best man. Come on. I'm not trying to pry into your marriage. I know that's your business. But what was it that was troubling Scott so much at the end?'

'I wouldn't know.'

'Anna.'

'We were in different worlds.'

'There's nothing you can tell me?'

'Nothing.'

We sat and said nothing. It had been a long way to travel to exchange silences. Carla was holding a biscuit which seemed to be as full of detail as an Elizabethan miniature. In a place as cold as that all you can do is try to light a fire with whatever comes to hand.

'Hell,' I said. 'I don't believe this.'

But the silence outvoted me two to one.

'Okay,' I said. 'Let's not actually have a conversation. But do you mind if I ask you some questions? All you have to do is answer. Monosyllables welcome. All right?'

She didn't answer.

'Do you know who the man in the green coat is?'

Anna glanced at Carla in elaborate amazement.

'Shall we take your pulse?' Carla said.

'The man in the green coat,' I said.

'What's this supposed to mean?' Anna said.

'Have you heard of him?'

'I've never heard of him.'

'Are you sure? He seems to have meant an awful lot to Scott. He wrote things down about him. He must have mentioned him to you sometime.'

'I've never heard of him.'

Who had? Maybe Sanny Wilson had been drunk. No. Ellie Mabon had heard of him, too. But I was beginning to feel like someone trying to fill in a census-form for the invisible man. Not known at this address. The rest of my questionnaire didn't yield much more in the way of significant answers. It was full of dismissive strokes where the words should have been. Not applicable, not applicable.

Fast Frankie White?

Unknown.

Sandy Blake?

Unknown.

Dave Lyons?

Known but hardly.

David Ewart?

Known at one time but not now.

Why sell the house?

To get away.

Why Edinburgh?

Why not?

Possible to see the boys?

Not possible to see the boys.

Why not possible to see the boys?

Boys away at swimming.

Boys at school here?

Boys at private school here.

Is there a toilet?

Jackpot. Whereabouts of toilet known. Directions supplied.

I didn't know whether I wanted to piss or puke. I shut the door and walked up and down, grimacing at the ceiling. I mouthed furiously at the walls and gave the print of a Degas ballet dancer the fingers. I briefly strangled a loofah. Purdah wasn't just a Muslim tradition. Women could withdraw into it any time they chose. Behind the veil, what was there? Another veil. Relieving myself, I realised I was being careful to hit the side of the bowl, presumably in case the noise profaned their feminine ears. I felt as if I was defiling the sanctum with male urine.

But I could hardly be doing that. For I noticed something as I washed my hands. This bathroom had been decorated for a man. I knew that instinctively because this place didn't interest me at all. That is never the case in a bathroom which is dominated by the sense of a woman's presence. I could go my holidays to those places. All the appurtenances of femininity intrigue me. A bathroom's a kind of confessional, where we admit to the inescapable physicality of ourselves, own up to the nature we lie about in public. I like the secret hoard of womanhood they can hold.

This one didn't rate. My instinct was confirmed when I

checked it out against a rational examination. There were some of what I assumed were Anna's things on the window-ledge – perfume, a couple of fancy deodorants, hair-colouring. But that was all. It was as if she hadn't moved in properly yet. The rest was too stark. As an interesting bathroom, this one's Laidlaw rating was nil.

I opened the mirrored door of the cabinet above the wash-hand-basin. There was a Wilkinson razor and blades, a jumble of pill bottles. There was a bottle of Aramis aftershave. I remembered Dave Lyons' proximity in Cranston Castle House. I remembered that he worked in Edinburgh. I remembered how he could say without thinking that Anna came from the Borders. I closed the cabinet door.

I began to wash my hands again very slowly. It gave me an excuse for waiting longer and it's a great aid to reflection. I decided my journey hadn't been wasted. Knowledge begins in establishing the dimensions of your ignorance. Anna had helped me to establish the dimensions of mine. She had taught me exactly what I didn't know.

All I knew was that she was lying. A baby with the cord not cut would have known more than she did. But what I didn't know was why. The interesting thing was why. The interesting thing is always why.

What did she have to hide? This house probably belonged to Dave Lyons. Was it loaned to her by someone who was just a friend in need? She wouldn't have to hide that. Was she set up in it by a lover? Was that what she had to hide from me? But then why would she have to hide that? What the hell did it have to do with me? It couldn't be that. Unless it was to protect Dave Lyons. Did she think I would tell his wife?

But her silence seemed too massively fortified. You don't build Fort Knox on the off-chance that someone may try to break in. You build it to make certain that nobody ever can. I thought her secret was a big one. Why did she have to hide it so determinedly?

As I was drying my hands, the phone rang three times. I was assuming that it was all right to pick it up now that I was no longer in the room. But then it rang again, almost immediately, just once, and I was forced to revise that conclusion. It had rung twelve times when I was in the room because there were people who phoned here that Anna mustn't speak to? They were presumably people who didn't know she was here. Perhaps a triple ring was a signal and prepared her to pick up the phone when the call was repeated. An interesting household.

When I came back into the living-room, Anna said, 'Speak to you soon. 'Bye,' and put down the receiver. I asked if I could use the phone. Nobody threatened to bar my way. I phoned the Crime Squad office and left a message for Brian and Bob Lilley. I left a pound note beside the phone.

'I'll leave you the money for that, Anna,' I said.

Anna was standing in the middle of the room. Carla rose to join her. I think they were telling me something.

'Well,' I said. 'Anna. Carla. It's been a gas. Let's do it again some time. When we're all dead.'

'That'll be soon enough for us,' Carla said.

That Carla was good at it. I wouldn't have liked to be her husband and be found in a compromising situation. She would probably feed you through a mincer. We parted. Nobody cried.

Isn't what people don't say so interesting? I had plenty of

time to contemplate how interesting it was as I tried to nego-
tiate Princes Street. I hadn't arrived anywhere with Anna. But
I had increased my determination to travel on. Her behaviour
was more full of questions than Trivial Pursuits. Another small
one occurred to me. Who had warned her that I was coming?
Dave Lyons? But how would he know? Her father? Or had her
father told Dave Lyons, who told her? With someone as well
hidden as Anna, a lot of things were possible.

I studied Edinburgh Castle. The evening traffic of Princes
Street was moving slowly enough to let me do a painting of
Edinburgh Castle. It was a strange place, I decided. There was
the uncompromising ruggedness of the rock and growing out
of it, like a natural extension, the old battlements. But I knew
that if you saw it from a different angle – say, Castle Street
– you would notice the more modern addition to it, like a
genteel country house. It was maybe a fair symbol of Scotland
right enough, of our duality. It would certainly have been fitting
as Anna's coat-of-arms, and perhaps mine as well, though I
hoped not. See how what it has been grows incomprehensibly
into what it is, survives by denying itself, as if the root of a
thistle should nourish a rose.

19

I decanted the water carefully into the whisky and watched them quarrel in the glass. Let us not rush pleasure. It was my first of the day and my last of the day, all I could allow myself when driving. I take a lot of water in my whisky. I think I'm trying to convince my liver that I don't really drink. Down there, whatever metabolic foremen are on shift may be confused. 'It's all right, boys. He's into the water again. We can relax. There's just a tincture of something in it.' By the time they've worked out what's going on, the crisis is over. Danger multiplies in the knowledge of itself, through panic.

I sat and watched the clouds pass in the mixture. Clear weather followed. I lifted my drink. Proust had his madeleine. I had my whisky. As I sipped, I saw this pub on countless other occasions and tuned into long, rambling conversations and wandered again through labyrinthine nights. Memory was held in a glass. Why do I drink? To remember.

I suppose I had chosen the Admiral as the place to meet Brian and Bob because of the associations it had for me. I've known a lot of pubs in Glasgow. I could gantry-stare for Scotland. But no bar has meant more to me than the Admiral.

Since I left University at the end of my first year, suffering from irrelevance-fatigue, a group of us had been meeting here once a month or so. Those innumerable nights began with myself and Tom Docherty, whom I knew from school in Graithnock. We had been joined over the years by various others but the hard core remained as Tom and myself, Vic Vernon and Ray Harrison. For more than twenty years, give or take long furloughs when one or more of us was out of the country, we had been coming here to discuss the books we had been reading, the lives we were living, politics, ideas, relationships. Those times were important in my life.

Tonight I sat alone and felt that the company of the others would have helped, especially Tom. If Morag Harkness thought I was mad, she hadn't met Tom Docherty. Come to think of it, I hadn't met him lately myself. His marriage had broken up, too, and he had vanished into a bedsit somewhere in Glasgow. Vic was trying to find out where he was. He was a writer and I assumed he must be writing now, doing what he called 'unravelling my entrails'. His grandfather, Tam Docherty, had been a legend in Graithnock before we were born, a street-fighter for justice. I sometimes thought Tom had carried the family tradition on to the verbal plane. It helped me a little just to think that he was somewhere nearby, trying to wrestle his experience into meaning. I wasn't the only obsessive in town. I toasted Tom with the last of my whisky, missing him.

For the moment I would have to settle for the less sympathetic presences of Brian Harkness and Bob Lilley. The way they were looking at me as they came in wasn't promising. Bob put his hand on my forehead.

'Do you want a second opinion?' Brian said.

When I came back with the drinks, Bob suggested to me,

as he had more than once, that it was perhaps the soda and lime that was clouding my judgment.

'It could be the sudden shock to your system. Taking in substances it's not used to.'

'I've had my quota. I've got to drive back to Graithnock tonight.'

'You're still not finished down there?' Brian said. 'I thought when you phoned us to meet you here, you had recovered. And you were back to stay in the real world.'

'It feels real enough where I've been. Full of deceit and lies. That's the real world, isn't it?'

'It's the same place we've been lately, anyway,' Bob said.

Brian was studying me with some curiosity.

'So you drove up here from Graithnock just to talk to us? That's quite touching, Jack.'

'No, I came through here from Edinburgh. I thought since I was passing through, I could catch up with you.'

'Edinburgh? What were you up to there?'

'That's where Anna is. I was talking to her.'

They exchanged looks that were a serious version of Bob's hand on my forehead. I imagined they were thinking of me encroaching on the widow's grief. They didn't realise you'd have to find it first.

'Anyway,' I said. 'What's the story with you two? You look as if you've been up to something more fruitful than me.'

They had a flush of purposefulness on them, the look of people who are convinced of the importance of what they're doing. Bob, with his healthy, open-air appearance, might have been happy with the way things were going on the farm. Brian, younger and more citified, might have had a good day at the

165

office. I felt a moment of envy, like a failed alchemist looking on at two happy dispensing chemists.

'Jack,' Bob said. 'More fruitful than you? Ploughing the Sahara would be more fruitful work than you're up to.'

'You don't know that.'

'Everybody knows that. But you.'

'We'll see.'

'When? When will we see? How long before you just admit that Scott's dead and leave it at that? Now you're chasing up Anna, for God's sake. Get a grip.'

'Leave it, Bob.'

'You take a week off work to do this? Why not just take a holiday?'

'You could use one,' Brian said. 'You really could.'

I caught unmistakably the modulations of prepared speeches. They were a duet.

'How about it, Jack?' Bob said. 'Give yourself a break for a few days.'

'You've done what you can,' Brian said.

I imagined them setting up their advice bureau between them before they came into the pub. I hate rehearsed scenes.

'Look,' I said. 'I've left my tolerance for lectures in my other clothes. Just give me what you have about Fast Frankie and I'll piss off.'

'That's another thing,' Brian said. 'What's Frankie White got to do with anything?

'That's what I'm trying to find out, for Christ's sake. To do that it would help to talk to him. And if I want to talk to him, it would be useful to meet him. And if I want to meet him –'

'Kentish Town,' Brian said.

'Kentish Town? Thanks. That really narrows it down. Brian, we both thought he was in London. Kentish Town's in London, right enough. But is that as close as we get?'

Brian smiled and took a piece of paper out of his pocket and passed it across. Brian had written on it Frankie's name and address and telephone number. I looked up at him. He winked. I had to admit to myself, if not to him, that it was impressive.

'You are dealing,' he said, 'with a finder-out of the highest calibre.'

'How did you do it?'

'Those who know know me.' He read the remark like a lesson from scripture. 'Those who know know that I know that they know. Those who know —'

'Uh-huh,' I said.

'Anyway,' Brian said, 'what use is it to you? What are you going to do? Phone him? You couldn't get Frankie White to tell you the truth if you had him in the same room with you. Along with several thumb-screws. He lies for a living. And you're going to get something out him on the phone? Be like guddling trout in a spate. And I assume your travels aren't going to take you as far as Kentish Town. I'm not sure my car would, anyway. Though probably your head would, the way it's working just now. And Frankie's very unpopular up here just now. With a fella we're interested in at this very moment, as it happens. Matt Mason. You won't get Frankie to come up here for anything. Take his chances with Matt Mason? Better volunteering to be a mugger in Beirut. What you've got in your hand is a piece of waste paper. It would take more than the SAS to get Frankie White out of London.'

One half of me could see what Brian was up to: discredit the information as he gave me it, so that I would be discouraged from pursuing it. The other half of me could see that he was probably right. I turned the paper over. The reverse side was empty.

'You're not that good,' I said. 'What about where he comes from?'

'Who?'

'Fast Frankie White.'

'He lives in Kentish Town.'

'That's where he lives. But where does he come from?'

'You want to know that as well? What's that got to do with it?'

'Brian.' I couldn't believe it. 'I specifically asked you. On the phone. To find that out.'

'Me? No, you didn't.'

'Jesus Christ! Ayrshire. I said it was Ayrshire. But I didn't know *where* in Ayrshire. That was the main thing. Shit! Aw, naw.'

Bob put his finger to his mouth, a man advising a small boy to be silent.

'You'd better tell him, Brian,' he said. 'Otherwise, the wee chap is going to take a fit.'

Brian smiled and produced another piece of paper.

'I was just trying to save you from yourself,' he said.

The paper contained an address in Thornbank, which is a village a few miles from Graithnock.

'It's his mother's house,' Bob said.

As soon as I knew I had the information, I relaxed. It struck me immediately that Frankie's address in Thornbank was probably worthless, since he wouldn't be there, and I couldn't take the time to go to Kentish Town. Why then did it matter so much to me? I realised I was feeding a compulsion. It was the mere possibility of finding out more about what had happened to Scott that was keeping me going. I felt embarrassed about inflicting my mania so unashamedly on them.

'Hey. Thanks, Brian,' I said. 'And, Bob. Thanks.'

'Don't go all nice and polite on us,' Bob said. 'That's when I'll really worry.'

'I'm sorry about all that,' I said.

'Are you hell,' Brian said.

We started to laugh. I felt as if I had just arrived, belatedly, in their company. Before, I hadn't been seeing them as themselves, just as a part of my preoccupation. Bob bought a round of drinks. We talked about how Brian's car was doing and the vagaries of Morag's car. Bob had recently won a cup at bowling. I asked him if he had ever played in Kelso. He looked puzzled but said he hadn't. Morag was still threatening to have me at their house for a meal. We decided Bob and Margaret should come along, too.

The room had widened for me. I was no longer seeing it through a tunnel. The bright warmth was soothing. The pub wasn't busy but there was a group of four girls and two boys at a table across from us. Their laughter was a pleasant sound. Brian saw me looking over towards them.

'Remember that?' he said. 'Real life?'

'Aye, it's good stuff,' I said.

'You should try it some time.'

'I intend to. But not this week.'

He bought another round. I became briefly so normal that I wasn't the first to bring the talk back to business. Bob Lilley mentioned the name of Matt Mason. He was nominally a bookie. It was an occupation he wore like a fancy coat which had a lot of secret pockets. There were some bad things in the pockets, including possibly murder. If you fell out with him, emigration wasn't a bad idea.

'What does he have against Frankie White?' I asked.

'That's vague,' Bob said. 'We think Frankie let him down in some way.'

'Frankie's let everybody down,' I said. 'It's what he does.'

'It's not what he does to Matt Mason,' Brian said. It's not what anybody does to Matt Mason. Anyway, Frankie's not involved in this one. At least, that's what it looks like. He's been away too long. That thing you said. About looking high up for the source. We think it could be Mason. He's in drugs. Meece was dealing. We think Mason was his wholesaler. He's the kind of business man who would cut off your franchise by the neck. He stops you dealing by stopping you breathing. Frankie has never been involved in anything as heavy as that.'

'What about the woman?'

'We've got a name,' Bob said. 'Melanie.'

'That's a good Glaswegian name.'

'But that's it. Melanie. No second name so far. We got the name from Meece's brother. But he doesn't know any more. Meece's family didn't mix with him too much. I don't know why. He was a fine upstanding man, Meece. We think if we find Melanie we've got a good chance.'

'Sounds like one she could have picked out of a book,' I said. 'If she was with Meece, she was using. Somebody clean with a junkie? Mixed marriages like that don't work. If she's using, she can't hole up for too long at a time.'

'We've thought about that,' Brian said. 'But maybe she's holed up with another junkie. Who gets her the stuff. One of the problems is Meece seems to have been the unknown citizen. He hasn't left too many traces. I mean, what else did he do? Besides stick needles in his arm?'

'That tends to be a full time job,' Bob said.

'He used to be a good driver,' I said. 'He used to drive for people. He was good. He could've U-turned a Daimler on a footpath. Put him in a car, he thought he was superman.'

'Melanie,' Bob said. 'Can't be too many of them around.'

'I don't know,' Brian said. 'Maybe in Hyndland there is.'

We talked round it some more while I finished my soda and lime and they sipped their pints. I wanted to get back to Graithnock before it was much later. It was maybe a sign of how our conversation had helped to calm my fever that pursuing leads wasn't my only reason for being eager to check in to the Bushfield. I was also very hungry. Before I left in the morning, Katie Samson had said she would have a meal ready for me when I got back.

I offered to buy them another drink but they were moving on as well. I didn't leave the bar with them because I wanted to use the pay-phone. Obviously, my fever wasn't completely cured. If I'd needed any confirmation of that, Brian and Bob provided it. When I stayed behind, their tolerant head-shakings made them look like doctors who have done the best they can for a patient who just won't take advice.

I tried phoning Frankie's number in Kentish Town. There was nobody in. The phone at the restaurant was engaged. I tried Jan's home number. She didn't use an answering machine, so that I couldn't even talk to her by proxy.

Nobody loved me. The way I was feeling about myself, I was in danger of agreeing with them.

20

Staying in the Bushfield was beginning to feel like a way of life. Buster's growl was becoming almost welcoming. Katie was annoyed that the food she had made for me and now had to reheat was going to be so dry. But I like it that way. I think it goes back to the time at school when I had an evening paper run and often ate after the others and acquired a taste for the overdone. I associate those meals with the warmth of home on cold nights. Katie didn't realise that she was serving me comfort food, a brief holiday in the womb. I irrigated the pleasing dryness of the food with glasses of milk.

'There's a woman in to see you,' Katie said.

I looked at her. She was being arch.

'It doesn't take Jack Laidlaw long. Aha. Women queuing in the lounge. Well, two of them actually.'

'Not much of a queue.'

'Oho. It's usually more than that, is it?'

'Katie. I carry pocketfuls of stones to fend them off. A fella's got to protect himself.'

The nonsense had a purpose. There was only one woman, besides Katie, who would know I was here. Ellie Mabon wouldn't want to advertise. She had presumably brought a friend to be less conspicuous. If Katie knew the name, she would know the association with Scott. Remembering Ellie Mabon's fixation that the world was full of nosy neighbours, I wanted to protect her privacy. I wondered if Katie suspected.

'So don't keep me in suspense,' I said. 'Who's the woman?'

'Ah don't know. It was Mike she asked. Ye know him. He didn't even ask her name. Mike's the kinna man could leave a telegram lyin' unopened for a week. Ah just saw them. Bonny women. The one that did the askin', she looks like that Lee Remick in the pictures. Ah wouldn't be standin' beside her at the disco anyway. Who is she?'

'How do I know, Katie?'

'Liar.'

But she left it at that. She went out of the kitchen. I finished eating and did my dishes, which is the only domestic chore I sometimes almost enjoy. I think I just like playing with water.

Ellie Mabon's friend was a woman called Mary Walters. She was attractive but tonight she was definitely playing the leading lady's best friend. Ellie had not become any more difficult to look at in the last day. There were quite a lot of people in the lounge and several of them seemed to find their eyes attracted to her from time to time. When the introductions were over and I went to get them a drink ('It'll have to be a quick one, we're just leaving'), a man at the bar spoke to me.

'Do you want any help carrying those over?' He widened his eyes and breathed out noisily. 'I won't even take a tip.'

Conversation didn't flow immediately at our table. We made some remarks about my soda and lime. Mary Walters was a teacher, too, and she had known Scott casually. We said nice things about him. There was no sign that Ellie, unlike Mary

Walters, knew Scott beyond the man who had appeared at teachers' conferences and on staff nights out. I was beginning to wonder why Ellie had come. If she had something to tell me, why did she bring her own gag? I was looking into her aquarium eyes and seeing nothing but the reflection of my own thoughts, not all of them as innocent as they might have been. Then Mary Walters went to the toilet. Ellie's voice became as urgent as a telegram.

'Mary doesn't know about Scott and me,' she said. 'But I couldn't very well come here on my own.'

'You've thought of something?'

'You mentioned Dave Lyons.'

'That's right.'

'There was a party at his house. Scott was there. I spoke to a friend who was there as well. She told me.'

I appreciated the effort Ellie had made. But I couldn't help feeling disappointed. She was delivering yesterday's newspaper.

'I know,' I said.

'But do you know what happened?'

'He threw a vase at the telly?'

Her disappointment made a small girl of her.

'I thought maybe you didn't know. It seemed as if it might be important. It must have taken something special for Scott to do that.'

'Your friend didn't happen to say what was on television at the time?'

Ellie's reaction wasn't much more reassuring than Dave Lyons' had been.

'Do you think that matters?'

'It might.'

'No. She wasn't actually in the room at the time. She just said some people had been watching a video.'

'A video?'

'Yes. Why?'

'Try to be exact about this, Ellie. Your friend said it was a video. It wasn't just a television programme?'

'What's the difference?'

'There's a big difference.'

Ellie considered it. 'She said "video". What she actually said, she said, "one of Dave's videos". I took her to mean something he had taped himself. Why?'

'Dave Lyons says he doesn't know what was on television when Scott had his brainstorm. But if it was a video, that seems less likely. Especially if it was something he had taped himself. It was maybe something he wanted his guests to see. It was at least something he would have to take out of the machine later. So he would know what they had been watching.'

'So what does that prove?'

'It proves he was lying. Why would you lie about something as trivial as that? Unless you had something to hide.'

'He's not the only one,' Ellie said.

'What?'

'With something to hide.'

I thought at first she meant herself. She seemed hesitant.

'Anna,' she said.

'What about Anna?'

'I didn't mention it to you yesterday. But there was something that was troubling Scott. Anna had someone else.'

'Who?'

'I don't know. I'm not even sure that he knew who it was.'

'It wasn't just a fantasy of his?'

'I don't know. But his conviction was real enough.'

Mary Walters reappeared at the end of the lounge. Perhaps she knew more than Ellie thought. She had taken her time in the toilet, possibly to give us a chance to talk.

'How long are you staying here?' Ellie asked.

'Maybe not after tonight.'

'Give me your home number then. In case I need to get in touch.'

As Mary Walters came towards us, I wrote my number on a beermat. As Mary Walters sat down, Ellie slipped the beermat into her handbag. We chatted pleasantly for a few minutes more and they finished their drinks and left.

The friendly Dane was at the bar with some others. He waved to me. But I didn't want one of those Bushfield nights that wander on into the morning. I had some more travelling to do tomorrow. Thornbank was one place on my itinerary. Troon was another. If Fast Frankie White wasn't in Thornbank, there must be people there who knew him. It was worth trying. If Frankie did happen to be there, I fancied my chances of getting him to tell me what I wanted to know. Dave Lyons was a harder proposition.

I recalled that image of him walking away from me in Cranston Castle House. I didn't know too much more about the smaller versions of himself that were hiding behind the veneered exterior. But I had some ideas. If I hadn't worked out yet how to unscrew the outermost Russian doll, I could maybe break it. I knew he was lying. I could prove it on the triviality about the television. I had the basis for one very strong suspicion: he was more than Anna's landlord. Let's see if the polish at least cracked. He had said he would be at home this week. That was the best place to see him. Liars are at their most vulnerable in their own house, because it's where the truth can hurt them most.

I finished my soda and lime, feeling such a clean-living man, and handed it in at the bar. The earliness of my departure evinced a chorus of disbelief and the suggestion that Katie should get my Horlicks ready. I promised I would bring them in some tracts on teetotalism tomorrow. Before going upstairs, I went across to the pay-phone in the hall.

I rang Kentish Town. Nobody answered. I rang the restaurant. I wished nobody had answered. It was Betsy, pleased to elocute precisely that Jan wasn't there. I rang Jan's flat. Standing lonely in a busy place, I thought how much I could have used a night with my friends. Where was Tom Docherty anyway? There are few sounds more forlorn than the phone of someone you love ringing out with no one to answer.

FOUR

21

Someone's death can be like a flare illumining where you are. You realise with a shock how far you have wandered from where you were intending to go, how strangely the terrain differs from where you had hoped to be. Driving to Thornbank, I was still held in the livid brightness of Scott's dying. The landscape was more than a landscape. It was also a private ordnance map of questions and messages to me. The countryside and the villages I passed through seemed to make an innocent statement about the coexistence of people and nature but the subtext for me was the strangeness of what I had become.

Outside of Graithnock, I drove past familiar fields where three of us had wandered a lot one summer. We would be fifteen, Davy, Jim and me. Jim's father had greyhounds and we sometimes took them with us. I remembered the private club of our laughter and the grandiose folly of our expectations. Jim died at nineteen on a motorbike. I had met Davy by accident a few years ago. He was an architect who appeared to be drinking what was left of his dreams to death. I was a middle-aged detective who liked to try and read philosophy, like someone studying holiday brochures in the poorhouse.

In the village of Holmford I passed a shabby council house I had known before they finished building it. I had been there with one of the first girls I took home from the dancing. I was seventeen and so was she. We missed her last bus and walked the few miles to Holmford. Seeing the doorless and windowless shell of the building, I carried her over the threshold. It wasn't a long marriage. We stayed there maybe a couple of hours, away from the eyes of others. We could have done anything without being observed. What we did was kiss and touch each other in many places with endless gentleness and sing songs. We must have sung about twenty duets. No doubt my performance would have earned me disbarment from the mobile stag party that was male adolescence in Graithnock at that time. But I didn't care. I acquired with my first interest in girls a conviction that whatever good things happen between two people looking for love are their own sweet secret and nobody else's business. And, anyway, I enjoyed what we did. I think the songs were a kind of making love, a shared dreaming, a faith in what would be, even if it didn't happen between us. Thinking of black-haired Mary and wondering how she was now, I wished her well. I wished her a good duet with someone kind. The house then, it seemed to me, was where I had been. The house now, I was afraid, was maybe where I was.

It's not just you that moves on. Places move too. You go back and you find that they are not where they were. The streets and buildings may remain, with modifications, but they aren't any longer the place you knew. The looker makes the looked at and what I was seeing perhaps was a kind of absence, a self no longer there. I had come into what I took for manhood among these parts of Ayrshire and they had meant much to me, not just as a geography but as a landscape of the heart, a quintessential Scotland where good people were my landmarks and the common currency was a mutual caring. Why did it feel so different to me today, a little seedy and withdrawn? Had I dreamed a place? Going through Blackbrae towards Thornbank, I recalled that big Pete Wells was dead. He had come from here, the father of a friend of mine at Graithnock Academy. I had enjoyed listening to him talking many times. He had been one of the strongest believers in the worth of people I had ever met and in the social justice that was coming. Thinking of him, I wondered what he would think of me and of what I had become. Stopping in Thornbank to ask the way to Fast Frankie White's mother's house, I felt as if I was asking directions to the faith Pete Wells had had. Was it still there and could I share it?

The house was in the middle of a terrace, a two-storey roughcast. As I walked up the path, I noticed that the curtains of the upstairs bedroom window were still drawn. I tapped the letter-box lightly. A woman opened the door. She was maybe forty, pleasantly strong-featured.

'Yes?

She said it quietly, as if conversation were a cabal. I found myself joining in the conspiracy.

'I'm looking for Frankie,' I said. 'I was passing through. I thought I would say hello.'

'You haven't heard?' she said.

'It's been a long time since I saw him.'

She glanced upstairs.

'Come in,' she said.

She ushered me into the living-room and closed the door.

'It's Mrs White,' she said. 'She hasn't long to go. A couple of weeks at the most. Frankie's upstairs with her now.'

I understood why Frankie White was home. Brian had said it would take more than the SAS to get him out of London. The death of your mother qualified.

'Ah'm sorry,' the woman said. 'Ah'm forgettin' maself.' She held out her hand. 'Ah'm Sarah Haggerty.'

'Jack Laidlaw.'

'You known Frankie long?'

'Quite a few years. Back and forward.'

'Ah was just makin' a cup of tea there. Ye want one?'

'That would be nice.'

She left the kitchen door open and we talked in a quiet and desultory way. The nature of her references to how Frankie was 'workin' in London these days' convinced me that she thought the work was legal. When she asked me what I did myself, I didn't want to mar her image of Frankie as an honest grafter. I said I worked for quite a big firm. In personnel. Involved mainly in recruitment. I was glad she didn't go on to ask me about working conditions as I was running out of euphemisms. She was full of praise for Frankie's concern for his mother. It seemed he had arranged leave of absence from his work in London to stay with her till she died. He didn't care if it cost him his job. There were people in Thornbank, she said, who spoke badly of Frankie, especially after what had happened lately. What had happened lately? She didn't seem to hear the question. Perhaps it was because the kettle was boiling at the time. But the gossips didn't know the real Frankie White. 'He loves that woman up the stair. An' he's a good judge.' Unlike a lot of people these days, he hadn't forgotten where he came from.

The picture she painted of Fast Frankie White as an upholder of the solid virtues in shifting times was an interesting departure from realism, the portrait as an abstract of improbable colours. Frankie was good-looking and unviolent and he dispensed slickness like a Brylcreem machine. But what he promised, you must never hope to be realised. He had a mouth like a dud cheque.

Yet in this place Sarah Haggerty's sense of Frankie seemed less ludicrous. The style of the room was familiar enough to me to be part of a whole contemporary trend in interior decoration: filial plush. In this case, it meant thick wall-to-wall carpeting, heavy wallpaper, a lot of ornaments and a fyfe-stone fire-place encasing a very elaborate metal-work gas-fire.

I liked the style fine not because it pleased the eye but because it pleased the heart. I had seen examples of it all over the West of Scotland. What it meant was gratitude. Its essence was that you should realise this place had very definitely been *decorated*. The person who lived here mattered to her family and this was their way of thanking her for enduring threadbare carpets and linoleum while she sacrificed to bring them up. If you were to judge Frankie White by what he had done for his mother, you came closer to understanding Sarah Haggerty's naive idea of him. I just hoped the video hadn't fallen off the back of a lorry. That would have been like making a crucifix out of stolen gold.

'Here we are,' she said. 'Jack, isn't it?'

'That's right. Thanks. Sarah?'

She nodded. I was glad to be one of the family before Frankie arrived. It should make our performance easier. I had been adopted just in time. Frankie came in.

I couldn't remember having seen Frankie White without his make-up. I was seeing him now. Even Pagliacci had a place where he took off the greasepaint. This was Frankie's. The flip attitudes were gone. The fear of what was happening to his mother still looked out of his face. Perhaps most revealingly for Frankie, who normally dressed in the sartorial equivalent of neon lights, he was wearing a woollen shirt, track-suit trousers and trainer shoes. Then he realised who it was he was looking at.

'Hullo, old friend,' I said, being not too subtle with the cue. 'I was explaining to Sarah that I haven't seen you for a while.'

'Oh, Frankie,' Sarah said. 'Ah was just sayin' to Jack here about yer mother. He hadn't heard.'

Trouble always travels in company, as Katie Samson would say. As if upstairs wasn't bad enough for Frankie, here was a policeman drinking tea in his house like an old family friend. What was happening to the world? Frankie didn't know. He stood in the middle of our charade like the only person at the masked ball who had forgotten his costume. I thought I had better not offer to shake hands in case he had a cardiac attack at the end of my arm. Sarah helped the situation unknowingly by getting a cup of tea for Frankie and saying she would go up and see his mother.

'You two must have a lot to talk about.'

Frankie was wondering what it was. He stirred his tea very slowly.

'What is this?' he said. 'Ah'm clean, Mr Laidlaw.'

'Call me Jack. We've got to keep up appearances.'

'Ah'm clean. Ah came up from London tae see ma mother

out. Ah'm not involved up here any more. Ah don't need this.'

'Frankie. I'm not here on official business.'

'Mr Laidlaw —'

'Jack.'

'Jack.' He didn't use the name with complete conviction. 'What polisman was ever anywhere that wasn't on official business? You mob don't have friends. You have informants. Who are ye kiddin'? You're lookin' for information. Ah don't give information. You know that.'

I did. Frankie White had never shopped anyone. It was what made him accepted among men a lot harder and more successful than himself.

'All right, Frankie. But this is personal information. It's not for use in the courts. It's just for me. Why did you fall out with my brother?'

'What brother?'

'Scott.'

'Who the hell's Scott? Ah don't know your brother.'

The troubled amazement in his eyes was not for denying. He was having a bad day and he didn't know where it came from. I told him Gus McPhater's version of the incident in the Akimbo Arms.

'Ah remember somethin' like that,' he said. 'Was that your brother? Jesus, he was wild. Runs in the family, eh? But Ah never understood what it was supposed tae be aboot. Ye no' ask him?'

'He's dead.'

I thought I saw an infinitesimal relaxation on Frankie's face. 'What happened?'

I told him.

'Ah'm sorry. That's hellish. Ah'm sorry. Jack. But Ah never knew what that was about. Ah think the fella was just drunk. Picked on me. Maybe he didny like the suit Ah was wearin'. He wouldny be the first.'

The way he used my first name confirmed my suspicions. False intimacy is treachery's favourite weapon. Judas kisses. The best way to knife a man is to embrace him as you do it. I decided I didn't believe him. He knew what I needed to know and he was lying. I felt my anger freeze me to the chair. I stared at Frankie. Drinking his tea seemed to demand as much concentration as threading a needle.

'Frankie,' I said. 'Tell me why Scott quarrelled with you.'

'Ah wish Ah knew.'

'Frankie. Ah need to know.'

'What can Ah say?'

'The fuckin' truth.'

'Come on. Ah can't tell ye what Ah don't know.'

We will take our little deceits to the edge of the grave. We will trivialise even death. Frankie White was staring the ultimate truth in the face and still he couldn't kick the habit of a lifetime: lie to the police. My compassion for what was happening in his life atrophied.

'Frankie,' I said. 'You're a petty crook. And you're not very good at it. You're a fantasist and a liar and a phoney. But you've got two things going for you. Just two. I suppose they're what hold you together. You've never touted to the polis. And if that woman Sarah's anything to go by, there are maybe a couple of people who believe in you as a good man. Like your mother. Your mother must think you're something special. What I'm going to do. If you don't tell me what you know. I'm going to make your name a bad smell everywhere. Not just in Glasgow. I know where you're living now.' I told him his address in Kentish Town. 'But before that. I'm going to go upstairs and tell your mother things that'll destroy her faith in you.'

We both sat still in the room for a couple of minutes, despising me. I thought of Pete Wells and knew I wouldn't have liked to look in his eyes just now. I had threatened to make an innocent old woman's dying miserable in order to get at her son.

'Frankie,' I said. 'I apologise. Of course, I won't say anything to your mother. It would be like pissing on my own mother's grave. I'm sorry. Forget it. Forget I asked.'

Frankie finished his tea.

'You know,' he said. 'The last week or so. Ah've had to look at maself in a different mirror. It's not nice. All that woman's done for me. An' what did Ah give her back? An' she still believes in me. It's probably all she's got to believe in. If she stops believin' in that, she'll know that all those years were wasted. In one way, Ah'm glad for her that she hasn't been out the door for the past few months. She hasn't heard what the village thinks o' me these days. May she never. That's what your brother was talkin' about. Ah honestly didn't know that's who he was. He was a stranger to me. But he knew me all right. And he knew what had happened.'

He lifted his cigarettes from beside the fire and offered me one. We lit up. I waited. He was talking to himself as much as to me. A question would have been an intrusion.

'Ah've been thinkin' all this week,' he said. 'Ah wish Ah wis more of a man. Not just for me. But for her. Ah mean, there she is. She hasny cheated the world outa tuppence change in the whole of her life. She could teach God fairness. She came through the sorest times an' made them intae a bed for me. An' whit does she get oot them? A fuckin' toe-rag for a son. An' Ah've been thinkin'. Ah want to give her somethin' to hold in her hand before she goes. Somethin' good. Some belief in me. Just so that she can shut her eyes on a good feelin'. It's the least she deserves. An' Ah've been wonderin' how Ah do that.'

He looked across at me.

'You're a respectable man,' he said.

'I think you could be confusing me with somebody else, Frankie.'

'Come on. Jack. Jack Laidlaw. If you're not, ye certainly look the part.'

I couldn't see where he was taking me.

'Jack. Ah'm even callin' ye Jack. Just like old friends. How about takin' that a stage further? Ah'll make a deal. Ah'll tell ye what ye want to know. An' you do one thing for me. You walk up that stair an' talk to ma mother an' be ma friend. Not many people round here come about this house these days. Sarah is it. For the rest, it might as well be a leper colony. At least while Ah'm in the house. But if you went up there. An' ye sat a wee while. An' ye told her what a good man Ah am an' how much ye believe in me. That would be something, eh? See what Ah mean? Could be like morphine for 'er. She'll float out in a dream. That's all Ah'm askin'. Help me to give her somethin' nice she can cuddle to herself till she gets tae sleep.'

He was finding it difficult to go on. But he did.

'You see, you don't know her. But she's worth it. This is a wumman that . . .'

'Frankie,' I said. 'Don't waste your breath.'

He looked saddened and hurt.

'For that generation of working-class women,' I said, 'I'd burn down buildings. I know how much they gave and the shit they got back. You don't have to convert a disciple. Just tell me what to say an' Ah'm yer man.'

He smiled at me and I smiled back and we were a momentary brotherhood – two reprobates who nevertheless understood the shared goodness they had come from.

'Ah'll leave the details up to you,' he said. 'Ah canny think of one thing in ma favour at the moment. Ye'll see why when Ah tell ye. Your brother knew something that had happened here in Thornbank three month ago. He knew Ah was involved in it. Don't ask me how he knew. Ah think he thought Ah was more involved in it than Ah was. But Ah was involved all right. An' he hated me for it. Ah couldny believe how much he hated me that night.'

I remembered Gus McPhater's awe at Scott's anger. That small, vicious altercation was about to clarify into meaning, like an insect noise that is finally identified.

'Dan Scoular's dead,' Frankie said. He paused as if he was still not fully used to the idea. 'The big man's dead. You know who he was? He was as good as ye get. Your brother knew he was dead. An' he blamed me for it.'

The name of Dan Scoular whispered a memory at me that I couldn't quite catch. Scott had mentioned him to me more than once. Something about how formidable he had been.

'A bit of a puncher?' I said. 'An ex-miner?'

'That's your man. You knew him?'

I shook my head.

'Well, what happened was. He was unemployed. An' Ah got him into a bare-knuckle fight. Wi' Cutty Dawson.' I was familiar with the name of the ex-heavyweight boxer. 'Dan won. But they thought Cutty might be blinded. An' as a loser he got no money. Big Dan wouldn't have that. So he's taking on the promoters next.'

'Who set up the fight?'

'Matt Mason and Cam Colvin. Dan was Matt's man. Cutty was Cam's.'

'So what happened?'

'Dan visits Cutty in hospital after the fight, finds out the score. He goes back to Matt Mason's, knocks him out and takes what he decides should be Cutty's wages. He delivers them to him. Can ye imagine it? He robbed Matt Mason.'

Frankie was right to find it an amazing story. The headline could have been: Gunfighter challenges the Eighth Army.

'Then Dan came back here. Hide in plain sight, right enough. Ah knew Ah was in the line of fire. Ah had it away to London. But Ah tried to take Big Dan with me. Ah warned him what he was mixed up in. You try to pick Matt's pocket, ye're goin' to leave yer hand in there. But Ah felt responsible. Not for what Dan did. Who could have imagined anybody would be as simple as that? But for setting him up for the fight in the first place. Ah made him the offer to come with me. Why didn't he take it?'

He seemed genuinely puzzled. I recognised the old Frankie White. Confronting a potentially transforming experience, he hadn't really changed. I sometimes wonder if we ever do.

Because his was a portable self, a suitcase on which the labels will vary according solely to personal need, he couldn't understand that a man might be fixed to a place by factors beyond self-interest.

'Thing is, Ah hear Cutty's sight's all right again. He didn't go blind.'

He appeared to be saying that Dan Scoular's stand had been pointless after all. I thought Frankie perhaps had his own problems of vision. He couldn't see that the big man was presumably protesting against the nature of things beyond the pragmatic.

'How did Dan Scoular die?'

'A hit-and-run driver. Dan kept up the joggin'. We used to do that for his trainin'. He went out one mornin' an' never came back. Seems he was found on the road. Ah mean, when ye think of it. They never found who did it.' Frankie looked at me like a small boy who wants to show his butterfly but is afraid you might crush it. 'Ah mean. It really could've been an accident. Couldn't it?'

'Sure, Frankie,' I said. 'And John F. Kennedy shot himself.'

'Aye,' Frankie said.

We sat in our own thoughts. I was glad mine weren't Frankie's.

'He was married?'

'Aye. Betty. Two boys.'

'They still live here?'

'Three streets away.'

'Where exactly?'

Frankie was staring at me.

'You're no' goin' there?'

'That was the idea.'

'Come on. What's the point of that?'

'Frankie. There's things I need to know. I still don't know what Scott had to do with all this. Do you?'

'Not a clue.'

'Maybe Betty Scoular has.'

'Rather you than me,' Frankie said. 'Betty never liked me anyway. She's a smashin' big wumman, right enough. But Ah'll admire her from a distance. Especially now. Ah just hope she doesny know Ah'm here. Though Ah suppose she's bound to. If thoughts could kill, they'd be buryin' me soon, not ma mother.'

I asked him where she lived and he told me how to get there.

'You've kept your bit of the bargain,' I said. 'You want me to speak to your mother?'

'You don't mind?'

'Why should I mind?'

'Well, Ah suppose Ah'm askin' ye to lie.'

'I've only two rules about lying, Frankie,' I said. 'Never tell them to yourself, if you can help it. Never tell them to anybody else unless they're benign. I've known lies that were gifts. A dying woman who wants to believe she looks the way she looked when she was eighteen. You going to tell her she's wrong? Of course, you're not. You're going to ask her for a date, aren't you? Anyway, who said you're the worst. I can talk nice about you without choking, don't worry, Francis.'

We went upstairs. There were two lamps with floral shades lit in Mrs White's room. She lay in bed, staring at the ceiling, while Sarah Haggerty talked to her from a cushioned wicker-work chair. Frankie introduced me as an old friend who had dropped in. Sarah said she would have to be getting round to her own house to check on things but would come back later. She said cheerio to me. Frankie went downstairs with her, perhaps to see her out, perhaps to let my creative version of him flourish without the inhibiting presence of reality. I sat down in the chair from which Sarah had risen. I smiled at Mrs White.

She had a face like a handful of bones and those pilgrim eyes of the dying. Most of the essential luggage of her life had gone on ahead and here she was waiting at a wayside station among strangers who had other business. The living are all strangers to the dying. It's just that they're too polite to tell us so. They are kind to our crass familiarities that mistake them for someone else. They do not tell us that we are the bores who have crashed a party for one, seeking company for our own terrified loneliness we have suddenly recognised in their eyes. The dying arrive at true politeness. Even if they scream, they only scream in so far as it is necessary. For who else can establish the rules for what is theirs alone? They cannot be unkind to us, for they leave us alive when they are not. She was kind to me.

'Hullo. Mrs White?'

'Hullo, son.'

Her eyes seemed to be taking an inventory of the room, not with any particular urgency but in an offhand way. It wasn't all that important but she might as well get it done with. Her look lingered on the curtains. But it wasn't possible to tell why. She looked at me. She knew immediately who I was supposed to be.

'So you're a friend of Frank's.'

'That's right.'

'He's an awfu' man, is he no'?'

'He's all that.'

'Uh-huh. Ah haveny seen you in here before, have Ah?'

'Ah've been away for years.'

'Ah sometimes think everybody's been away for years, son. Whit are we gonny do wi' him?'

'Frank? He'll be fine, Mrs White. He's a good man. An' he's doin' well these days. Don't you worry.'

'D'ye think so, son?'

'Ah do, Ah do. Yer son's a success. He's a much respected man.'

Her face enlivened slightly. We had found an old tune she liked and we could play it together, maybe evoking happier days when even Frankie looked like a coming man instead of what he was now, a shifting mirage of promises that never got any nearer.

As we talked, I realised I knew her. I should do. I had seen her often enough, on buses, in shops, in innumerable houses of my youth. She was my auntie, a woman who lived along the street, a friend of my mother. She was one of a courageous multitude of women who without too much fuss made all of our lives better than they would otherwise have been. I found it no hardship to tell her many lies about her son. In any case, they weren't lies to her. They were the truth of her dream and it was a dream that she had earned and that no one should take from her.

We exhausted the topic of Frankie's wonderfulness, at least as far as I was concerned. I had started to feel that if we went on much longer I might finish up believing it myself. I saw how tired she was and said I had to be going. She held out her hand and I took it.

I felt the painful loss of any person of true worth being taken from us. I think for a moment I half-believed that if I could hold her hand hard enough I could keep her here. Her hand was precious with old skin and fading warmth. I did not know what to do. I leaned across and kissed her because her brave ordinariness was so beautiful and because she was so utterly of our kind and because that is what happened.

Frankie was waiting for me at the bottom of the stairs.

'You want to earn *her*?' I said. 'Be better. I'll try as well.'

I came out and closed the door.

22

Betty Scoular was like an impressive house in bad repair and she didn't seem bothered, as if the owner was away from home and she was only leasing it. She was tall and striking. But she wore a jumper that was beginning to gather small nubs of rolled wool and her skirt sat slightly asymmetrically on her hips. She had slippers on. The few flecks of grey in her hair seemed to have gone unchallenged for some time. The eyes watched me dully as she stood in the open doorway. She said nothing.

'Mrs Scoular?' I said. 'I'm sorry to bother you. My name's Jack Laidlaw.'

The expression of venom the name evoked in her face took me aback. It was like watching someone you didn't know stick pins in your effigy. Her eyes found a focus. The lens was malice.

'You're a bit late, are you not?'

'I'm sorry?'

'Dan's three months dead. Three months.'

'Yes, I know. I'm sorry.'

'That's nice. I don't see your brother with you, anyway. Is he too ashamed to come?'

'Mrs Scoular. My brother couldn't make it. A bad case of death.'

Her eyes cleared suddenly with surprise. I had arrived in front of her at last. The world for a moment became more than her widowhood. Her bad thing hadn't ended all the bad things. They were still happening to other people. She found it hard to believe. Perhaps her grief had made her a pedant of its forms. This was something at least she was interested in.

'How?' she said.

'He was run down by a car.'

She closed her eyes and put her hand to her mouth.

'Oh my God,' she said. 'Does it never end? They must have known that he knew.'

Hope can take strange forms. As she spoke, I had a sense of having arrived at the meaning of Scott's death. He had known something he shouldn't and had been killed for it. The quarrel with Fast Frankie White had demonstrated that he knew. Fast Frankie had told Matt Mason. Matt Mason had done the rest. It was simple. It was clean. And it absolved the rest of us. His death was a crime in which we weren't involved. But that self-delusion lasted about three seconds. I had been told about the driver of the car that killed Scott. He was a newsagent with three children, who would never live as casually again as he had lived before. There was no way he had been part of a murder.

Betty Scoular seemed to have forgotten about me. She was staring past me into the street. Perhaps she was having difficulty associating all that had happened recently with the place where she thought she had been living.

'Do you mind if I come in?'

She turned away and I came in after her. If I hadn't closed the door, it wouldn't have been closed. She was standing in the living-room. It might have been a street she didn't know and her looking for directions. The room was well furnished but untidy. It was where a purposeful woman had begun to lose her purpose. It was essentially tasteful and attractive but the essence had been diluted somewhat with abandoned newspapers, books open on a table, clothes over a chair. She sat down in an armchair. I came and sat across from her.

'Mrs Scoular,' I said. 'Why were you so angry with me at the door?'

'You mean you don't know?'

'I've never met you before. I didn't know of you until today.'

'But you knew Dan all right.'

'I never met your husband. I've got a vague idea I've heard Scott speaking about him.'

'A vague idea? You bastard. You can sit there and talk about vague ideas.'

'It's all I *can* do, Mrs Scoular. I've got no choice.'

'Scott told you the danger Dan was in. And what did you do about it? You're even too late for the funeral.'

'Scott knew about this before your husband died? How?'

'How do you think? Dan told him. So that he could pass it on to you. His policeman brother. The great protector.'

No wonder she hated me. I had found out more about my brother than I wanted to. I couldn't believe he would renegue on such a crucial commission. For Scott's sake, I was hesitant to tell her the truth. But there were enough lies and silence already surrounding this matter and, anyway, filial love was not quite at the full just then.

'Scott didn't tell me,' I said.

'What?'

'He didn't tell me. I don't know why he didn't tell me. But he didn't.'

'Oh,' she said, turning a vowel into a brief keening.

She didn't apologise for maligning me in error. Why should she? That sound from her mouth came from far beyond the shores of etiquette. Where she was, I imagined, was in that place after a dying where you keep coming upon small, related fragments of the fact that give you yet another perspective on its enormity – the shoes that will never again be worn, the favourite cup, the letter addressed to the person whose eyes are closed forever. Scott was yet another one who had let her husband down. The terribleness of Dan Scoular's death was renewed in that attendant detail. We teach ourselves the worst things by degrees. They are too big to be absorbed at once and so we memorise the pieces as we find them until we can bear to look at last and see our sadness whole. She had stumbled on another fragment in the meaning of her grief that she was trying to put together. She was sitting wondering where it fitted in.

I was lost inside my own wonder. Why does every answer ask another question? I now knew how you could die twice. By representing in my brother's mind someone who had died before. I knew why Scott had been so angry with Fast Frankie White. I knew a lot more than I had known when I set out from Glasgow – which seemed more than three days ago. But everything I knew resolved itself now into a more puzzling question: why had Scott not told me what Dan Scoular had asked him to tell me?

That drunken moment in my flat came back to me. Scott

had sat up on the floor in the early hours of the morning. There was something he had to tell me. It became 'I am leaving Anna.' But was that what it had truly been? I recalled the tension in his face before he spoke, the prelude to a most difficult thing to say. Perhaps he had failed to say it. The immediate relaxation on his face after he had threatened to leave Anna reminded me now of the expression people have when a joke successfully defuses extreme tension. He must have been leaving Anna a hundred times. It was a safe diversionary tactic that brought him back to where he had been for so long, allowing him to subside again into sleep. What was it he had almost confronted then? The need to tell me about Dan Scoular?

And if it were, why couldn't he say it? That was a conundrum I couldn't see past. There was no reason he couldn't tell me, that I could think of. Except, it slowly came to me, one reason. The reason was guilt.

I have been long enough wandering through the shadows of other people's lives – the violence, the betrayals and the hurt – to be aware of the power of guilt. It is often a malignant power, for it is those desirous of the good who feel it most and, when they do, it can intimidate them into conformity with natures smaller than their own. It can make them so ashamed of themselves that they condone the shameful acts of others. Self-contempt leaves you ill-equipped to challenge the immorality of anyone else.

Towards the end, Scott had been expert in self-contempt. Had guilt closed his mouth? But, in my imagination, I could not see any connection between what Scott might have done and the kind of threat Dan Scoular had faced.

'Mrs Scoular,' I said. 'How did Scott know your husband?'

Renewed contemplation of her misery seemed to have gentled her rage against things for the moment. She shook her head.

'They had met in Graithnock. Playing indoor football. Dan liked him so much. How could your brother let him down like that?'

'I don't know. I can't believe it. You're sure your husband told him? He didn't just say that he would?'

'He told him. I remember the night Dan said that he'd told him. I remember he said, "Should be some kinda deterrent." You've been a name in this house for a while.'

'I wish I'd known.'

'I wish you'd known Dan,' she said. 'I mean, I don't kid myself. We had our troubles. And maybe the marriage wouldn't even have lasted. But nothing would've stopped me loving him. In whatever way it turned out it had to be. I couldn't not, in a way. You don't see two of him in your life. I disagreed with him a lot. But then I disagree with the rain. It doesn't stop it raining. He was himself. He went wherever what he believed in took him. If it was over the edge of a cliff, that's where it was. And it was over the edge of a cliff. Wasn't it?'

'I'd like to have met him.'

'Yes, you would. After it, I resented him so much for it. I still do when I remember to. Leaving the boys and me like this. In some way, I'll never forgive him. But then I knew I wasn't marrying an insurance policy. I've sometimes thought, "What has he left the boys?" But money's not the only inheritance. Maybe theirs is not a bad one.'

Talking a kind of epitaph had calmed her, like paying another visit to the grave. I saw briefly how she must have been and how no doubt she would be again when she had won her way out of her present pain. Her attractiveness was beyond cosmetics. It came from the natural grace of a strong presence. She looked at me steadily.

'How do you know about this if your brother didn't tell you?'

'When Scott died,' I said, 'I wanted to find out why. I came down to Graithnock to ask around. I heard about what had happened to your husband.'

'Who told you?'

It occurred to me that Frankie White didn't want her to know he was in Thornbank. Frankie had enough problems of his own.

'A couple of people in Graithnock knew about what had happened. They told me.' I wanted to move her away from Frankie's hide-out. 'By the way, there was nothing suspicious about Scott's death. It was definitely an accident.'

'Are you sure? Maybe you think Dan's was, too.'

'You don't, obviously.'

'I don't believe in the tooth fairy either. You know Matt Mason?'

'Yes.'

'He killed Dan. That's what happened.'

'Yes, it has to look that way. But to do that, they would have to plan it. How would they know so much about your husband's movements?'

'It could've been Frankie White. Do you know him?'

'I know who you mean.'

'I hate him. I always will. I could believe anything of him.'

'But he's been in London, hasn't he?'

'So what?' She shook her head. 'But I don't really think it was him. There are some things even he's not capable of. He'd be too busy saving his own skin. His poor mother. She's dying, you know. Such a good woman. To have spawned that.'

'If you're sure it was Matt Mason,' I said, 'why haven't you done something about it? Like tell the police.'

She gave me a stone look, a rage so still and cold I was transfixed. I realised how volatile she was, living still between extremities of response, trying to find a stance towards what had happened which could hold in balance all the things she felt. The phone rang. I was glad.

It was someone called Gordon. 'I'm all right, Gordon,' I heard her saying. 'I'm all right.' She responded quietly to whatever he was saying. 'Not now,' she said. She put down the phone. She crossed towards the sideboard.

'Do you want a drink?' she said.

'Better not. I've got the car there.'

'Well, I will.'

She poured a large vodka and topped it up with lemonade. She came and sat back down opposite me.

'The boys have lunch at school,' she said.

I had a glimpse of the little deals she must have worked out between the pressure she was under and the demands made on her by her former standards. It would be all right to have a drink late morning if her sons didn't see her.

'I don't usually do this,' she said. 'Just sometimes.'

No doubt the way my presence reopened hurts in her had helped to make this one of the sometimes. She sipped her drink. I thought she had forgotten what I said. But she hadn't.

'I sometimes think nobody else notices what is happening,'

she said. 'You ever get that feeling? It's like the rest of the world is mad. It carries on regardless. Did I tell the police? What planet did you come from? They did a lot for Dan, didn't they? Anyway, enough people in Thornbank told the police. This village knew what had happened. And this village loved Dan Scoular. I sometimes think they loved him to death. They encouraged him to try and stand for more than one person can stand for. And he died of it. I don't blame them. They've done their best. And they'll forget. I won't forget.'

The fixedness of her eyes was hypnotic.

'You want to know what I did? The more nothing happened, the stiller I became. I became very, very still. Because I understood something. If they could do that to my man, they could do it to my sons.' She put her finger to her lips. 'Sh. Don't move. They've been telling you lies. How safe it is out there. It isn't safe. Bad animals out there. And nobody can control them. They move when they choose. And they do what they want. That's true.'

She nodded at me confidentially. Some might have thought she was the one who seemed mad. But she wasn't mad, just too sane to play along with the rest of us. She had wakened from her sleep-walk to recognise the minefield we call normality. She had found a way to admit to herself the prolonged terror of living. Some people never do.

'So I've been here. In this house. And I do the necessary things. I look after my sons. I make the meals. I wash the clothes. But it's like keeping house on the edge of that cliff Dan went over. That phone-call. That was Gordon. I knew him before Dan died. He's been wanting to know if he can help. I don't know if anybody can help. I know I have to go on living.

But I haven't worked out how to do it yet. It's as if something more has to happen. Or it'll be like leaving Dan unburied.'

'I'm sorry,' I said.

'I don't want another mourner,' she said. 'I think I want a champion. Someone who'll get justice for Dan Scoular.'

'Well, I don't know that I qualify. But I can try.'

She almost smiled.

'That would be something,' she said.

She took another mouthful of her drink. She was alone. I had become just a looker-on.

'Is there somewhere in Thornbank I can get a meal?' I said. 'Even champions have to eat.'

'I'm sorry. Not here. Another time it would have been. But not these days. The Red Lion. They do pub lunches. That's where Dan did his training.'

'Okay,' I said.

I stood up.

'This,' she said. She held up her glass. 'It's all right. This isn't permanent. It's just that I know I have to face what's happened. I can't hide from it. And this sometimes helps. But it's only for the time being.'

I believed her. I know I face my own despairs by letting them take place. I don't deny them with displays of determined nonchalance. They're too real for that. Deny grief and it becomes a sapper, shallowing your nature. You have to go through sadness as you would go through the Roaring Forties. You batten down and let the bad winds blow. They will bring you to yourself.

'I believe you,' I said.

I left her waiting for the weather to clear.

23

I had lunch in the Red Lion. Before eating, I stood at the bar with a tomato juice. I was becoming a connoisseur of soft drinks. The place was fairly dilapidated. There were maybe half-a-dozen people in. The talk seemed to be of imminent closure. The barman, whose name was Alan, had a face like a Christmas tree, every vein a fairy-light. He had decided he would have to sell out to the brewers. He couldn't understand where all the takings he used to have had gone. I thought he might look in the mirror for a clue. He was drinking doubles. But then again maybe I was just jealous.

He was talking to a man called Wullie Mairshall. I knew because at one point the man said, 'This isny Simple Simon talkin'. This is Wullie Mairshall.' The barman said, 'Thanks for pointin' that out. Ah wis gettin' confused there.'

The talk of closure became talk of the mess Thornbank was in, became talk of Dan Scoular. His name was mentioned with a reverence I couldn't imagine any living person managing to justify. But sainthood is always posthumous. The still breathing Frankie White appeared to be in no danger of canonisation. An outbuilding Dan Scoular had used as a gym was still being preserved as he had left it, it seemed. The barman was adamant that it would stand as a monument to 'the big man' as long as he was still owner.

I had ordered beef olives, potatoes and vegetables. When the food came, I sat at a table by a window, taking a glass of exotic soda and lime to wash it down. Wullie Mairshall deputised as a waiter. He brought me condiments and cutlery in a paper napkin, with the suave injunction, 'Dig in, big yin.' When I did, I realised the food was very good. Whoever was responsible for the falling-off of trade in the Red Lion, it wasn't the cook.

I didn't eat alone. The meal, the menu apart, was my mental version of a Roman banquet. First you eat with them, then you give them the thumbs down. The companions of my mind were Dave Lyons and Matt Mason. They sat with me at table, whether they wanted to or not. I studied them. It was them or me, I had decided. Or rather it was them or what Betty Scoular and Mrs White and Scott stood for. I was just the champion of their cause, as Betty Scoular would have it, since nobody else had bothered to turn up. Let's make an arena. I would.

I had solved one half of a mystery. I would go the whole way, however I could. I had discovered the surrogate man in the green coat. His name was Dan Scoular. I would find the real one. Do not bet against me. But discovery is not merely knowledge, it is obligation. Matt Mason had killed Dan Scoular. All right, I didn't know that this was true. But I believed it.

If I had belief in the fact, without proof of the fact, what could I do? I couldn't plant the evidence that would establish the apparent proof, as some of my less scrupulous colleagues might have been prepared to do. That isn't what I do. It isn't what I do because it leads to madness. To pretend that subjective conviction is objective truth, without testing it against the constant daily witness of experience, is to abdicate from living seriously. The mind becomes self-governing and the world is left to chaos. That way, you don't discover truth, you invent it. The invention of truth, no matter how desperately you wish it to be or how sincerely you believe in the benefits it will bring, is the denial of our nature, the first rule of which is the inevitability of doubt. We must doubt not only others but ourselves.

So I would doubt my own conviction for the moment. But I would find a way to test it. It is not enough to think the truth is there. It needs the breath of our acknowledgement to live. I had to find out how to give it the kiss of life.

The original commission I had given myself – to know what lay behind my brother's death – had clarified itself into a double purpose: to find the man in the green coat and to nail Dan Scoular's killer. It looked already as if circumstances had combined them and events were beginning to fit the shape of my compulsion. Maybe that's what compulsion does for you.

The name of Matt Mason kept coming up. He was suspected twice: of Dan Scoular, of Meece Rooney. He was a ubiquitous man. People as busy as that can sometimes get careless. Their sense of detail may blur. Also, if he had done these things, he was their deviser, not the person who physically carried them out. This meant that, with every action he was responsible for, there were witnesses beyond himself. If I could rifle their knowledge, unlock it with threat or fear, I could come at him. I wanted that.

I had two possible sources of access. One was the

information Brian Harkness and Bob Lilley might have. The case they were working on must have taken them into various areas of Matt Mason's life. The second source was Fast Frankie White. There had to be more that Frankie could tell me.

In trying to fulfil the other half of my self-determined task, I could think of only one way forward. It went through Dave Lyons. So that's the way I would go. Whatever the man in the green coat meant, I was convinced he knew. The man in the green coat was a message from Scott's life that I had to understand. Others had given me such fragments of its meaning as they could: Sanny Wilson, Ellie Mabon, David Ewart. But they were like people who have learned by chance some incidental phrases of a code. Put them together, they didn't make a meaning. But Dave Lyons knew the code entire. Anna understood it as well, I suspected. But if she did, she had learned it second-hand. She merely kept its secret in trust for someone else. Who? Scott was dead. It could only be Dave Lyons.

He was the one I had to get to. He had been present when a secret had begun to be kept. It was presumably a secret shared by four. 'It was something that happened when he was a student,' Ellie Mabon had said. David Ewart had thought of the four of them being out that night in Glasgow while he was in Rutherglen. The next morning, he believed he had looked at the suicide of youth, the death of idealism. Of the four who might have been present at that death, one was dead himself. Another was just a name. Another wasn't even a name. That left Dave Lyons.

I didn't expect him to tell me all that he knew. He was too well prepared for me, too well fortified. There was no way I could prove that he must know about the man in the green coat. But there was also no way for him to deny that he knew Sandy Blake and the anonymous English student. If I could find them, I might find people who were worse at lying than Dave Lyons was. It was unlikely that I would find anyone who was better at it.

Mental incantations over. It was time to see if I had found a way to conjure forth the truth. Let's begin.

I crossed to the battered pay-phone in the bar and looked up the phone book beside it.

'Hullo,' Frankie said.

'Hullo, Frankie. It's Jack Laidlaw.'

'Yes. You saw the lady in question?'

Frankie was sounding more like the old Frankie, the man I had grown to know and distrust.

'I did. I need to speak to you again.'

There was a pause during which I could imagine Frankie trying on different reactions.

'Ah. That could be tricky.'

'Why? You're still there, aren't you?'

'Well, yes. But.' His voice went down to the basement, where things are kept that not everybody knows are there. 'What it is. Ah've got a couple of cousins here. Tae see ma maw. Know what Ah mean?'

'Frankie. I don't intend to burst in with a warrant. We won't be surrounding the house or anything like that.'

'Still an' all. They might twig who ye are. Could be embarrassing. Ah'd rather they didn't meet ye. No offence.'

I was tempted to invite him to the Red Lion. But he had a point, I grudgingly admitted to myself.

'Tell you what I'll do, Frankie. I'm in the Red Lion. I'll

drive down to your place in ten minutes. I'll wait outside. You come out or I'll come in. Okay?'

He was in a one-way street. It wasn't where he wanted to be but it was where he was.

'Okay,' he said.

24

I didn't have long to wait at Frankie's house. He was out before I could turn off the engine. As he came down the path, I could see he was himself again for the moment. He was wearing slacks and an expensive-looking suede jacket. The cravat was colourful. As he climbed into the car, his after-shave almost nipped my eyes. At least it wasn't Aramis.

'Where to, man of discretion?' I said.

'Anywhere. As long as it's outa here. Ah don't think we should do the motorcade through the village. If they see me, it won't be ticker-tape they're throwin'. Turn left down here.'

The tension suited him. It was his natural habitat. Indoors, he had seemed drained, uncertain of himself. Now he was alive with energy, glancing round all the time, tapping his hand on the top of the dashboard as he leaned forward. It was because, I think, Frankie needed a role. This one was the big-time crook revisiting his small-town background, where he was misunderstood and unappreciated.

'Straight on,' he said. 'Jesus. I hate coming back here. Not just the thing about Dan. It was always a pain. Like standin' in front of one of those mirrors at the shows that makes ye look wee. Head for the hills.'

It didn't take long for us to come out into the countryside.

'Dan used to do his roadwork along here,' Frankie said. 'Him runnin', me on the bike.'

Training for a fight seemed a bad purpose to which to put such gentle country. It was soft farmland, greening richly towards summer. When I die, I thought quite cheerfully, this is where they bring me, back to Ayrshire. And don't cremate me. Let me fertilise a place I love.

'That's Farquhar's Farm,' Frankie said. 'See that wee hill there? We used tae sit on the top of it for a rest. Big Dan did it the first day we were out on the roads. An' it became a habit with us. Every day for a fortnight. We'd sit there an' talk.'

On instinct, I drew in at the gate to the field. As the engine died, I worked out where the instinct came from. I was going to try and get Frankie to tell me what he wouldn't want to tell me. The place might help. If he had any ghost of loyalty to Dan Scoular, this could be where it haunted.

'We'll get some air,' I said.

I climbed over the gate into the field and Frankie followed me, being careful about his slacks. I walked to the top of the hill and sat down. Frankie sat beside me after spreading a handkerchief on the grass. Thornbank was visible from here.

'Dan Scoular's view,' I said.

Frankie followed the direction of my look.

'Aye. Big Dan loved that place. Looks nice from here, right enough. Not so good up close.'

'How do you mean?'

'Like the pictures ye used to look at in the children's books. Remember? Say, a farmyard scene. It always looked that nice. They never showed ye the henshit on the tail-feathers. Or the sow eatin' anythin' that would stay still long enough. Yerself included.'

'You just don't like the place, Frankie.'

'Does the place like me?'

'Maybe it has its reasons.'

Frankie selected a stalk of grass for chewing.

'You mean what happened to Dan? That wasn't me. It was more likely that place that killed him. The values it gave him. They don't work in the real world. No heroes there. Maybe that's yer murderer there.' He nodded at Thornbank. 'Maybe that's what killed him.'

'We both know what killed him,' I said. 'It's called Matt Mason.'

'I don't know that,' Frankie said quickly.

'Frankie!'

'I don't *know* it.'

'All right. That's even better.'

'Better?' Frankie took his piece of grass out of his mouth, as if it tasted strange. 'What do you mean?'

'It means you can talk freely. You're not shopping anybody. You don't know enough to do that.'

'Ah don't know enough to do anything. Ah've told you what Ah know.'

'Just tell me about the fight, the people involved.'

'Come on, Jack. Ah can't do that. It's not what Ah do. It's like you said in ma maw's. Ah've got ma sense of maself.'

'Your sense of yourself? A good man died partly because of your sense of yourself. Bury it. An' don't invite me to the funeral.'

Frankie shivered. There was a slight wind combing the grass

gently. It wasn't enough to make it cold. The draught had to be internal. Frankie was looking at Thornbank.

'You ever get that feeling?' he said. 'That something's happened before. Ah've just had it. That first day. We sat here. An' Dan was tryin' to find out what was really goin' on. He wanted to know who the people involved were, too. Ah could've told him more.'

'So tell more now.'

'What's the point? He's dead.'

'You're not. Are you, Frankie? Your obligation to him doesn't end with *his* death. It ends with yours. We gave your mother a goin'-away prezzie there, didn't we? Something to make her feel better. But it was just fancy wrapping-paper, Frankie. There was nothing inside. Why not put something real in it? Like respect for Dan Scoular.'

'Ah wouldn't know where to begin.'

'Anywhere.'

'What are ye hopin' to do with it, like?'

'I'm going to try and get Matt Mason.'

'Jesus, you better be early up.'

'Frankie. All o' that's my problem. All I'm asking. You tell me what a lotta people know already. That's all. You're not informin'. Christ, there musta been hundreds at the fight. Just give me a back-dated ticket, that's all. You won't be involved in anything that happens. In fact, the way Matt Mason feels about you, you might be taking out insurance.'

I think perhaps that thought swung it, like a quote from the book of self-preservation, which had for a long time been Frankie's bible. Staring at Thornbank, he started to talk. Maybe the town, seen as he must often have seen it in childhood from places like this, was like a photograph from his past, reminding him of who he used to be.

He told me Eddie Foley had been involved in things in the capacity of fixer, as he usually was. Tommy Brogan had been Dan Scoular's trainer in Glasgow. Dan and Frankie had lived in Glasgow for a week before the fight, in the Burleigh Hotel, which was where Jan had worked.

'Ah saw you there,' Frankie said. 'Wi' a good-lookin' big wumman.'

'When?'

'While we were stayin' there. It was late at night. You came in wi' her and went up in the lift. You were well on.'

'Well on? You must've mistaken me for somebody else, Frankie.'

'Aye. Anyway, Ah would've said hullo, of course. But Ah didn't want to disturb ye.'

'That was nice.'

My glibness belied my feelings. The thought of Dan Scoular and me sharing the same building that night was an eerie one. I had been within yards of a man whose death would affect my life, without ever meeting him.

As Frankie talked on, I didn't know what I could possibly do with the information. He described a disco afterwards and some kind of party at Matt Mason's house. All of these events were part of the most dramatic experience he had had, something that had cleft his life in two, and so, once started, he spoke of them in that compulsive, fragmentary way we speak of things when we know they have defined us but we're still not sure what the definition is. I had become an eavesdropper. Frankie's pain was Frankie's pain. I sympathised but there wasn't much I could do about it. In any case, in the scale of things any price he was paying hardly compared with the price Dan Scoular had paid.

All I was trying to do was find pieces of the happening I could weld into a purpose of my own. It wasn't easy. The one thing that interested me so far was Eddie Foley. Eddie had always interested me. He was one of Mason's men unlike any of the others. He was a genteel criminal. In his gentility might be his vulnerability. While I was wondering about that, Frankie said something that interrupted my thoughts. He was talking about a woman in Mason's entourage who had apparently fallen very heavily for Dan Scoular.

'What did you say her name was?' I said.

'Melanie.'

'What's her second name?'

'McHarg,' he said. 'Melanie McHarg. She went loopy for big Dan. Ah think she thought he was the answer to all her prayers. She used to speak to me on the quiet about him. Ah think she imagined he was her ticket to a normal life. See, Melanie's a funny one. Ye'd think the kinna life she's led, she'd know the story. But a wee bit of her still believes in Santa Claus. She's a romantic, Ah suppose is whit she is. Buys a Mills an' Boon book wi' every packet of heroin.'

'She does drugs?'

'Do weans like sweeties?'

'Would she know Meece Rooney?'

'Meece supplied her. Certainly at one time.'

'You know her, Frankie. If she was in trouble, who would she go to?'

'Take yer pick,' Frankie said. 'Ah mean, don't get me wrong.

Ah like Melanie. Always did. But let's face it. She's not a house, she's a hotel. A lotta men've stayed there.'

'But there must be somebody she would turn to.'

'Might be Meece.'

'Anybody else?'

'Could even be Matt, Ah suppose.'

'What if it couldn't be either of them?'

Frankie's very mobile head became still and, in its slow turning towards me, the instinct of chatter became the wisdom of silence. His wide eyes stared at me. A parrot had just turned into an owl.

'What's goin' on here?' he said.

'Meece Rooney's dead,' I said. 'Melanie won't be turning to him. Matt Mason's the man that arranged the retirement. Melanie won't be turning to him. She was living with Meece. Meece seems to have been fiddling the accounts. They killed him and left him beside the river. Maybe for easy disposal. So who would she turn to now, Frankie? Who's left?'

Frankie seemed to be trying to see beyond the horizon. Maybe what he was looking at was the prospect of his own death.

'Ah don't touch this,' he said. 'That's it. Ah don't touch it.'

'Frankie.'

'You're not on. Ah don't touch it.'

'Just give me a name.'

'Ah'll give ye a name. Frankie White. Ah'd like to keep it off a headstone for a while yet. Come on. You know this man. You can go for him if you like. Maybe you'll get a medal for it. Me, Ah'll just get dead. Maybe Ah'm next already.'

'Maybe you are. And if you are, I'm your best bet.'

'Some bet. A three-legged horse in the Derby. Ah don't fancy your chances, Jack.'

'You don't have to. I do. You silly bugger. What's to lose? You tell me, nobody else knows. It just gives me a better chance of stopping him. If I can't, you're where you are already. You're getting to bet with my money. Take the chance.'

He did.

'You know Marty Bleasdale?'

He was a man from Newcastle who had been a social worker in Glasgow until dealing with the endless mayhem of other people's exploding lives had made him shell-shocked. He went rogue. I liked him. He seemed to have decided that he was a revolutionary caucus of one. He was half-crazy and wholly sincere. He lived on the edges of criminality because, as he had once told me, 'villains are less dishonest than the rest of us.' He played in a jazz-band and sometimes worked at the Barras but where the eating-money came from wasn't entirely clear.

'I know Marty Bleasdale.'

'He's your possibility. Marty's a kind of one-man Samaritan Centre for a lot of people. He's helped Melanie before. She sees him as some kinda patron saint. Ah think because he never tried to screw her. She might go there.'

Frankie wasn't talking any more. Our heads had parted company, mine trying to work out how to get closer to Matt Mason, Frankie's presumably how to get further away.

'Thanks, Frankie,' I said.

'Oh, don't say that,' Frankie said. 'Ah hate to hear a polisman sayin' thanks. It usually means ye've said somethin' that ye're gonny regret. Any chance of a lift?'

Outside his house, we sat a moment in the car.

'Well,' Frankie said. 'Ah can't wish ye luck. It's against ma religion.'

'That's good,' I said. 'With the kind of luck you would wish me, Frankie, I could be in terrible trouble.'

He smiled.

'I hope your mother feels no pain,' I said.

'Aye.'

He looked quietly terrified of many things. He had his reasons.

'Honourable,' he said.

'Sorry?'

'Honourable. That was Melanie's word for big Dan. Honourable. The most honourable man she'd ever met, she said. Ah wonder what it means.'

'I don't know, Frankie. I suppose it's one of those things it's up to other people to see in you. From where I'm sitting, maybe there's a bit of it in you at that.'

'You couldn't point it out to me?'

We both laughed. I watched him walking up his mother's path, wearing his jauntiness like someone else's clothes.

25

In Graithnock I had to find a Clydesdale Bank with a hole in the wall. The introduction of the Autobank has allowed my life to inhabit an intermittent fantasy of solvency. I have always looked on money as if it were a species of bird unhappy in captivity. It never sings there. Before autobanks, my only technique for getting access to more money than I had involved mournful conversations with an understanding bank manager in Byres Road. Now, after each heartbreaking performance in which the applause took the form of an extended overdraft, I could forget the seedy realities of finance and for a time draw money when I chose. The notes that slid towards me assumed a proper meaninglessness. They might as well have been Monopoly money, part of a game in which I had marked the cards and drew only the ones I wanted. Collect £200. Do not go to jail.

My vulnerability being covered with money, modern society's figleaf, I went to a florist's. I bought a large bouquet of flowers of indeterminate genus. All I knew was they looked good to me. I went to a newsagent's and bought cigarettes, a newspaper and a box of chocolates. I found an off-licence and managed to get a bottle of Talisker. I put the flowers, the chocolates and the whisky in the boot of the car. I drove to the Bushfield.

Katie was in the kitchen. When I went in, Buster and I exchanged our usual greetings. He growled at me and I told him that I hoped his third brain-cell arrived soon.

'You two,' Katie said. 'Ah think ye secretly love each other. Scartin' an' nippin' is Scots folk's wooin'.'

'Aye. Don't call the banns yet anyway, Katie.'

'Ye're early the day.'

'I've got bad news for you,' I said. 'Maybe ye should sit down. I go back to Glasgow tonight.'

'Ah wish ye'd told me earlier,' Katie said. 'We coulda put the bunting an' the streamers out. It's no' often we get something to celebrate in the Bushfield.'

'It's all right, Katie. Ah know ye're just puttin' on a brave face.'

'That's right,' Katie said. 'The laughter's just hysterical. Actually, Ah *will* miss ye. At least, you're no' boring. A different mood for every minute. Ye're like that thing they used to say in "Monty Python". "And now for something completely different".'

'We better square up here, Katie.'

'How d'ye mean?'

'That's Monday, Tuesday, Wednesday night. And meals and everything.'

Katie turned another page of her magazine.

'Jack, it's the first break I've had the day. It's the only break I'll get the day. Don't bother me wi' business. I'll see ye before ye leave. Also, I've got something special for ye to eat the night. Ah haven't worked out what it'll cost yet. Probably more than the rest of what ye owe us put together. Ah'll see ye before ye leave.'

'Okay,' I said. I turned at the door. 'It wouldn't be Buster a l'orange, would it? That would really make my night.'

She stared up at me from her magazine.

'More like char-broiled Laidlaw.'

I went up to my room and sat for a while. I looked again at my personal collection of Scott's paintings. 'Scotland' reminded me somehow of my father. I think it was because of the suggestion in the picture that the public reality of Scottish experience was denied in private lives. For my father, the method he hated had been to translate the demotic of Scottish traditions into a bland standard English, losing most of the meaning in the translation. For Scott, the method had been what? To simplify the darker realities of our lives into bogus tourist images? To deny the truth of what we were in order to live more comfortably with lies? But wasn't that what we all did, what society taught us to do? Wasn't that perhaps what Scott and his student friends had done when faced with what-ever truth was represented by the man in the green coat?

I looked at the faceless one again. The sense of Scott's guilt had occurred to me forcefully in the Red Lion earlier today. Now, staring at the painting afresh, the element of guilt seemed to me so obvious. I remembered what John Strachan had said the first time I saw the five at supper and was wondering what their strange conclave meant. 'Maybe the four are feeding off the man in the middle.' Also if, as I had decided, it was a pastiche of 'The Last Supper', what else could it mean but guilt? It was an echo of the primal treachery, betrayal of God. Scott had been an atheist. But that Christian symbol could have a humanist reading. In his terms, it could mean treachery against people, the denial of kinship with others. Was it belief in the necessary shared humanity of all of us that had been sold for thirty pieces of silver? Who then was Judas? Or, given the same face on each plate, were they all Judas?

I was looking at a public confession of private conspiracy. Scott had wanted that there should hang, in the house of friends he believed in, an admission of guilt. Anyone could see the painting, though not anyone could understand it. What he couldn't find the means to declare directly in his life, whether through fear or coercion from others or the addiction of habit, he had acknowledged here in code.

I could read some of the code now. The bearded men were no longer so well disguised. The stem of the flower that bloomed to the head of a serpent was held in Scott's hands. His was the creativity that gave not sustenance but poison. The man with the ring was Sandy Blake, the healer who could dispense sickness as well as health. Did the double masks of tragedy and comedy belong to the unknown man? Had he become an actor? They had been watching television at Dave Lyons' party. Had he been what they were watching? Had the apple of knowledge been bitten by Dave Lyons? If so, maybe I could get him to share some of that knowledge with me.

I rose from the bed where I had been lying and straightened out the coverlet. I gathered the dirty clothes I had worn since Monday and put them in one of the plastic bags I always keep in my travelling-bag. I put what was for washing at the bottom of the travelling-bag. I emptied the pockets of my leather jacket and put it in next. I would be wearing the blazer. Maybe it would help Dave Lyons to believe that I wasn't fresh off the farm. I put the rest of my things on top and zipped the bag half-way along. Why do clothes always expand between unpacking and repacking?

I lifted the paintings and carried them carefully down to where the car was parked in the forecourt of the Bushfield. I slid the paintings in beside the flowers and the whisky and the chocolates. I retrieved David Ewart's ashtray from the back seat and put it in the boot as well. I closed and locked the boot.

I collected my travelling-bag from upstairs and put it in the back seat of the car. I made sure the car was locked. When I went up to my room for the third time, I noticed the bottle of the Antiquary beside the bed. It was over half-way gone. But then so was the week it was designed to see me through. It had kept faith with me. Had the beautiful, dark woman?

I took the glass from the circular metal holder above the washhand-basin. I poured out a modest measure of whisky — purely for ceremonial purposes, you understand. I ran the water till the feeling on the back of my hand matched the word on the tap. I topped up the whisky with water almost to the brim. I set the glass on the bedside table, wiping its base first with a towel. I took the bottle down to the car and put it in the glove compartment.

Sitting on the bed for the last time, I lifted the glass and toasted the distance gone, the distance to go. While I did that, I resolved that I wouldn't go back to my flat tonight. Firstly, I couldn't face it. That place was a cottage-industry that manufactured loneliness. I wanted the sense of people around me, even if I didn't know who they were. Secondly, I knew there were people I needed to talk to in a neutral environment.

The flat wasn't it. I might have to aggress on their lives. When you do that, you don't let them know where you live. The fox doesn't advertise its earth. I would book into a hotel. It wouldn't be the Burleigh, because for me it was ghosted with Jan's presence, not to mention Dan Scoular's. I didn't need that. I would book in somewhere else. I rose and rinsed the glass and put it back in its holder.

I went downstairs to get change from the bar. Two men who, I suspected, had been introduced by the emptiness of the place were talking football. Mike was on duty. We exchanged a few words. He was a man more pleasant than he knew how to show. I went to the pay-phone in the foyer.

I remembered the number of the Grosvenor Hotel. Some of the staff there knew me. Since splitting with Ena, I had been a few times, just to be not in the flat.

'Oh, Mr Laidlaw,' the woman said when I stated my case. 'Hold on.' Then, 'Listen. We've got a nice corner room. It's like a small suite. How about that?'

That was fine. I tried to put a face to the voice and I thought I succeeded. Her kindness made me feel welcome. I phoned the restaurant. It was Jan who answered.

'Hullo, busy woman,' I said.

'Jack? How are you?'

'The better for hearing yourself.'

'Where are you?'

'I'm in Graithnock. But I'm coming to Glasgow tonight. I wondered if I could see you. Later on.'

'Not tonight, Jack. It's impossible.'

'Tomorrow? Dinner?'

When you love somebody, even their silence talks. Her

pause was telling me I was no longer a personal necessity, just a social possibility.

'Yes. All right. Let's do that. Listen. Will you phone me at the flat tomorrow? I've got to rush now. We're just getting organised here.'

'I'll do that.'

'Great. Take care.'

'You too.'

When love begins to leave, one of its exits is through the mouth. Words that were endlessly prolix with the need to try and share everything become as cryptic as an exchange between sentries guarding closed borders. The omens were bad. One week, Jan had said. It sounded as if the jury was in early. Maybe Betsy, counsel for the prosecution, had done a good job. Maybe, to be fair, I was simply indefensible.

I phoned Brian Harkness's number. It was Morag who answered. While she kidded me, I put my banter on remote control. Talking to Morag, what I was really doing was that thing we do when our own relationship is foundering. I was envying Morag and Brian their ideal partnership. You know your sense of them is false but you can't help it. You keep wondering: what the hell's wrong with me? How can all those sleek cats be in there in the warmth, purring at each other, and I'm still out here in the cold, freezing my arse off on this wall and mewing at nothing? I recovered sufficiently from my self-pity to become briefly practical. I gave Morag the names of Melanie McHarg and Marty Bleasdale. I told her what I knew about them. I asked her to tell Brian I would be at the Grosvenor tonight and maybe he could call me there.

I phoned Ena but there was nobody at home. Putting down

the receiver, I had a vision of a dread future, with myself as the phantom phoner, haunting other people's lives for news of the real world.

Katie's special meal helped. It was coq au vin. Seemingly, that first night in the Bushfield, one of my unremembered confessional moments had related to coq au vin as one of my favourite dishes. It was good, except that she had overplayed the onions a bit. If there's a heaven, there will be no onions there.

With good eating done and dishes washed and an awareness of something ending, I tried to pay Katie for my keep. She wouldn't consider it. I think it was a kind of present from her to Scott. I had suspected it might be this way. I resorted to Plan B. I collected the day's purchases from the car and gave her the flowers and the chocolates. As I carried them in to her, I was embarrassed by my lack of originality. But I think the very corniness of it perhaps touched her. She was pleased and we embraced in the kitchen. It wasn't a long embrace. Buster, with undiminished acumen, assumed I was attacking her and barked like a pack of fox-hounds. I left her putting the flowers in water. I took the Talisker through to Mike. He thanked me.

On the way out, I stopped at the pay-phone. I rang Troon. Dave Lyons' voice answered. I put the phone down. He was in.

26

It was a fortress, wasn't it? There were no electronically controlled gates or invisible seeing-eyes, at least as far as I could make out. You turned through the gate off Marrenden Drive and there it was among its trees, very large in weathered sandstone. It was, on the face of it, more accessible than my small flat with its double doors guarding nothing but the debris of a dishevelled life.

But the sense of openness was illusory, I felt. It wasn't just that I could detect the signs of an elaborate security system. It wasn't just the leaded windows that seemed more a way of looking out than seeing in. It was the awareness of strange proliferation in the building. There were outcrops and oddnesses around its edges. I wondered what shapes the rooms were and what might be in them. Two dozen paces through my flat would have told you all. Here, I suspected you might still not know where you were once you were in. It would have unexpected shadows and secret places. I thought of ghosts, not supernatural beings, just those self-projected creatures of the mind, old deeds that can haunt us more the more we deny them. No wonder ghosts traditionally frequent big houses, it occurred to me. There's more room for guilt there.

I pulled the bell. It was a woman who answered. She was wearing a skirt and blouse. Her deferential air suggested I might have more rights here than she had. This was where she worked. I had started to explain what I was doing here when Dave Lyons appeared behind her.

'That's all right, Janice,' he said. 'I'll get this.'

I nodded to him and he stared at me. He waited, looking over his shoulder to make sure that Janice had gone. He looked even more authoritative than he had looked in Cranston Castle House. He would. This was his territory.

'What are you doing here?' he said.

'I just want to speak to you.'

'But I don't want to speak to you. Where did you get this address?'

'The same place I got the phone-number.'

Something occurred to him.

'Did you just phone there? Not long ago.'

'That's right.'

'And hung up.'

'Well, I didn't think you would invite me down if you knew it was me.'

'Oh, you're right. You're very careless for a policeman. That was a nuisance phone-call. Risky thing to be doing.'

'I'll deny everything. Come and get me, copper.'

'What an arsehole,' he said. 'Move your car. If that's what you call it. It's blocking my driveway.'

I tugged my forelock.

'Aye, zur,' I said. 'Right away, zur. After we've talked.'

'We've talked all we're going to,' he said. 'You've spoiled a lunch for me already. You're not going to waste my evening.

I've had more meaningful conversations with the talking clock.'

The door was open but it wasn't open. The doorway might as well have been filled with reinforced glass. I wasn't getting in.

'It won't take long,' I said.

'Get lost,' he said and was closing the door.

'Does your wife know about you and Anna?' I said.

Now the door was really open. He looked as if he couldn't believe the garbage someone had dumped on his doorstep. I think I shared his feeling to a degree, but to a very precise degree. What I had said was a malignant thing to say. But in handling such potentially toxic material in my own nature, I had a couple of protective thoughts, like rubber gloves. First, I would never have used such knowledge beyond this conversation with him, though he wasn't to know that. (And the expression on his face told me this was knowledge, it was no longer guesswork.) Second, I wasn't yet convinced of his right to moral outrage at my remark. But I still felt like averting my head from the smell of my own behaviour.

'Come in,' he said. 'I'd ask you to wipe your feet but how do you wipe the rest of you?'

Maybe that was fair enough. We crossed a wide hall with a wooden staircase leading up from it. The windows at the bend on the stairs were filled with stained glass. He took me through a large, open, wooden door, which he then closed. I assumed this was where he had come from when Janice answered my ring.

We were in a kind of personal trophy-room. There were a couple of small silver cups, maybe for golf. There was a piece of Caithness glass and three sombre certificates that were awards of some sort for industry. A careful arrangement of photographs on the wall showed groups of confident-looking men enjoying the importance of their own company. A leather-topped desk dominated the room. I had met its brother in Edinburgh. The desk-lamp was lit, its narrow beam focused on sheets of paper. I felt the intrusiveness of my presence in this man's preoccupations.

'I suppose you'd better sit down,' he said.

I sat in a leather swivel-chair near the outer edge of the desk. He crossed to the small window and put his hands in his pockets, looking out. I noticed an antique-looking vase resting on top of a bookcase. I thought its pattern was as complicated as the interweaving lives I had stumbled among. Now that I had breached his sanctum, I experienced a reluctant awe at having invaded the private recesses of another person's life. He was still looking out of the window. There wasn't much to see out there except the obstructing branches of a tree. But he seemed to be able to see far, for he began to describe the view.

'I'm going to marry Anna,' he said. 'I tell you that so that you'll understand what the information means. That your seedy investigations have found out. This isn't some hole-in-the-corner affair we're talking about. You're playing around with people's lives here. Linda. My wife. She can't have any children. Anna and I are hoping to have a family. But I care about Linda. She's not too strong emotionally. Anna has agreed to give me time to prepare her for all this. It'll help Linda if I leave her on my own terms. If Anna's not involved. We can do it amicably. I need a little time to do that. To arrange things. I'm asking you not to interfere with that. For my wife's sake. That's all. I can understand how you feel. Anna being Scott's widow. But Scott wasn't exactly a saint himself, you know.'

'Not even approximately,' I said.

'He was having an affair with a woman called Ellie Mabon. Why don't you check that out?'

'I did.'

'Jesus Christ. You really are a seedy one.'

'Mr Lyons,' I said. 'I want you to stop saying that. All I've been trying to do is find out some truths about my brother's life at the end. If the truths turn out to be seedy, you included, don't blame me. You don't accuse the X-ray of the cancer. And don't parade your moral rectitude in front of me. As far as I can see, it's just a long view of nothing. Like a flea on stilts. And this sudden confidential talk is crap. Open day at a nuclear plant. All that means is you're only going to see what doesn't matter. That's not what I'm here for. Keep the moving details of your private life. I'm not sure I could believe them anyway. Maybe you *are* concerned about your wife. Or maybe it's financially healthier for you to arrange the break-up this way. How would I know?'

I had swung the chair towards the window and was watching him. He turned towards me.

'What is it you want from me?' he said.

'Just information. A modicum of honesty.'

'About what?'

'The man in the green coat.'

'Not that again. Who the hell is the man in the green coat?'

'You don't know?'

'Not a clue.'

'You do remember as a student sharing a flat with Scott?'

'Briefly, yes. It wasn't exactly one of the highlights of my life.'

'Do you remember someone called David Ewart?'

'No.'

'You're sure?'

'I'm sure.'

'He came to see about renting the flat. When you and your friends were moving out. He was a first-year student.'

He was starting to laugh.

'Is this supposed to be a serious question? I'm supposed to remember some student coming to look at a flat? What do you think I did? Made a note of it? "Dear Diary, a wonderful thing happened today."'

'But it seems to have been a memorable day. Or at least the evening was. Something happened that night.'

'That would make it novel, right enough.'

'You don't remember all going out together that night?'

'We went out together quite a few nights. I don't remember any one night in particular. I shouldn't imagine any of us did. The idea was usually to get pissed.'

'That night Scott destroyed his paintings.'

'Did he? I don't know about that.'

I realised there was no way I could prove that he knew about that night. My only hope was to concentrate on small, specific details.

'Who's Sandy Blake?'

He thought about it carefully.

'He shared with us as well.'

'What happened to him?'

'He became a doctor.'

'Where is he now?'

'He's in South Africa.' He was smiling. 'I don't think I have his address.'

'What about the fourth one?'

'The fourth what?'

'The fourth student. There were four of you sharing the flat.'

'No. There were only three.'

'David Ewart says there were four.'

'Who the hell's David Ewart? I lived there.'

'I think I'm wasting my time,' I said.

'I think you're wasting everybody's time,' he said. 'Especially mine.'

'Well,' I said.

I stood up and wandered vaguely about the room.

'The door's that way,' he said, nodding.

I paused beside the bookcase. I touched the vase gently.

'Leave that alone,' he said. 'It's very, very valuable.'

I lifted it in one hand.

'Put it down,' he said.

'You're a liar, Mr Lyons,' I said. 'I assume your wife's in?'

'What if she is? That's worth a lot of money. Put it down.'

I started slowly to throw the vase from hand to hand.

'I don't care about that stuff, Mr Lyons. Just about the real things.'

'You would know what these are, I suppose.'

'I know what they're not. I'm still looking. Tell me, what's the secret of your success?'

'What I am I've made myself.'

'And used a few other lives as the material. There are no

self-made men. They all use other people as spare parts. Who was the fourth?'

'There was no fourth.'

'My palms are sweating,' I said. 'I can't keep this up. When it breaks, I'll break something else. Until Mrs Lyons comes. To see . . . what . . . the noise . . . is.'

He said nothing.

'Fuck it,' I said.

I threw the vase up until it almost touched the ceiling and made to put my hands in my pockets.

'Michael Preston,' he shouted.

I caught the vase about four inches from the floor. The surprise of the name almost made me miss, for it was familiar to me. In the hearing of that name, I realised the deviousness that had been Scott's life. That he had known Michael Preston and never mentioned the fact to me was amazing. Michael Preston was a very well known television presenter, his name the kind that was liable to crop up in a lot of conversations. I straightened up slowly.

'You're mad,' Dave Lyons said.

'Just angry,' I said. 'Mad's a lot worse than this.'

I replaced the vase where it had been.

'So that's who was on television that night,' I said.

'I wouldn't know.'

'No. Of course, you wouldn't.'

I looked at him. He had rediscovered his anger. This wasn't how people treated him. His mouth was sealed with rage.

'I'll unblock your driveway,' I said.

27

I was in the shower when Brian phoned me at the Grosvenor. I had intended it to be a luxurious experience. In the Bushfield I had only had access to a bath. Now I could have hydrotherapy as well as wash myself. But the pleasure was short-lived. I hadn't even finished singing 'The Other Side of Nowhere' by the time the phone rang.

I was still dripping as I took the call, trying to towel myself. It wasn't a long conversation. We talked a moment about Marty Bleasdale and Melanie McHarg. Brian and Bob would be looking for them tomorrow. They would phone me at the hotel and leave word if I wasn't there. Brian suggested I should get an early night so that I could be fit and fresh to carry on with my mania in the morning.

I finished drying myself. I pulled on a sweater and a clean pair of underpants. I combed my hair. I filled out an Antiquary and watered it. I stood at the window and looked down on to Byres Road. It felt good to be back in Glasgow. I thought of David Ewart's ambition for his retirement. It wasn't a bad one.

I watched the cars pass, the people walking in the street. I saw endlessly criss-crossing preoccupations, not noticing one another seriously, pursuing their own strange loyalties. Strange and questionable loyalties, I thought, including my own. We were moles that lived in the light, following painstakingly constructed tunnels of private purpose.

My week so far had been one of those tunnels. In its determined progress it had broken into other people's secret places, disturbing the still air, bringing an alien and upsetting presence. In the calmness of this moment, I could acknowledge how abrasive I had been. I regretted that, but not too much.

For although I admired loyalty, I reflected, it could have strange side-effects. Frankie White's loyalty to a malignant ethic had allowed his friend to be buried in a very deep silence. Anna's loyalty to Dave Lyons had amputated her husband from her life with clinical coldness. Dave Lyons' loyalty to himself made everything else irrelevant. In our haste to get to the places to which our personal and pragmatic loyalties lead us, we often trample to death the deeper loyalties that define us all – loyalty to the truth and loyalty to the ideals our nature professes.

I was faced with a labyrinth of commitments in which, it seemed to me, people kept to their exclusive space and pretended it did not connect with other corridors, where bad things happened in their name but not in their hearing. Given that, I could see only one way to proceed. Each of the people I was dealing with had presumably more than one loyalty. Let's strike one against the other and see if a spark of truth came out of that. Let's force them to a choice of loyalties.

Eddie Foley, for example, was a faithful minion of Matt Mason. It seemed there was no way he would betray him. But Eddie Foley was also a devoted family man. He lived two contradictory lives. Let's make them confront each other, the nice man and the criminal, and see who won the fight. I would start with him. It wouldn't be easy. From here on, I might have to be somewhat more abrasive. I drank reluctantly to that. When the world decides to take away from you, without explanation, a part of what matters to you most, you'd better challenge its indifference, some way or other.

And the meek shall inherit the earth, but not this week.

FIVE

28

K now thine enemy. I hoped I knew Eddie Foley. I had parked the car and was walking towards Rico's in Sauchiehall Street. One reason I hoped I knew him was that, if I did, he would be there at this time. There was another reason that was more complicated.

I needed him for what I was planning to try. I needed that my assessment of him should be accurate if the plan I had was to work. Like all of my plans, it wasn't too tightly constructed – more free verse than rhyme. A plan for me is impulse with, hopefully, intelligence on its back. The rider will work out what the destination is as they go.

There are as many variations of criminality as there are of social conformity. Just as the apparent openness of rectitude will have its hidden places where foul things may moulder in the dark so, in the shadowed lives of those outside the law, may sometimes be found concealed honesty and naive ideals. We may think of evil and good as separate states but they have no fixed borders. Any one of us may pass between them without declaring anything. We are all born to parents with passports entitling us to travel freely in both.

Eddie Foley was an interesting example of dual citizenship.

He was a criminal whose wife was a woman of seemingly unimpeachable decency. Married to Eddie, she may have been naive but she was honest. He had a daughter who was a teacher, a son who was studying agriculture. His love of family was no pretence. There had never been a whiff of womanising to his reputation. Word was he watched television a lot. He was not without cultural interests. I knew that he and his wife had membership of the Glasgow Film Theatre, where they seemed to go quite often. He had told me once that he was looking forward to having grandchildren.

In his private life he was a model citizen. At work, it was different. His job was enabling evil. He didn't fire any guns. He just kept the chambers oiled. He had worked with Matt Mason for a long time. Mason knew his own people. He knew what Eddie would do and what he wouldn't, the delicate nature of his functions. Eddie would never be present when the sore things happened. He saw no serious crimes. Extreme violence and death were noises off in his life. But he understood people and he was a skilful administrator. He was a fixer who fixed what he was asked and took his wages.

The endless adaptability of our compromises fascinates me. Bring a child up in a locked safe with an eye-slit at the bottom and I imagine it would learn to spend much of its life standing on its head, because that's the way it sees the world. The compromise that was Eddie Foley's life was a prize specimen of the species. He was a caring husband and father and a gentle citizen, who helped to arrange anonymous mayhem. He had a civic conscience that was housebound, a violence that was abstract.

I had often wondered how he did it, how he kept walking

the tightrope back and forth across the chasm of contradiction that divided the two halves of his life. Approaching Rico's, I thought maybe his case wasn't so strange – extreme but not strange. Perhaps the cost of guaranteeing the safety of his own had been the blunting of his conscience towards others. That wouldn't make him strange. That would make him one of many – not some incomprehensibly alien expression of our lives, just demotic in italics. Big-scale or small-scale, comfort costs. Winners feed off losers. It was the system. Eddie was just playing the system.

His security was the insecurity of others. Like a lot of us, his security might be his weakness. He was a careful man. He had his family safely to one side. He helped Matt Mason but not so that you would notice him doing it. He opened doors. Others went through them to do whatever was to be done. You wouldn't catch Eddie out on small things. But if Mason fell, you could maybe bury Eddie in the debris. I wondered if I could frighten him with that.

For perhaps Eddie had been too careful. He had never been in prison. He had never even stood trial. Elaborate security can be a trap. You can spend so much time making sure that others can't get in, you may not realise that you can't get out either. I didn't think Eddie could survive outside the life he'd made for himself. He was habituated to its forms. Prison would destroy him. Conviction would destroy his family. I wondered how the very contemplation of such things might affect him. We would see.

He was there. I saw him through the window, seated at a table at the back, facing towards me. I paused beside the menu-card and watched. He was framed in the O of Rico's, like a photograph of father in the family album. He had his glasses on. He was reading the newspaper. I went in.

Rico's is a café bar that opens early in the morning for breakfasts. It lets in a lot of light and it's spacious. With the unpretentious metal-topped tables and the mosaic paintings on the wall and the bottles behind the bar, it imparts that civilising sense of being in a bistro. The rack of newspapers suggests you needn't hurry. The place can give you the feeling that mornings are not a bad idea. It evidently gave Eddie Foley that feeling. This was where he regularly came for a late and leisurely breakfast.

He didn't look up as I reached his table. He was halfway through a croissant and his coffee-cup was almost empty. The paper was the *Daily Mail*.

'What's the news, Eddie?' I said.

He looked up over his glasses. Something that was perhaps caution came into his eyes and went. He smiled. He had a nice smile. He looked as if children would like him.

'Jack,' he said. 'You going to join me?'

'Oh, yes.'

'Ah haven't seen you for a while.'

'Ah'm livin' quiet.'

I had sat down opposite him and a dark-haired waitress came up to ask me if I wanted anything. She had such an attractive, unforced pleasantness, you felt your day had earned a bonus just by meeting her. I ordered coffee.

'Yourself, Mr Foley?' she said. 'How are ye doin'?'

'Ah could use a refill, Jennifer. Add this to mine.' She took his bill-tab as she went. Eddie folded his paper with one hand and pushed it to the end of the table. He took off his glasses and stowed them carefully in a soft red leather case and put it in an inside pocket. He looked slightly less avuncular that way.

'Here,' he said. 'Ah heard about yer brother. Ah'm sorry. That was bad.'

'Aye.'

It struck me suddenly that I had been thinking of Scott in a different way in the past few days. The obsession had subsumed the grief. That was one way to staunch your tears.

'That was a waste.'

'It was,' I said. 'But he hit the car more than the car hit him. Laidlaws can be careless people, Eddie.'

'Not all of them.'

'Listen. I don't think *I'm* going to win any medals as an insurance-risk.'

Jennifer came with the coffees. I milked and sugared. Eddie took his as it was. He broke off a piece of croissant, began to chew.

'You don't want something to eat?' he said.

'I've eaten, thanks. So what's the word of yourself, Eddie?'

'Same as ever, Jack. Same as ever. But you know that, don't you?'

'Hm?'

'Jack. When did Ah get on to your social calendar?'

'This is true.'

'So what's this about?'

Jennifer was back with the amended slip. She laid it beside Eddie and went away. I reached across and lifted it to look. It was printed in that faint blue type that looks as if it's dissolving. I could just about make it out. It said £5.50.

'Ah'm gettin' that, Jack,' Eddie said.

'Okay.'

He was watching me. I continued to hold the slip of paper in my hand, studying it.

'This bill's wrong, Eddie,' I said.

He took it from me and looked at it. He had to get out his glasses. He counted his way through the small column of figures.

'No, it's right,' he said.

'The bill's wrong.'

He looked at me over his glasses.

'You owe a fuckin' sight more than that, Eddie Foley,' I said. 'An' ye're gonny pay.'

His right hand took off his glasses in slow motion. He looked round Rico's. He looked back at me. I nodded.

'Time to divvy up,' I said.

His hand slowly abandoned his glasses on the table.

'What's this about?' he said.

'It's about the firm you work for is going to go out of business in the next few days. I'm the liquidator.'

He turned his head slightly sideways to look at me. He seemed to be trying to see past my words to the joke that must lie behind them.

'Could I see your credentials, please?' he said, smiling.

'You're seeing them. Me. Believe them or don't. And don't smile, Eddie. Don't smile. Or I'll arrange for you to lose your teeth.'

It was the strangeness of the threat that convinced him. We had never spoken to each other before except either in a friendly way or through an agreed ritual of jocular enmity.

He knew that I had changed the terms on which we were meeting. I watched his eyes try to work out where he now was.

'What's happened?' he said.

'You know what's happened. You always did. The difference is that now I know as well.'

His breathing wasn't relaxed.

'Like what?' he said.

'Your boss has lost it, Eddie. Talk about misjudging the market? He's killed two people in the last three months. I think it's called over-extending yourself. Who the hell does he think he is? Attila the Hun?'

'Ah don't know what ye're talkin' about.'

'That's fine. Just as long as I do.'

'Ah don't. Ah really don't.'

'Dan Scoular. Meece Rooney.'

'Ah don't know what ye're talkin' about.'

'Hey! What d'ye think this is? A lavatory pan? Talk shite somewhere else.'

'But Ah——'

'Eddie!'

He froze. His eyes were nervous as a mouse along the wainscot where there is no exit.

'Don't do that. This is away past telling wee fibs to the polis. Stay quiet if ye want. But let's not sit here saying what we both know is crap.'

He subsided gently, staring at the table.

'Listen. I'm making an assumption about you. That you didn't actually do the things. That you weren't directly involved. That's not what you do. If I'm wrong, then you'll know I'm wrong. And when I go out this door, you better move fast and far. Because it'll be you I'm looking for. But I don't think you did.'

He had no impulse to talk now. He looked as if he was seeing his lawyer in his head.

'Because I think I know what you're like. Know what I think you're like, Eddie? You're like a maintenance worker at Dachau or somewhere. You might convert the showers to gas. You might make sure the doors lock properly. But you wouldn't actually kill anybody. You're nice that way. You do a practical job and go home and forget about it. Seems a few of them did that there. In those places. Go home and play with the kids. Forget about it.'

He was fingering his glasses.

'Well, I'm here to remind you, Eddie. Time to stop playing at wee houses. You owe. Now there are two ways you can pay. Reluctantly or of your own free will. The first way will come dear. I'm going to get Matt Mason. I know he's the head of what happened. Who the obedient bodies were, I don't know. But I will. You stand in my way, you're going, too. Everything goes. Your lifestyle. The way your family think of you. The lot. If you help, you get to keep your family's sense of you. You stay out of jail. That's it.'

His hand was gripping his glasses, clouding them.

'You're right, Eddie. You're not on my social calendar. I don't like you. You're like a permanent flu virus in everybody else's life. You leave them vulnerable. But Mason's cancer. I'm going to cut that bastard out. You can be part of the operation or part of the tumour. No other choice.'

I made to sip my coffee but it was getting cold. I took out

a cigarette and lit it. I knew Eddie didn't smoke these days. Maybe it was so that he would be there when his grandchildren came. I had said what I had to say. The way he took it was the way he took it. I would be going on from here, whatever. I smoked for a time.

'I'm not agreeing with anything,' Eddie said. 'But could you be more specific?'

'There's a way I can do this where you're not directly involved. Only you and me'll know. And maybe a colleague that I know I can trust.'

'What if *I* don't trust him?'

'Hey, Eddie. I'm making this contract. You sign it or don't. That's all. Who told you you had rights here? You gave them up when you took them off other people. You're with me or I'll fuck up your neat life permanently. The way you've helped to fuck up other people's. Like to the death.'

He looked at his coffee. He looked at his newspaper.

'So what would be involved?' he said.

'I don't know yet. For the next two or three days, we keep in touch. You give me your number. If David Ewart leaves a message, that'll be me. You don't get back on it soon, I'll know you've renegued. But when you get back, you phone me in my own name at the Grosvenor.'

'What kinda deal is that?'

'It's the only one I know how to make just now.'

'But Ah don't even know what ye're askin' me to do.'

'Neither do I. I just want you there in case I need you.'

'For what?'

'Whatever it is, it'll meet the terms I've stated. Nobody'll know that you're involved.'

'How can you say that if you don't know what ye're askin' me to do?'

'Because when I ask you, you can judge. You don't like it, you get out. I'll just have to waste your life. You're covered.'

'Oh, thanks. David Ewart?'

'David Ewart. It's a harmless name.'

He put his glasses in their case, put them in his pocket. He took the glasses back out and put them on. He reached for the newspaper at the end of the table. He tore off a piece of the margin. He wrote his telephone number on it and passed it to me. I checked it and folded the paper neatly and put it in the ticket pocket of my blazer. Eddie replaced his glasses in his pocket. We sat together, feeling apart.

I wasn't fooling myself about what had happened. So far, this meant nothing. All Eddie had done was play for time. All he had given me was a phone number. I could have found that in the book. He had made a gesture that was either a handshake or a wave but nobody knew which yet, not even him. But at least I'd caused a draught in his safe house. There was a broken window somewhere he hadn't known about. He would be wandering around his premises for a time, trying to work out where it was and if there was anything he could do about it.

'What about Matt Mason?' I said. 'What's happening just now?'

Eddie's look told me to back off. He wasn't working for me just yet.

'He's in Glasgow?'

'He's not in Thailand.'

'Nothing happening?'

'Oh, yes,' Eddie said. 'There's a big caper on tomorrow.'

'What's that?'

'A children's party.'

'A what?'

'A children's party. Matt's got twin nieces. They're eight tomorrow. He's very fond of them. So he's havin' a big party for them in the house. He's got more room than their parents. Millie's going.' Millie was Eddie's wife. 'It'll be her first time in the house.'

'You not going?'

'Ah'm supposed to go to the football. Ah haven't seen a game for a while.'

'A children's party? Nice.'

'It will be,' Eddie said. 'It'll be great fun for the kids. All the twins' friends. Some of their parents. It'll be quite a houseful. You're not plannin' to raid it, are ye?'

I put out my cigarette.

'Okay for you to get the bill, Eddie?'

'Ah thought that was the idea.'

We looked at each other.

'Eddie,' I said. 'I know what's happened here. Between us. You can go away from here and tell Matt Mason everything. Tell him to protect himself. It's your choice. But that would be a foolish one. You know why? Either I'm serious about this or I'm not. If I'm serious and you don't tell him, you can save your family's peace of mind. If I'm serious and you do tell him, your life's over as you know it. If I'm not serious, who needs to know about this anyway? This conversation might never have happened. One last tip. I'm serious, Eddie. I didn't know Dan Scoular. I wish I had. But I like people who liked him. That'll do me. I'll take their word for it. Dan Scoular's dead. I'm going to lay Matt Mason's future at his grave like a bunch of flowers. It's up to you to be part of the bouquet or not. Thanks for the coffee.'

As I came out, Jennifer called goodbye and waved. I was sure Eddie would give her a good tip. He was generous that way.

29

Hunting is largely waiting, I suppose, whether you're hunting animals or people or understanding. I remember Tom Docherty telling me how he went about writing. It was in a letter, the only one he ever wrote me. He suffers from what he jocularly calls epistolary paralysis. That time he was living in Paris and experiencing the moody glooms.

'Writing? Who needs it? When you write, here's what you do. You go alone. You build your hide round yourself from whatever is available – broken relationships, gathered hurts, remembered joys, wilful routine. You wait. You try many different baits. You let everything escape – no matter how good it looks or what praise the catching of it would bring you – but the one you're waiting for, the one you know you must get. You're prepared to lose yourself rather than it. Meantime, you feed on whatever scraps there are to hand, iron rations of the self.'

I was thinking of him as I came back to the hotel. One of the pleasures of his presence in my life has been that he is a great completer of half-thoughts. You offer him a vague perception and he takes it from you, cleans off the gunge and gives you it back, having shown you how it works. He clarifies you to yourself.

Here he was, doing it again, even if he didn't know it. For I saw in his description of where he had been a clarification of where I was. Eddie Foley was part of the bait. But what he was designed to catch wasn't really the quarry I was after. I wanted Matt Mason all right. But he was just a stop along the route, not the destination. If we caught him, he was for Brian and Bob. He was what they were hunting. Let them take the credit.

I was waiting for something bigger, at least bigger in my terms. I was looking not just to catch whoever had snuffed out two lives but whatever it was that had snuffed out a lot of lives, though it might have left them still moving around. I wanted to locate the source of the defeat in David Ewart's eyes, the remorseless hardness in Dave Lyons', the avid self-interest in Anna's. Had the death of Scott's idealism been suicide or murder?

As I ate my lunch in the downstairs restaurant of the hotel, I also experienced an echo of the loneliness Tom had been writing about. There had been a message left by Brian Harkness that they had some leads on Marty Bleasdale. Instead of making me feel part of a team, the communication had left me feeling more isolated. I thought of Bob and Brian doing what they do and knew that they were pursuing ends different from my own. False proximity becomes a measure of real distance.

That feeling had been intensified by my call to Jan before I sat down to eat. I had phoned her at the restaurant and she was there and able to talk, though not for long. We agreed that we would meet at the Bona Sospira tonight for dinner.

'How will I recognise you?' she said.

'It's only four days, Jan.'

'They've been long ones. Tell you what. Why don't you just come as yourself? I hope you've worked out who that is by now.'

Had I? Maybe, in Tom's sense, I had lost myself rather than lose the thing I was after — at least lost my comparatively familiar sense of myself. It wasn't just time I had put between Jan and me but emotional distance as well. She obviously felt it. And so did I. I wanted very much to meet her but I wasn't sure how fully we could meet. In examining the terms of Scott's life, I had been examining the terms of my own. The price you pay for arriving at a personal vision is the loneliness of having to live with it. I had a suspicion that my bill was on the way.

I looked round the restaurant. I saw an elderly couple eating with dignified slowness, a family whose children were just managing to impose public standards on what was normally a domestic experience, what I assumed were three business women, an American couple nearby whose clothes suggested they had confused Glasgow with Miami. The apparent completeness of their involvement in ordinary things made me feel even more isolated and alien.

My hotel room didn't help. I found myself opening drawers as if I might find there a clue to my identity, a personal equivalent of the Gideon bible. I found, appropriately enough, emptiness. I was reminded again of Tom Docherty. He has written a lot in hotel rooms. His theory is that they are such sterile and anonymous places that they make him write, if only to react against the void, to prove to himself that he exists. I looked at the hotel pen and the sheets of hotel paper. But I opted for the phone.

I phoned the BBC for the third time today. If Michael Preston were there, I was only a couple of hundred yards away. I could catch him before he escaped. But Mr Preston, it seemed, was still out on location somewhere in Glasgow. They couldn't tell me where.

I switched to my secondary obsession, like a driver transferring to his emergency fuel-tank. Something Eddie Foley had said interested me. It had started up in my head the process of refining my raw determination to catch Matt Mason into the vague possibility of a method.

I phoned Edek Bialecki. Edek was a sound-recordist and a sound man. He had worked with the BBC for years until a general disillusionment and a very specific straitening of finances had encouraged him to move out into freelance. He worked for independent companies and sometimes contracted back into the BBC for particular jobs. His father had been a Polish prisoner-of-war in the early 1940s and had stayed on to marry a Scottish girl. Edek had three loves: his wife, his children, and machines. His wife and children sometimes struggled to keep up. Jacqueline kept his mania in perspective. She had once said to me solemnly, 'The marriage is in trouble again. He's seeing a new console.' Jacqueline had also had an interesting effect on his speech. Edek had always been a terrible swearer and, after their marriage, it had led to rows until they found a compromise. Edek's swearing was, as it were, put on a diet, allowed just the one indulgence. That was why he was sometimes referred to as Bloody Edek. Jacqueline was a woman of some will-power. You could have told that from her voice. One hullo was enough.

'Hullo, Jacqueline,' I said. 'It's Jack Laidlaw. Why are you not working?'

She was a freelance film editor.

'Jack! You know another film editor that's working, do you?'

'I don't know another film editor.'

'They've probably all died off. If you're looking for Edek, he's working today. Praise the Lord.'

'What is he doing?'

'He's at Black Cat. A studio discussion. But they won't have started recording yet. Be setting up. They're doing the programme this afternoon.'

'I might try to get him there.'

'Do that. The couch is still here, by the way.'

There had been a phase when I spent a few nights there, debating many aspects of the world with Jacqueline and Edek.

'I'll try it again some time.'

'Good. If you give us some forewarning, we can buy a distillery. It took Edek three days to recover the last time. Cheers.'

Edek was at Black Cat Studios and able to come to the phone.

'Hullo. Is that bloody you, Bloody Edek? Jack Laidlaw.'

'You haven't got the style for it,' he said. 'No sense of timing. So where've you been?'

'I'm not too sure. Listen, Edek. Are you free over the weekend? Say, tomorrow and Sunday?'

'I'm not working. Why?'

'I'm not sure yet. I just want to know if I could call on you, if it was necessary.'

'You mean professionally?'

'That would be the idea.'

'So what's this about?'

'I don't know entirely yet. It might never happen. But I'm working on something. If it turns out the way I think it might, you could do me a right favour. Wouldn't take more than a couple of hours. Are you game?'

There was a brief pause.

'Here, Ah love mysteries,' Edek said. 'Are you a real detective, mister? Could Ah be helpin' you to catch a criminal an' everything? If Ah do it, can Ah get a gun home wi' me? To play with. Just for the weekend.'

'Thank you, Edek,' I said. 'Is that a yes or a no?'

'Could be. Come on, Jack. Phone me once you know what it is you're asking me to do. If it's making a recording of a shoot-out, forget it. Those bullets ricochet. I'll have to go here. Get in touch, will you? And, hey. What about sometimes getting in touch just to go for a drink or something? I like doing simple things sometimes.'

'We'll do that,' I said. 'So where do I get in touch with you?'

'I'll be at the house all day tomorrow. Bloody domestic bloody bliss.'

Talking to Edek hadn't given my feeling of disorientation any significant point of connection with the things that were going on around me in the city. I was still left waiting for something to happen and I was still not sure what it was. But renewing contact with Edek gave me another idea.

He had introduced me to a woman who worked in the BBC. He and I had been in the Ubiquitous Chip when she came in. I had met her several times since, in there, and we had talked a lot. I phoned the BBC again and asked for Naima Akhbar. When she came to the phone, it took her a moment to locate me on her mental map. But the sounds of recognition sounded enthusiastic. I explained that I was trying to find out where Michael Preston was filming today. He knew my brother and there was a message I wanted to pass on. It was fairly urgent. Naima would see what she could do and call me back. I gave her my number at the hotel.

I lay on the bed and smoked a cigarette. I said, 'Come on, come on, come on.' Naima did. The phone rang.

'Hello, Jack?'

'Naima. Ya beauty. What's the word?'

'Sunny Drumchapel,' she said. 'It's a programme on unemployment in Scotland. I got a look at the shooting schedule. This afternoon, it's supposed to be Drumchapel. If they keep to the schedule. Which doesn't always happen.'

'What, in the streets? In a house?'

She gave me an address.

'It's a boy who's unemployed. Michael Preston's going to interview him. The schedule has them starting at two o'clock. They should be there by now. But these things take a long time to set up.'

'Naima. Have I told you lately that I love you?'

'You can tell me in the Chip some time.'

'At great length.'

'Uh-huh. We'll see you there then. Take care.'

'Thanks, Naima.'

30

I knew Drumchapel, alias the Drum. A lot of people there wrestled with the bleakness of a badly conceived place. The decrepit council houses were a past promise of social improvement that had turned into the fact of deprivation. Today I saw dogs roam like the disinherited spirit of the place. Jennifer Lawson, whom I had first met as a brutalised corpse, had lived here. The place had its associations for me. But Michael Preston was not one of them.

I had my sense of him though. Television can make us familiar with strangers. We often look at the faces on it with more concentration than we look on the faces of friends. He was urbane and very articulate and he appeared to put that articulacy at the service of more than his own career. I had read an article about him in a newspaper which claimed that he had never made a programme he didn't believe in utterly. I had always liked him. He seemed sincere and his voice had the rhythm of natural speech – not the way voices sometimes sound on the box, as if they had been punctuated by computer. His public voice had the tone of integrity. If his private voice matched it, conversation with him should be less of a pin-ball game than it was with Dave Lyons.

I drove past Ardmore Crescent, where Jennifer Lawson had lived. That was the first case I had been on with Brian Harkness — strange bonus from a bad death. I worked my way through the cold geometry of streets that were like an industrial estate manufacturing disillusion. I knew I had found the house when I saw three cars parked outside, two of them estate cars. Someone had visitors, and visitors who needed space in their vehicles for a lot of equipment. As I locked the car, I saw a television light at an upstairs window.

The outside door of the house was ajar. Pushing it open, I saw a young man coming down the stairs. He was wearing jeans and a sweater and a Barbour jacket. He was carrying a canister of film. He nodded to me on the way past. He was with the BBC and obviously thought that in some way I came with the house. I decided to accept the freedom of the building he had bestowed on me.

The uncarpeted stairway led up to a long, dim hallway at the end of which the door was slightly open. Voices came from beyond it. The wooden floor creaked as I stepped on it, already haunted with departed people. I opened the door to the living-room and went in.

Strange image of the times: a kind of theatre made out of real hardship; designer deprivation. The room was so raw as hardly to suggest an interior at all but rather one of those make-believe houses children may put together on a waste lot from other people's cast-offs. The walls bore the scars of previous failed attempts at decoration, overlaid with the scrawled graffiti of names. The uncovered floor had one patch of carpet in the middle — a raft of identity sinking in a sea of anonymity. A burst sofa and two chairs were all the furniture, looking as if they hadn't been delivered but dumped.

Yet surrounding this construct of serious need was enough expensive equipment, had it been sold, to make the room a showpiece. There were powerful lights, sound machines, an impressive film-camera mounted on a tripod. Around these stood more than half a dozen people. Some of them obviously were there with the equipment. The others, two teenage boys, were friends who were there to see the show. Each side apparently took me as belonging to the other and my presence was barely remarked.

Beside the camera, out of range of its lens, Michael Preston sat on a metal box. The object of his attention, as of everybody else's, sat on the sofa opposite him. They were a boy who might have been eighteen and a girl who could be hardly that. Between them a girl of maybe one year old was sitting. The child was the true denizen of the room, someone already being defined by her habitat. The pinched features had faint sores around the mouth and the unchildlike listlessness of the eyes seemed to lag behind the movements around them, a cripple trying to follow a parade. Even someone insensitive enough to miss the statement the room made about the way some people live couldn't have missed its meaning as reflected in her face.

From Michael Preston's interview, which was already in progress, I learned that the two older children were the parents of the third. The mother was wan and shy and didn't say much. The father had the kind of youthful face one glance at which made me think, with a sinking feeling, that they could book the cell now. It might lie empty for a few years yet but it was going to be needed. I liked his face. It was a 'so what?' face. He had seen enough already to know that he wasn't exactly born to win and, if his life was never going to have much in the way of material substance, it could at least have style. The old felt hat was a part of it. The expression beneath it was saying to every stranger, 'Doesn't bother me'.

Their names, it emerged, were Julian and Marlene. I wondered what unconsciously shared dream in different council houses had spawned the poignancy of the names. We call you Julian and Marlene and, by the sympathetic magic that is in names, you will grow mysteriously to fit them and be different from us. But the only difference was perhaps that, while their parents' poorness had been part of a cohesive community that gave at least the support of shared values, theirs was part of a widespread rootlessness. The magic hadn't worked the way it was supposed to. But then a few of the essential ingredients had been missing, like opportunity and social justice.

Michael Preston conducted the interview gently, establishing a trust. His accent gradually modified itself until it was hardly distinguishable from Julian's. Seen in the flesh, he didn't match the sense I had had of him. He looked smaller and more vulnerable. But then fame's just borrowed clothes. I can't imagine that anyone's reputation fits them.

Listening to Julian, I heard the banality of hopelessness. Futility had become so familiar to him that it was a casual idiom in his mouth. He told of a temporary job he had had, the small amount of money they had to try and live on, the incidence of mugging in the area, their incompetence in bringing up the child. The appallingness of his situation was muffled by two things: his cocky self-defeating acceptance of it and the mediating requirements of the camera. His life was being processed into a piece of television.

The way in which the reality of his life was being made over into a viewable artefact had come home to me when the camera-man suddenly said, 'Oh God! No! Stop it there.' There was, he said, 'a hair in the gate'. The drama of his performance shattered any atmosphere of naturalness Michael Preston had managed to create. When the interview resumed, Marlene had become terrified of the moods of the camera and kept glancing at it as if it might sprout a headful of hair this time. Julian, invited to repeat the last thing he had been saying, started not to talk but to perform.

Looking on at the end of the interview, I felt I recognised where I had been several times this week – a place where people knew unjustifiable things had happened and were happening but had tried to give the truth they knew elocution lessons, so that form became the criterion, not content. I began to worry about the man who was central to the shaping of the truth that was emerging here. I didn't want Michael Preston to give me a carefully packaged version of what I sought to know. As soon as he said, 'That'll do us. Cut', I crossed towards him. I was beside him as he straightened up from his box.

'Mr Preston,' I said. 'I'm Jack Laidlaw.'

His eyes took a moment to come back from his interview. He looked at the child, he looked at me.

'It doesn't matter how pure you think your motivations are,' he said. He was talking to himself. 'You always feel you're exploiting people in these things. You're Scott's brother.'

'That's right. Could I talk to you for a minute?'

'Well, just a minute. We're going to set up outside for a piece to camera. I'll have to look at my notes.'

While they were clearing up, we wandered through to the kitchen. It was no more homely than the living-room had been. You could believe that the main thing they cooked here would be stale air. We could hear the technicians prepare to move on, having plundered the room of its few minutes of voyeurism. Standing in this place of disadvantage with this man who exuded well-being, I felt at last as if the disparate lives I had been moving among recently were coming together. Public rectitude was meeting private accusation. It was as if Dave Lyons were being introduced to Dan Scoular. But would they talk?

'How did you find me here?' he said.

'Through the BBC.'

'Nemesis, right enough,' he said. 'A Detective-Inspector calls. You're persistent.'

'I've had to be.'

'I've been expecting you,' he said. 'But not in a house in Drumchapel.'

'I suppose Dave Lyons would phone you.'

'That's right.'

The honesty of the admission was hopeful.

'So you know what I want to talk about.'

'I do. And we'll do that. But not here. And not now.'

'Why not?'

'It's a long story. And I'm under the cosh to get this programme finished. I've another interview to do today. And we've got editing time tonight. Tomorrow I'm working as well.'

The hope I had felt receded. He must have seen it in my

face. He wrote something on the back of one of the pages of notes he had in his hand. He tore it off and gave it to me.

'That's my address,' he said. 'Tomorrow. Late afternoon or early evening you can get me there. Bev, my wife's having a dinner party. But I can talk to you before it.'

I thought about arguing but I had no choice.

'You wouldn't be going to synchronise stories, would you?' I said.

The look he gave me was hard with pride.

'Listen,' he said. 'I belong to me. When my mouth opens, it's my words coming out. Nobody works me from the back.'

'Mr Preston,' I said. 'I hope that's true. I've been a long way round the houses here. And I'm getting tired of it. Somebody better speak to me straight. I hope it's you.'

'Well, you'll find out tomorrow, won't you? I'd better get out.'

He spoke briefly and kindly to Julian and Marlene, who were nervously elated with the experience of having been on television and seemed to be looking for somewhere to put their energy. He ruffled their daughter's sparse hair. When I came outside with him, the camera was already set up in the middle of the road. He took up his position on the pavement. I walked to the car. I unlocked the door but stood and waited. Somebody checked that no vehicles were approaching and he began to speak to the camera.

'Any social contract is a two-way agreement,' he said. 'It's one thing to make the people serve the economy. But the economy must also serve the people. If we disadvantage the present of one section of society, we disadvantage the future of all society. The children of the well-off will not just inherit the wealth of their parents. They will also inherit the poverty of the parents of others. Even self-interest, if it is wise, will concern itself with the welfare of all. Not just the poor will inherit the bad places. All of us will.'

He had delivered the words strongly and clearly but at that point one of three boys who had been standing on the pavement opposite shouted, 'Ye're aff yer heid'. Apparently, the sight of a man talking precisely to no one in particular had been too much for the boy. They were obviously going to have to take the shot again. I got in the car and drove off. Michael Preston was an articulate man, I was thinking. I hoped he didn't lose his articulacy overnight.

31

I had once seen Marty Bleasdale defuse a potentially ugly incident in a pub. A man who had picked an argument with him was beginning to get threatening.

'Has anyone ever told you,' Marty said, and those around him waited for the telling insult, 'that you've got pianist's fingers?'

The remark had arrived from so far away that the other man contemplated it as if an alien had landed. Then he managed to fit it into the context he was trying to create.

'Ah could rattle out a tune on you, anyway.'

'Do you do requests?' Marty said. 'Ah like Prokofiev. Something from *Romeo and Juliet*.'

The tension dissipated in laughter. The man hesitated, then laughed along. It had seemed an almost accidental dismantling of threat but it involved two qualities which Marty had in plenty. One was skill in dealing with people. He may have felt his years as a social worker hadn't effected much improvement in other people's lives but they had certainly made Marty very difficult to nonplus. He had not only obliged the man's aggression to force its way through laughter. He had also made the man express it not in his own terms but in Marty's. By the time the classical allusions turned up, the man wasn't too clear about where he was or what the rules were.

The other quality was nerve. Like a bomb-disposal expert, Marty was able to deal calmly with an explosive situation because, if his techniques didn't work, he had prepared himself for the consequences. I think the man understood that. The person from whom the outlandish talk was coming was rough-faced and pony-tailed and dressed like someone who wasn't worried what other people thought, and his eyes didn't flicker. Marty had a certain style. He gave the impression that circumstances were meeting him on his own terms.

That was why, when I received word at the hotel that Marty was rehearsing with a new group at the Getaway, I felt some uplift in my spirits. Whatever practical results a conversation with Marty might or might not have, it shouldn't do my mood any harm. When I went down the long flight of stairs that led to the basement bar, I found Brian and Bob were the only two customers. They were drinking beer. From the rehearsal room at the back of the place interesting sounds kept starting up and breaking down into cacophony.

'It's the happy wanderer,' Bob said.

'Excuse me, sir,' Brian said. 'Could you direct me to the nearest murderer?'

Brian's remark was a mocking echo of one I had once made. Ricky Barr, the owner, came over.

'At last, Jack,' he said, 'you've decided to come where the culture is.'

'If Marty Bleasdale's culture,' I said.

Ricky was one of the more benign expressions of success. He had made a lot of money in the music business before buying the Getaway. Now he provided a venue for all kinds of struggling musicians and gave them rehearsal space and recording facilities at minimal rates. His ambitions were fulfilled, he had a happy family life and he wanted to share the superflux.

'What are you drinking?' he said.

He brought Brian and Bob beers and myself a whisky and water.

'I'll see if they can spare the maestro,' he said.

'I'll talk to Marty on my own,' I said to Brian and Bob.

'Oh-ho,' Bob said. 'We set up the interview and then get locked out the room.'

'You know what Marty's like,' I said. 'One polisman makes him jumpy. Three could cause a fit.'

'It's all right,' Brian said. 'We're just happy to have been of service.'

'Who said you have yet? Depends what kinda mood Marty's in. He might decide to tell me nothin'.'

I went to the other end of the big, split-level bar and sat down. As Marty came out of the rehearsal-room with Ricky, his eyes checked off Bob and Brian. Marty was wearing a baggy shirt and jeans and cowboy boots. He had a fine, silk scarf knotted round his neck.

As he sat down at the table, he said, 'Ah feel surrounded. Three's a crowd, eh?'

'They're not involved, Marty. Just the two of us.'

'That's nice.'

Ricky brought him a drink.

'What's that?' I said.

'Jack Daniels,' Marty said. 'That's what Ah'm on this afternoon.

Ah change ma tastes by the hour. Got to try everything in this world.'

Disconnected sounds were still coming from the rehearsal-room.

'Rehearsing?' I said.

'What?'

'I didn't think you rehearsed jazz.'

'Tomorrow'll be the first time we've played together.'

'But Ah thought you were supposed to improvise with jazz.'

'Oh, is that what you do? We're just building the trellis. Give the roses room to grow. Rambling roses.'

'Hm.'

'Do yourself a favour, Jack. Don't try to be clever about it. Just come and listen.'

'I'll see if I can manage.'

'Anyway, you're not here to write a preview. Are you?'

'I want to find Melanie McHarg,' I said.

'Melanie Who?'

'Do yourself a favour, Marty. Don't try to be clever about it.'

We sipped our drinks and smiled at each other and Marty looked round the room.

'Ah've met her,' he said. 'Of course, Ah have. So what?'

'So where is she?'

'Ah've met Thelonius Monk, too. Ye want me to tell ye where he is?'

'You could save that for later. I want to find her, Marty.'

'Good luck. If Ah was her, ye wouldn't find me. She's had enough troubles lately. Ah'd be off an' runnin'.'

'But you're one of the places she would run, are you not?'

275

'Not known at this address,' he said. 'Ah'll have to get back to the clarinet.'

'Before you do,' I said.

I could see Brian Harkness and Bob Lilley laughing and nodding at something they were talking about. Ricky was standing against the counter, reading a newspaper. The jazz-group in the rehearsal-room was making aural shapes I didn't recognise. In those three mysterious preoccupations, I felt how the meaning of things withholds itself and hides among the endless banality of its proliferations. I sensed that, if this moment, too, were allowed to pass without revealing its small cache, the truth Betty Scoular knew was there might never be declared. The only pressure I could put on Marty was the truth. He would have outmanoeuvred anything else.

'The reason I want to talk to her. It seems obvious that Matt Mason wiped out Meece Rooney. It looks as if he also killed another man. About three months ago. Melanie could help us get at Matt Mason. Ah think she might also help herself. She must be trying to come to terms with her past. And see if there's a future. Maybe if she stopped just being the victim of her life. The way it looks as if she has been. And started to pay it back. Make it take on a shape she gives it. Maybe that would help her. I think they call it rehabilitation.'

I hoped the social worker's instincts weren't quite dead in Marty. He looked through me, as if he were checking my file for trustworthiness.

'What way could she help?' he said.

'I've got an idea. Something she could do for us.'

'What would that be?'

'That would be for me to ask. And for her to decide yes or no. Not for you to decide, Marty.'

'You goin' to put pressure on her?'

'There would be no pressure. Just ask her and let her make up her mind.'

'She's tryin' to come off it cold turkey, ye know. She's not in great shape. The way she is, a twig droppin' on her be like a fallin' tree. Timber. You'd have to leave it entirely up to her.'

'That would be the deal.'

'Ah'll see.'

He finished his Jack Daniels.

'See quick, Marty,' I said. 'Time's short here.'

'It's shorter than you think,' Marty said. 'Melanie's leavin' for Canada tomorrow.'

'Then let me talk to her today.'

He thought about it. He shook his head.

'No way. That way we narrow her choice. She might feel pressured into it. What Ah will do. Ah'll see her tonight. Ah'll speak to her. Ah'll let ye know if she wants to meet you. That's it.'

'It's maybe not enough. It doesn't leave us a lot of space for fancy footwork. I can't see her till tomorrow?'

'Jack. Maybe you can't see her at all. How do Ah get in touch?'

I gave him my room number at the hotel. As an afterthought, I also gave him Jan's telephone number. Going back to rehearsal, he turned.

'Oh and, Jack,' he said. 'Don't try to put a tail on me, eh?'

'Who would I get to do the job?' I said. 'Your shadow's got trouble keeping up with you.'

I joined Brian and Bob at their table. The vagueness of my arrangement with Marty didn't impress them. It didn't impress me much either. The music reflected the continuing uncertainty of where I was – all the disparate elements I had tried to bring together still hadn't fused, were still looking for the timing and inter-connection that would make them cohere. Jan was a part of that uncertainty. Where had I found the arrogance to give Marty her phone-number? I didn't know what she had decided. Maybe after dinner tonight I'd be lucky to reach her by postcard.

32

There are public places on which our private lives have an imaginative freehold, because of their associations. La Bona Sospira was one of mine. It was where Jan and I had our first meal together. We had gone back often since then.

You came in, through a narrowly unimpressive frontage, to what wasn't so much a bar as an ante-room to the restaurant. I had always enjoyed that room. It was like a bridge between two cultures. You stepped in off a Glasgow street and the room said: okay, you're Scottish and you want a drink, you have a drink; but we're Italian and any drink you have here is just a prelude to some serious food. The gantry was minute, telling you not to get excited. The decor was banal but so what? Bring your own dreams and any place is special.

This was where I had brought a few of mine. Tonight I wasn't sure if they could live here any longer. I was nervous about meeting Jan. I loved her and I needed her and I thought she loved me but I didn't think I was what she needed. That worried me because, many romantic fictions notwithstanding, most people will eventually go with what they need, not what they want. Think of Meece Rooney. That's why drug-dealers do so well.

I sat down at one of what I had always assumed were beaten brass tables. I hardly know one metal from another. But I had always assumed they were beaten brass. I felt vague about myself. Guido turned up, as Guido often had.

'Jacko,' he said. 'It's nice to see you.'

'Nice to be here, Guido.'

'The glorious Jan will be here soon?'

'That's the idea.'

'I bring the menus. But, first, I bring a drink. We have a little of the Antiquary.' The third syllable seemed to go on a long time. 'This for you?'

'That's great. Marcella's well?'

'Marcella is too well. She's so strong, it frightens me.'

Guido went away and came back and brought two menus and a stubby glass of the Antiquary and a jug of water. I had left the car at the hotel. I topped the glass up with water.

I looked at a menu. The food was inventive but so were the prices. I had once suggested this connection to Guido but I wouldn't do it again.

'You want Volvo,' he had said, 'you buy Volvo. You want Alfa Romeo, you pay for Alfa Romeo.'

The problem was, I reflected, I had for a long time been paying for Alfa Romeos I couldn't afford. My finances were a disaster. My one piece of luck in that area was that Freddie, my landlord, was someone I had known for years. The rent he charged for the flat was ridiculously cheap. Beyond that, all was crisis. Once I had set aside what was for Ena and the children, the rest was carrion money, just there to feed the vultures. They had been constantly circling for some time now and my cunning plan had always been to ignore them. When I finally collapsed in a heap of putrefying debts, they would no doubt come and get me. In the meantime, just keep running.

I was starting on my whisky as Jan came in. I had just kissed her, tasting the coolness of the evening on her cheek, when Guido arrived like a heat-directed missile that only homed in on women. His small rotundity surrounded her. He buried her in facile compliments, which Jan received delightedly. I suppose if someone is showering you with flowers, it would be churlish to notice that they're plastic.

I had to admit that she was due some compliments. As Guido elaborately unveiled her, taking her grey woollen coat like a gigantic matador's cloak, she stood in a plain, tight, black dress that declared every pore to be perfectly in place. She sat down and the area around the table brightened.

'You look incredible,' I said.

'That's how I feel,' she said. 'You look tired.'

'That's not how I feel.'

We smiled opaquely at each other. We were circling. Few people can be more distant than estranged intimates.

'How's your week been?' I said.

Before she could answer, Guido was back to make a ritual presentation of her Campari and soda, a large ruby for the Queen of Sheba. He fussed and Jan graciously accepted his fussing.

'My week?' she said, as Guido left. 'Unbelievable. You know we closed last night?'

'Sorry?'

'The restaurant. We closed down last night. For renovations We're getting far more business than we can handle. We're extending the restaurant into the coffee-lounge. Even then things'll be tight.'

I didn't mention that all of this was a surprise to me, because perhaps that was my fault. If you've been down in a diving-bell for over a month, you can't expect to keep up with the news. But her failure even to hint at it, previously, suggested to me not accident but deliberate policy.

'I would've thought,' I said, 'that the obvious night to close down would be a Saturday. This way, you're losing the two best nights of the week.'

'Oh, we can afford it. It's been going unbelievably well. The reason for closing Thursday. You know what it is? We wanted to prepare the place for one last thrash before the decorators move in. Tomorrow night we're throwing a party. All the people who've helped us and some of our regulars. We're making the biggest Boeuf Bourgignon in the world. It'll be some night. You must come.'

Her invitation had all the intimacy of a business-card.

'What about you?' she said.

She leant towards her Campari, as if she needed a prop, and I noticed a sudden stillness in her. She was staring at the table. The defencelessness of her posture gave me a glimpse of the vulnerable woman behind the glamour, renewed the intensity of my feelings for her in an instant. Jan had once said to me after making love, 'You make me frightened of me.' I had known what she meant, for I felt the same way. Those moments we had shared defied pragmatism and were therefore difficult to accommodate in the light of day. I had a feeling that was difficult to accommodate now. I would have rather we had each other on the metal-topped table than go through these charades. She glanced up and we were sharing a look directly for the first time since we had met tonight. Our eyes were a mutual confession: we are a joint compulsion. The acknowledgement made her defensive again. She looked away.

'What about you?' she said. 'Have you sorted things out?'

'I'm trying.'

'Oh, not still that.'

'Still that.'

She lifted her drink and stared at it and sipped and looked round the room. She had moved away from the admission our eyes had made. She had remembered there were conditions to it I still hadn't met.

'Oh well,' she said. 'Meantime, some of us have to live.'

'I suppose we're all trying to do that.'

'I mean live in the daily world. You're so unrealistic.'

I found that an interesting observation. I respected the difference of Jan's life, the validity of her personal preoccupations. But I wasn't quite prepared to concede that running a successful restaurant made you expert in the nature of reality.

'The world moves on, Jack,' she said.

'Aye. But where to? That's what's worrying me.'

She took another sip of her drink and smiled at the passing Guido and became a busy, successful woman again. The passionate look we had exchanged might have been between an attractive scuffler in the street and a sophisticated woman, while her Daimler was stopped briefly at the lights. She opened a menu.

'Nice Campari,' she said.

Any evening has its motifs. Those were ours, evasive mannerisms and an impulse to strip each other in the restaurant. During the meal, we tried to talk seriously about our lives but the conversation remained somehow oblique. We seemed incapable of meeting in no-man's-land. We just kept checking the other's position and reinforcing our own. We were outmanoeuvring each other so effectively, I wondered if we would ever connect.

I asked, 'How's Betsy doing?'

'Better than you would like,' Jan replied.

Jan said, 'You seem to have been talking a lot to Morag Harkness.'

I said, 'That's because she answers the phone.'

I said. 'Barry Murdoch been around much?'

'Barry Murdoch's always around,' Jan said. 'So what? I know some people who aren't.'

'You're a bit too vehement about Anna,' Jan said. 'You sure you haven't got a thing for her?'

'I have,' I said. 'It's called a Gatling gun.'

And so it went on through the jolly meal, a cross between a minuet and a sword dance, where you had to watch where you stepped in case you found you were bleeding. What I think we were doing, really, was devoting an entire evening to one of those long, askance looks lovers sometimes give each other in their minds, that could roughly translate into what-the-hell-am-I-doing-with-this-one? Our lack of contact had perhaps emphasised to each the difference of the other. Sometimes Jan would look at me as at something surprisingly quaint, as if she were thinking, 'I never noticed that you had two noses before'. Sometimes, for sure, I must have been doing the same.

What Jan was realising about me, I suppose, was that my relationship with her hadn't smoothed my edges as much as she had hoped. I could order Pinot Grigio with the food, right enough, but while we drank it I still talked about the streets and swore occasionally. I might mention Shakespeare's name but it might well be linked with that of Meece Rooney or Frankie White. That had always bothered Jan about me. I refused to pigeonhole my nature into separate social identities. I was the same person whatever room I entered. I would make adjustments out of consideration and politeness, like trying not to swear in front of someone I knew it would offend or not using a big word to someone I thought wouldn't understand it. But there would be no pretence of being who I wasn't.

Jan and I had argued about that a lot. Once I put the question to Tom Docherty when we were drinking. I didn't connect it with Jan. I just posed it as a generality. Tom related it to writing, as he does with a lot of things.

Another of the shorter sayings of Chairman Tom: 'It's like literary criticism. It's nearly all about register. There's a lot of po-faced crap that gets highly praised because of its tone of voice. "I'm serious, I'm cultured," it's telling you all the time. Bollocks. The serious and the cultured don't even have to mention the fact. It's coming out their pores already. They just do it, they just create. Often laughing and swearing as they go along. Same with people. "There are things you say, things you don't say, times to say it, and times not." Some more bollocks. The idea of register in language is mainly just fences shutting out most of the reality we should all be sharing. There's only one serious human register and it accommodates everybody: truth, in the most generous form you can find it.'

That would do me. Maybe that was why I was a policeman who read philosophy. I could understand both Albert Camus and Matt Mason. I had better. They were both telling me important things about the way we live. They were both part of the same world. It was my world, too. It had to be. There was only the one world to choose from.

What I was realising about Jan, I suppose, was how alien this attitude was to her. There was a time she had been more tolerant of the wind off the streets I had often brought into her life. But lately she seemed to be waiting more and more impatiently for me to close the door on its blowing. That wouldn't happen. Tonight she seemed to understand that. She listened with a weary silence to the things that were concerning me. So I stopped talking about them.

I saw that she thought all of those people I had been talking to and all of those strange events others got themselves involved in had really nothing to do with this bright and pleasant room we were sitting in, nothing seriously to do with the life we might have together. I didn't think that. This place was connected to those places. Any place she and I went to together would be. I could sit here and enjoy a good meal and love looking at her but I couldn't make the pleasure erase those other things or somehow discount them. All I wanted to do tonight was to be with her. But I cared very deeply what happened in other places tomorrow. I hoped Marty Bleasdale found Melanie McHarg. I hoped Melanie McHarg would help me. I wanted that Dan Scoular's death should have honour and that Scott's death should be understood. If they weren't, any life Jan and I could have together would be the less.

It seemed to me Jan thought I could live in two stories, the one where these other things happened and the one that she and I would write together. That couldn't be. I could only live in the one continuous story – different chapters maybe but the one plot, if you had the sense to follow it.

But while our minds were behaving like strangers, our bodies were arranging an assignation. It was happening in spite of ourselves. She touched my leg instinctively below the table in contradiction of what she was saying. I lost the thread of my objections and was left simply enjoying her eyes. As our pre-determined sense of ourselves proceeded rather pompously through the evening, together but apart, the desire to make love to each other followed furtively, like a down-and-out who had nothing to commend him but his need. I think we both knew he was bound to confront us.

Perhaps that's why, after the restaurant, we went into a pub for a drink. We were allowing time for the unadmitted truth of what we felt to catch up. We both became slightly drunk and finished, by no route that I can explain, making our way into the restaurant to get to her flat.

The restaurant was in an alleyway in the West End. Jan's flat was above it and had a metal work balcony which I liked. The flat had an outside door that you reached by means of a stairway. It could also be entered through a back staircase in the restaurant. Why Jan should decide that we had to go in through the restaurant I do not know. There may have been a logic at the time, now lost forever.

Inside the restaurant, all was pleasantly dim. Light came in from the streetlamps outside, as if filtered through gauze. Each empty table, draped simply in pink cloth, floated like a lotus in a pool. I moved with effortless grace among the tables and barked my shin very painfully on metal. I thought I was going to scream. After a brief, soundless dance, I looked down. I saw an object I had always hated.

It was a large metal flowerpot. It contained a lot of money, mainly coins but with quite a number of notes. It was supposed to be a unique tradition of the restaurant. The idea was that, since everybody who worked here was well enough paid, any tips were put into the flowerpot. Once the amount of money became impressive, it would be given to charity. I didn't mind the thought so much. But I despised the public, patronising style of it. It was enough to make me worry about Jan. I was exhausted trying to connect with her anyway. The flowerpot palpitated, along with my leg, into a symbol. It blocked my way. This route I may go no further. Jan was still talking, oblivious to my pain.

'But we'll have an alcove. Leading through to where the coffee-room is. It'll be like a room inside a room. Privacy inside privacy. More whispery than the main place.'

'Hey, Lady of the Manor!' I called.

She turned towards me. Having thrown her coat off, her body was the only sheer presence in the vagueness of the room. She was looking at me quizzically.

'I've had this,' I said. 'For God's sake, take your pants off and put them round your mouth.'

I was as shocked as she was. But her shock became assurance more quickly. We looked at each other without the mediation of accidental circumstances or deliberate mannerisms and accepted the challenge. It was as if some kind of smoked glass were no longer between us – say, the window of a Daimler had come soundlessly down. She was face to face with the scuffler in the street. She smiled and waited to speak. When she spoke, it was just the one word. The word was a name. She said the word gloatingly, as if she were a spider that had found a species of fly it particularly enjoyed dismembering.

'Sexist!' she said softly.

'All right,' I said. 'Take your pants off and put them round *my* mouth. Even better. I love the taste of you any way it comes. But let's just meet.'

She stared at me.

'Well,' she said. 'If you're that desperate. You know where they are.'

If I hadn't known, I would have found out. She was standing, still as a startled animal, as if she had caught the sudden whiff of our own nature and knew we were its quarry. I came towards her. I did not touch her. I stood close to her and took her scent. That woman smell, may it always fuse every light in my head and teach me to wait again till my senses glow in the dark.

I reached down very gently. My fingers did not touch her. With both hands, I found the hem of her dress at the outside of each leg. I eased her dress up, very slowly. There being no attack, there was no resistance. As the cloth came above her thighs, it struggled and, in that feeling, the sensuality of her hips seized me more potently than if I had looked or touched. When the dress was crumpled round her waist, I released it and it stayed there.

In the half-dark, the whiteness of her thighs shone above the stocking-tops. Her legs were strong and beautiful. To my awed reverence they might as well have been the pillars to some temple. The white brocaded pants concealed her darkness. I knelt down and softly began to lick the insides of her thighs. I became engrossed, as if I had found my life's work. She began to moan faintly. The sound grew, part pleasure, part complaint, like an animal that wanted to leave its lair but was afraid to. All the words of the evening had translated into this – a licking tongue, inarticulate noises, the sounds of need. Her legs were trembling and they did not so much part as they thawed open.

I reached up with both hands and pulled her pants down. The pants were pretty but they were an ugliness compared with what they were hiding. As I eased them over her ankles and she stepped out, her legs buckled and she closed on me like a trap I wanted to be caught in.

On the floor we stripped each other with an urgency that precluded the need for technique. It happened that we became naked. The rest took place beyond much that we could do about it. Such lust doesn't submit suggestions to a committee to be ratified. It descends like a visiting divinity out of the machine and says, 'You'll do this and this and this. And then you'll do that.' We did. We ended with Jan sprawled naked across one of the tables, her hands grasping its edges, her buttocks hoisted in the air, and me serving her manically from the back. The idea of making love on the table in La Bona Sospira had, unintentionally, managed to fulfil itself. We had found a way past our pretences to ourselves. Pleased to meet us. The smart detective was a gasping, obedient servant of his phallus. The suave business-woman was an abandonment of beautiful, welcoming flesh. Oh, the lies we tell in the daylight about what we are in the dark. We came finally together with a terrible shuddering I thought I might not survive. The force of the moment shook me like a rat. I felt the strength of her loins would pull me outside in.

I fell across her. We lay. I lipped her back, like someone trying to convince himself he is still alive. 'Oh, darling, oh,'

Jan said. She didn't move. She lay spread-eagled, as if she had been fused to the table. It was a while before either of us said anything else. We had to wait for the intensity of what had happened to leave. Somehow, it didn't seem right to speak in its presence. It was Jan who spoke again, reintroducing us to practicality.

'We're beside a window,' she said. 'I suppose we'd better move.'

I pinned her to the table.

'No chance,' I said. 'I'm going to keep you here for good. Make us own up to what we're really like.'

'Could be awkward at the party.'

'Don't care. And they can decorate around us. Could make the place's name. How's this for trendy decor?'

'Some people might object.'

'More likely to follow suit. Or follow suitless. We could start the revolution right here. Own up. Strip off. Make love.'

'Or we could just get the jail.'

'No problem. I'm a policeman.'

'Oh, I know.'

I had said the wrong thing. It was a cold shower after love, diminishing our intimacy. Our difficulties were gathering again in the room around us. I tried to disperse them.

'I'm glad you bought strong tables for this place.'

'I better remember to change the table-cover,' she said, 'before the hygiene-inspector comes.'

But the levity didn't quite work. We eased ourselves apart and gathered our clothes together. The table reverted to a place where business-deals would be made over lunches and people would act out their fictions of success and self-sufficiency. At least we had blessed it with a kind of human truth.

We took on our problems with our clothes. As we made our way upstairs naked to the flat, we carried our social identities in our arms, our separate commitments, our mutually exclusive purposes, the continuity of our differences. We couldn't stay naked for each other. We hadn't resolved our dilemma, just rendered it irrelevant for a time. We were content with that for now.

Upstairs we lay in bed and held each other in the darkness. We shared skins. We touched hair. We said soft things we hoped came true. Before I slept, I realised that this was the closest thing to home I had, this fragile tent of feeling I could share with Jan.

The phone ripped through it.

SIX

33

D awn can be a nuisance. It keeps turning up whether you want to see it or not, making noise, repeating a lot of things you know already, breaking your concentration by demanding your attention. Why can't the world leave lovers alone?

I watched Jan struggle with the phone as if it were a new invention she hadn't yet got used to. When she had finally worked out which end went where, it didn't seem to help much.

She said 'Sorry?' and 'What?' and 'Who?' Her voice was hoarse. It made several false starts, tuning up in preparation for another day. As she listened, her eyes wandered blindly round the room, feeling for a familiar object that would remind her of where she was. They came to rest on the Jim Dine print of different-coloured hearts.

'Who is this again?' she said and waited. 'Who?'

She turned round to look at the time on the alarm clock. It was half past eight.

'Oh, yes,' she said. 'He's here.'

She turned towards me and gave the phone across like a piece of evidence that incriminated me. Her eyes were passing bitter judgment.

'Hullo,' I said.

'Jack? Marty Bleasdale.' The Newcastle accent wore a trace of Scots like a tartan scarf. 'Sorry about this. Ah don't seem to be exactly a welcome caller.'

I was aware of Jan lying beside me, communing with the ceiling in disbelief.

'It's all right,' I said neutrally, hoping Jan might think I was talking about my health.

'The reason Ah'm phonin' so early. Melanie gets her flight today. Early evenin'. She wants to talk to you. Ah thought from your point of view, the earlier the better.'

'That's right, Marty,' I said.

I had to meet her. It was a chance I couldn't pass up. It was the surest way I had to come closer to Matt Mason. But at the moment it was also a way to move further from Jan. I felt the assessing stillness of her presence.

'Tell you what,' I said. 'Can you and Melanie come to the Grosvenor about ten? That'll give me time to get there. Shave and stuff. We can talk.'

Jan turned away from me on the bed. I gave him the room number.

'We'll be there.'

'Thanks, Marty. Cheers.'

I put the receiver down but the connection was still there in the room. We had been estranged by the presence of others. I looked at the back of Jan's head. It was rejecting me as she felt I had rejected her. I was aggrieved that she was aggrieved. But as I leaned across her and replaced the phone on the bedside table, I caught the smell of her hair and touched the gentle warmth of her skin. I started to kiss her neck and stroke her.

I was aware of her body relaxing sensuously. But the voice came out cold and precise, a computer in a boudoir.

'You sure you've got time?'

'Come on, Jan,' I said, mouthing her arm. 'I don't take an hour and a half to wash and shave. That was all part of the subtle plan, give us some time.'

'You don't fit *me* in between appointments.'

'Jan. Don't say that. I've got to talk to these people. And this is my only chance. I've spent a week trying to crack this. I think today maybe I can do it. Just give me this space. I'll see you tonight.'

'Which one of you will be coming?'

'Oh, Jan.'

She didn't speak. I began to feel the outline of her body under the covers. She went soft and then stiffened. She pushed my hand away with her arm. I lay with my emotions all dressed up and nowhere to go. I tried to touch her again.

'No way,' she said.

I looked at the ceiling.

'Not even position 42?' I said.

'Piss off.'

I kissed her hair and got out of bed. As I was putting on my clothes, it started – one of those quarrels that grow out of a triviality, a hairline crack that causes a subsidence.

'Who was that person?' she said without looking at me.

'That person?'

'That person. The one who makes Cheetah sound cultured.'

I stood with one leg in my trousers. It was not the best posture from which to project righteous indignation. But I'm a natural improviser.

'Hey,' I said. 'That's Marty Bleasdale. As you would know, if you'd paid the politeness of listening to him. He may not have as many plastic cards as Barry Murdoch. But he would make five of him as a person.'

'Where did Barry come from?'

'I didn't know he had left.'

In the pause I managed to get my other leg into my trousers.

'How did he get this number?'

'Jan. You know I gave it to him. How the hell else would he get it?'

'You *gave* it to him? *You* gave it to him? So you knew you were going to spend the night here. I didn't have a choice? I seem to be the last to know. Maybe I should check my engagement diary out with Marty bloody Bleasdale.'

'It's not like that,' I said. 'You know it. I just hoped I would be here. It's happened before, you know. In case you've forgotten. I gave him the number in case. He obviously phoned the hotel first. Then tried here.'

'How many other people have you given my number to?'

'Nobody else. I don't have to. You're good enough at doing that without my help.'

That was a mistake, one of jealousy's blind swipes that connects with nothing and just leaves you vulnerable to the counter-punch. I tried to duck it by buttoning my shirt and looking for my tie.

'I've had enough,' she said.

'Look, I'm sorry. I shouldn't have said that. I —'

'No,' she said. 'It's not that. It's everything. This isn't a house to you. It's an office with a bed in it. And it always will be. There always will be strangers in it. You bring them with you.

I don't want to know about their lives. I've got my own to live. I think I better learn to live it without you.'

I had found my tie. Making a knot in it became a very slow process, almost ceremonial. I sensed that perhaps I was dressing for a final departure. This conversation was our relationship in miniature, compressed but exactly detailed. The central motif was the conflict between Jan's need to live towards ourselves, what was in here, and mine to live towards what was out there. I didn't see how the conflict could be resolved. The fault was mine. I almost garrotted myself with my tie. The anger was not against Jan. It was against myself and also against something I hadn't yet located. Perhaps today I would. Then she said a strange thing.

'Jack. Why does darkness fascinate you so much?'

I put my jacket on and stood there. I tried to answer honestly.

'Maybe because I see it almost everywhere,' I said. 'And a lot of people trying to ignore it.'

She lay and I stood with that statement stretching between us like a terrible distance. I tried to cross it. I went to the bed and bent down and kissed her face. Her cheek was like ice beneath my lips. It didn't thaw.

'I'll see you tonight?' I said.

'Will you?' she said. 'I don't know if either of the people we were last night can be there.'

I came out and closed the door and stood a moment on her balcony. It looked like being a nice day. I wished I could have shared it with her.

34

Even for a messenger of darkness, which is presumably what Jan would have seen Melanie McHarg as being, practical preparations have to be made. At the hotel I showered and shaved and dressed. I ordered continental breakfast for two — orange juice, croissants and coffee — to be delivered at ten o'clock. It arrived a couple of minutes before Marty Bleasdale knocked at the door.

They came in and Marty introduced us. Melanie McHarg had an appearance that caught the attention. But she was a sketch of attractiveness rather than its fulfilled image, a sketch that seemed to be undergoing erasure and alteration. Her body moved gracefully but it wasn't the way you felt it should be. It was too fine-drawn. The features of her face needed filling out. The dark hair lacked sheen. Only the eyes were vivid. They were bright blue, honest and startlingly vulnerable. She was wearing jeans, blouse and black cotton jacket.

Marty said, 'Ah'll leave you two to talk. Ah'll be downstairs. Take it easy, Jack.'

I nodded and he went out. We sat down at the low table. Breakfast allowed us to deflect our awkwardness into small actions. I poured the coffee. She sipped orange juice and picked at a croissant. She took neither milk nor sugar. I took both.

'Thanks for coming to talk to me,' I said.

'I've heard of you,' she said. 'The people I used to mix with sometimes talked about you. They weren't exactly fans. But they did have a grudging admiration. It made me think I could trust you.'

'I hope so,' I said.

'Marty's told you about me?'

'Some,' I said. 'I hope you make it out of the drugs.'

At the mention of her situation, her eyes looked even more naked. I saw how raw she must be, as if her skin didn't quite cover her.

'So do I,' she said. 'Anyway, I'm leaving for Canada today. For a while. I've got a sister lives in Oshawa. It's outside Toronto. Maybe I'll find I've still got some kind of life to live.'

'Of course, you have,' I said. She looked about mid-thirties. 'You have.'

'How did you hear about me?'

'I've got a brother just died,' I said. 'Thirty-eight.'

I didn't know why I said his age. Maybe I was still accusing the world of a misdemeanour. Her eyes stared at me with immediate compassion. She had the openness of pain to share the pain of others. We looked at each other as if we had met a while ago.

'And I went down to Ayrshire. Where he lived. I suppose I've been trying to understand his death. And I talked to a lot of people. One of them was Fast Frankie White.'

She began immediately and very loudly to cry. The name had unlocked her. I was astonished. I stood up and went across and put my arm round her. I was assuming she must have been involved with Frankie at one time. But it wasn't that. As she started to talk through her tears, I realised that it wasn't Frankie himself evoking the reaction but bigger things that his name stood as cipher for, like a phrase of a song evoking past times.

The weeping breached her self-containment and a lot of words came out. It was an autobiography in fragments. The impromptu abstract I made of it as I listened suggested that it wasn't exactly a unique story but it was not less moving for that.

I could imagine how good-looking she had been in her late teens. A Glasgow jeweller whose name I knew had taken her up. His name had been in vogue in the city at the time in certain places. He would be in his late twenties then and living what passed for the fast life. There were cars and trips abroad and a lot of parties. He introduced her to many people, including Matt Mason, and to a style of living as progressive as a merry-go-round. When he jumped off, landing softly on his money, he left her there.

Her chief talent had been her looks and she admitted she had used them. I felt that she was mourning more than lost time. She was grieving for what she had allowed time to take from her in the going.

'I kept my vanity for a while,' she said. 'But I lost my pride.'

'I'm terrified,' she said. 'You know what frightens me most? I'm afraid I can't love anybody. Vanity can't do that. Only pride can.'

Her fear, set against the confused and broken details of her life, made a kind of sense to me. Thinking she was using other people, she had let them use her in small, seedy ways.

Her vanity had been pleased by the flattery of being used. ('I'm still attractive, I'm still liked.') Vanity can use using but it can't use love. One reaffirms vanity, the other calls it in question. She had become addicted to other people's uses for her and, when they waned, she made the addiction chemical.

Dan Scoular had happened to her between the soft dependency and the hard. She had seen him as someone she could love. When that chance went, she didn't believe in the chances any more. He had reminded her of where she came from, values she had lost, and with his departure from her life any pretence of recapturing them went too. She knew herself a long distance from where she should have been and no way back. She settled for letting herself use Meece and Meece use her. It had been a fragile union, balanced on a needle point.

As she mentioned Dan Scoular yet again, I gathered from her remark that she did not know he was dead. I weighed the hurt she didn't know with the hurt she did, and I thought one might help to absorb the other. I told her. I held her shoulders while they shook like wings that had lost the power of flight but were taking a long time to accept it. She became eventually very still and very quiet.

'Excuse me,' she said.

I released her. She took her handbag and went into the bathroom. I looked at the cold coffee. I thought of being in Rico's with Eddie Foley. I wasn't doing well with coffees. Maybe some year I would finish one. I rinsed out the cups in the wash-hand basin and put them on the tray. I noticed the croissant she had been plucking at. It lay in several pieces on her plate, less a meal than a blueprint for a meal.

I was staring at the croissant when I decided. I couldn't ask her to do what I had intended to ask her to do. She was too wounded. She had been through too much to be put through any more.

When she came out of the bathroom, she had done her face skilfully but the make-up was a mask from behind which the eyes looked out warily. She sat back down.

'How did Dan Scoular die?' she said.

'He was run down by a car.'

'Run down?'

'We think Matt Mason killed him. We don't know that. But we think he did.'

'And Meece?'

'Well, what do you think?'

She nodded. Though the eyes were still nervous, the face set cold around them.

'Why did you want to see me?'

'There was something I thought of asking you to do.'

'What's that?'

'No,' I said. 'It was probably always a wild idea. And the way you are just now, it's just not on.'

'Tell me.'

'Let's forget it.'

'Tell me.'

I told her. She stared a long time at the floor.

'Could I have a drink, please?'

'What do you take?'

'Gin and tonic would do.'

I broke the seal on the drinks cabinet and gave her what she wanted.

'I think I'll join you,' I said.

I found another tumbler in the bathroom. I poured out a miniature of whisky and filled it up with water. I put the empty bottles in the bin. I sat down opposite her while she thought about it.

'All right,' she said. 'I'll do it.'

'Wait a minute,' I said. 'You should understand the details. And there's somebody else involved.'

I explained to her. She took another sip of her drink.

'All right,' she said.

'Maybe you should think longer about it.'

'I'm leaving anyway,' she said. 'Maybe this is one way to pay my respects to Dan Scoular before I go. And Meece as well. Meece wasn't all bad, you know.'

We clinked glasses. I gave her some more time.

'So I can phone these people?'

She nodded. I phoned Edek Bialecki. He would come to the hotel immediately. I phoned Eddie Foley. I arranged where I wanted him to meet me. I phoned Brian Harkness and asked him to bring Bob to the hotel. Reception said they would page Mr Bleasdale and ask him to come up to the room.

When Marty found out what we were proposing to do, he tried to dissuade Melanie. But she stayed firm. I think I went down in his estimation. He refused a drink on the grounds that he didn't like attending wakes. The arrival of Edek made Marty disown the whole proceedings. He stood looking out of the window while we discussed things. Looking at Melanie's jeans, Edek said she would have to change.

'Ah know where we can check out some costumes. We should be able to get something.'

'Make it a shroud,' Marty said.

35

Davy, the disillusioned architect I had met up with again a few years ago, had a theory about houses. It is true that he expounded the theory to me when we were both drunk. It is also true that we had just finished holding a kind of conversational memorial service for Jim, our mutual friend who had been killed at nineteen when his motorbike went under a lorry. We had been remembering the preposterous hopes of that year when we were all fifteen and wandering the fields of Ayrshire with the combined imaginative vision of three Columbuses staring out at the Atlantic. Therefore, Davy's theory may have been less coherent and perhaps more dark than he had wanted it to be. It expressed the immediacy of a sad mood as well as the general unease of a troubled life. But I think he meant it all right and I think the sober man would have ratified the findings of the drunk one.

'Theatre,' Davy had said, his forefinger tracing out an immediately vanishing pattern in the spillage on the table in the bar. The noise around him drowned his voice the way the liquid defied any shape he tried to give it. But he had found something he meant and he had to say it.

'Theatre,' Davy said. 'That's what houses are, you know.

Just theatre. All buildings are. Charades of permanence. They're fantasies. Fictions we make about ourselves. Right?'

With the prescience of the drunk, I was nodding in agreement before I knew what it was he meant.

'Right,' he said. 'What do the pyramids mean, for example? They're a lie, that's what they are. Okay? What are they supposed to mean? The immortality of the Pharaohs. Right? Are the Pharaohs immortal? Are they hell. The Pharaohs is long gone, don't worry about it. Empty bandages and some pots of entrails. That's the Pharaohs. So what do the pyramids really mean? Mortality. The corpses of all the people it took to build them. The pyramids are a lie. They mean the opposite of what they say.'

He sipped a little more whisky, sending it in pursuit of his thoughts.

'Well, most houses are lies, anyway. If we just built them as shelters, that would be fair enough. If we say, look, we're a pretty feeble species and it's cold out there and we need all the help we can get to survive, that makes sense. Let's make wee shelters and hide in them. That's honest. A tent's honest. But as soon as we go past function, we're at it. Big houses aren't an expression of ourselves. They're a denial of ourselves. We're not saying, see how feeble we are, but look at how important we are. Right? We're saying we could be here forever. We're a permanent fixture. Houses are one of the main ways that we tell lies about ourselves. They're public statements of security and stability and achievement that deny the private truth. They're masks. They're where we play out roles that aren't us. Just theatre. Look at houses carefully.'

I was trying to take his advice. This house in Bearsden, in

Davy's guide to house-watching, was presumably enacting a domestic comedy. It sat in soft sunshine. The well kept grass looked too green to be true. The French windows were open. Children kept spilling through them into the garden and being shepherded by adults back into the house where the party was taking place. From this distance, the performance was in mime.

The audience consisted of four men sitting in a car parked on the hill above the house, looking down on it. We were a mixed audience, as all audiences are, each bringing his own experience, his own preoccupations, his own interpretation to what we were watching. Edek, the mechanical man, was just there for the acoustics. He was an extension of his machinery, not so much concerned about what would happen as concerned that it should happen clearly. Brian Harkness was being a bit blasé as if he just wanted the performance over without any mistakes being made. Eddie Foley, I imagined, had to be the most fraught of us. He would take the drama for real because it was real for him, a possibly life-changing moment where he was both watcher and participant.

Myself, I suppose I was looking for a highly personal denouement to the first part of a double bill. I had another play to go to. I was aware of Michael Preston waiting to say his piece and I was hoping he hadn't learned his lines from Dave Lyons. The scene, as they say, would be an apartment in Glasgow. There would be played out the coda to my week.

But what would happen there was related to what happened here. They were interconnected, the legal hypocrisies reflecting the illegal ones in endlessly duplicating mirrors until they made a warren. I was hoping not just to incriminate Matt Mason but to move nearer to understanding where I had been this week, where I had been for a long time. As I looked at Matt Mason's house, I thought of Scott's house and Dave Lyons' house. I thought of our house in Simshill, where Ena and I had for years enacted a marriage that was a concealment of mutual loneliness.

Eddie Foley coughed. Nobody said anything. We were waiting for the entrance that would transform the scene for us. From our high position, we could see the taxi come along the street beneath us. As it stopped at the opening to the driveway at the front of the house, a small girl came running out of the French windows at the back, followed by Matt Mason. He was wearing slacks and a polo-neck sweater.

The small girl seemed to be upset about something. As Matt Mason caught up with her, she stopped. Melanie McHarg stepped out of the taxi. Matt Mason put his hand on the girl's shoulder and crouched down to talk to her. Melanie McHarg was paying the driver through his window, which is not a Glasgow idiom, since payment is usually made inside. I thought maybe she didn't use a lot of taxis. Matt Mason straightened up and took the girl's hand, apparently distracting her by showing her the garden. The taxi moved off. Melanie McHarg adjusted her blue lightweight coat over her wide-skirted floral dress and went out of sight towards the house.

Matt Mason looked like any dutiful husband spending a weekend in the garden with his family. From this far, he seemed an identikit of suburban man. But my knowledge of him provided me with some harsh close-ups. I was aware that the hand gently holding that of the small girl was aggressive with expensive rings, wore wealth like a socially accepted knuckle-duster. I saw the thinning hair, the hard face, the grey irises flecked with ice that could put a frost on anything they looked at. I saw him where he was, not where he seemed to be.

Margaret, his wife, stood at the French windows and said something to him. He let go of the girl's hand. His wife came out into the garden. They talked briefly. He stared at the ground. He went into the house. Margaret took the girl's hand and followed him in.

'Hello, hello,' Brian Harkness said in a whisper.

Even from this distance, Margaret Mason walked like a carnival of womanhood.

'Bloody activate,' Edek said. 'Bloody activate.'

He rolled down his rear-seat window and balanced his leather-cased receiver on the sill. He pulled out the aerial. He checked the connection to the tape-recorder on the seat, which he had insisted on telling us was a Nagra. ('State of the bloody art, don't worry about it.')

'Is this going to work, Edek?' I said.

'Is up to her now, isn't it?' he said. 'There's no more I can do from here. She's got a mike in her brassiere. Connected up to a first-class transmitter. Taped to the outside of her thigh. That was hard work. Jeez, the things you have to do for your art. I even picked her wardrobe. Now it's in the lap of the gods. Or the breast of the goddess, maybe.'

He was doing mysterious things with some of the knobs on his machine.

'I hope she hasn't interfered with the bloody wiring,' he said.

The garden was empty. The building looked charming and beautiful, a picture in an estate agent's window. Then there was a sudden crackling and the house was haunted by a dark voice.

'In here. Your timing could've been better.'

Rendered metallic by the recording equipment, Matt Mason's voice was low and harsh. Abstracted from gesture or facial expression or social context, it emerged without concealment, just itself. It cut into the silence of the car like a serrated knife.

'So, Melanie. To what do we owe the pleasure?'

There was a pause. Melanie's voice, when it came, seemed barely there. It impressed itself on the surface of the silence as delicately as fingerprints, seeming almost to fade as it happened. It made you listen intently.

'Matt, I'm sorry to be bothering you.'

'So why are you?'

'Matt, you know what's happened.'

'Do I? What's that?'

'Meece is dead.'

'Uh-huh? Siddown, Melanie.'

The material of her dress rustled through the microphone as she sat. The length of the silence made me wonder if we had lost them. I looked round at Edek. From his position at the open window, he winked.

'So that's the news, is it?' Matt Mason said. 'You came to tell me that?'

'I was livin' with Meece.'

'I know that. Come on, Melanie. Do you think Ah just arrived on the bus yesterday?'

'I miss him, Matt. I miss him so much.'

'What is it you miss? Your supplier? Is it money you want, Melanie?'

'No. No. I'm tryin' to come off it.'

'Is that right?'

'What happened, Matt? I can't understand it.'

'You don't have to. Let other people do that. Now if you need money, Ah'll give ye some money. If you don't, that's up to you. Either way, you'll have to leave. We're havin' a party here. You're not exactly addin' to the atmosphere.'

I was hoping I hadn't underprepared. I had simply suggested that Melanie should go to Matt Mason and ask about Meece Rooney, and possibly Dan Scoular. I had chosen not to rehearse her because I was afraid she would give herself away if she tried to follow a script. She wasn't exactly in shape for handling complicated instructions. Now I wasn't sure she could improvise a response to such a summary dismissal. I leaned into her silence.

'I can't leave, Matt,' she said.

'Sorry?'

'I can't.'

'Ah don't think you heard me. You *are* leaving.'

'No, Matt. No.'

'Come on! Get —'

The tape-recorder fed us a confusion of noise — rasping sounds, what could have been a chair falling, strange poppings.

'For Nagra read aggro,' Edek said.

'To hell with this,' Brian said.

He put his hand on the ignition. I gripped his wrist. Brian stared at me.

'He's givin' her a doin',' he said.

'Behave,' I said quietly. 'This is a war. It's not a skirmish. We'd do Melanie a lotta favours breakin' cover now. The cell door's open. Sh. Let's see if he walks in.'

We waited. I could hear Eddie Foley breathing directly behind me. The first clear sound that came back to us was of Melanie crying. Brian's look judged me hard.

'Come on, Melanie,' I said. 'If just one person turns up and defies their fear, we've got a chance.'

I was watching the house. Three children, two girls and a boy, had come out into the garden. They were playing what looked like an improvised game of tig, a way of touching one another, of learning one another without admitting that's what they were doing. Receding and approaching, running away and hoping to be caught, they were a beautiful innocence, human relationships at play. Behind them, the house seemed to me menacing, an adult corruption that was already threatening to thwart their lives. They did not know the inheritance the house was giving them, what lay at its heart, the continuing conflict between violence and hurt.

I stared at the sunny garden, the red tiled roof, the white walls, the shining windows. This was where we were, all right – a place where violence dressed nice, injustice wore legal robes, venom smiled sweetly, unnecessary suffering was ignored and hypocrisy was honoured. I thought of many of the people I had met this week. They lived here, too. And like polite house-guests, they wouldn't break the rules. Their continued residency depended on that conformity. To break the rules was to put yourself at hazard.

I realised that nobody I had met had been quite prepared to do that. They might have whispered the odd secret to me but they wouldn't stand up and risk themselves to challenge the lies of others. If we were to expose the truth of Matt Mason's life, Melanie was our last chance.

It was a strange thought. Here was a woman who had more reason than any of us for running and hiding. Life had battered her remorselessly. She had been used by men. She had been on drugs. She was hanging on to what remained of her sense of herself by her fingernails. Who could blame her if she had decided her only allegiance was to herself? It would take a lot of courage to do otherwise.

We were still waiting. When Matt Mason spoke, I understood that his long silence had been to give her time to compose herself.

'Okay? You ready now?'

There was another silence.

'No.'

I could have cheered. That one word was defencelessness refusing to be intimidated.

'Get up and get out of here.'

'No. I need to understand what happened to Meece. I feel as if my life's over.'

'Not yet it's not. But that can be arranged.'

On the wildness of that remark I heard the conversation swing in the direction we needed it to go. The weird experience of a helpless woman defying him had made Matt Mason careless. This didn't happen and, since it didn't happen, his reactions lost their judgment.

'I need to know about Meece,' Melanie said.

'You know about Meece. Everybody knew about Meece. He was a piece of shit. You know what he was up to. You were in it with him. Ye're lucky ye didn't join him. Thank *me* for that.'

Brian looked at me and raised his eyebrows. Eddie Foley

sighed behind me. The children were still playing in the garden.

'Meece? I'll tell you about Meece. What were ye doin' with him, anyway? You used to have a bit of class. Remember Dan Scoular? The love of your life? That was a man at least. Remember what I did for you? I brought you to my house. Ah let ye meet real people. Look at ye now. Listen. You want to mourn for somebody, mourn for Dan Scoular. He's dead, too.'

I assumed that Melanie's distraught state would conceal the fact that the information came as no surprise.

'You know who killed him? Meece. The demon driver. That's right. It's not him you should mourn for. He took out as real a man as I've met. Just for the money. Only the wages weren't enough, were they? He's got to give himself a regular bonus. He thinks he's too important now. He's got a hold on us. A special case. He was a special case, all right. So I put him in one. Wooden.'

The only sound for a time was Melanie crying. The shock of what Matt Mason had told her must have been severe. He wasn't finished.

'So now you know.'

A matronly woman appeared at the French windows, drinking a cup of tea and watching the children.

'You're lucky to be alive. Ever say anything about this and you won't be.'

The conjunction of the homeliness of what we were seeing and the savagery of what we were hearing was hard to bear. I heard Eddie Foley gasp faintly and I realised that the woman was Millie, his wife. It was as if she were standing unaware in the crossfire of contradictions that were his life.

'Who would believe you, anyway? Hophead. Get out.'

There were sounds of movement, of breathing. The stillness in the car was total. We saw Melanie appear at the end of the driveway. She was walking blind. The machine went dead. I looked round at Edek. He made a wiping gesture with his hand. He had decided her tears were private. I was glad she had remembered to turn left out of the driveway. Bob Lilley would be waiting for her round the corner. She went out of sight. The children were still playing in the garden.

'Nice man,' Edek said.

'I think it's a good idea for Melanie to leave the country,' Brian said. 'Mason might get nervous about what he's said.'

'He won't have time to,' I said.

I turned round to look at Eddie Foley. He was pale.

'A woman as brave as that deserves to be protected,' I said. 'Some woman, eh?'

Eddie Foley stared at me. He nodded infinitesimally. I took it as thunderous applause.

'What, we going in for him now?' Brian said.

'No,' I said. 'We keep to the arrangement. We go to the Getaway.'

Brian drove. Once we were well into the city again, Eddie touched me lightly on the shoulder.

'Pull in anywhere here, Brian,' I said. 'We'll let Eddie off.'

I got out of the car with Eddie and we walked a few yards away. We stopped. I waited.

'So what is it you want from me?' Eddie said.

'You know what I want, Eddie. Matt Mason's just put himself in the nick. You heard him do it. There's nothing you can do for him. But you saw Millie. She was enjoying the view. Though her view is a bit restricted. You don't want to open her eyes too wide, do you? You can maybe still convince her you were a dupe.'

'What price?'

'Somebody else has to go inside with Matt Mason. We know Meece Rooney killed Dan Scoular. Who killed Meece Rooney?'

'There were two of them,' he said.

He looked along the street. He was taking his farewell of what he had been.

'Tommy Brogan and Chuck Walker.'

Both were known. He looked into my face. I nodded. He turned away. He became just a part of the busy street.

36

Bob Lilley was standing outside the Getaway when we arrived. The three of us came out of the car. Edek had his recording equipment in a leather shoulder-bag.

'Melanie's inside,' Bob said. 'So it was good?'

'She was good,' I said. 'The rest just followed.'

'So?' Bob said.

'So,' I said. 'Brian knows the score. You and him can go and get the clearance. And we will proceed in a very direct direction. Tommy Brogan. Chuck Walker. Matt Mason last. You've got to build the cage before you catch the tiger. Okay, Brian?'

'We'll get back-up, Jack,' Brian said.

'Sure. But you and Bob should make the pinches. It's your case. You do it yourselves. I just want to be there.'

'We've really got them?' Bob said.

'Well,' I said. 'It does look slightly promising.'

Edek and I came into the Getaway. The place was quite busy, mainly with young people. It was good to be reminded that other things were happening besides my preoccupations. While we were looking round, a voice spoke behind me.

'What are you doing here at this time? It's hardly your scene.'

It was Ricky, mine altruistic host.

'They let me out the Eventide Home for the day,' I said.

'Marty's over in the corner.'

'You do us a favour, Ricky?' I said. I gave him a tenner. 'You get somebody behind the bar to bring us a pint of Eighty, a whisky and water, a gin and tonic and whatever Marty's drinking? And one for yourself.'

'You want table service now?'

'Just this once, Ricky. And a drink for whoever brings them over?'

'I'll put it to the committee.'

Marty was brooding over a whisky that was dark enough to be a Jack Daniels. None of the young people had claimed the seats at his table, perhaps because the battered authority of his presence discouraged them. With his rough face and the eccentric pony-tail, he looked like somebody who had come to his own terms with experience and might act unpredictably out of them. We sat down with him.

'How's Melanie?' I said.

'Not so good,' Marty said. 'She's in the toilet. Doin' repair work. She had a bad time?'

'Threats were made. But they won't be carried out.'

'Ah hope not.'

'Melanie's going one place, Marty,' I said. 'Matt Mason's going another. Never the twain shall meet.'

'Ah don't know. Malice can wait a while. An' it's got long arms. You're goin' to have to use the tape.'

'Maybe not. We'll see.'

A young man arrived with the drinks. While we were sorting them out, Melanie came out of the toilet. She was dressed in her jeans and jacket again. She was carrying a couple of plastic bags which she offered to Edek. The small plastic bag contained Edek's microphone and transmitter, which he put in his leather shoulder-bag. I took the larger plastic bag and looked inside. It contained the dress and the coat.

'Why not keep these?' I said.

'What?'

'You looked good in them. You like them?'

'Yes. They felt good to wear.'

'Then keep them. They might remind you of the day you did something really brave. Said, to hell with being a victim.'

Edek looked at me.

'I'll pay,' I said.

'Not out of police funds,' Melanie said.

'Out of the pocket, Melanie,' I said. 'It's not a bribe. It's a gift. Personal. All right?'

She smiled and nodded. Taking the bag back, she put it on the floor beside her chair. There came a brief, good time like a furlough from the front. Melanie was just about due to go for her flight and the excitement of where she was going softened the bleakness of where she had been. In spite of herself, she became animated. It was good to see. Marty's worries for her seemed to relax. She said she was glad to have confronted Matt Mason and to know the truth of the recent past. It might make the future less haunted. When Marty gently chivvied her about catching the flight, I saw, as she glanced round the room, a glimpsed fragment of the girl she must have been – interested in everything, nervous as a thoroughbred mare. We all stood up with her. We said our goodbyes. She embraced me.

'You're some Melanie McHarg,' I said. 'You did it all. The rest of us have just been on the sidelines. Good luck.'

'The odds are against me, aren't they?'

'The odds are against us all. So what?'

Then she said a nice thing to me. It was about time somebody did.

'Why weren't you the first policeman I ever met?' she said. 'It might have made a difference.'

I found an envelope in my pocket and wrote my name and number on it. I tore off the piece of paper and gave it to her.

'You're in trouble,' I said, 'you ring. Over there or back here. If it's just talk you need, we'll talk. If things are getting heavy, we know ways to get heavier. Don't be afraid.'

'An' what about me?' Marty said.

'If you could just learn to behave yourself, Marty, you would do us all a favour.'

He pouted a kiss at me.

'While Ah'm waitin' for you, Jack. I will. I promise.'

As they were leaving, Edek looked at me. He nodded towards Marty.

'Does that mean what Ah think it means?'

'I don't think he was serious.'

'Ah know, Ah know. But –'

'Yes. That's Marty's tendency. He just deals with it on his own terms. The way he does with everything else. Anyway, who stole your scone? You've been very quiet. What are you thinking?'

'I'm thinking,' Edek said, 'that I'm glad I'm a sound recordist.'

'Explain the mystery of your utterance, wise man,' I said.

'I'll explain all right,' Edek said. 'You're going to do

yourself in, Jack. That stuff at that house today. You think you can handle that and stay yourself? No chance. Ah don't even want to go near it. I want to do my job and have a pint and be with Jacqueline. Maybe climb the odd Munro at the weekend. You ever tried hill-climbing? You should. Each Munro is over three thousand feet. That's high enough for me. You like risk too much.'

'What's the risk?'

'The risk is to you. You're spending your life in a contagious diseases unit without inoculation. What have you got in your life to counteract the bad things you live among? No marriage. No structure to your life. Why do you do it?'

I began to wonder if he had been talking to Jan. I was glad that Bob and Brian came in.

'Officialdom is with us,' Bob said. 'Shall we go?'

I nodded. Edek was still looking worried about me as we left. I didn't realise I was about to find out why.

37

Oedipus lives. I had spent a week demanding that the malefactors come forward and show themselves. I hadn't thought that I might be one of them.

Brian Harkness had an address for Tommy Brogan and one for Chuck Walker. But Chuck Walker might be a problem. He was a younger man, in his thirties, and where he was on a Saturday afternoon could be a lot of places. He might be at the football. He liked gambling. He might be with one of the women who had discovered the expertly concealed secret of his attractiveness. He had been involved with many women, usually briefly. I had wondered about that. I had sometimes thought that his girlfriends had all been determined to prove once and for all that romantic love really doesn't exist, so that they could get on sensibly with their lives. If that was what they wanted to learn, they had come to the right teacher.

'I've put Macey on him,' Brian said in the car. 'If he can find him, he's going to phone in with the word. I hope it's not to tell us he's part of a football crowd.'

'That would be all right,' Bob said. 'He would be in the stand. These days, Chuck sees himself as above the terracing.'

'Right enough,' Brian said. 'Macey's word is that he's

involved with a high-tone woman. He'll be drinking daiquiris next.'

'In a pint dish,' Bob said.

'Then I hope he's had a few by the time we get to him. Might make him easier to handle. I don't fancy one to one with him.'

'We've got the two back-up cars.'

'That's right. If one car just stuns him, we can always knock him out with the other one.'

Tommy Brogan should be easier to locate. He had the social life of a leopard. Wanting only the company of his nearest and dearest, he lived alone. He had been briefly married but announced his equivalent of a Muslim divorce suddenly one night in a pub by dismantling a man who spoke to his wife: 'I batter thee, I batter thee, I batter thee.' His wife's punishment was to be banned from his company forever, which was a bit like exiling someone to the Riviera.

His was one of the bleakest spirits I had so far met. He had done some boxing at one time and something in him was still waiting for the final bell. The staple diet of his life was keeping his body fit. A treat would be using it against someone else. I remembered Frankie White telling me that he had trained Dan Scoular. That must have been a strange convergence for the big man: welcome to the planet Mars.

He lived on the way out to Rutherglen. We put a car at each end of the street before we drew up at the door. It was a reconditioned tenement but the street door still opened without mechanical control. One floor up, the nameplate said 'Brogan', nothing else, as if telling the world not to get personal. Bob Lilley knocked at the door. The footsteps that came towards it were light. He opened up and took in the three of us, face by face.

'If it's for the Policemen's Fund,' he said, 'Ah gave.'

'Can we come in?' Bob said

'Well, Ah don't know anybody that's found a way to stop your lot from doin' that yet.'

He walked along the hall into the living-room. We closed the door and followed him. He was in his stockinged feet. I was surprised again at how comparatively small he was. His reputation exuded size. Seen now, he was quite small and neat, like a frame on film before it is projected. The projector was his preparedness for violence.

He stood in the middle of the floor and looked at us. I saw him in his habitat. It was a very tidy room. The newspapers were in the elasticated newspaper-rack. The glass coffee-table had nothing on it. On the sideboard there was one large, framed photograph of an elderly woman. I assumed it was his mother. It was certainly someone who would never speak to strange men in pubs. It was a room where nothing would happen except what he decided, until today. The television, which he had perhaps turned down before he came to the door, was showing sports results. It broadcast a routine that was no longer audible.

'Yes?' Tommy Brogan said into the silence.

'We're here to arrest you for murder, Tommy,' Bob said and gave him the official caution, word perfect.

Tommy Brogan looked at the television as if he was checking an especially interesting result. He looked at Bob.

'Ye wouldn't happen to have the name of the murderee on ye, would ye?'

'Meece Rooney,' Bob said.

'Meece Rooney? What kinda name is that?'

'Put your shoes on,' Bob said.

'This is crap,' Tommy Brogan said. 'Ah don't even know the man.'

'We'll show you photos,' Bob said. 'Get ready, Tommy.'

'Who told ye this?'

'We just know.'

'No. You don't know. Because it never happened. Ye're makin' a bad mistake here. Ye'll finish up lookin' pretty pathetic.'

'Not quite as pathetic as Meece. Come on.'

'Well, it's your funeral. Ah'll come with ye.'

'That's nice,' Bob said.

Tommy Brogan made as if to move and then paused. He assessed the three of us. He seemed to be making a decision. His look to me was saying something like, 'If it wis just one against three, Ah would win. But there's more of ye out there, isn't there?' The moment tremored on a dangerous silence. He stirred and crossed the floor and sat down to put on his shoes. The unfulfilled possibility he left behind him opened a chasm in my preconceived sense of things. It was a dizzying prospect. I would have thought there was no choice but to come with us. But he had, however briefly, imagined an alternative. In that realisation I glimpsed the terrible logic of his life. Faced with nothingness like stone, he was always tempted to paint on it in blood the violent shape of his will.

When he went through to the bedroom to get ready, Brian went with him. Bob and I looked at each other. I walked about the room.

I was angry. The anger came from a disproportion between the offence and the reparation. This was all? Those wilfully damaged lives, those invented deaths were to be paid for so casually. A small, unfeeling man would put on his shoes and jacket and be chauffeured to jail. In his indifference to what he had done, he enraged me even more than he had in the doing of it. This wasn't enough. Something more, a black angel whispered in me. I hoped he came out of the bedroom fighting. But he walked calmly back into the room wearing a sports jacket, with Brian after him. He went to the television and switched it off and turned and smiled at us. The bright images of a football game fused into black behind him. As casually as he had darkened the lives of others, he would accept the darkening of his own. I understood he was in prison already. What more could we do to him but exchange one cell for another? Perhaps there are those who cannot be punished more because they are their own punishment.

The message from Macey was that Chuck Walker was in a bar with the sophisticated woman. Macey would be waiting outside. He had told us where to meet him. Driving there, with Tommy Brogan handcuffed in one of the cars behind us, I barely noticed the day. The sense of anti-climax in me was like inertia. The unexpected reawakened me.

Macey wasn't there. The three of us got out of the car to look around. Bob went and told the other policemen to stay in their cars. While Brian and Bob and I were standing in the busy street wondering what to do next, Brian suddenly said, 'There he's!'

I thought he meant Macey. Some distance away I saw Macey's sharply dressed figure signalling to us among the people. It was a few seconds later that I noticed what Macey's signals meant. Chuck Walker was in the street with a tall, blonde woman. They were an interesting couple, the lady and the rottweiler. They were nearer to us than Macey was. They were coming towards us. Even as we saw him, he saw something else.

It must have been an amazing image for him, like glancing sideways in a mirror and seeing a skeleton's head. He had already passed the first police car when he looked casually into the second and saw Tommy Brogan in the back. Then he saw us over the heads of the crowds in the street. He spun and noticed the other car. He turned back towards us and then he wasn't there. There were the people jostling in the street and there was the woman among them, still unaware of the suddenness with which relationships can end. Seeking to avoid bumping the passers-by, she was holding up the expensive plastic bag, which presumably contained something they had shopped for – instant memento.

We were trying to force our way through the mob and the other policemen had come out of the cars and there was no sign of him. We were separated and moving around aimlessly when I looked through the window of a café. I saw the man behind the counter looking around him. Something had happened he didn't understand. I went in. The place was busy and some of the people at the tables had the same ruffled appearance as the owner, as if a sudden wind had blown through the place. I stared at the owner. He was frightened. He looked towards his back shop.

As I went through there, I heard the sound of a door being kicked open. Locating the sound, I saw the outline of Chuck

Walker. His shoulders almost filled the doorway. He had his back towards me. Ahead of him was nothing but high wall. As he turned back, I thought I might just live long enough to regret that all he had had in front of him was wall.

As he rushed me, his body filled my vision. I knew what I wanted to do but that isn't always a great help. The punch I tried to throw was deflected like a gnat. He hit me in the stomach and then something, his fist or his forearm or his elbow, jarred into my neck. I fell through the doorway back into the space behind the counter. He was on top of me and he had a knife. I stayed very still. I saw the mole on his cheek. I saw the gargoyle malevolence of his face, the eyes lit eerily as if a torch were under them.

'You're ma hostage, polis,' he said. 'If they don't let me pass, you're dead.'

For a moment I agreed. I could see my name in the obituary column. He trailed me to my feet and, as he did so, I jabbed my index finger and my forefinger in his face, one for each eye. Stumbling, he hit his hand on the hot-plate, where an abandoned egg was crisping. The knife fell. I kicked him in the balls. His body buckled. His head happened to be about six inches from the hot-plate when I caught it. I held it there. If my hands could feel the heat, his face must have been scorching.

I had thought I was hunting evil. I had tracked the quarry down and found me. The café, the place where people eat and chat, volleyed away from me. I felt it disappear, sucked into darkness, and I was alone with my rage, and with my hands on a man who stood for an almost total contempt for other people. In that moment I hated him in a way that frightens me still. There was nothing he could do to me now but I still held him there. I felt what I can hardly believe I felt. I said what I am ashamed to have said.

'Do you want fried face?' I said.

He felt the seriousness of the offer. And he screamed. I was near in myself to what I had loathed in others. His animal terror broke down into garbled speech, the plea to be human.

'It was Brogan,' he was saying. 'Tommy Brogan. Did it. He did it. Not me. Not me. He did it for Mason. Ah was just there. Ah'll tell you. Ah'll tell you.'

'Not enough,' I shouted.

'Jack!'

It was Brian Harkness. The café came back. The other policemen were with him. People were standing at their tables, staring at me. A woman was hiding her small son's face. Brian pulled me away and Bob Lilley put handcuffs on Chuck Walker. I suddenly saw the separateness of Chuck Walker's enormous hands, enclosed together in the metal, like a predator in a glass case. It was glass in which I could see my own reflection. As we came out, I felt it was like one of those occasions you see memorialised in newspaper photographs, when they're leading the criminal to the car. But the way people were looking at me, I was the one who should have had the coat over his head. With Chuck Walker stowed in the second car, we stood in the street.

'I wouldn't have done it,' I said.

I was talking to myself.

'No,' Brian said.

Bob didn't say anything.

'Anyway, let's go, Jack,' Brian said.

'No,' I said. 'You two get Mason on your own.'

'What? Jack.' Bob wasn't taking me seriously. 'Behave. You've got to complete the circle.'

'There's circles inside circles,' I said. 'I've got another one to complete. There's a man I have to see. Brian, you do me a favour? When you've sorted this out, you dump my stuff at the flat? The bag's in the boot. And there's an ashtray I bought. And don't forget what's left of the Antiquary. I might need it. Oh, and a couple of paintings.'

I gave him my spare keys to the flat. That was what made them accept that I wasn't coming with them.

'When'll we see you?' Bob said.

'Monday at the latest.'

'What about tonight?' Brian said.

'Maybe. We'll see. Good luck. When you're lifting Matt Mason, make sure you don't drop him.'

'You watch yourself, you,' Bob said.

They went into the car. I walked for a little, a very little, till I found the first bar. I took two whiskies fast, waiting to see if they would remind me of who I was. I felt strange to myself. I was still hollow with anger. I sat staring ahead and talking to no one and smoking and trying to calm myself. I came out of the pub and went by a very roundabout route to Michael Preston's flat. But by the time I arrived I wasn't significantly quieter. The flat had its own door to the street. It was a woman who opened it.

'Jack?' she said.

'That's right.'

'I'm Bev.'

The accent was Australian. We shook hands. She preceded

me up the stairs. She moved well. Michael Preston appeared in the hallway at the top. He shook hands with me.

'Jack and I'll talk in the study, Bev,' he said.

'He always hides the good-looking men from me,' she said.

'I must be the exception that proves the rule,' I said.

He took me into his study and closed the door.

38

The story of the fox in the tunic has haunted me since schooldays. I can't remember which teacher told me it. But some forgotten day in some forgotten classroom, an adult casually told a boy a story, perhaps as incidental illustration of some more important matter, and the moment went into the boy's mind clean as a knife and left a scar there. The scar may have healed into a fairly wilful shape, as scars will, but this is how I remember its origins.

In Sparta, if I can trust that teacher, it was all right to steal. The crime was in being found out. A Spartan boy one day stole a fox. He hid it in his tunic. I wouldn't mind going back now as an adult and asking that anonymous teacher a couple of questions. He stole a fox? He hid it in his tunic? I assume foxes were wild even then, so maybe he stole it from someone else's land. Maybe what he did was poach it. But it must have been either a very small fox or a very large tunic. Perhaps it was a baby fox. I don't recall.

What I do recall is the impact of what followed. On his way home, the boy met a family friend who detained him in conversation. I've often wondered what they talked about — perhaps the price of sandals. As they passed the time, maintaining the social niceties, the fox began to eat the boy's stomach. Not only did he avoid saying, 'Wait a minute. I've got a problem here'. He also managed to keep his face so composed that his friend had no idea of what was happening to him. They talked. They parted. By the time the boy came home and could acknowledge what was going on behind his public image, it was too late. His very entrails had gone public. He died. He became, it seems, a kind of Spartan hero, representing the ideals of their society. Some society.

I don't think that was so heroic. It was formidably tough, all right. But I think he would have come closer to heroism if he had breached the accepted rules. I don't think the boy should have said, 'That's right' and 'Yes' and 'Really?' No wonder the Spartans gave us the word laconic. I think the boy should have said, 'Listen. I don't want to talk about this shit. There's a fox eating my guts away. All right, so I stole the bastard. Do what the hell you want. But I'm not having this.' Something like that.

For me as a boy the story was first of all simply a stunning event. It left my mind gaping. Subsequently, more meaning gathered around it in my head. The shock of disbelief became a slow sense of recognition. I thought I saw in the behaviour of the Spartan boy a metaphor for how we live. I realised that it wasn't just in Sparta that people smile and nod and talk trivialities while their self is unseaming. It was what we were all taught to do. Certainly, in Scotland, I decided, a lot of us had evolved social conventions so cryptic they almost amounted to mime and must be sustained, no matter what tragic opera was unfolding in the head.

I had come to think that the story had stayed with me so

determinedly because it contained this central significance. After talking to Michael Preston, I began superstitiously to wonder if there was another reason why that anecdote from an old culture had claimed my attention beyond rationality. For it was the story of my brother's life. It had lain about my awareness for many years, patiently, as if it knew its purpose and I didn't. Then, suddenly, in the small, comfortable study of a spacious, attractive flat early on a Saturday evening, I looked at it again, that familiar hieroglyph, and saw in it the features of my brother's face.

The realisation brought a terrible stillness to me. I had knocked at all those doors and at last one had opened and brought me to a place from which I did not know how to go on. Michael Preston sat and told me what I had become so desperate to know. I had looked into so many blank faces, listened to so many unhelpful voices that I went to him ready to force my way past his defences. Instead, he simply invited me into the truth. Once there, I wasn't so sure it was where I wanted to be.

Discovery is not merely knowledge, it is obligation. I had decided that, sitting in the Red Lion in Thornbank. It came back to haunt me in the West End of Glasgow. I had gone into Michael Preston's room with eyes like weapons. I came out with eyes like wounds. I strode towards his flat. But I wandered away from it. The streets I had known most of my life were strange.

Since I didn't know what was to be done, it didn't matter what I did. I walked. I went into pubs. I observed the bizarre purposefulness with which other people moved and talked. I saw a man in passionate conversation with his friend and then, going to the bar, heard that he was discussing the ridiculous price he had been charged for garage repairs. I watched a woman watch herself in the mirror as she chatted. I went to several places. I drank a lot. I wandered through the evening like a wraith, feeling substanceless.

Only my head was rabidly alive. I had to think that Scott had probably committed a kind of suicide – not through a deliberate, conscious act but through a deliberate carelessness that was inviting the worst thing to happen. I could imagine he had lived so long with the fox that he couldn't take the pain any more. He, too, had died of a guilt he couldn't declare.

The anger I had set out with this week had found so much to feed on. I remembered talking to Jan at Lock 27 about Scott's funeral. I had thought that was anger? Look at me now. My anger had grown on Dave Lyons and Sandy Blake and Michael Preston. And Anna. I remembered my feeling in the car after talking to the stranger outside Scott's old house. Muzzle the dog, I had said to myself. How did you muzzle this one? That had been a chihuahua. This was a Great Dane. I felt such rage.

But that day in the car I had also told myself that my rage had to find an address to which to go. Now I knew it never could. For it was a rage not just against certain people, Chuck Walker or myself, but against the terms on which we have agreed to live. My quarrel was with all of us. Where did you go to deliver that one?

I went anywhere my feet took me. One of the places must have been the Chip, for I have a memory of talking to Edek and Jacqueline and Naima Akhbar. I have not much memory of what was said. I remember the concern on Naima's sweet face. I think she told me a Muslim saying that was supposed to help too, But it couldn't have worked because I have forgotten it. I'm left with an impression of many people jostling as we drank, as if someone had installed a gantry in a football crowd. And then I was outside again.

Why I did what I did next, I don't know. I went to the party in Jan's restaurant. A less likely party-guest than I was at that moment it would be hard to imagine. I was drunk but it was an odd, dislocated drunkenness. Some cold, bleak part of me was watching the meanderings of the drunken part, like a sober man who is too weary and indifferent to help his befuddled friend and can only look on as he stumbles into places that he shouldn't go. I think perhaps I was trying to reconnect with the city, where I felt like an alien, by plugging into the energy of others as if it were a generator.

There was certainly plenty of energy at Jan's place. The party was going well. Music was playing. Some people were dancing. Talk was loud and laughter louder. In the midst of these festivities I suddenly appeared, girt in rough thoughts, like John the Baptist at a disco. Someone had left the restaurant door unlocked. As soon as I entered, Betsy clocked me and her face had an attack of dyspepsia. She came across at once and bolted the door – securing the locks once the burglar is in. Then she went to tell Jan, who was talking to Barry Murdoch. Barry had one arm round Jan's shoulder. I reckoned from the way Betsy was speaking to Jan that she wasn't bringing her the good news. She was warning her of impending trouble. I saw Barry scan the room until he found me. He gave me the long, macho stare. It was like looking down the barrel of a pop gun. Jan came across.

'Are you all right?' she said.

'What's all right?' I said.

'Uh-huh. I see. It's one of your metaphysical nights. Well, we're just trying to have a party.'

'Let the party proceed,' I said grandly.

'Oh, thank you. Will that be all right? Listen, Jack. You're welcome here if you can behave yourself. But I'm not having any trouble.'

'Could Ah talk to you, Jan? About Scott?'

'Jack. You ever heard of timing? Enjoy. If you can. I'll maybe see you later.'

She went off to mingle. Unable to have what I needed, I made for what I needed least of all – another drink. It was white wine I thought wouldn't have been out of place in a vinegar bottle.

'The champagne's finished,' someone told me.

'It is, it is,' I said darkly.

That opaque exchange, as if we were speaking different languages, crystallised how alien I was to the others. I wasn't part of the occasion. I was something unnecessary that had been added, a quibbling footnote to the text of their enjoyment. I wandered about the place, wilfully editing their pleasure into the significance it had for me.

If I had been them, I would have thrown me out. It would have saved us all embarrassment. People were talking loudly to one another. They were being pleasant enough. But I heard them talking about house prices and cars and business-deals and I decided that this wasn't a party. It was an auction. I saw the flower-pot of money that had attacked me. I managed to be polite in refusing a woman's offer to dance. If she wanted me as a partner, I wasn't the only one who might be well advised to go easy on the drink.

I took another glass of wine as the night suddenly caved in on me. I couldn't reconcile this convention of the terminally self-satisfied with the bleak world I had been wandering through outside. Davy's idea about the pyramids came back to me – all those wasted lives to construct a false, exclusive certainty, a habitat for wilful egos. I thought of Scott and Mrs White and Dan Scoular and Julian and Marlene in Drumchapel and Melanie McHarg. Somehow, I wanted a way to invite them to the party. Unfortunately, in my confused sense of things, I found it.

There was a wild logic to my madness. I decided that I wouldn't pick a fight with Barry Murdoch. I stopped myself from haranguing a group who were explaining to one another how the poor create their own problems. With great difficulty, I refrained from demanding that Jan talk to me about Scott. Yet these minor triumphs of comparative wisdom only led me relentlessly to an absolute folly, a way to offend in one move every single person at the party.

I don't know where my inspiration came from. But I suddenly found myself wrestling with my arch foe, the pot of money. Those closest to me were nonplussed at first and then amused. I suppose they thought they were witnessing one of those impromptu moments of cabaret that can happen at a party – the drunk woman's dance on the table, the man who decides he can balance a bottle on his forehead. Drunkenness can give you surprising strength, just as rage can. I had both of them on my team at that time. I managed to lift the pot off the floor, to a spattering of derisive applause. As I made my way across the restaurant with it, legs splayed, struggling, people parted to let me pass. I had become an interesting curiosity. Was this my party piece? Was this what I did to get attention, being unable to say something witty or arresting? Perhaps it was. By the time I was standing facing them from behind the table where the food was, the room had gone silent. People were watching me, some with amusement, some in puzzled expectation. They possibly thought I was about to dedicate the money to a favourite charity. I suspect some of them believed it was a pre-arranged event. They seemed to be waiting for a formal speech. It was a short one.

'You bastards!' I shouted. 'Eat money. It's all you can fucking taste.'

I decanted the money carefully into the biggest Boeuf Bourgignon in the world. As I did so, I shook the pot meticulously along the full length of the dish, as if to make sure the ingredients were properly mixed. The coins rasped against the inside of the pot to shower on to the stew and submerge in it, instantly indistinguishable from the food. The notes fluttered and settled on the surface like some novel topping of yuppy haute cuisine. I stood looking at them, holding the charity pot that contained nothing but verdigris.

Into a vacuum of astonishment rushed a hubbub of shock. I was confronting a hydra of contorted faces. Voices bayed outrage at me. Five or six men, Barry Murdoch among them, started towards me. I wanted them to come ahead. The first one to reach me would be wearing a metal flowerpot for a hat.

'Stop this!'

The stridency of the voice froze the room.

'This stops now!'

The voice was Jan's. Everybody waited, held in their poses.

'Nobody will touch that man. Nobody. Jack, you leave now. Leave!'

I set down the flowerpot, which was as empty as my sense of myself.

'Betsy. Let him out. And nobody touch him. Don't dare.'

I passed through them like somebody walking among statues. Betsy let me out and locked the door behind me. I stood on the cobblestones of the alleyway in the soft rain. And drunkenness, like a false friend who was only there for the wild times, deserted me at once. I felt I had nowhere to go. I felt I had no one to be. I seemed to have consumed myself in my own grand gesture. I stood in a void and was simply a part of it. The rain was more real than I was.

'Jack.'

It took me some time to locate the voice. It was Jan, standing on her balcony. No place was ever further away or less attainable than that balcony. Once she knew I was seeing her, she threw something down to me. My hands reached out automatically and caught it. It was a plastic bag. It didn't weigh much.

Romeo in middle age: you won't have to climb up to the balcony, which is maybe just as well. Juliet will stand there and fire down at you whatever you need, and even what you don't need.

'Just in case,' she said, 'you ever imagine you've got a reason for coming back here.'

She went into the flat. I looked in the bag. There were some of my clothes there. Maybe they were telling me who I was – Tom Docherty's iron rations of the self. They brought me back from the disorientated wildness of what my mood had been, reminded me that living is a matter of small practicalities. Postures solve nothing. Action, not movement. It was necessary to re-engage with the small practicalities. I decided on the first one.

Taxi-time.

SEVEN

39

And on the seventh day I rested. It's exhausting trying to remake the world in your own image.

As I let myself into the flat, carrying my little parcel of rejection from Jan, the phone was ringing. Moving hurriedly through the darkness, I stumbled on something and cursed it. It hadn't been there when I left. Had the furniture been mating in my absence? I lifted the phone.

'Where are you?'

It was a good question. I would have to give it some thought.

'We're having a slight gay-and-hearty here. You should be the guest of honour.'

It was Brian Harkness. He sounded like a town-crier. I had to hold the ear-piece side-on to my head. There was the sound of merriment in the background.

'Jack? Is that you? What are you doing there? We're in the Getaway. Behind closed doors. A mob of us. Marty was great tonight. They're all asking for you. That doesn't happen often. You should cash in on it while it lasts. Get over here. We've done it, we've done it. Mason, Brogan and Walker. How's that for a half-back line? Signed, sealed and delivered.'

'That's good.'

'Matt Mason still hasn't believed it, I don't think. You should have seen his face. When we were bringing him out, he looked as if he'd never seen a street before. As if he didn't recognise where he lived.'

I thought of Betty Scoular staring out of her doorway. Matt Mason had earned his alienation from himself.

'So are ye comin'? Even Big Ernie Milligan's here.'

'That's a good enough reason for stayin' away. I'm having my own wee ceremony here, Brian. Thanks all the same.'

'Ah can imagine that. Come on, Jack. Get outa there.'

'Not tonight. I'm tired.'

'Well, listen. That meal's still on. This week. Morag says you have been warned. No excuses will be accepted.'

'No excuses will be made. I'm looking forward to that.'

'Bob and Margaret as well. We'll have a night. Listen. Jack. Are you all right?'

'How do you mean?'

'I mean, you've laid the ghost?'

'Oh, I think so. I'm not sure where I've laid it, right enough. But I've laid it somewhere.'

'No more trips to funny places? I mean, I need the car.'

'I'll see you on Monday.'

'Okay. Take care.'

'Enjoy.'

'Oh, Jack. Bob Lilley says you're the best. You could cobble a solution out of anything.'

But the cobbler's children, they say, are always the worst shod. I couldn't solve the problems of my own life. When I put on the light, I saw that I had tripped over my travelling-bag. I hadn't thanked Brian for delivering it. Scott's two paintings were leaning against a wall. The Antiquary, sadly diminished, stood on the sideboard along with the green ashtray from David Ewart's workshop.

I would have liked to give him Michael Preston's version of how idealism died. I felt I owed it to him. But then it was the story of a criminal act. Some of those involved in it were still alive. If I told David Ewart, it would have to be an anonymous account, with names omitted to protect the guilty.

At least later today I could phone Betty Scoular. Dan Scoular's death was going to be paid for. That might help her to let the grave settle and go on to wherever her life was taking her. I hoped so. This place needed women like her at full strength, not debilitated by the unjust wounds that had been inflicted on them. I might also phone Fast Frankie White. At the moment he deserved to have whatever fragile peace of mind his nomadic sense of himself was capable of. I hoped his mother was finding a painless way to go. I could still feel the echo of her gentle, dying hand in mine. I wished Melanie well. At least we shouldn't have to use the tape.

I drew the curtains. The place looked slightly less bleak that way. It didn't change my mood but it put a blindfold on my loneliness, so that it had nothing to compare itself with. I opened the plastic bag Jan had given me. Two shirts came out, then two pairs of underpants, then three socks. They were unwashed. I could imagine her wrenching them from the laundry-basket in her anger. I smiled wryly to think of that one buried, subversive sock. Parting is never easy. Something of the other will remain against your will. But, in this case, not for long, I could imagine. There was still something that weighed lightly in the plastic bag. I reached in and brought out a packet of cigarettes. I opened it. There were three cigarettes inside. In the pettiness of the gesture I saw the finality of her dismissal. Maybe she would fumigate the place to complete the process.

It was cold. I put on the gas fire. I unzipped my travelling-bag and put away such clothes as weren't to be washed. Then I took what was for washing and put it in the washing machine. For some sentimental reason I did not care to examine, I included the odd sock. I suspect I was imagining myself as some embarrassing variant of Prince Charming. If I were ever again to match it up with its neighbour, I would be with my own true love. No wonder I hid from my motivation. I took the washing powder from under the sink and filled the white plastic drawer. I closed the machine and started it up. The sudden noise in the stillness reminded me with a shock that we were in the early hours of Sunday morning. I switched the sound off at once, grimacing to myself. I stood in the kitchen and started to worry about what living alone was doing to me. Perhaps I would finish up existing inside a private time-scale of impulse and compulsion.

I went back through to the living-room to escape from the now-I-must-do-the-washing impulse and found another one waiting for me. I had to hang Scott's paintings. Home handyman not being one of my more impressive personas, it took me about twenty minutes to find a hammer. I took two picture-hooks from the bedroom where, on renting the flat, I had put up photographs of the children. I could repair their desecrated shrine when I bought more hooks. I hung the five at supper above the fire-place and 'Scotland' on the opposite wall, hammering furtively and intermittently.

The bottle of the Antiquary had two drinks left in it. I filled out one and watered it in the kitchen and came back through. It wasn't so cold now. I put my blazer over the back of a chair and sat down at the fire with my whisky. I took a sip and looked at the five men. Scott, Sandy Blake, Dave Lyons, Michael Preston. And the man who was still unidentified. Not even the colour of the coat was accurate.

'It was brown, as I remember it.'

Even our guilt we shape into our own needs. Scott had spent a long time shaping his. I confronted it at last.

'It was brown, as I remember it.'

Michael Preston's voice had brought home to me how even shared actions can separate us. His sense of what had happened that night after the impromptu party in the flat with David Ewart remained clear and it troubled him still but not as it had troubled Scott. I thought of Dave Lyons. Did anything trouble him? I thought of Sandy Blake in South Africa. Maybe for him guilt was geographical.

'We got drunk that night,' Michael Preston had said. 'It was a celebration, after all. Three of us were finishing up. Sandy still had some time to go. But he was saying goodbye to us. It was one of those nights when you're young and you feel the possibilities. Know what I mean? We went on a pub-crawl. I suppose we felt like the new aristocracy visiting the peasants. We all thought we had so much potential then. Our horizons seemed limitless. I remember saying not unportentously that I was going to write the house down. Scott was going to paint. Dave Lyons was going to do something of great scientific value. I don't know what Sandy was going to do. Maybe find the cure for cancer. All I've ever written are commentaries for television programmes that may have helped to pass the time in a few living-rooms, that died with the credits.'

He lifted the paper-weight and turned it and replaced it. We sat watching the imitation snow-storm fall gently on the miniature house. He stared at it till it had subsided.

'I sometimes think I might as well be living in that house,' he said. 'Hermetically sealed in my career. That night. I remember Scott warning us all against succumbing to the system. He had a dread of settling for too little. This was only a beginning, he was saying. It would all be meaningless unless we related it to what mattered, to where we came from. We were all from working-class backgrounds. The chance we had was held in trust for others, he said. Whatever talents we had belonged to the man in the street. Each of us had to find our own way to reconnect with him. Find him, bring whatever gifts we had to him, and he would teach us how to use them. Without him, what we had learned was useless. It was a good speech at the time.'

He ran his hand along some of the clip-binders filed on one of the shelves beside him. On the back of each was something written in felt pen. I assumed they were the titles of projects he had been involved in but I couldn't read them.

'Tell you the truth,' he said. 'I think it's still a good speech. These.' His forefinger played along the binders. 'These are Preston's Thesaurus. A personal dictionary of synonyms for futility. They make a long study of nothing. The longer I live, the more I think Scott was right that night. I wish I didn't.'

He looked at me and I thought I saw in his eyes how the depth of the wish was measured by its hopelessness.

'We came out of the pub that night,' he said. 'Thrown out of the last one at time-up. It was pissing with rain. Coming down in sheets. I think in our euphoria we were almost offended that the weather wouldn't match our mood. We doorway-hopped for a spell. We reaffirmed what we were going to achieve. Like a pact. We addressed the weather like King Lear. Telling it to behave itself. We didn't want the feeling we had made among us to stop. We were busking an end to the night that would match the grandeur we felt in it. Then, from some final doorway, somebody saw a car. I don't know who saw it first. All I remember is there we were talking about it. It was an old A40, pretty beat-up. It was parked across the street. There were no lights in the buildings around us.'

They decided to steal the car.

'It was a group decision, I suppose. I remember that my own clever contribution was to say, "Property is theft. Let's thieve it back." The idea was just to drive it close to the flat and leave it there. No harm done. Even if they traced us to the flat, we'd be off by tomorrow. It was just a joy-ride.'

Breaking in was easy. Dave Lyons connected the wires. They drove off. As he reached that point in his story, Michael Preston held his hand up, forestalling my question.

'We were all driving,' he said. 'Don't ask me to define it more closely than that. We were one group mood. The way it can get sometimes. All of us broke into the car. So all of us drove it. We accepted that among us afterwards. I still accept it. I know Scott did. Maybe one pair of hands on the wheel. But four intentions. There's no reneguing from that.'

He stared into my scepticism and didn't flinch. I saw the strength that had enabled him to live for so long with something he hated to live with. Wounds sometimes heal into hard places.

'I was there,' he said. 'I remember the shared madness. I think they call it hubris. That wasn't just a car to us. It was an ego-machine. That wasn't just a road. It was our road, where we were going, what we would become. We were all shouting instructions. Naming destinations. "Take us to our leader." "Next stop: the meaning of the world." "Drop me off at the next planet." "Self-fulfilment here we come." That kinda nonsense. The car was fogged with our lunacy. The rain hammering down outside didn't hear us. And then it happened. Jesus, I don't know where he came from. It seemed to me he reared up out of nowhere. He might as well have been born full grown in the headlights. It was as if he came out of the impact, not the other way around. He was a brief shape in the air. Like Icarus. Only difference is we were the arrogant bastards. It was him that took the fall. The car stopped. That's the loudest rain I've ever heard. Or ever want to hear. It was like living under a waterfall. One you know is never going to stop. You're going to live the rest of your life with the sound of it in your ears.'

He lifted the dagger that was his paper-knife and his face was so clenched and dark he might have been contemplating using it on himself. He sat still for a moment as if he was still listening to the rain. He looked at me.

'That was your man in the green coat,' he said. 'Except that it wasn't green. It was brown, as I remember it. But then maybe that was just the rain. He was lying mainly on the pave-ment. He was the stillest thing I'd ever seen. He was balding. Not a face you'd notice normally. One of those that make up the numbers. An extra in a thousand pub-scenes. Could've been anybody. He was lying with a terrifying awkwardness.

That's been the shape of a lot of my nightmares. Sandy Blake examined him. He wasn't dead. But he said that he was getting there. And no way would he live. We had found the man in the street all right. And it looked as if we had killed him.'

I have dreamed many times that I have murdered someone. Those are the most frightening dreams I have ever had. The terror, I think, comes from the sense of irrevocability. I am in a place from which it is impossible to go back. I have become someone I never wanted to be and I must be that person forever. Waking up with the sweats, I have experienced a feeling of immeasurable relief. I tried to imagine never wakening up.

'The only blood,' he said, 'was coming from under his head, where it had hit the road. We tried to argue with Sandy. But he said he was losing his heartbeat. We were shouting in whispers to each other. And the rain was drowning out everything. Terror, people talk of it loosely. That was terror. Imagine your life frozen in one long, long accidental moment. You have to move to unfreeze it. And you're too terrified to move. Because there are only two ways you can go. And both of them are badder than you ever imagined anything could be. You can take him in and he'll be dead already. And you'll be just drunken bastards who have killed a man with a car. Your lives are over before they properly got started. Or you can leave him there. And maybe nobody will ever know except yourselves. But the rest of your life is based on leaving an innocent man to lie dying in the rain. Nice choice we had made for ourselves. You fancy it?'

I didn't say anything. His bitter smile was just a scar across his face.

'We made our choice,' he said. 'Or panic made it for us.

The longer we stood, the more chance we would be found. And have no choice. Scott was crying. We more or less had to wrestle him into the car. We drove away. We left the man there. We left him there. We left him there. He's there still, I think, for all of us. Except poor Scott. He's erased that image at last. We abandoned the car somewhere and went back to the flat.'

He sat very still, staring straight ahead. His voice took on a dead quality, as if he were repeating a text he had learned painfully by heart.

'University,' he said. 'I don't know if you went there. I thought I had graduated earlier, that summer. But it was that night in the rain I really graduated. I found out who I was. And that I didn't like who I was. And that I never could. I mean, I had loved all that grappling with great minds. The moral questions. Then suddenly, in one night, the issues were real. We were living the questions. Seminars? Did we have a seminar that night. We talked into the light, though I don't know that we ever found it. Scott still wanted to go back. That we should give ourselves up. I felt like that myself. Dave and Sandy were against it. I couldn't see how I could live with this. I still don't see how I have. But I have. It was Dave who finally persuaded me that there was nothing else we could do but live with it. He said we had all acquired certain abilities. The most valid respect we could pay to the man we had killed was to fulfil those abilities. Anything else was anti-life. If we gave ourselves up, we were destroying ourselves for a moral convention. For what good could it do? It wouldn't bring back a dead man. It would simply waste our lives, bury such abilities as we had. A terrible, irreversible thing had happened. We could either sacrifice ourselves to no purpose. Or we could find the strength to live with it and fulfil our lives as best we could. I came to accept that. We were three against one. But we needed four. Scott couldn't implicate himself without implicating all of us. His conscience wasn't his own. It was all or none. That's when he wrecked his paintings and tore up his books. We let him do it. Because I think we knew what it meant. That he had given up on his self-belief. And would have to find out how to live without it. Which was what we needed.'

There was a knock at the door and Bev, his wife, looked in. As he saw her, the softness that suffused his face was striking. It was not an act of concealment, so that she wouldn't know the dark things he had been saying. It was a spontaneous admission of love.

'You two old wives,' she said. 'I've made some coffee.'

She brought in a tray with coffee and biscuits.

'I hope this one's not boring you,' she said to me.

'Never that,' I said.

As she put down the tray, his hand rested briefly on her hip. It was an instinctive expression of affection.

'Don't use up all your anecdotes,' she said to him. 'You've got the dinner-party.'

'I'll just steal some of yours,' he said.

'Then I'll tell the punchlines early.'

She went out. He nodded at the closed door.

'She's my life,' he said. 'She's got a spirit stronger than ten Sumo wrestlers. She knows about this. But she doesn't know I'm telling you about it. I'll tell her tomorrow. This dinner-party matters to her. Truth is, I wouldn't have been telling you. If Scott hadn't died. That's changed things for me.'

He pushed the biscuits towards me, sipped his coffee.

'Interesting, isn't it?' he said. 'The ambiguity of things. I can talk about the mockery that's my life and sip coffee at the same time. I can sit in my own guilt like an armchair. We're strange things. I sometimes think our lives are a contract with the impossible. If we're going to live together, we have to sign that contract. But most of us know we can't really meet its terms. So we insert our private clauses in small print. And don't mention it to anybody else. Only the best of us try to abide by the contract. And the attempt often destroys them. Like Scott. You take us four. When we left that room that morning. We had an agreement. But that was an unfair agreement. It obliged the best of us to abide by the terms of the worst. It denied Scott's nature. Which was to follow the honesty of his idealism to the bone. It was a death-sentence. We killed Scott as well as the other man. Think of it. I've thought of it. A lot I've thought of it. Dave would survive. What else would he do? It's all he was born for. Sandy? There are people who wander the world like dinosaurs. They don't know evolution happened. They eat, they sleep, they shit. When they get the chance, they copulate. If they manage to keep doing all of them, they don't know anything's wrong. That's Sandy. I don't resent him. I pity him. For myself, I think Bev saved my life. She's allowed me to believe in some part of myself that stayed decent. But Scott took the pain most, for all of us.' He looked at me. 'I'm sorry.'

He was right about the ambiguity of things. What do you do when you've heard the news that changes the significance of your life forever? You finish drinking your coffee. You don't make some profound statement that matches the enormity of what you've heard. You may ask a weird, tangential question, like an uncomprehending child wondering what colour the car was that has killed his father.

'Why do you think he dressed him in green?' I said. 'You said his coat was brown. Why would Scott do that?'

'I think I know,' he said. 'I should do. This has been my life's study in a way, hasn't it? The methodology of guilt. I've thought about how we've all handled it. We didn't exactly keep in touch. Who needs to stare their own hypocrisy in the face every day? Although I think Dave tried to stay close to Scott. He was monitoring him. In a chain of lies, honesty's always going to be the weak link. But that wasn't friendship. It was supervision.'

I thought of Dave Lyons' relationship with Anna. Had that begun as part of the supervision? I realised the riskiness of his having an affair with Scott's wife. If Scott had found out, nothing was more likely to make him break and declare publicly what had happened. Why had Dave Lyons involved himself there? Had he not been able to stop himself? Had the very danger of it intrigued him? Would it have remained clandestine if Scott hadn't died? Even the certainty of our duplicities will multiply into doubts.

'Sandy,' he said. 'I see him as a kind of moral idiot. He has no sense of the other. He just is. For him, I would imagine, the problem wouldn't seriously exist if it isn't acknowledged. Justification is not being found out. Dave is different. I think in a strange way he took his subsequent strength from what happened. He had been to the worst place and survived it. If life couldn't break him there, what else could it do him? He had found a secret. The way things work. There are no avenging angels. No poetic justice. There's only the law. Avoid it and you're running free. All you have to deal with is the inside of your head. Dave could do that all right. And I can see why. I've tried to think of it with his head. I've tried to think of it with everybody's head I can imagine. You know how I think he might have squared it with himself? Think of it. The very fact that you can flout the law like that proves how little it means. It's just a set of rules for those who happen to get caught. And if you can make a mockery of the law and thrive, it would be a bit immodest to think you were the only one. Wouldn't it? Dave knew his guilt must also be a lot of other people's. It was the nature of the game. That was a find. It was like splitting his private atom. He understood the structure of things. Hypocrisy wasn't a weakness for him. It became a strength. It wasn't social death. It was the lifeblood of career. No wonder he's such a successful man. It's quite simple, really, when you think of it. The bad have limitless capacities. The good are constrained. The hypocritical good have got it made. They have a structure of conformity that is plainly visible from the outside. Inside it, there are subterranean passageways in which anything is allowed to happen. That's Dave. Me?'

He stared at his desk. He smiled. It was a shy, vulnerable smile, less pleasure than pain with a mask on.

'Don't laugh at this,' he said. 'What I think I've done with it is try to be as good a man as I can be. Bev became the meaning of my life. Her and the kids. I wanted that things should be right for them. Beyond that, just do the best I can for everybody else. That's all. The house, everything's in Bev's name. I've got a horror of possessions. Anything in here that's mine, Bev bought for me. Every year I set aside whatever I can for charities. I've never knowingly cheated another person since that night. I've never been unfaithful to Bev. It's pathetic, isn't it? To think that changes anything. Because I still shared in what happened. And it still happened. And this may be technically Bev's house. But I live in it comfortably enough, don't I? And it's still built on the bones of a dead man. My life remains a lie, no matter how white I try to make it.'

He stared at me. The meaning I took from his eyes was something like: judge me as hard as you like, I can add to your severity.

'Scott,' he said. 'Well, you know, don't you? Who are the bitterest people in the world? The failed idealists, I would think. We made sure that Scott was one of them. But we couldn't kill his idealism. We just gave it cancer. He still kept it in him but it became grotesquely tumoured. If he couldn't undo what had happened and he couldn't admit it, he could make it the most important thing in the world. The man we killed came to stand for everybody who's a victim of our socialisation, the wholeness of our nature we lose in order to fit in to society. I think that's why he gave him a green coat. I suppose he saw him as natural man. To meet Scott's needs, he couldn't just be the man we knocked down and killed with a car. That's what he is for me, right enough. But who am I to say my way of living with it is nearer the truth than Scott's? For Scott, I think he was the part of ourselves we kill. In order to be able to go on living with the pretence of being who other people think we are. I'll show you something.'

He opened one of the top drawers in his desk. Whatever he was showing me must matter to him, since he kept it so conveniently to hand. It was a plain postcard with a handwritten message. He passed it across to me.

'Scott sent me that a couple of months or so ago.'

I read it slowly.

'See what I mean?' he said.

'I think so,' I said.

'You can keep it,' he said. 'Evidence, eh?'

I put it in my pocket. So now I knew. At least, the facts were in my head. It might be some time yet before they reached my heart. But some unsatisfied instinct persisted in me still, like a hand automatically fixing the hair on a corpse.

'Who was driving?'

'I can't tell you that,' he said.

'Was Scott driving?'

He stared at the floor. He stared at me.

'Look. Because he was your brother and because he's dead. I'll tell you this. Scott wasn't driving. But that's all I tell you. The other three of us were driving. All right? A deal's a deal. No matter how foul the terms. Honour among the dishonoured. It's all I've got left. As it is, you've got enough to blow us all away, I suppose. That's up to you. I sit at this dinner-party tonight and I don't know when the lights might go out on my life. I can live with that. I've lived with this, I can live with that. Maybe a part of me wants you to do it. I think it's only Bev and the kids I would worry about. Dave and Sandy, with them I've kept the bad faith. But when Scott died, that changed the terms for me. When you came round, I knew I had to tell you. For Scott's sake. He deserved it. I've told you. You do with it what you will.'

I was afraid I would just have to endure it. I had thought earlier tonight, on my wanderings, that I might have to bring this case to court, as well as the death of Dan Scoular. But why? What would we achieve? The resurrected pain of an unknown man's family, the damaged lives of a lot of innocent relatives who didn't even know the perpetrators when it happened. There are griefs we must try to put right and griefs we must endure. This guilt was not absolvable. All I could do was take my share of it. I took the secret into myself.

But I would live with it on my own terms. Dave Lyons wouldn't win. That must not be. There are other things we can do with our capacity to betray one another besides condone it. We can quarrel with it till we die, as Scott had done in his way.

I thought of Scott now, trying to see him whole. I knew that there was in me a recurrent tendency to think back to the excitement of new beginnings and regret the ends they've come to. The bitterness that can give rise to is bearing false witness to life. I thought that the essence of life lies not in the defeat of our expectations but in the joy that they were ever there at all. Life's a spendthrift mother. Once she has given what she has, it's ungrateful to complain that she didn't have the foresight to take out an insurance policy on your behalf. You just say thanks.

I did. He was my brother and that made for pride in me. I loved him in his anger and his weakness and the folly of his dying as much as ever I loved him in his strength and in his kindness. I found no part of him deniable.

And his last gift to me from the grave had perhaps been a more intense vision of the blackness in myself. It gave me a proper fear of who I was. In trying to penetrate the shadows in his life I had experienced more deeply the shadows in my own. I was his brother, all right. The beast he had fought, that ravens upon others, slept underneath my chair. I would have to try and learn to live with it as justly as I could. Beware thyself.

I had finished my whisky. I rose and filled out the last of the Antiquary. I put the empty bottle in the cupboard in the living-room. It's where I keep some objects that matter to me as memory-hinges. They are all quite worthless, to be thrown out with my body. But they serve to remind me of some of the things I believe are important.

I watered my drink in the kitchen and came back through. I remembered the card Scott had written to Michael Preston. I took it out of my pocket and stuck it in the corner of the frame of the five at supper. I sat down. Later today, I would see my children. I would begin again to try to be a good father to them. As I finished my glass, I looked at Scott's card. I couldn't make out the writing from here, but that didn't matter. I had read it over so many times since Michael Preston gave me it that I knew it by heart.

'Four experts had an appointment with an ordinary man. They needed him to ratify their findings or anything they achieved would be meaningless. As they drove to meet him, they knocked down a man on the road. He was dying. If they tried to save him, they might miss their appointment. They decided that their appointment, which concerned all of us, was more important than the life of one man. They drove on to keep their appointment. They did not know that the man they were to meet was the man they had left to die.'

I wished I had more whisky.

Turn the page for an interview with William McIlvanney, author of the Detective Laidlaw trilogy.

'A crime trilogy so searing it will burn forever in to your memory. McIlvanney is the original Scottish criminal mastermind'
CHRIS BROOKMYRE

A LAIDLAW INVESTIGATION

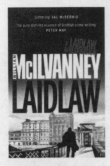

Meet Jack Laidlaw, the original damaged detective. When a young woman is found brutally murdered on Glasgow Green, only Laidlaw stands a chance of finding her murderer from among the hard men, gangland villains and self-made moneymen who lurk in the city's shadows. Winner of the CWA Silver Dagger Award.

£7.99 – ISBN 978 0 85786 986 9

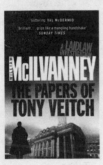

Eck Adamson, an alcoholic vagrant, summons Jack Laidlaw to his deathbed. Probably the only policeman in Glasgow who would bother to respond, Laidlaw sees in Eck's cryptic last message a clue to the murder of a gangland thug and the disappearance of a student. With stubborn integrity, Laidlaw tracks a seam of corruption that runs from the top to the very bottom of society.

£7.99 – ISBN 978 0 85786 992 0

An interview with William McIlvanney

by Len Wanner

William McIlvanney was born in Kilmarnock in 1936. The fourth of four resourceful miner children, he discovered his love of literature and learning in what used to be known as 'modest circumstances'. Back then the old phrase denoted the lack of fashionable experience in spite of solvent respectability, but at times it has also connoted a family economy that places its greatest stock in the life of the mind. Such was Mr McIlvanney's good fortune. At home he soon learned how to invest benign aggression, be it in spirited debate, Kilmarnock Academy, or Glasgow University, and the payoff has been rich. To 15 years of teaching English he has added 15 books in fiction and non-fiction, poetry and prose, two Scottish Arts Council Book Awards, two CWA Silver Daggers, a Saltire Society Scottish Book of the Year Award, a Geoffrey Faber Memorial Prize, a Whitbread Award, a Scottish BAFTA, etc.

Yes, Mr McIlvanney is highly prized, but versatility is deemed a division, not an addition of assets, and thus his due fame, the routine repetition of praise, has been delayed by the variety of his writings. Starting with *Remedy is None* in 1966, he has written such critical and cultural classics as *Docherty*, *Laidlaw*, *The Big Man*, *Walking Wounded*, *Surviving the Shipwreck*, and *The Kiln*, and on every page, be it that of a novel or a short story, an essay or a poem, he has championed the courage of our doubts. Only let his clear, undecorated language linger in the ear, and you begin to hear your own questions, feel as his protagonists do, and see them the way he does: unblinking, unafraid, and understanding. We know these people like ourselves, for although they belong to the past his power of intent makes of them the here and now.

Speaking of which, Mr McIlvanney has done for our time what Sir Arthur Conan Doyle did for his. He has created an archetype with an all-access pass to his fictional as well as our factual society. Starting in 1977, his Inspector Jack Laidlaw has led a procession of Scottish writers around the world, and since their shared success, his service to crime fiction has been seen as the source of Tartan Noir. *Laidlaw*, *The Papers of Tony Veitch*, and *Strange Loyalties* have enlightened generations of readers, not least as to the term's intentions and the author's imitators. This is why he has been charged twice, first with selling out and ever since with deeds of note. Having refused the funds of a series franchise, he has remained commercially undervalued, he has been rated a writer's writer, and he has given the Scottish crime novel a new lease of life.

The genre's debt to Mr McIlvanney is immeasurable. The man has shown that there are no formulas, not in literature and not in life. He has done so by mining the gap between purpose and performance, by reminding us that we all live within touching distance of the tough, the troubled, and the tested. That this can seem hopeless is the sign of a sensibility formed when stoicism ruled thoughtful minds; yet reading any one of his genre-defining works leaves one as heartened as the generosity of his spirit. When we met for the following interview in a Glasgow bar, he took my questions like his gin & tonic: slow, stirred, and with a smile. Talking in prose, he tipped the conversation with poetry as if he knew it was loose change and his last suit will have no pockets. Could a man do more to bewilder the public?

According to Ian Rankin, you were supportive of all your literary heirs in that you gave Scottish crime writers their own mongrel tradition. How did that happen?

I had just written *Docherty*, and although I found al[...]
research fascinating, I had contemporary starvation, so I[...]
to connect with the present again. This is going to sound te[...]
but I heard a voice. It sounds like Joan of Arc, eh? So the [...]
clues I had to Laidlaw were things he was saying. He was qui[...]
an abrasive man and I knew I wanted to write about him. As a
convert who came to Glasgow from Kilmarnock I always loved
the place, so I thought I'd write about contemporary Glasgow
from the point of view of somebody who would have to go to
the bad places. I didn't want it to be some Cook's tour of the
city, so I made him a cop. I wrote a first draft of about 40.000
words, and when my agent told me it was a runner I went back
to work on that sketch. It was a strange experience. Some of it
I loved, but for a long time I didn't know where it was going.

As for the effect *Laidlaw* has had, I wasn't aware of that until
people like Val McDermid said to me: "You started it all." Did I?
I've been quite moved that folk regard me as a forerunner of
Tartan Noir. In my old age, it's like getting a pension of esteem
you didn't know you were going to get. Even the main man, Ian
Rankin, wrote me a letter when he was living in France, saying
something like: "It was you that made me realise these books can
be something worthwhile, so I want to dedicate my second book
to you." I lost the bloody letter. I met him years later and apol-
ogised, but I felt bad. I could have got a book dedicated to me,
and I blew it because I'm so disorganised.

Is there any chance of you writing a fourth Laidlaw?
I don't know. Sean Connery phoned me once and said: "I've got
a window for a film. Do you have any ideas?" So I wrote this
thing called *Streets*, a film script of about 80 to 100 pages, and
Laidlaw comes into it tangentially. I thought it was quite a good
idea, but I'm not telling you what it was in case anybody steals
it. Connery shot me with a silver bullet. He said: "My secretary
really likes it, but I think it's more a book than a film." He's

ight, so I left it at that. Anyway, there's that idea and
nother one for a final Laidlaw, but I don't know. The way
e is so disorganised. It's like the laboratory of some Baron
kenstein, with inert projects lying all over the room, waiting
r the lightning flash that will galvanise them into life.

When we were trying to make a film of *Laidlaw*, we were
all sitting in this room, just a wee bit short of the money, and
this nice woman said: "Tell you what, let's just keep the money
we have and get Willie to play Laidlaw, instead of trying to hire
Connery or some other actor." I thought: "What a terrific idea!"
Then everybody in the room burst out laughing, and I thought:
"Well, maybe not." I've always thought that was my chance of
fame gone. Too late now, because a tough Glasgow detective
with a Zimmer doesn't quite hack it. To get back to your question, I'm always haunted by the ghosts of what I have not done,
and Laidlaw is one of those ghosts. If there's anything coming,
it'll be the sunset for Laidlaw.

When Laidlaw is asked why darkness fascinates him in
***Strange Loyalties*, he answers: "Maybe because I see it**
almost everywhere, and a lot of people trying to ignore
it." Do you share his night vision or why did you switch
to his narrative vantage point?
It's very difficult to answer that honestly, Len. I'm not entirely
sure why I made it first person. In my awareness, Laidlaw had
developed so much as a character that he could speak for himself,
and the one thing I hate doing is boring myself while I'm writing
– it's bad enough to bore the reader – so I thought: "I don't want
to write about him in the third person again, and the first person
might liberate Laidlaw."

When *Laidlaw* came out, a few journalists complained he's too
bright to be a policeman, but I know a lot of bright cops, one of
whom was head of the serious crimes squad and he'd been writing
poetry all his life. To make it feasible for Laidlaw to read Unamuno,

I just let him speak for himself, so in the end it really li~~t~~
me. For me, *Strange Loyalties* is Laidlaw most fully realised, a
there were another one I think it would be first person again.

In the same novel, *Strange Loyalties*, you mention a pub, 'The Getaway'. Were you aware enough of Jim Thompson to want to get away from conventional crime fiction?
Not much, really. I hadn't read much other crime fiction and most of what I had read I was dubious about. Agatha Christie? Even Raymond Chandler, whom I love, made me think: "Wait a minute. This detective's head is made of ferro-concrete." When my detective gets battered, he won't just walk on. Also, in a 'whodunnit' the question 'Who did it?' takes over everything and buries a lot of valuable stuff in its pursuit, so I made it a 'whydunnit'. In the beginning of *Laidlaw* you know who did it, so the questions you ask are: "Why did he do it?" And: "What's going to happen to him?"

So, if I'm right about the gestation of *Laidlaw*, I would say I was aware enough of crime fiction to want to do something different from what I'd seen. It was a new area which fascinated me and which I thought was underdeveloped. I'm not saying that I could grandly develop it, but I could at least try to suggest that there's more here. It seemed to me that it usually fought as a flyweight and it could fight at least as a middleweight.

Were you worried there might not be more here for much longer if you wrote a Laidlaw a year or how do you explain your 'arid periods'?
They were arid in terms of book production, but I don't think that's what writing is about. Writing is about writing. The book production is very much a secondary issue, so when the publisher said to me: "Do one a year." I thought: "Are you kidding? That's like a factory." I'm not saying that good writers don't do that, but *I* didn't want to do that. I was trying to develop and enlarge myself in those intervening years, but it's also fair to say that I

lazy, and to me the hassle of a book is quite severe. It
a lot out of me, and whenever I write a book I rediscover
lack of confidence. For me, every book I've written has
:en a bit of a trauma where I thought: "This is maybe bad.
Who's going to want to read this?" I've never lost that.

Alan Sharp once wrote an essay about Scottish football. When
Billy Bremner failed to score and take us to the next level, he
was down on his knees with his face buried in his hands, and
Alan said: "I know that moment. It's a Scottish moment – the
moment you're found out." I suppose I've always had a bit of
that: "This time, *this* time they're going to see the emperor is
bollock naked here." Besides, although I'm not saying it's feasible
or that I came remotely close to doing it, I always wanted to
believe in the next book in advance and know: "Something new
is here, some progress has been made."

Is the joy of writing its autonomy?

Yes, but it's not autonomy in a self-confident sense; it's autonomy
in a dangerous sense. You realise that you could fall on your arse
every time you do it, and it's that risk that is exciting – the defi-
ance of the risk. Life is a haphazard means of precipitating fiction
for me. I come to a place and think I'd like to write something
that accommodates these things. I try to create something of
interest, and if I'm lucky I create moments of truth, but it's
always a risk.

Is it fair to say that you and your characters are preoccupied with the shifting roles in their lives – who am I here?

I suppose so. I've spent my whole life intermittently asking myself
that. I think if you don't do that you miss half the truth. If you
don't realise you're playing multiple roles and ask yourself which
one is truly you, you miss the game. In a lot of ways life is a
performance. That doesn't mean you're pretending, but that

you're adopting a stance more confident than the c
allow, and it loses a frisson if you don't admit you're ן
on thin ice. Some game to play this – it's great fun and
Sometimes, the ice will go, but you live with that. You con:
re-examine yourself, and you're lucky if you give yourself a ר
mark, but you go on. There's the constant asking of "who am
here?"

Is literature about faith to you and your characters whose high hopes end in high tragedy?
Absolutely. To me, Shakespeare is a kind of locum God. In the absence of a God I can believe in, he explains human nature to me more than anybody else I've ever read. I don't think life's about success; it's about the honour of the endeavour. I'm old-fashioned enough to believe in honour. You live towards others as honestly as you can, and if you live honourably, you go to your grave on your own terms. To me, part of the greatness of people is taking on the bad stuff and not visiting it upon anybody else. Wilfully inflicting unnecessary pain on others pygmifies the species, although I must have done my share of that. Somebody like Laidlaw is a massively imperfect man, and he might visit it on folk that he thinks are cheating at the game, but he doesn't invade decent people's lives with it. I don't know if he's a tragic figure, but he's a tortured figure. He's trying to be honest in the midst of endless pomposity and dishonesty. He's an awkward man, but I like him, and I agree with him most of the time. If we had the courage of our doubts, not of our convictions, the millennium could be here.

You've described detective work as "a balancing act of subtle mutual respects. You hoped to give small to get back big." How has that worked out for Laidlaw and yourself?
I've certainly got back big. The man who organises the Glasgow

invited me to speak next year because it's been 35
Laidlaw came out. It was like saying: "Dear Willie, do
se how old you are?" Not until you mentioned it, no. I
idea that I would be as lucky as for serious writers of
e fiction to say I was helpful in releasing the genre in Scotland,
though I'm not sure they're not being too generous. It's nice
of them to think so, but it hasn't made me think I can sit back
and rely on it. It matters because it gives you the energy or the
chutzpah to go back into that place where you write and where
you're on your own, but it doesn't matter once you're back in
that padded cell, trying to rediscover the honesty of what you're
hoping to say.

When did you first see yourself as a writer?
When I was 17, I went to the headmaster and said: "I'm giving
up Greek, Sir." – "Why?" – "Because it's interfering with my
reading." He said: "Don't you mean you're reading is interfering
with your Greek?" – "No, Sir. If I'm not going to be a writer,
I'm not going to be anything." Another time, I was sitting in a
library at Glasgow University, revising for a history exam with a
friend, Frank Donnelly, when a wee latticed window suddenly
blew open. It was a weird feeling, so I took out my notebook
and wrote it down. When I looked up, Frank was staring at me
and said: "I think you should watch that, Willie. They could take
you away for that." It was a compulsion I had then, and it's developed, but I don't mind it because it was part of my almost
lifelong compulsion to try to be a writer.

How do you write?
I write with a pen. If it doesn't go through my system and straight
onto the page I don't quite believe it, so everything I've written
in my life, I've written in longhand. My favourite pen is a fineliner,
and I've never typed in my life, never used a computer. I'm not
proud of that, mind. It's just what I do.

Which aspects of writing do you think ca[...]

All you can do is encourage writing. I don't think [...]
writing. I can understand why people teach plot, tho[...]
know how good I would be at that. I tend to work it ou[...]
along, but it's valid for people who want to write to have w[...]
teach them. I'm just not going to be one of them. It depends
the writer, but I think somebody who really feels a powerfu[...]
compulsion should watch out about taking too much advice from
anybody. You don't want to theorise it to death.

Writing is ultimately an inexplicable compulsion, and there
may be valid ways to assist that process, but I wouldn't know
what they are, and I tend to believe in the power of writing
that doesn't need it, but maybe I'm wrong. When I taught creative writing classes, I didn't tell people how to write. I encouraged them to write and to see that defying my advice was
possibly as valuable as following it. Creativity is intelligent
passion – passion with a jockey on its back. You must have the
force to write, but you should also try to have the intelligence
to direct that force. And eventually you have to be your own
jockey.

Looking back now, do you know why Laidlaw's marriage failed?

No. I'm not entirely sure. He never told me. It's probably his
intensity about his job. He's so aware of the outside that he can't
quite focus on the inside. He can't relax in his domesticity. The
two coexist in a contradictory way, but I think there are other
factors. He gets involved outside his marriage, but I don't know
if he's due my flagellation, because he's a troubled man, which I
quite like about him. He's so involved in the nature of things you
can't always trust him to relate to you directly, which makes him
a detective version of a writer, relating his own experience to
that of others. At least to that extent, he may be a wee bit like
a writer.

promises normalcy. It makes it more difficult to ... y into society. Writers may be good at kidding on, ... s just that the writers I love are always a bit outside. ... u imagine making Kafka comfortable? Nah. The difficulty ... that you're some amazing genius, but that what you're ... ng to do is so bizarre, which is to live life and overtake it. ... s like disembowelling something and trying to make it live again, which is why serious writing is a troublesome thing to carry. It's a gig my life could have been easier without, and, whether or not it's screwed up my life, it's certainly complicated it. Without being melodramatic, writing is like living a parallel existence. Just as your real life feeds into your fiction, your fiction feeds into your real life, so I don't think writers move through life with the same smoothness as some nonwriters may do. Graham Greene claimed every writer must have a chip of ice in his heart, and he mentioned a painter who once confessed he couldn't help but notice the way the light struck his wife's head as she lay dying. There's a bit of you that records as you experience, and that mild split personality can be a bit troublesome, as you're not just living your life but looking on at it at the same time.

Do you have any literary regrets?

Some, inevitably. When I wrote *Laidlaw*, they said: "Do one of these a year and you'll be a millionaire." I thought: "But I don't want to do one of these a year." I didn't want to get trapped because there were other things I wanted to try. That was in the 1970s. Occasionally, at two in the morning, I now think: "Aye, I wouldn't mind the 1970s back. I could have made a right few quid." But that's a joke with myself. I don't really regret that. That was how I felt then. I have this half-baked dream that before I die I'll look at all my unfinished writing and make final decisions about what to bin and what to keep, but although I have maybe about 12 undeveloped ideas for novels, I can't regret not having written them, because if I can find the energy, maybe the potential for writing them is still there. Although obviously the older I get, the less likely that becomes.

What do you wish you'd known when you started writing?
I think I know a lot of things now that I didn't know then, but I don't wish I'd known them then, because that's the way I was then, and I respect that. Also, I don't think that my knowledge now is so impressive that it would have made a great difference to my life. Most of what I think I know has gone into my words. It's hard to be as innocent as I was then, but that innocence was a very valuable commodity and I hope some of it remains.

For the full 9000-word interview, please see *The Crime Interviews Volume Two: Bestselling Authors Talk About Writing Crime Fiction* by Len Wanner (published by Blasted Heath, 2012)

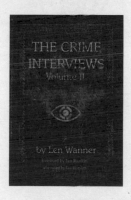

CHANNELLING GREAT CONTENT FOR YOU TO WATCH, LISTEN TO AND READ.